1983

Novels by Morris Philipson

BOURGEOIS ANONYMOUS
THE WALLPAPER FOX
A MAN IN CHARGE
SECRET UNDERSTANDINGS

Secret Understandings

a novel by

MORRIS PHILIPSON

SIMON AND SCHUSTER · NEW YORK

This novel is a work of fiction. Names, characters, places and incidents either are the product of the author's imagination or are used fictitiously. Any resemblance to actual events or locales or persons, living or dead, is entirely coincidental.

PUBLISHED BY SIMON AND SCHUSTER
A DIVISION OF GULF & WESTERN CORPORATION
SIMON & SCHUSTER BUILDING
ROCKEFELLER CENTER
1230 AVENUE OF THE AMERICAS
NEW YORK, NEW YORK 10020
SIMON AND SCHUSTER AND COLOPHON ARE
REGISTERED TRADEMARKS OF SIMON & SCHUSTER
DESIGNED BY EVE METZ
MANUFACTURED IN THE UNITED STATES OF AMERICA

1   3   5   7   9   10   8   6   4   2
LIBRARY OF CONGRESS CATALOGING IN PUBLICATION DATA

Philipson, Morris H., date.
Secret Understandings
I. Title.
PS3566.H475J8   1983   813'.54   82-19548
ISBN 0-671-46619-4

This book
is dedicated
with loving admiration
to
the past life of
my grandmother
JENNY ALDERMAN
born 1867 .... died 1950
and
with fatherly love
to
the future life of
my daughter
JENNY PHILIPSON
born 1966 ....

SECRET
UNDERSTANDINGS

LETTER FROM SHELAGH JACKMAN
TO HER SISTER, ADRIENNE MARKGRAF, IN LONDON

New Haven, Connecticut
September, 1973

Darling!

What do you imagine the serpent looked like before God cursed it? You know the serpent I mean—the one who lured Eve into offering the apple to Adam. According to the New English Bible (Oxford and Cambridge) that I'm using, the serpent is referred to only as the craftiest of all the animals— and nothing more; there is no description of it. And in what way was it crafty? Don't you think what it looked like would have made a great deal of differ- ence to how crafty it could be? You see, if a serpent became what we know it as—no legs or arms, crawling on its belly—only afterward, as a consequence of the curse of God—then, of course, it couldn't have looked like that before it was cursed. So what was its appearance at its craftiest? This is the kind of question Father would have loved. But then, he'd have put two research as- sistants on it and come up with the seven hundred most interesting-looking images of the serpent in Western iconography. That isn't what I want. That's not why I'm asking you at all. I mean—forget art history; I just want to know what you imagine the serpent looked like . . . because you've seen so many snakes in disguise.

Joking aside, let me tell you what this is all about. Of course, I've jumped into the middle. I always do; you understand that. But this is really very flat- tering. I've been offered a chance to illustrate a new (abridged) edition of the Old Testament. Really, from a commercial publisher's point of view, it's like being awarded the Victoria Cross. Having done battle for years in the trenches of illustrating all sorts of inane children's books, to have a chance at the Bible—just like Gustave Doré! it's an apotheosis. I've looked that up in the O.E.D.; it means—the elevation of a human being to the rank of a god. Dig that! I feel exalted. Of course, I didn't tell him that I haven't read the Old Testament since I was ten; but he didn't have to know. I doubt that he's ever read it. By "him" I mean Freddy Tiejens—the creative director of the juvenile department at Harvest House. Most of the books I've illustrated during the past half-dozen years have been on commission from him. Since the lot of them are, generally speaking, pedestrian—forget the prizewin- ners—it never occurred to me that what he asked me to see him about in New York last week was going to be the bloody Holy Bible.

9

Actually, you would have adored the situation. He took me to lunch at Caravelle. You remember him, don't you? I've described the lout. He's tall and scrawny; intuitively smart, if uncultivated; shy, nervous—born and brought up in some hamlet in Ohio; didn't know what an artichoke was until he passed forty. But with an uncanny sense of what sells in children's books. Remember when he suggested I do the illustrations for a book on sewage disposal—*Waste*—and I thought it would be a catastrophe, but it sold thousands of copies. It turned out that children are crazy about what happens to "doo-doo"; the point is: he knows what will sell. And now—in the middle of the nineteen-seventies—he's decided that religion will be "in" again. He's terribly eager for an Old Testament and a New Testament. I don't know whom he's going to commission to do the life of Jesus, but I'm ecstatic to have the Fierce God rather than the epigone.

Anyhow, we went to lunch and there we were between elegant food and softly sounding background music, the New York publishing sharpie and the provincial artist talking about whether Adam and Eve should be blond or brunette, dark-eyed or blue-eyed. But of course his own eyes never met mine. It's absolutely the Manhattan disease. No one looks you in the face. He's talking to me and thinking about Jehovah and whether the Garden of Eden had artichokes in it, and at the same time staring beyond me, looking to the left and right, continually wondering if someone will appear who is more important, whom he has to ass-kiss, or less important, so that he can snub him. I swear, New Yorkers must have the most overdeveloped and wearied eye muscles in the world. If you think that ordinary animals constantly have to be perceptive about the sudden appearance of a friend or an enemy, they have an enviably soft life compared with the New York publisher at lunch or at a cocktail party wondering about whom he ought to be talking to rather than the person he's with.

Anyway, I'm thrilled about the assignment—but certainly didn't let him know that; one has to be very indifferent if one wants to get anywhere in New York. Father and Mother would have been excited too, don't you agree? A third-generation agnostic illustrating the Bible! Art and commerce are what counts; if you can create something new and beautiful—and make money out of it—from the Old Believers, so much the better. Most of the artists Father admired were rotten nonbelievers who lived in velvet off the patronage of semibelievers who kept them painting their equivalents of illustrations for children's books. I think they would have roared with proud laughter if they knew.

Well, at least, Father would have. Mother was such a stick. What did she laugh about? Oh, I remember, you don't agree. I'm sorry I mentioned Mother, but I don't want to rewrite this page. Forget I mentioned her.

Well, since last week, I've actually read Genesis and begun making sketches. I have nine months and sixty-four pages and feel it's a noble challenge and I'm riding high. What else can I tell you? While I was in New York, I stayed over with Claire, who is rehearsing for a new play. She really will be a good actress! and looks more like you than ever; it's the high cheekbones. Morgan, on the other hand, is not only more remote and "his own person" but took me out to dinner a little worried, as if unsure of whether I'd embarrass him. I think he's afraid of waiters who carry trays about at the level of his head. It's occurred to me that if we had not accidentally named him after the most successful banker in the history of this country he might never have gone into finance, although sometimes I have difficulty in locating his name. I have to think through all the notables of his firm—Merrill Lynch, Pierce, Fenner and Smith—before I can remember "Morgan." But he is a dear boy—at a distance; and Claire is radiantly happy. Both of them are working hard, very much on their own—that is: off our backs. But you don't care about things like that.

I suppose what I ought to tell you is that I have a grotesque pain in my "little inside" and have finally decided to see a doctor, which I will do today. I dread the thought that he might tell me to stop drinking. I adore the case of Port you sent; there are still five bottles left. The Judge is no judge of Port, but I am. Bless you.

Which, for no particular reason, reminds me of Walter Webster. Isn't it odd that I should still know him? Do you recall him from the time he was a student of Father's at the Warburg Institute before the war? He's an old and important professor at the university here now, and I take him to New York with me whenever I drive; well, at least half the time. It's peculiar that he should be the only link here between the life of those days and my life now. Naturally, he's just as harmless as he was then, but with Mother and Father dead and you at such a distance, it turns out that only he stands as a "marker" against which I measure my own aging as I watch him grow old, and whom I can remember as he was (if not as how I was) in the old days. It's rather funny that he takes me out for lunch to places like the St. Regis and the Ritz Carlton in thanks for driving him back and forth. He's exactly as solicitous as he was years ago when he brought gifts to Father. In those days it was a question of whether the cigars or the brandy were "to your liking." I think I actually remember him asking that, but maybe I'm imagining it. And now, over lunch at Lutèce or the Plaza Oyster Bar—all these years later!— he's asking me, "Is that the way you like it? Is it all right? Too well done? We can send it back if it's not . . ." Oh, I remember why I thought of him—his ordering port after lunch. After lunch! darling; imagine. No one else in America does. He is amusing. I must make him call on you the next time he's in London. He worships Father. It's a little disconcerting to see a man in his sixties still worshiping his professor of forty years ago. But then, it was Father.

11

I must get ready for my doctor's appointment. I think I'll wear black lingerie. Write to me soon. And meditate about the serpent. The craftiest of the animals in the Garden of Eden. What could it have looked like?

Shelagh Jackman had been writing in bed, propped up against pillows, with a leather portfolio supported by her raised legs. She screwed the top back over the wide point of the fountain pen and placed it on the letter. As she pushed the folder away toward the edge of the bed, lowered her legs, and stretched, the ache in her side became acute. Breathing deeply and slowly, she attempted to remain immobile until the pain subsided, but she grew impatient soon enough, threw off the covers, and stood up, ignoring it. She tightened the belt of her blue cotton dressing gown around her and looked for her slippers, then decided she didn't need them. The morning breeze, coming in from the partly open window, was balmy. At the low chest of drawers, where her husband had left the breakfast tray, she took a sip of tea and found it too cool to enjoy. The Judge made breakfast—tea, toast, and marmalade—and brought it to her after he dressed each morning; he sipped his tea in the armchair opposite her in bed while he glanced at the morning newspaper. They barely talked during breakfast, but they were happy to be in each other's presence. This morning she suggested he get his hair cut. They were back only two weeks from a vacation in Alaska. She was a little over fifty, and they had been married twenty-eight years. He was ten years older than she. They had not made love for a few months. Masturbation, she thought, is second-best—but not a close second.

Shelagh brought the jump rope out of the closet and began her half-hour of exercise: sit-ups, knee bends, and isometrics. She showered briskly, washed her hair, warmed it with a blow dryer—her auburn hair, brushed out in broad wings about her head—and set about putting on her makeup standing in her slip before the mirror over the bathroom sink. She was pleased with both her face and her figure. She benefited from good habits. They give you the advantage, she used to tell her children, of not having to decide about everything all the time. Establish a good habit and you can forget about thinking what to do for a while. It gives your mind freedom. You can daydream while you're doing exercises if you no longer have to decide whether to exercise. And daydreams refresh the human spirit. There are enough new decisions that have to be made every day.

Such as which dress to wear. She looked about the bedroom with its French Provincial furniture, the filmy white curtains fluttering slightly over the window ledges; saw her reflection in the mirror above the chest of drawers; and noticed her slippers half-hidden under the armchair. She put them away on the floor of her wardrobe and slipped off the pink padded hanger a long-sleeved dress of Italian knit jersey in navy blue with gold braid piping along the shawl collar and running down the front and around the waist. It would be ideal in this September weather. She pulled it on and zipped up the back. She was wearing a fragrant cologne and wanted no jewelry other than her platinum wedding ring and the silver ring with its tiny watch concealed under a mount of marquisettes.

When she threw back the sheet and top blanket to air the bed, her writing case fell to the shaggy green rug along with her letter to Adrienne. She tucked it under her arm and put the pen into her handbag. Writing weekly a letter to her sister was another good habit; it relieved her of ever wondering whether she wanted to write her sister this week or not.

Shelagh Jackman paused at the doorway and surveyed the comfortable bedroom. It had been her fancy to wallpaper only the ceiling with the pattern of bouquets of flowers against splashes of a pine-green background, and run strips of it like columns upholding the four corners and over the woodwork on the doors and windows, while the walls remained white. Tied in with the black-green of the rug, the effect of it made her feel enchanted in a spacious bower, forever springlike. The only pictures on the walls were enlargements of favorite photographs of her two children, mementos of their early youth. She left the door open behind her.

Flowers had always been important. When she had descended the stairs and placed the leather portfolio on the hall table, she stared at the bowl full of orchids there: three sprays of yellow-and-brown-spotted demitasse cups of blossoms entwined on strips of bark that lay at the bottom of the porcelain bowl. It had been the Judge's most extraordinary gift—for their fifteenth wedding anniversary—to have the orchid hothouse built over what had been a small back porch. They did not live extravagantly or ostentatiously. They owned only one car, and not a new one at that; the Judge walked to his office. Their house was not in a fashionable suburb. But he did love to collect first editions, and they shared a passion for travel.

The pain in her side had stopped. She walked through the living room and dining room back toward the kitchen, taking pleasure in the way the cleaning man, who came in every other Monday, had done his job. The windows were sparkling, the carpets vacuumed, the furniture polished. At the kitchen counter, Shelagh sat on the high stool reading over the list of groceries and meats she had made up the night before and then telephoned to place her order. She would come by to pick it up in a few hours. While she spoke on the phone, she fingered the yellow blossoms of a begonia plant that she had potted and brought in from the backyard the day before: each circular flower made up of a series of discs like a clutch of petticoats that belong in a doll's house. She would repot the plant in one of the Chinese urns and keep it in the living room. She felt that all about her there was order: neatness, cleanliness, subdued or cheerfully bright colors, and restful quiet. The silence of the empty house; the invitation to be herself, as if only alone is anyone herself—not called upon to function in relation to anyone else. Even in writing the letter to her sister, Shelagh recognized the particular tone of voice, the pitch, the timbre that changed for that performance. Not myself, she thought, but myself-for-my-sister, which is as different as myself-for-my-husband is from myself-for-my-son: each a calibration of the instrument slightly altered from the others; each on a slightly different wavelength, for a different condition—so that the signal sent would be accommodated to the receiving station; so that the particular set of assumptions would be maintained on both sides and the message would get through. She thought, wryly, as she went back to the front hall for her handbag, And now I shall be myself-for-my-car.

It was no distance at all to drive to the doctor's office, but she needed the car for marketing afterward. Shelagh drove the large black Chevrolet into the parking lot behind the apartment house on York Street where Dr. Connolley's suite of offices was located on the ground floor. In walking around the Crown Street side to enter the building through the front door, she was aware of two little children scampering ahead of her as a blind man turned the corner toward them. A thin man, in his early twenties, wearing a light windbreaker, khaki slacks, and sneakers, with a long slender white cane tapping the space before him in staccato semicircles back and forth as he moved into the cleared place. The two little boys stopped for an instant, trapped between the hedges on the street side and the low brick wall along the parking lot. Suddenly both of them jumped up onto the brick wall, somehow more in fear of being touched by the blind man or even by his long white stick than out of concern for removing obstacles from his path. The fear of contamination. Moving in the opposite direction, Shelagh stepped between two hedges to leave the sidewalk free for him. The blind man passed, the children ran the length of the brick wall, and she proceeded around the corner to the doctor's office.

It was eleven-thirty. She appeared exactly on time for her appointment. It was not necessary for her to wait more than a few minutes before she was shown in.

Quentin Connolley stood up and walked around his desk to greet her. He was tall, broad-shouldered, and trim; his complexion was ruddy, but his white hair and white beard—like a Viking's, Shelagh thought—made him look older than he was. Probably no older than she. His only child was a boy of about twenty. He took her hand to shake in both of his. "How nice to see you." He had a broad smile, and it looked as if all those large bright teeth were his own.

"Yes," she agreed. "Except under these circumstances."

"Oh, don't take a doctor's visit seriously. Lots of people make appointments just to be with me for a little while." They both laughed. He did not direct her to sit in the chair opposite his desk. Rather, still holding her hand, he led her to the leather sofa under the window and sat down with her there, side by side. "I haven't seen you since you went off to Alaska. How was the safari?"

"You don't safari in Alaska. You backpack."

"You didn't carry a pack on your *back*, did you?"

"No, the outfitter packed our gear on mules; we rode horses."

"You *look* wonderful."

"It was a grand trip! Those crystal waters deep down between jutting peaks of snowcapped mountains. Like the Norwegian fjords. The clean air. The sleeping bags. The mist. The rain. The smoked salmon. Marvelous. I wouldn't have missed it for the world."

He continued to hold her right hand in both of his. She withdrew it, to snap open the mound of marquisettes and look at the time. "You may have thought this is a ring; but it's a watch."

Nonchalant, Dr. Connolley pulled back his left cuff and twisted his watch around his wrist. "You may have thought this is a watch," he said. "But it's a ring."

Having established the note of familiarity, if not intimacy, of cheerfulness and ease, he asked forthrightly, "What's the trouble?"

"Pain. Aches. Odd feelings. . . ."

"How old are you?"

"Fifty-one."

"You're right on time."

"I've never been to see you before."

"As if I hadn't often wondered why."

"I'm healthy! I haven't been to a doctor in *years*."

"That's nothing to be proud of."

They had known each other for five or six years, since her husband, the Judge, had begun playing in a golf foursome with Connolley, Conrad Taylor, and Henry Warner. They had been to dinner or parties at each other's homes, run into each other at concerts or the theater. They were social acquaintances. Now, they regarded each other cautiously.

"Well, I am a proud person."

"You're British, aren't you?"

She chuckled. "As if that accounted for it. Well, no, I'm not. Or rather, only partly."

"I thought you were. Your accent . . ."

"I'm an American citizen. 'Naturalized'—the hard way. I was brought up in England. I lived there from 1933 until I was married in 1945. But I'm originally from Vienna."

"Vienna? I would never have imagined." He stared at her now, adjusting to the information, trying to see her in a different light: as if associations of distance, danger, drama had altered his focus. "Your family fled from the Nazis?"

"Of course."

"But you're not Jewish, are you?"

She smiled at his naiveté. "You didn't have to be a Jew to be an enemy of the Nazis. My father was a prominent Social Democrat. If we hadn't left, he would eventually have been arrested."

"How old were you at the time?"

"Eleven."

"And then you grew up in England—right through the war?"

"In London." She found his surprise amusing and asked, "How did *you* spend the war?"

"In medical school. But I was in Germany during the first year of the Occupation."

"How long have you been in private practice?"

"Twenty-five years."

"Well, what do you say you try to treat me?"

Silent for an instant, he then burst out laughing. "But of course I'll try," he said. He took her hand again to raise her from the sofa and led her to the chair near his desk. He seated himself on the other side and drew from a drawer a medical-history form. Shelagh thought what a remarkable self-indulgence it was for him to be wearing a white jacket not of stiff linen or flimsy nylon but of raw silk.

She had survived all the ordinary diseases of childhood, and no unusual one. She had no history of diabetes, tuberculosis, any broken bone or mental disease. Her father had died of pneumonia, because it had gone undiagnosed, at the age of sixty-eight; and then her mother had died of a sudden heart attack at the age of sixty-two. She had given birth to two children, normal and healthy, suffered two subsequent miscarriages, and had a tubal ligation ten years before.

"Where?" Dr. Connolley asked. "Who was the doctor?"—still writing.

"In London. I visit my sister there once a year. The doctor's name was Peacock. I think he's dead. I haven't seen a doctor since then."

"In ten years?" He was shocked.

"I haven't been ill.'"

"That's no reason not to see a doctor."

"You *are* American!"

He pushed away the form and folded both hands before him. "Now, what's wrong?"

Shelagh described the discomfort, the occasionally sudden stabbing pain, and the more frequent nagging ache. She stood up and placed her open hand against her right hip. "In from here," she said; "my guess is about two inches in and one inch down."

"For how long?"

"On and off for up to an hour, every day or at least every other one."

"No, I mean: since when? How long ago did it start?"

"Before we left for Alaska. About six weeks or so."

"What have you taken for it?"

"Nothing. I haven't seen any doctor."

"Aspirin?"

"No."

"Painkiller?"

"I don't have any."

"Tranquilizer?"

"Never touched the stuff."

"Sleeping pill?"

"Took a phenobarbital once—and slept for twenty-four hours." She shivered at the recollection.

His conclusion was that "You may be naturalized, but you're not yet a typical American."

"I like Bourbon."

"Well, that's a redeeming feature." He stood up. "It may be ovarian or musculoskeletal. Don't be disturbed. It doesn't sound like anything serious at all. We'll have to see the results of some tests. Let's start with your going into the examining room next door. My nurse will take urine and blood specimens and an X-ray of your chest. Then come back and we'll continue in here. All right?"

"You're the doctor."

It was when she returned to his office and sat close to Quentin Connolley, his thigh touching against hers, her sleeve rolled back over her upper arm, with the bulb on the blood-pressure manometer pumping tension through the black cuff against her flesh, that Shelagh felt disheveled, somehow tousled, as if forced to become negligent. It displeased her, and she could sense herself becoming stiff-necked.

"Why are you tensing like that?" Dr. Connolley asked.

"I'm uncomfortable."

He unwound the black cuff and removed it from her arm. "I'd like to make you comfortable." He began to stroke the pink flesh where the pressure in the viselike black material had squeezed her arm.

She looked up suddenly into his eyes, blue eyes with pale blond lashes. He was not looking at her arm, where his hands stroked her smoothly, with a slow, sensuous back-and-forth motion. Neither of them showed any facial expression. They stared. They waited. He leaned forward and kissed her on the lips. Then he drew back and said, "I've always thought you were a marvel—a remarkably lovely woman." The steady motion of his hands on her arm now moved apart, one hand toward her shoulder, the other meandering down her lower arm toward her wrist.

"I've always thought you were a lecher," she said softly, huskily, in a tone of objectivity.

"Just because you didn't respond doesn't mean you didn't respond. Shall I check your heartbeat? Your pulse rate now? Take your blood pressure again?"

"Is this a new substitute method, instead of having the patient run in place for five minutes?" She was looking for her handbag and saw it to the side of her on the leather sofa. She drew her sleeves down into place and looked about the office to the doors through which the nurse or his secretary or some other patient might enter. And then she let a large smile warm her face. Her heart was pounding. "This is rather funny," she said.

"What is?"

"Playing Doctor." She chuckled.

"I haven't taken advantage of you. I haven't violated you in any unprofessional way."

"Unprofessional!" She laughed.

"Or unethical." He was unsure of the degree to which he would have to defend himself.

She said, smiling, "You are an indecent exposure."

"A negative of an indecent exposure. You haven't seen the print made from it yet."

Shelagh said, "I'd better leave now." But she remained seated.

"Let me kiss you again."

She lifted her hand. He looked at it uncertainly at first and then, taking it firmly in his—bending it back, to her surprise—he stroked his cheek and his beard with her palm. She released her hand from his and stood up, smoothing down her skirt. Putting her hand on her hip near the source of her pain, she considered: "Obviously, it's nothing serious."

"On the contrary," Quentin Connolley replied. "I could fall in love with you."

"I was referring to the other problem: the one I had before I came here today."

"Have I added to your problem?" he asked hopefully, almost with self-congratulation.

"What have you added to the bill, I suppose, is more to the point." She bent over to pick up the handbag and, in the same instant, swerved away before he could pat her. "There are some things a woman is never old enough to disregard."

"Old? You're in the full flower of your beauty. You are"—groping for the word, he arrived at—"majestic. Your violet eyes, your chestnut hair . . ."

"Tint, tint," she interrupted.

". . . are glorious. You can't keep me from falling in love with you."

"I can keep me from coming here again."

"You mustn't do that. Besides, you'll have to learn the results of the tests." He turned to scan the calendar on his desk. "They'll be back by Friday. You must come here again on Friday. Say, three in the afternoon."

Shelagh did not reply.

After she had turned her back to him and opened the door to leave, she heard him say: "I'll have my secretary phone to remind you."

From beginning to end, the whole visit could not have taken more than forty minutes. Shelagh Jackman walked very slowly along the street, around the corner, along the route where the blind man had tapped his way, back to the parking lot, placing one foot before the other carefully, deliberately, keeping herself from breaking into a run. But she was charged with a rush of energy, with the delight of guilty excitement. For what excites me most, she thought, is to be desired, to feel attractive, to be coveted. How long has it been since I experienced that shock of shared implication? That excitement of an unexpected invitation to share a new pleasure? That invitation which has no basis other than declaring: I must desire you because you are desirable? It was at that moment, standing still before the door of her old car, that she was conscious of feeling the presence of her pubic hair, the nipples of her breasts, the skin at the underside of her knees. She had been made sensitive to the facts of her sensual existence by the stroking of her arm, by his kiss, by the pressure against her thigh. She had been in contact with a man who wanted to seduce her. Suddenly she laughed out loud, and got into the driver's seat of the car trying to make a joke of the whole encounter. I'm no more sensible than I was at sixteen, she thought, trying to wipe the smile off her face. Excited by the attention of a lusty Viking. I didn't even get a prescription for a painkiller out of the visit, she realized, remembering why she had put herself in his hands to begin with. But she had difficulty starting the car.

Where was she to go?

What could have possessed him? His wife is no beauty, but she is charming and vivacious and adores him; why shouldn't he be content? Why did he have to disrupt her life? But not her whole life. She tried to laugh again, but this time it was hollow and no help. It was not that she liked having her feelings disrupted; she liked being challenged, being given the option to take it

19

seriously or not. After all, how often is a woman over fifty made to feel desirable, lusted after, or worthy of lying to?

She backed the car out of its space and drove it forward out of the parking lot feeling that the rush of energy that the erotic excitement charged her with had been added to the power of the automobile. Dr. Quentin Connolley had made a pass at her. Where did that expression come from? Shelagh wondered as she drove toward Orange Street: bullfighting?—when the matador draws the attention of the bull with a turn of his crimson cloak over the concealed sword? Or is it from the *paseo*, when the girls of the town walk around the plaza in one direction while the boys walk in the opposite direction; all they do is glance at each other—but always aware of the possibility that a glance will linger, a look may become a stare. For a glance is enough to supply you with all the information you require—the contours, the shape, the gait, the tone of the other person—but a stare lingers into the exercise of the imagination, no longer asking to know about the present but attempting to fathom a conceivable future. It was such a stare that she had shared with Quentin Connolley. He had not been looking at her but through her, to a future event as he wished to imagine it. One has only to be blind to a stare like that in order to destroy such a hope. He had made a pass. Had she made the mistake of encouraging him?

Shelagh Jackman double-parked outside the grocer's shop and opened the trunk of the car. As the butcher's boy brought his package out along with the bag of groceries, she caught sight of Mrs. Henry Warner coming out of the store, and shouted, "Kate! Hello, there. I haven't seen you in ages. We were away in August, and then you went away."

Kate Warner was a handsome woman, younger than Shelagh. Their husbands played golf together.

"Isn't this weather glorious?" Shelagh was uncertain whether she was basking in the warm sunlight or in Quentin Connolley's stare. She wanted to talk with someone; she joined Kate on the sidewalk. "What are you up to?"

"I've been shopping with the children. The little ones. Jonathan has just left to start at the University of Michigan. . . ."

"Already? I think of him as a 'little one.' "

"No. It's come to this." She pretended to sob. "Off to college. And the two younger ones go back to day school first thing next week. I've been buying them clothes all morning, and notebooks, and apples for the teacher." Kate Warner held two baskets of strawberries in her hands. She wore a skirt and vest made of gray pin-striped flannel as for a man's suit, but a long-sleeved blouse of pale beige silk with a dark chocolate tie at her neck held in place by a cameo, the elegant Italian profile alabaster white against an oval of milk chocolate. She smiled comfortably. "The children are in the car waiting for me." She nodded toward the corner of the street.

Shelagh thought her a very attractive person, both feminine and strong. "Have you had lunch?"

"Haven't thought much about it." And then, holding up the bright red strawberries, as if to apologize for them: "These are for dinner. I just thought we'd drive home now. The children don't need any other rewards."

"But you do," Shelagh said quickly. "I'd love to have you all for lunch. One never does anything spontaneously anymore."

"That's true." Her words carried the weight of calendars, appointment books, schedules.

"It would be fun," Shelagh urged.

"For the two of us, yes. But I have the children with me. You wouldn't mind?"

"I'd be delighted. The children can see the orchids—or make things in my studio. And we can talk." They looked at each other with the pleasure of old social acquaintances who were suddenly confronted by the opportunity of becoming friends. "We've lived in the same world long enough to get to know each other," she said, laughing.

Kate Warner sighed. "The truth is, Shelagh," she confessed, "I don't think I can find your house. The only times I've been there, Henry drove the car. It's in a hidden street, isn't it?"

"We keep it secret. Lynwood Court. But it will be easy for you to find. Follow me. If we get separated, just keep going up Elm Street to where Broadway begins."

"Yes."

"Christ Church is at the corner. The big red stone one. Looks like a fortress in India. Don't go right up Broadway. Go left past the brick Fire House—the one that's been made into a restaurant. One short block past that corner—Park Street—and take a sharp left: that's Lynwood Court. It's only one block long."

"I remember."

"Mine is the fourth house on the left. Dark brick. Federal period. I'll pull well up into the driveway. You can park behind my car. You'll never find a parking place on the street."

Not only the Warner children, Peggy and Gabriel, but Kate herself had never seen any home like this. What the Jackmans had done was buy two tall, narrow joined row houses in the late 1940s and break through inner walls on each of the three floors to connect them into one house; from the facades on the street they continued to appear as two houses. They had not doubled the size of most rooms—the rooms in each house retained their own character— but what seemed a small house from the outside simply went on and on from wherever one entered it. Two rooms in the second building served as the Jackmans' library; the second master bedroom had been made into Shelagh's studio.

"It has such charm," Kate Warner said. "So formidable—not to say Spartan—from outside, but so expansive and cozy. . . ."

"One of the things I remember best about Vienna when I was a child," Shelagh said, "was the apartment house I grew up in. The stone archway of the entrance—though maybe it was plaster—was carved into the shape of two giants—two 'Atlases,' I told myself—who held up the building on their backs. It was tremendously dramatic, especially for a child with a lively imagination."

"What if they let go?" Kate asked.

Shelagh chuckled. "Exactly! I came home every day wondering if they would still be there or whether the building had collapsed because they'd taken off."

"Vienna . . . ?" Kate began to ask.

"But that was the only thing that was dramatic about it—the outside. The inside was rather dull. Whereas, in London, afterward, it became apparent that the outsides of houses were uniformly dull and the insides were lively, well-kept secrets: just like the people," she concluded. "Let's make lunch," she said, taking the two children by the hand—the girl of almost nine, the boy almost seven, in orange short pants and white T-shirts, moving soundlessly in their sneakers across the Oriental rug of the living room and squeakily across the hardwood floor of the dining room as Shelagh led them to the sunlit kitchen at the back of the house. "The orchids are on the other side of that wall in a greenhouse that's moist and warm." She made it sound like one of the Wonders of the World.

Shelagh had no peanut butter or jelly; her children were both grown. But Peggy and Gabriel were willing to eat tuna-salad sandwiches and drink milk even if it didn't have chocolate syrup in it. Kate and Shelagh ate the tuna and tomatoes on lettuce and drank Chablis. Beyond the kitchen window, the huge evergreens and spruce in the backyard concealed the houses nearby; the children trained their eyes on the birdhouse hanging outside the back window, awaiting the appearance of the promised family of cardinals.

But then the children became surly, made snarlish faces at each other, and one kicked the other under the kitchen table.

"You did that!" Gabriel snapped.

"It was your fault." Peggy smiled, a false smile.

Kate pulled Gabriel's chair a foot away from the table.

Gabriel whispered, "You're a liar."

His sister replied, "You're a pest."

Apologetically, Kate asked Shelagh, "Would you believe—sometimes they get along beautifully?"

"Of course." Shelagh looked at the clean, well-dressed, healthy children who were expected to be proper if not pleasant at all times and said, "But you have to expect them to push each other around some of the time. It's like flexing your muscles to find out how strong you are." Gabriel liked that.

"The oldest is off to college," Kate remarked, as if to prove she'd done some things right.

"Where did you say he's gone?"

"Ann Arbor. The University of Michigan."

"That far away . . ."

Kate did not pick up the invitation to bemoan the distance. She was still trying to make her peace with that.

"When the children have finished lunch, I can show them the orchids and then my studio. I can set both of you up with paper and colors and you can be artists for a while. Would you like that?"

In disbelief, Gabriel said, "Orchids!"

Peggy wondered, "Studio?"

"Mrs. Jackman is an artist." Kate looked to her quickly. "Or should I say illustrator?"

"I wish there were the term 'imagist,' " Shelagh replied. "I'd love to be called an image-maker."

"Mrs. Jackman illustrates books, you know," Kate was prompting her children. "Remember the book called *Waste*? You loved that. Mrs. Jackman did all the pictures for that book."

Both Peggy and Gabriel turned their attention to Shelagh. Gabriel stared at her with the mute surprise of one trying to comprehend: because all things that did not grow on trees must be made by human beings, he was asked to believe he was now in the presence of such a person—one who *made* things. Peggy was uncomfortable at having to think that a "maker" stood between her and the pictures in *Waste*. She had been happily unaware of any person's having drawn the pictures, let alone that her mother knew the woman. Peggy did not like attention to be drawn to her for the things she made. She felt embarrassed for Mrs. Jackman.

"What would we draw?" Gabriel asked.

"Do you prefer to draw things you observe or things you imagine?" Shelagh asked.

"What I can see!" Gabriel asserted.

Peggy said quietly, "What I make up."

"Well, then, you can both be happy. Let's put all these dishes in the sink and take a stroll." When Shelagh held each child by the hand, she said,

"First we'll go from this house into the next house and see the orchids. There's no direct connection between the kitchen and the 'glass house.' " She led them back through the dining and living rooms into the front hall, where the double vestibule formed a wide, welcoming entrance to both houses.

Gabriel said, "It's like having a secret house."

"Everyone should have secrets," Shelagh confided to the children. "It makes you feel special." She looked back at Kate—whose expression was worried or disapproving. Shelagh imagined she was afraid 'secrets' would mean concealing, would lead to the children's not telling her the truth; the woman was concerned at every instant with bringing up her children correctly. Or she was distressed to watch another 'mother' influencing them, when she alone should be responsible for their education: a lioness?

The living and dining rooms of the parallel house taken over by the Jackmans had been made into a library for the Judge's large, elaborate, and valuable collection of books. On the oval mahogany table in the center of the inner room was displayed Shelagh's collection of brass objects and crystal paperweights. There were molded brass buckles and saddle joiners and knobs and clasps; paperweights the size of baseballs, clear glass to the bottom, where imaginary flowers in rosettes of bright circles, packed tight together like hidden treasures, were magnified into magical underwater gardens. At the far end of the library stood the French doors that opened into the orchid greenhouse.

It was a humid hothouse. Shelagh switched off the source of moisture and, as the pumping machine stopped sounding, cranked open the louvers of a window to let in fresh air. The room was small, but all four of them stood on the wooden slats across the floor between the broad counters on both sides along which the pots were filled and above which, suspended from hooks on steel rods along the glass ceiling, hung hundreds of red clay pots seemingly spilling the profusion of their extraordinary variety.

"Some of them are as tiny as my fingernails," Peggy said.

Gabriel's comment was "They don't look like orchids."

"Oh, don't be disappointed. We have one here for you." Shelagh drew up from the back of a counter a standard white orchid with golden lines like caterpillars along the center of three petals. "Just like certain ladies wear at their fiftieth wedding anniversary," she said.

"That's more like it," Gabriel agreed.

"Would you want to draw this one?"

"Yes."

"All right. We'll take it with us."

But Kate and Peggy were fascinated by the small waxen cups of color— mauve and tiger-lily, bone-white, specked with green sequins. "You cultivate these from seed?" Kate asked.

24

"In a sense, we bring them in from everywhere: Tanzania, Singapore—there are superb orchid farms there; South America, Africa. They usually arrive already attached to branches like these twigs or on a strip of bark."

"And they don't need soil?" Kate asked.

"They root in the air," Peggy supplied brightly.

"They cling," Shelagh explained. "They're called epiphytes because that means they take their food from rain in the air. Their seeds are blown by the breeze, and wherever they find a haven—something to cling to—they can grow, as long as it's warm enough and moist enough."

"Do you breed them and get different species?" Gabriel asked.

"No. We can't even keep up with the variety that already exists in the wild. This is the most variegated of all plants. There are thirty thousand known species *in nature* before you count a single cultivated orchid."

Kate was surprised. "But that should make them seem ordinary, whereas they're thought of as *rare.*"

Shelagh replied, "One jungle's 'ordinary' is another continent's 'rare.'"

Peggy said, "I think I'm going to faint."

"Let's go," Shelagh ordered. "Here, Gabriel, you carry your model."

He took the pot, with its shallow bed of brown bark instead of soil, and held the large ivory-and-gold orchid carefully before him as he led the group back into the library. After closing the louvered window and switching the moisturizer on again, Shelagh drew the glass doors together behind her, ran her hand across the wetness on her forehead, and sighed with pleasure. A virile man had found her desirable today. She had felt again that upsurge of excitement implicit in an unknown future. Then she led her guests upstairs to her studio.

"Gabriel—Peggy—I think you might like pastels or Magic Markers. What do you say?"

Peggy chose the hard, bright colors and Gabriel the soft, chalky ones.

"Here are drawing pads," Shelagh continued, "one for each of you. Gabriel, you sit here on the high stool at this flat table. Peggy, you take the swivel chair at the tilted drawing board in front of the window." In the array of pens and brushes and file cabinets and a lightboard, suddenly the two children had been set to their tasks in an orderly, simple manner, like being told it was rest period at camp. The adults wanted to have a little time for themselves. The children were not happy about the whole idea, but they silently followed orders. Shelagh led Kate back down to the library. "Would you like a Sherry?" she asked, and then poured out two glasses from the decanter on a side table.

They sat in comfortable armchairs facing each other before a window next to the fireplace. "I don't know how you did it," Kate began, both weary and envious.

"Did what?" Shelagh asked.

"Survived raising your two children and lived to seem sane: you know—all together."

"Oh, that . . ."

"I don't think I'll make it."

"You take it too seriously." Shelagh sipped her Sherry and then said, "The secret of success is simple: think of your children as adopted. Then whenever they do things you think well of you can take pride in what they learned from you; but if they disappoint you or dissatisfy you, you can blame it on genetics—tell yourself you couldn't have done anything about it."

Kate laughed nervously. "You're joking."

"That's my point—see the joke in it. You don't have total control over how they develop. Then don't presume to total responsibility. Actually, I got this advice from a theologian who learned it the hard way. He had three children of his own and then adopted three orphans. He knew what he was talking about."

"Well, I suspect what saved you is having a career of your own. You were an artist before you were a mother, weren't you? Illustrator? Image-maker?"

"Yes, that's true, I was."

Shelagh sensed resentment stemming from Kate's own lack of similar "status" and anticipated her asking: "How did that come about?"

"Well—from childhood; my father was a great art historian . . ."

"Yes, I know: Sir Hans Markgraf. My husband has all his books."

"Really? I haven't read all of them. It's a pity—his writing, I mean. The books are so solemn. None of his charm, his humor, comes through in those books of his I've read."

"But he was an amusing man?"

"Enormously. He had a great sense of play. Whimsy, the British would say. I'm afraid there isn't as much whimsy nowadays as there used to be."

"No," Kate agreed. "There's so little time for anything but what's 'purposeful.' "

"That takes me back to my drawings. Of course, as the daughter of Sir Hans Markgraf I was aware of—exposed to—all sorts of works of art from the day I was born. There was always sculpture, paintings, etchings, drawings, woodcuts—you name it—all over the house. And my father took me to museums and to see the collections of friends or acquaintances from the time that I could walk."

"You just came by it naturally," Kate concluded.

"Not at all. I was terribly inhibited. I felt I shouldn't draw unless I could do marvelous things, superb things; priceless, timeless, glorious things."

"But then . . . ?"

"I would hide my drawings. Or tear them up. Or burn them. That was the turning point. I must have been about fifteen or sixteen. My father walked in when I was destroying a clutch of drawings in the fireplace. We talked and talked and talked. I was so crestfallen; he was enchanting. He told me never to try to judge my own work—like giving it a grade at school. I could never be my own student as well as my own teacher. He said never to despair that something I did wasn't worthy of lasting forever. Nothing lasts forever. To think rather of everything I made the way certain ceremonials are carried out in India. There are all sorts of festivals in India for which 'image-makers' create masks, costumes, decorations of the most imaginative kinds—sumptuous in purple, vermilion, green—fierce or lyrical; out of papier-mâché, you know. And in the end they destroy them all. It goes up in flame. Even the flames are decorated—with saffron thrown through the air into the fire, cedar shavings, eucalyptus leaves. The whole ceremony ends in an auto-da-fé. It is self-consumed."

"Yes," Kate agreed, vaguely.

"That's what my father urged upon me. To paint or draw with no further expectation than that the creation was self-consuming. To consider it something for the pleasure of a festival that would end in its own ashes." She paused, and then added, "He was a very wise man."

"How did he know so much about India?" Kate asked. Shelagh poured more Sherry, and they both sipped the wine.

"India was a hobby with the Viennese in my father's circle. I believe they thought of it as the most exotic and complex country in the world. The most remote—with an elaborate cultural and religious life more different from what they were familiar with than any other 'high' civilization. Many Middle Europeans went to study there. Think of Eliade. And when push came to shove, many of them thought of emigrating there: India. Or Ireland."

"Ireland? Why Ireland?"

"For the same reason. Exotic. The most unspoiled and unique island in Europe. Celtic art and all that sort of thing. They imagined the Irish to be noble savages . . ." She laughed. ". . . until they found out they were only savages."

Kate frowned. She was the daughter of good socialists; no one was permitted to be a cultural snob. Still, she had never been to Ireland or known anyone who had.

"The Irish preoccupation," Shelagh continued, "explains my name. I suspect my parents knew more old Irish folklore and myth than anyone in Dublin. In any case, I was given the Irish form of the name 'Sheila.' "

Kate said, "Fascinating . . ." And then, "I wonder how the children are doing."

"You worry too much. You can't breathe for them, you know. . . ."

Kate drew back and then shifted the subject. She asked, "How did you and the Judge come to meet?"

"Well, of course, he wasn't a judge in those days. It was during the war. He was stationed in London, at Grosvenor Square, and had a letter of introduction to my parents from Walter Webster. Do you know Walter?"

"No."

"He's here at the University now. Professor of art history. But before the war he was at the National Gallery in Washington—it was the Mellon then—and he knew Chester in those days. The future judge was a clerk to one of the Supreme Court justices. Walter Webster had been a student of my father's at the Warburg Institute in the middle 'thirties."

"I see. Some sort of intellectual community of interests"—as if looking at a genealogical table in her mind's eye.

"Not quite. Chester doesn't have much interest in art."

"But it was Webster's connection with your father that brought you together."

"True. Why do you ask?"

"It's amazing how anybody finds a husband these days," Kate said with a smile.

"But not a lover," Shelagh added quickly. "You can pick up the man who sits next to you on a bus; but it's still preferable to marry someone who is introduced through a family connection."

They chuckled, somewhat uneasily.

"I met Henry at a party in New York," Kate offered, wondering about the future of her children.

Shelagh savored the feel of Quentin Connolley's hands luxuriating on her bare arm.

"Women must stop thinking about marriages," Shelagh announced, "or it will ruin their social lives." And both women laughed, rather unsure of themselves.

"It's all so much balderdash," Shelagh's father would have said, because he had learned British English in the 1890s and the word was current then for nonsense—silliness. "Balderdash" came to Shelagh's mind as she waved goodbye to Kate and her children from the steps of the front door, watched the boy and then the girl waving their rolled-up drawings in response from the back seat of Kate's white convertible. Nonsense, she repeated to herself. This effort to make conversation. In "converse," what is it we give and take?

She closed the door behind her with a sudden sense of distaste. As if to free herself from such feelings she briskly washed and dried the dishes and glasses in the kitchen, then, in her studio, replaced the pads of paper, pastels, and Magic Markers in their proper locations, and returned the conventional orchid to the hothouse. Standing at one of the mahogany tables in the library, Shelagh gazed about the double room to see if she had left her diary there and found it on the mantelpiece, with a ball-point pen lying nearby. Actually, it was a bound manuscript book of blank pages. She bought one—of a different-colored binding but the same size—each year on her visit to London. She sat in the chair where she had been facing Kate Warner and reread the final line of the last entry. *"Sometimes I think I must be the only person left in the world who keeps a diary."* Now she began a new page with the date and the word *"Nonsense."* And then made these notes:

Lunch with Kate and her two kids. Odd conversation. Full of "How to_____" questions. How did you become an artist? How did you and Chester meet? How does one survive raising children . . . ? Why am I irritated by that? Respectable questions; a way to make intelligent conversation. What's wrong with it? Somehow abrasive or intruding—that excessive American assumption that everything of importance to know is in method, technique, means to an end. How do you flatten your stomach? How can I keep a soufflé from falling? How can I improve my wardrobe, my garden, my grammar, my muscle tone, my mind? Always How. Never What for? What good is it? What's it worth?

No. It's not Kate's fault. I don't fault her at all. I want to like her. I do like her. I blame myself. It was I who determined the answers. Why did I respond to each of the questions in the quickest, the most glib, the most superficial way? As if I couldn't trust Kate to accept more serious replies. Or maybe the situation, the time, the manner of the moment called for only the skin-deep reactions. Even then, there's so much skin that covers all those events; why choose those particular little patches? Why not be bold and tell someone else what you would tell yourself?

My goodness—how did Chester and I meet? During the war. During the blackouts in the days of the V-2. He appeared in my parents' home. He was sent to my father by a former student—like a CARE package. No, he chose to use a letter of introduction to an important person in London. He knew nearly no one else in London, let alone any "important" person. My father had just been knighted—on one of those mid-war honors lists, to show that the government had not forgotten what we were fighting for: survival, yes; but the freedom of the life of the mind. For the glory of beauty and thought. It was all very heady. My mother wandered about in a daze for weeks—remembering she had been born Ilse Löwe in Innsbruck, youngest child of the high school principal, educated to become an eye doctor—and now she was Lady Markgraf, to be presented at Court. My father thought it very amusing, a good deal below the Rothschilds' buying a baronetcy. But he was gratified.

Chester Jackman came to tea at four one afternoon. He was so tall and thin, but broad-shouldered, I thought: If he stands sideways he will look like a piece of wallboard with a big head piked on top. Not quite that; he looked so strong in a flat way, I was made aware of my strength in rounded ways. He wore an American Army officer's uniform, kept his large hands fanned out on his knees, and ate scones as if my mother had just invented them. My father found him "original"—an intellectual American was something of a cross between the noble Celts and the exotics of India. Imagine a man from New England who played the cello and practiced law and came from a family that had settled in the New World during the reign of Maria Theresa in Vienna.

Chester came to tea on Thursdays for four weeks in a row. It was only on the fourth visit that I knew he desired me. I had been barely conscious of him, so filled was I with my own concerns at the time. I recognized him; he seemed amiable; that was enough. But on the fourth visit we were left alone for a few minutes—inexplicably. And I sensed his passionate contemplation of me. Not a word was spoken. I was wearing a light blue shirtwaist dress and old straw slippers from Sicily. I had done nothing to attract his attention to me. Nevertheless, I recognized in his gaze, in his mien, his tension, that he found me desirable. He struck me as enormously powerful and in control of his powers: a warrior who could pounce, but chose to bide his time. He stared at me, as if he were invisible and I the object of his impersonal admiration. I had never before felt so excited in my life: and yet I made no move, no gesture; expressed nothing; drank my tea: wanting him to stand above me and announce, "You're mine!" I would have accepted it. What he did say was "I've loved you all my life; and now I've found you."

That is how we met. I did not need passage to the United States; I would have remained in England happily. I did not need a lover; I had desirable and desirous young men. I needed a man I could admire, a man of self-respect who wanted me and made me feel exquisite, made me feel that he wanted me to be with him forever. That was how I came to "meet" Chester. How well we met! Could I have told that to Kate? She didn't ask me how well we met.

Or: how I "survived" raising children? How can one answer that decently or honestly, or honorably? I was lucky, I suppose. I never felt the preposterous demand of being their "creator." I didn't know what the devil I was doing with Morgan, the firstborn; I was uncomfortable and awkward; unsure of myself—alone in a country without grandmothers. Whom does one ask for advice? The "how-to" people? I wasn't yet American enough for that. I suckled him and played with him, and kept my distance. Perhaps he suffered. He was insecure, and so as a grown-up he longs for safety and certainty. He thinks he'll find it in a lot of money. Maybe he will. With Claire I was a different person; I had experienced one child before, and she was a girl. I was endlessly loving and relaxed. They don't break! So there you have it: Morgan was nervously treated with kid gloves and now he needs to feel as secure as a gilt-edged bond. Claire was fondled confidently, as adored and enjoyed as possible, so what she's equal to is adventure. It isn't a question of how one survives bringing up children; they grow, they learn from you. They begin to live their own lives—which were "their own" from the very beginning. You can't really do very much damage . . . I think! They imagine their own dreams; and all you can do is encourage them to dream the dream forward. They are themselves and they belong to the world (not to you!), and thus, you "survive" the responsibility of having brought them forth. Could I have said that to Kate?

Besides, survival isn't interesting. It assumes a demand on you to overcome a situation you hadn't chosen, but found thrust upon you. Survive children? On the contrary: the joy resides in watching a child become himself—unfold, take shape, sharpen: not the way a crystal forms in the residue of a solution, but the way a flower becomes itself. From the earliest bud the flower is potentially there, and you have the pleasure of watching it form and take color the way Sweet William grows: the green leaves spreading out the base along the ground, the stalk stretching up, the top of it beginning to reveal pinheads of pale buds that gradually open into rosettes of burgundy or pink or white or circular patterns, dramatic combinations of colors, the patterns repeated again and again in the cluster, mysteriously made clear by repetition: blossoming! One doesn't "survive" that; one revels in it.

Why couldn't I have said that to Kate? Well . . . people don't speak that way to each other. That's why they keep a diary. "Articulate, only articulate!" my father said. "Try to become as articulate as possible. In your drawings as in your speech—even if only to yourself." And I've always liked talking to myself.

How did you become an artist? Could I have told Kate, "At the age of fourteen I learned from a girlfriend that if I took the life drawing course at the Slade, I could look at athletic male models in the nude"?

Shelagh left the pen and the diary on the end table, telling herself she must get back to work in the studio. She lowered the amber acetate shield over both windows facing west, and the afternoon light in the room turned to a soft golden hue as if from glowing kerosene lamps. Shelagh brought the portfolio with her first sketches for the Old Testament up onto the light table, untied it, and began to look them over critically, as if they had been drawn by someone else.

The Garden of Eden struck her as too formal—nearly Versailles. There were the river and the four streams, but the flora would have to be changed. It couldn't be an English garden, either: too casual. Something in between, orderly but not too neat, where art imposes control over nature without transforming it; nothing like hedges cut into the shapes of animals, or flowers trained into a sundial. The figure of Adam was fine—manly, unselfconsciously resting from the work for which he had been created: "to till the garden and care for it." But shouldn't he wear a beard? What would he have shaved with? she wondered, smiling to herself. Eve was languorously beautiful, if a somewhat idealized version of Claire. But a space for the serpent remained empty. What could it have looked like before it was cursed? It must have had arms and legs before, if only after the curse was it condemned to crawl on its belly; what made it so successfully "crafty"? Shelagh stared at the drawing blankly, while hearing the sounds of the silent house—an unanswered telephone ringing in a building across the street, a car door slammed shut, birdcalls that sounded like "Do we? Do we?"

She would have to come up with the serpent another time.

Turning the thin sheets of the drawing paper, she regarded with pleasure outlines for the expulsion from the Garden; but was dissatisfied by the cherubim holding a sword "whirling and flashing" to guard against anyone approaching the Tree of Life. The flashing and whirling looked like the fireworks of a Catherine wheel; it might be better with choppy Cubist fragments. She would have to revise that too. Cain and Abel were well drawn, and instead of the scene with the impact of murder itself, Shelagh had designed a view up from the ground where Abel lay dying—to show Cain's face in fear or remorse. Cain begot Enoch, and Enoch—Irad. Eve bore a third son, Seth, "in place of Abel," and Seth begot Enos. And so on and so on: Enos and Enoch; beget, beget. For ten generations unto Noah. Shelagh had outlined a play of generations down the page with the rhythm of a cataract, as in a great torrent flowing over boulders.

It took only ten generations before God "saw that man had done much evil on earth and that his thoughts and inclinations were always evil and he was sorry that he had made man on earth . . ." and decided: "I will wipe them off the face of the earth." But for one righteous man, Noah.

Shelagh stared at the hardwood floor, thinking God was ready to give up after only ten generations. She had counted the "begats"; there were no more than that. He hadn't got what He wanted. Only ten generations and God saw that the whole world was corrupt. As simple as that: wipe 'em out! The disappointed God. Revenge for not being pleased. With the exception of Noah, the dutiful servant. So He drowns everyone and everything except for those in Noah's ark—and the begats begin again. Twenty generations mean twice as many disappointments, so at Babel, when they try to storm into Heaven, He smites them each with a different language and scatters them all into enemy camps. God and the servant problem. Couldn't get what He wanted. Some creator! She laughed; for Shelagh had often enough gone through thirty drafts before a drawing of hers pleased her.

She remembered having once given notice to a nasty servant who was slovenly and broke things; unabashed, the woman had accepted the dismissal by saying, "Oh, I know, everything here turns on your pleasure"—as if that were a put-down. And Shelagh had instantly replied: "Not on my arbitrary 'pleasure'; on my *judgment*." The distinction was beyond the maid, who snorted, and then stole two bottles of perfume before she left that afternoon. So Shelagh revised the thought: often enough she had made thirty drafts of a drawing before it satisfied her judgment.

For judgment is the great meeting point of thinking, feeling, and acting; it knots them together in real life. All comes woven into its proper design when a decision must be made to behave in a certain way: knowing, intuiting, needing to make a choice, issuing into an understanding that spells out both: how it will have to be; and why it should be so. Shelagh had gone from thinking of God as judge of His creation, to the artist as judge of her drawings, to the return of Chester Jackman—the Judge; and thought of making dinner ready.

In the kitchen, as she stood with her hand on the door of the refrigerator, in the corner of her eye Shelagh caught sight of movement in the backyard next door. The yards were not large behind the houses on Lynwood Court, near to the center of the city. Her own yard was dominated by a blue spruce beyond which, on the left, she could see the steeple of the chapel of St. Thomas More, and on the right, above the slate roof of Pierson College, the black weather vane above the small golden dome. But her aged next-door neighbors, the McGraths, had always been fond of gardening, and around their square of grass, framed by a fence of white birch trees, they cultivated a wide border of flowers. During the many years that Shelagh had lived in this house, she had watched the McGraths decline into decrepitude.

Now Virginia McGrath, in her ninetieth year, moved toward the purple asters one inch at a time; she leaned with both hands upon an aluminum walker that made her appear to be isolated on a tiny balcony wherever she went. Her small gray head was bent forward; a shapeless tan raincoat covered a hollow form revealing bare spindly legs; their flesh, drooping like loosely draped stockings, ended in black-and-yellow sneakers. She moved the walker forward one inch and stepped in close behind it. Shelagh then observed Archibald McGrath hobbling behind her. His head was entirely bald, and the thick lenses of his spectacles in large black frames, stationed at the center of his long, sharp nose, appeared to make his eyes bulge out of his head grotesquely. He was as short as his wife and as slender, in a black suit worn over a white undershirt, and he moved with the unpredictable twitches of a skeleton

33

whose joints are silting up with arthritis. Using a long-handled garden hoe as a cane, he came jerkily forward until he stood abreast of his wife. Virginia McGrath pointed down between the asters; Archibald McGrath weeded with the hoe.

He had been an accountant who was already retired a quarter of a century before, when Shelagh had first met him. He must be in his early nineties too, she thought. Their children must be in their sixties. They never came to visit. The McGraths never had visitors. In the old days, before Virginia's stroke, they used to walk together around the garden hand in hand, first thing in the morning and last thing at dusk. They seemed so intensely devoted to each flower that Shelagh imagined they had a different first name for each one of them. It was a long time since she had seen them holding hands. Then a painful memory came to mind. A few months before, in the darkness of a spring evening, Shelagh had happened to be standing by the open kitchen door for a breath of air when she heard the harshness of Archibald McGrath's voice next door shouting, "Don't tell me about your bowel movements. It's bad enough that I have to help you to the bathroom. I don't want to hear about your bowel movements!" Shelagh felt cold sweat break out along her forehead at the thought of it. The suffering of senility, the impairments of old age. Even their house was decaying—at least what Shelagh could see from the outside. The brick walls were in need of tuck-pointing. Ivy grown over the drainpipes choked the gutters. Not having been repaired or painted for years, the woodwork around each of the windows, cracked open first and then inhabited by spiders, appeared to be turning to soft mold. But the excellence of the garden was maintained. Weeding did not cost any money.

Chester Jackman called out, "Shelagh?"—as a question—while he closed the front door behind him.

It had often struck her that he was saying, "She—*là?*" as a mixture of English and French meaning "Is she there?"

"I'm in the kitchen," she replied.

When he stood in the doorway he found her adding anchovy toast to a small tray of deviled eggs.

"Just like Werther and Charlotte," he said.

"You don't have to pine for me, darling," she laughed. "I'm yours, I'm yours."

He put an arm around her shoulder and kissed her on the right cheek.

"How about a Campari and soda?" she asked. "I'll take these hors d'oeuvre into the living room."

They sat in the corners of the Queen Anne period sofa, turned toward each other. Chester had placed drinks and the napkins on a small tray next to the platter of hors d'oeuvre on the low Chinese trunk with elaborate brass hinges that served as a coffee table between them.

"You're early," Shelagh observed.

"Bored," the Judge stated. "I wish we were still in Alaska."

"But it's been such a beautiful day. Why were you bored?"

"Trivia," he explained. "Nothing but trivia."

"You can't expect to make a major decision every day," she said, smiling.

He laughed. "Why not? You do. You decide on what to make for hors d'oeuvre; you choose which dress to wear; you draw a picture of something that never existed before . . ."

If he was being sardonic, Shelagh decided, she would not rise to the bait. "The truth is, you like your life as much as I do mine." They sipped their drinks, they ate the hors d'oeuvre, they patted their lips with the napkins; Chester Jackman took a cigarette out of his jacket pocket, struck a match to light it, blew out the match, stood up to fetch an ashtray to the Chinese trunk, and seated himself again heavily on the sofa. Shelagh glanced at the four paintings of the seasons by Archimboldo on the wall behind them, and then, opposite them, at the dozen Chinese plates that decorated the wall above the fireplace, and turning her face back to look at her husband's, she returned to thoughts of his day in court. "What was so boring about it?" she asked.

"Postponements. Setting trial dates."

"Did you send anyone to Discovery?" she asked, with a twinkle in her eye.

"Why do you think that's so funny?"

"It's the idea of ordering somebody to discover something." She would occasionally drop in at the courthouse, sit at the back of the chamber, and watch her husband on the bench.

"It only means that lawyers on opposite sides of the case have the right to learn what documents and other evidence their opponent intends to present at a trial."

"Why should one have the right to find out what his adversary might want to keep secret until the big moment?"

"This is not a course in jurisprudence," the Judge declared with a mock gruffness. "Was there any mail today?"

"No."

"Any calls? Any word from Claire or Morgan?"

Shelagh shook her head, no. "But I ran into Kate Warner and her two younger children. They came back and had lunch with me here."

"Nice Kate," the Judge said approvingly. "That sounds pleasant." He leaned forward toward his wife and reached out to take her hand in his.

"Now . . ." he began slowly to ask: "would you be good enough to tell me what Dr. Connolley said?"

"Ah, that's what you're being prickly about." She gave his hand a little squeeze and then released it, to reach for a slice of anchovy toast. "There's nothing to worry about yet because he hasn't told me what to worry about yet."

"What does that mean?"

"He took some tests; and I'll have to see him again when he has the results. But he didn't make any guesses and he didn't seem in the least upset. So I don't know anything more than before I went to see him."

The Judge exhaled a long jet of cigarette smoke with a sigh.

What went unsaid was that they were both doomed to age and that they lived in a culture which offered so many methods for prevention of disabilities that if one became ill or infirm, one had to live with the guilt of having lacked forethought or having been unequal to taking appropriate action at the right time; as if to die would be the ultimate failure of one's moral responsibility.

"So . . ." Chester Jackman concluded. "It is to be continued."

"Yes. I'll see him again at the end of the week." In the instant of saying that, Shelagh Jackman realized she wanted Quentin Connolley to try to seduce her. She regarded her husband, stubbing out his cigarette and reaching for the long, cool glass. He is aging, she thought; there is much more gray in his hair, heavy pouches under his eyes, and a wearied slackness in his body that is not to be explained by boredom. She had lived with him through the extraction of most of his teeth, wiping his face dry when he burst into tears after the laughing gas wore off. Her own teeth had always been flawless. But there he was, over sixty, tall and lean and strong. The sun lowered itself behind the houses across the street and the light suddenly faded from the living room. She saw her husband in silhouette: his high forehead, prominent nose, sensuous lips in an almost lantern jaw; the black-and-white polka-dot bow tie stood out against the white shirt, and his blue glen plaid suit grew darker. His legs were crossed, and the sole of one shoe touched carefully against the brass fitting at one corner of the Chinese trunk. Shelagh stood up, saying, "I must put on some lights," and moved to the four corners of the room switching on the lamps.

He said, "I don't want anything to happen to you."

She came back to stroke his cheek and then, feeling called upon to change the subject, declared: "I don't believe I told you about my dream last night." Sitting down again in her corner of the sofa, she continued: "I was a child again in my parents' house in London, about fifteen or sixteen years old, when a friend of mine—it was Evelyn Knops—and I decided we must get away. So we went off on a trip. We were in New York, then in California . . ."

She laughed. "It was somewhere in San Francisco that I was stricken with regret. We were spending all that money and I hadn't asked my parents' permission or let them know where I was. So I returned. Morgan was in the drawing room, which surprised me, but it was he who told me that spending all that money didn't matter, it was perfectly all right. And then my parents amazed me by confessing that they hadn't noticed at all that I had been gone."

Her husband said, "Well, I'd take that to mean you live a very secure life." When they chose to tell each other their dreams, they tried to interpret them. "You must feel that you can do whatever you like, and that between your parents and your children, you're going to be supported and affirmed."

"But I went home with a bad conscience."

"To be made to feel all right about it."

" 'Between my parents and my children . . .' " Shelagh echoed her husband. "And where were you?"

"I can't say. It was your dream." He smiled.

Am I more concerned to have the approval or reassurance of my parents and children than of my husband? she wondered; but did not state it. "And what about neither my father nor my mother missing me? Not recognizing that I'd gone away?"

"But you haven't," the Judge remarked. "It's they who've *gone away.* . . ."

"What a thought! That actually sent a chill down my spine." She held her elbows and squeezed herself for warmth.

"You never left them 'without permission,' " he persisted. "But they passed away without yours."

"I don't think we're interpreting a dream; this is more like a game of word association." True, she thought, they are gone, in the sense of no longer being physically present, for all that she could not think of them as gone to somewhere else. Not gone *away,* as when in childhood she had returned home to find her mother still away at her office or her father gone for a lecture trip and she had worried about how soon they might come back. But they were not gone from her. She lived between two generations, two layers of time—the unchangeable past of her parents and the unknowable future of her children. Her own life was a stretch of time that merged on either side with those two layers of before and after.

Suddenly she said: "How did you survive the children growing up?"

"Why do you ask?"

"Kate Warner asked me, and I didn't treat it very well. Tried to make light of it."

"I knew you were about to change the subject."

"What subject?"

"Your dream."

"Oh. . . . We had enough of that, don't you think?"

"I love the musical notes on which you say 'don't you think'—like do-re-mi."

"I love our desultory conversations." She smiled to herself, partly because Chester had once explained to her that the word came from *desultor*, the Latin term for the athletes, in horse races in the Roman Colosseum, who would leap from the back of one horse to another and another as the horses ran around the track.

"I'm not sure I *have* survived the children growing up," Chester said, chuckling half to himself. "I think about them a lot of the time. I don't miss the anxiety, though," he added quickly.

Still facing forward as if staring across the room, Shelagh looked at him from the corner of her eye. She would not criticize him. The time for that was long past. But what did he know of anxiety? Of how much more than he she had had to suffer those pangs of uncertainty: Would her daughter walk home *safely* from the roller-skating rink? She was only eleven, but didn't want to be called for; her friends' parents never picked them up. Where was Morgan at twilight on a bitter cold day in winter when he should have been home from school at three? Was that merely a cold, or a strep throat? Would Claire be able to pass her exams without sleep—having stayed up to study all through the night? While Shelagh knew the ways in which other women—American-born women—resented their husbands' lack of involvement in bringing up their children, she hadn't expected her husband to be the coach/buddy/Scout leader her friends seemed to expect of their husbands. And still she and Chester had had disagreements over how much time he might spend with Morgan, if not with Claire; but those arguments had evaporated a decade ago. Nevertheless, she said, "I thought I had a monopoly on anxiety about their growing up."

"I was very much here for them, whether you thought so or not," he replied, adding, "whether you thought it was enough or not."

"Well, it's over." She sighed. "Whatever we could have done we did."

For a moment she thought of him as having been "there" for the children the way the furniture and the refrigerator were: to be made use of. But that was unfair. No; it was true that he was *there* in the way her father had been for her—living his life before her; and what she saw of it and what she gained from it—how he solved problems, what he did to entertain his children, how his critical conversations with her mother demonstrated what they valued and what they disapproved of—amounted to teaching by example. Chester had been like that for her children. Even his humor was like her father's.

"Do you remember," she said, "that first time, soon after Morgan earned his driver's license, when we allowed him to take Claire in the car to a drive-in movie—how miserable with worry we were until they came home around ten at night?"

The Judge replied, "Of course I remember. Morgan put a dent in the right front fender."

"Oh, I didn't give a damn about the car. I was afraid of losing both my children in one fell swoop."

"Well, that's only natural. The car was insured. It was the children who weren't."

"I miss the giggles," Shelagh said suddenly. "Remember? Sometimes Claire and a friend would be in her bedroom—how old could they have been? twelve? thirteen?—and the uncontrollable laughter would flow for half an hour. It would ripple through the house. I could hear them in my studio or in the kitchen. I never hear anybody giggle nowadays."

Chester ruminated: "I suppose in the same incident that made me believe Morgan might become a financial wizard, I became nervous that he had criminal tendencies."

"What was that?"

"Don't you remember? He figured out how to mail a letter without putting a stamp on it. He would address it to himself and for a return address he'd fill in the name and location of the person he wanted the letter sent to; so it was delivered where he wanted it to go, marked, "Returned to sender.""

"Oh, yes, now I recall."

"I think he was heartbroken when I explained to him that what he was doing was not only illegal but immoral."

"Yes, yes—I remember—when he was in college he told us that incident made it possible for him to understand Kant's *Ethics*—you know: what if everybody did it . . . ."

"Right."

"I don't think he has 'criminal tendencies.' "

"Everybody wishes he could be the exception to the rules." The Judge shrugged his shoulders. "All rules."

"But there were times when he was the most darling child," Shelagh began enthusiastically. "Think of when we were in Manhattan at Christmastime. Claire went to someone's birthday party, and we took Morgan ice-skating in Central Park and then over to Rumpelmayer's for cake and hot chocolate. What was he—ten years old?"

"Yes, yes. I'll never forget it." Chester finished his drink and smiled at the recollection.

Rumpelmayer's! Shelagh was happy to be in that idealized re-creation of a Konditorei smelling of Sacher torte and vanilla beans: the perfection of a child's dream of a European ice cream parlor, all pink and white, done up in ribbons, decorated with dolls and stuffed animals and candy boxes to take

away as presents. Morgan ate a banana split and then a strawberry tart, drinking one hot chocolate after another, and they felt cozy in the late-afternoon
warmth, in a booth near the front window looking out on snowflakes beginning to fall casually onto Fifty-ninth Street and across the way into the Park.

"Are you happy?" Shelagh asked her son—an unnecessary question, perhaps calling for an expression of appreciation, a vote of confidence.

The child looked from her to his father and back at the elegant table; he
put down his fork and lifted his middle finger and thumb together to his lips,
kissed them, and blew the kiss into the air, saying, "I think I'm in heaven."
They laughed with joy. She remembered his connoisseur's smile, his boule-
vardier's gesture. Where had he learned it? Shelagh wondered. From television? from his classmates? Had she or Chester ever done that? It was the
quintessential expression of Morgan's childhood: old for his years, endearing,
with the charm of a child who wishes to please grown-ups, probably using
words he doesn't understand but assumes that they do. A very early instance
of self-consciously acting a part for the pleasure it would bring his audience,
his benefactors, his patrons; and at the same time: true.

"We have been very lucky," Chester said, "that our children have turned
out as well as they have."

"Claire—" Shelagh began uncertainly; "Claire will have a harder time of
it. Trying to be an actress is much, much more chancy than being a stockbroker."

"You are more *sympathique* with your daughter than with your son," the
Judge stated without implication of criticism.

Shelagh ignored the remark. "Elsie and Clifford Rostum have splendid
children."

"Conrad Taylor's daughter is a serious worry."

Shelagh added to the inventory: "The Connolley son is in good shape.
Kate Warner's older boy is starting college at Ann Arbor. But she frets too
much about the younger ones. Do you think we should add Henry and Kate
to the group for dinner on Saturday night?"

Chester closed his eyes and thought about it. "Cliff and Elsie are coming . . ."

"Brita; and Walter Webster . . ."

"Conrad and Isabel?"

"No. Dr. Rosenblatt and his wife?"

"How many are we, then?"

"Only eight, including us."

"Oh, I think that's enough. I like eight."

"I like ten."

"Too many."

She patted his knee. "Eight it is. We'll ask Henry and Kate another time."

"And Quentin and Ellen . . ."

Ah, Quentin Connolley, Shelagh pondered—what will the future make of him?

Tonight was to be a relaxed evening at home with no obligations. They had been to the house of the psychiatrist Dr. Rosenblatt the night before—Chester played in the string quartet with Mrs. Rosenblatt, Marcia Flower, and Brom Kirkill. Shelagh listened with the other spouses. No homework tonight, no show to attend, no lecture, no meeting, no concern, no deadlines to hurry up to. They would have a simple dinner and clean up together afterward. Chester would play the cello; Shelagh would read or knit, write letters or add to her diary. Late in the evening they would examine the orchids: check the humidity, marvel at the new growth, the waxen beauties gradually disclosing themselves; regret the desiccation of the older flowers turning brown. Thus they enjoyed themselves, each other, and peace.

And that was how they did enjoy the evening. After their meal, they settled themselves in the library. At first, Chester took from the shelves of his estimable books the first edition of Judge Learned Hand's *The Spirit of Liberty* to find one of the essays he wanted to look at again, standing up, his back supported against the mantelpiece; Shelagh nestled into the burgundy velvet armchair with her long needles, the chubby skeins of azure and royal blue wool trailing along the Oriental rug like two terrier puppies pulling on strings. She was knitting together the light and dark blues into a warm winter pullover for Claire. From the living room a performance of Prokofiev came over the radio. When he had finished what he wanted to reread, Chester replaced the book on the shelf; disappeared in order to switch off the music and then returned to bring his cello out of hiding from a library corner; sat on one of the tall wing chairs; set his music on the stand before him; and began to limber up.

Shelagh looked at him thinking: Most men relax from their work by doing nothing; they watch movies and get drunk. Chester refreshes himself from work by doing a different kind of work: making music. And then she realized, with a silent chuckle, that she was knitting for the same purpose. Shelagh wasn't sure what Chester was playing, although it sounded to her like Scarlatti. This was their plateau; this was the high level at which they had arrived—separately and together: they were themselves, alone and together, after a day's work, "recreating" themselves, as the antique vocabulary would have it; as their children would put it: by doing their own thing. It became them; it fulfilled them. Playing the cello involved no action on the part of the Judge that affected the lives of others; the music he made—as he often jokingly said—was a victimless crime. For his wife, knitting a sweater was a

41

homely activity that realized someone else's pattern; she was relieved of the need to create something that had never existed before—as she felt both free and compelled to do in her illustrations. They did not speak. There was no need for speech. He played the cello in resonant solitude, and she knitted the sweater privately in nearly soundless motion: both according to predetermined instructions. They had determined neither the pattern of the music nor of the sweater; but both of them relaxed, and accomplished their pleasures, by carrying out instructions. In the rest of their lives they had to determine the directions and the instructions; their hobbies offered them respite from those demands. They knitted sweaters and they performed music with the aid and comfort—the advice—of others. It struck Shelagh that "the advice of others" was a fact that filled her with reassurance; she was not alone and in need of reinventing the wheel. She could benefit from those who had come before. She was an inheritor, an heir in the best sense; and so was her husband—making lovely music at the suggestions of a Neapolitan composer of the late seventeenth century. They created what they could in their own houses, and in their "rest periods" they were reinforced by the lives of others who had lived before them.

"I got a really lousy haircut this time," he said as they undressed in their bedroom. "I have to find a better barber."

"I don't ordinarily think of you as vain," she replied, "but if you don't like that haircut, darling, I think you ought to take it up to a higher court."

They laughed comfortably as she switched off the light in the room and, plunged into darkness, they silently accepted the expectation of sleep. After all the years of marriage—nearly thirty years of marriage—they were not "lovey-dovey"; but they maintained a practice they had established in the first year they lived together: instead of their saying "Good night" before falling asleep, the last words they spoke—each to the other—at the end of every night were "I love you." It had seen them through their battles (even when it sounded like an accusation or a curse), and it had capped their happiest days: the highest common denominator of their sense of communion, for all the mystery of it. Chester was obviously extremely weary and eager to sleep, for he seemed to hurry into kissing her cheek and saying "I love you." She echoed "I love you," kissing him in turn. He sighed and turned onto his left side. She lay on her back, parallel to him, on the right side of the bed.

She was not prepared to fall asleep immediately. Chester was blessed with facility to drop off to sleep in the blinking of an eye, but Shelagh often daydreamed or made plans or meditated for an hour or more before sleep came. Her eyes grew accustomed to the pale light—the slivers of dull silver that shone from the streetlamps below, filtered through the shuttered windows and the organdy curtains, to make the bunches of flowers visible across the ceiling. Embowered, she thought, quoting to herself a line of a poem: "Nature I loved; and next to Nature, Art."

She had not yet drawn up a menu for Saturday night, but Cliff Rostum was so fond of rack of lamb. She'd find out if she could get a good one in time and plan the meal around that. She must confirm that Mrs. Yates would come to help cook and serve dinner. Also buy more wineglasses; why did they break so frequently?

She had not done well by Kate Warner. Something in the way she expressed concern over her children had rubbed Shelagh the wrong way. There was an undertone of fear, if not panic, in her voice. What was it? A note of self-pity; yes, that was the trouble—the sound of an unspoken complaint that she might not get *her way,* might not be satisfied as she felt she ought to be: the dread of being disappointed, unable to effect the degree of control over—influence on—her children to the extent that she desired, or imagined to be her right or her responsibility. Yes, that was what bothered Shelagh, because it had never been clear to her just what that responsibility ought to be for herself as a mother: resenting the need to try to determine the answer. All the important things in life are determined by instinct, she consoled herself.

Chester uttered a thin groan, and as he rolled over onto his back, his right hand hit her left arm. Gently she moved it closer to his side, thinking, We learn to accommodate to each other: his side of the bed and mine. Parallel and inturned: accommodated. First we learned to see each other, to admire and enjoy each other; then we came to see through each other—to discover what could not be altered or improved or escaped; then we came to see that it is better only to see each other . . . we come together; and we separate; and we come together again.

But it has changed as we grow older.

Chester let out a low whistle of a snore. Shelagh urged him to turn over onto his left side again and pushed the pillows up under his head. He became quiet. She stroked his shoulder, then turned away onto her right side.

What has changed, as we grow older? she asked herself. When we were young, he fell in love with me and his body wanted to make love all the time; I had only to invite, to lure, to suggest—I had only to touch him in certain ways—for him to leap into lovemaking with me. It was the perfect combination of desire and opportunity. I felt so endlessly desirable that it was as if I had the power to raise him from the dead. What is changed is not his love for me or his desire to make love, but what his body will permit—for while the spirit is willing, the flesh is weak. And so the illusion is shattered. It is not my power over him that enthralls and calls forth the evidence of love—as in a magic trick in which a prestidigitator has only to clap his palms together for a bouquet of flowers to appear between his hands—but the unpredictable power of his body that occasions itself fitfully and to which I accommodate,

43

for now I am at its mercy—saddened and shamed to know that my lures, my fascinations, my powers to attract have lost their magic. I deny it; I conceal from myself the simple truth that we have reached the opposite end of a trajectory of our history. In the beginning, he wanted to make love with me even more often than I wanted him to; and now we are at a point where I want him to make love with me more often than he is able to. It never was a matter of magic, despite the fact that it appeared to be. It never was in my power alone. We were always the victims or the beneficiaries of our bodies.

We accommodate. We accept the inescapable. And try not to grieve. Try not to notice the false teeth in the glass on a shelf in the bathroom. See the blue water and the foam atop the "denture cleaner," without seeing the false teeth. All things fade. All things fade away. And nevertheless, life goes on: less satisfactorily, as on a reduced income—the way the McGraths live next door; but be that as it may, life continues to go on.

She was reminded of what had become the classic example of that truism in the family of her parents. It had occurred in May or June of 1945—about six months after she had met Chester. The war in Europe was just over, although the war against Japan still went on. Their house was in an old section of Golders Green, near Hampstead Heath—almost like living in the country, while half an hour from the center of London. It was late afternoon on a spectacularly beautiful spring day, and by coincidence, both Adrienne and Shelagh had separately left their work a little early in order to arrive home in time for tea. Theirs was a simple house of the early nineteenth century, with a dining room, kitchen, and laundry on the ground floor; a sitting room, study, and sun room on the first floor; and bedrooms in the two stories above. During the days when Sir Hans worked at home—reading, thinking, and writing out his lectures—the large doors that otherwise were concealed in the side walls between the two main rooms were drawn closed, shutting off the study so that he might be undisturbed.

When Adrienne and Shelagh arrived that day, they found their mother in the sitting room just as the maid wheeled in the tea wagon—with sandwiches and cakes on the lower level, dishes and the tea service on top. The room was formal and cozy at the same time. Of course, there were books on all the tables, even scattered about the armchairs and the sofas, spotting the bright yellow chintz, with its bamboo designs, dark blue and Moroccan red with the bindings of scholarly tomes left in odd corners; and on the walls hung their framed Goya etchings, a copy of Archimboldo's *The Four Seasons*, an oil painting on a wood panel by Dante Gabriel Rossetti, along with six watercolor sketches, landscapes and seascapes of the Aegean islands, that her father's maiden aunt Greta had made during her trip to Greece in 1862. Flowing through the long windows, the spring sunlight gilded the frames of pictures, the piecrust edges of walnut tables, the large Mexican mirror on the wall, and warmed the faces of Shelagh and her sister staring down at their mother, who arranged to serve the tea and the boiled water, the powdered milk or the slices of lemon, and the miniature cubes of sugar. The parlormaid in a dove-gray dress stood at attention at the side of the tea wagon, awaiting instructions.

Sir Hans did not appear. Adrienne looked at her wristwatch. Their mother ran her hands over the high waves of her white hair, looked at her fingernails, smoothed down the pleats on her black wool skirt, sighing. Her husband was almost always exactly on time. But instead of his spreading apart the doors and arriving from the next room like an honored colossus, they heard a sob, then one deep-breathing gasp after another, until the chilling sound turned into a wail: a miserable, quick-panting series of heartbreaking moans rising into a shrill bleat—uncontrolled, her father no longer able to contain his crying, profound crying.

Shelagh's mother thrust herself up from the armchair, rushed to the doors, and pulled one aside, allowing her to move directly to his side. He was seated on the black leather sofa, his head in his hands, bent nearly in half, his shoulders almost at the level of his knees. His back heaved with sobs uncontrollably.

Lady Markgraf said, "My darling, darling, what is it?" patting his back, stroking his balding head, warming his arms. "Sweetest, tell me . . ."

Around him in a semicircle, scattered on the rug at his feet and on both sides of the sofa, lay newspapers and magazines, British, French, and Swiss, with photographs and articles attesting to the discovery of Nazi extermination camps: for the mass murder of Jews; for the elimination of all Jews from Nazi-dominated Europe. The revelation of the secret accord of the—how many? six, eight?—men who had dictated the policies of Germany during the war to murder all Jews, though keeping it a secret from the rest of the world. The public disclosure of genocide was verified, if incomplete.

"What is it?" Shelagh's mother pleaded, holding Sir Hans's head in her arms, tears welling in her own eyes at the sound of his horrendous sobs. "Why are you crying?"

He got a grip on himself. His tears stopped coming. His breathing continued in less frenzied spasms. He made an effort to speak, but that was choked by a new torrent of crying, until, finally, he regained himself, spread out his hands and arms over all the scattered magazines and newspapers, and brokenly articulated: "I'm weeping for humanity"—and again burst into tears.

Lady Markgraf grasped him more closely into her embrace. He sobbed, his whole chest heaving, his face still hidden in his hands. She rocked him, lovingly, whispering, "Shush . . . shush . . ." Adrienne and Shelagh stood like telephone poles in the sitting room, staring at the pitiful scene, useless, powerless as dumb animals.

45

The parlormaid, who stood next to them in the doorway unobtrusive, without makeup, simple in her dove-gray dress, her straight brown hair parted neatly in the middle, obviously wishing to be helpful, suddenly remarked: "But sir, it's time for tea."

Of course, she meant well. But for all of them—Sir Hans, his Lady, and their two daughters, transplanted Austrians, semiaccepted foreigners—*that*, yes, that statement alone was the ultimate British response, the quintessentially English reaction. "But sir, it's time for tea" had, ever since, echoed down through the years for them as the imperturbable attitude of sang-froid of the English confronted by chaos or confronted by the overwhelming, the incomprehensible, the unspeakable, that which is appalling beyond belief, but believed: the Nazis *did it!—nevertheless,* "It's time for tea!"

The gigantic implication of that "nevertheless" was not to leave any of them for the rest of their lives: Nevertheless. Six million—million, million!—Jews may have been murdered; half of all the Jews in the world; but by George!—*It is time for tea!*

Lady Markgraf cradled her husband's head in her arms. Shelagh and Adrienne hurried the parlormaid out of the sitting room and closed the door behind them: their parents had to be alone for a while. Through the closed door they listened as their mother commiserated with their father. When the sobbing stopped, they reentered the room and served tea to their parents; shared the silence with each other; wondered at the sun through the lace curtains, setting in the west; and knew of no way to dissolve their embarrassment or express the vulnerability of their human sympathy. They did not know how to grieve for humanity; they could only stare at the ashen, appalled face of their father, who himself had stared into this horror, the ultimate depravity of inhumanity. For whatever he, as an Austrian, with some connections to friends still on the Continent, had heard rumored or implied in the previous few years about the extermination of all Jews, he had not, as a humanist, been able to believe the worst. Now he could not disbelieve. The sudden impact of the revelation did not make him embrace his family as if, clutching them close, he might show that he was their defender, that they would care for each other, and he would protect them against the criminal and insane of the world. He sipped his tea, his reddened eyes looking from his wife to the faces of his daughters; impassive now, numbed, powerless to secure their safety in any absolute sense.

Her father had brought about the one change that saved their lives—by emigrating to England when it was still possible. Count Tolstoy had not been so lucky. In the 1800s Tolstoy had thought about it, written letters about it, talked about removing himself and his family to Britain, escaping the Russian despotism. But he was not able to carry it off. Instead, he tried to persuade his wife to agree to giving their estate over to the peasants and for them to live simply in a caretaker's cottage. The Countess thought he was mad and fought him to his dying day. She survived only for the Bolsheviks to give the estate over to those who worked the land, allowing her to live out her widowhood in a caretaker's cottage. What if Tolstoy had emigrated to England when he wished to do so? Sir Hans Markgraf often asked that question, in the 1940s, of strangers or dinner-party guests, to stimulate a conversation of hypothetical imaginativeness. Shelagh remembered that he had posed it to Chester Jackman on one of his first visits to their home. "What do you think would have become of Lev Tolstoy if he had settled in England in the 1890s?" And Chester replied: "He would have felt free to go on being the world's greatest novelist instead of feeling compelled to act as midwife to the Second Coming."

"Of course—that's it! Of course," her father responded. "Political freedom allows the creative artist to imagine reality; under a despotism, the best he can do is to fantasize Utopia." Sir Hans had approved wholeheartedly of his daughter's marrying Chester Jackman.

But what could she imagine that her father expected to become of her— emigrating to the United States? Shelagh answered herself: as little as she could know of what would be the future for Claire, wanting to have a career as an actress in New York. As a person, Claire would become more and more herself. The responsibility of a parent, Sir Hans had once said, is to bring up children to be independent enough to survive *well* the death of their parents. To that purpose, Shelagh felt, both Morgan and Claire had been well brought up; they each had a sense of independence; they would survive well. Their characters were adequately formed around cores of self-respect and responsibility to "the Tribe" for them to manage in the world—honorably to themselves and decently to others. But no one can foresee the future: except for a range of possibilities. How will Morgan or Claire face up to what they should resist? How will they recover if they aren't able to resist? Or if they are frustrated by their demands not being met, by lack of chances, challenges, or choices? Their fates will depend as much on the accidents of the temptations and obstacles thrust in their way by the world around them as on how they would behave if their own wishes were realized just as they dreamed them forward. Even wishes and dreams aren't all that clear-cut. What could she expect for her children? At least, expectations tie hopes into the surrounding world of opportunities. How they become more and more themselves will depend on how they respond to the surprises of the world. Either they will accept their fates and take pride in being themselves or they will reject their fates with resentment and dissatisfaction and never merge their wishes and their opportunities into genuine identities.

Had she achieved that for herself? Shelagh wondered. Did she have a genuine identity? It is harder for a refugee, an émigré, a displaced person to accept her fate because the opportunities and the expectations change in different circumstances. What one needs first is to feel safe from danger, safe against harm—and able to exercise her own abilities. But it is one thing to feel relatively secure; it is another to be fulfilled. Even though one never *knows* the future—Shelagh smiled in the dark—there is no society that hasn't tried a way to find out: through oracles, soothsayers, fortune-tellers. Her own future had been told to her once in Hong Kong some years before.

The children were young teen-agers, and a sitter had been found to stay at home with them while Shelagh followed the Judge to an international congress of jurists in Japan and then on holiday in Hong Kong and Taiwan. Their room at the Peninsula Hotel in Kowloon opened out to a view of the harbor and the mountains of the main island across the bay. They were tourists taking home movies of the boat people at their fishing; the tailors who made three-piece suits in twenty-four hours; a tiny ancient walled city; the students at the new Chinese university; the endless couples of affectionate friends and groups of families all holding hands as they meandered among the overstocked shops in labyrinthine bazaars. They were driven to the northern limit of the colony and allowed to stand next to the warning sign at the frontier and look across into the forbidden country: Communist China, at the border of an endless plain of fertile fields shimmering pale green under a low sky of light fog.

One evening, accompanied by a guide from the hotel, they rode the ferry across to the main island and wandered along the docks through the stalls of a farmers' market and a flea market toward the outdoor stage where a Chinese opera was being performed. The spectacle appeared to be interminable as well as incomprehensible to them, a pastiche of ballet, opera, and drama. But comfortable in the balmy air, at some distance behind hundreds of others in the audience, they perceived the costumes as shots of rainbows through prisms, and the jangled singing sounded like the birdsongs of swooping and hovering eagles high above uncharted mountains. Late in the evening but long before the performance came to an end, they urged the guide to start back to the hotel.

On their walk toward the dock, in one of the aisles through the flea market, they stopped to watch a seated elderly man playing idly with a collection of small objects on the surface of the narrow table before him. No one else was watching as his fingers touched the coins, the seashells, the pebbles, the feathers. His haphazard gathering of small things struck Shelagh as the most pathetic group of objects in any of the stalls or booths they had looked at; but the man himself did not appear to be poverty-stricken. His was a bulky figure of an elderly man, his dark complexion deeply lined, but his long, sparse white beard neatly combed and the top of his head covered by an embroidered cap.

48

The guide saw Shelagh contemplating the man and explained: "He is a fortune-teller. He is from the north of China," and added with satisfaction, "but I can understand his dialect."

Chester chuckled. "Would you like to know you fortune? Want him to foretell your future?"—only half-deprecating, nudging her slightly with his elbow.

With a sudden rush of eagerness, completely unexpected, she said, "Yes, I want it. How does he do it?"

The guide spoke with the old man and then translated for the Jackmans: Shelagh was to choose some or take all of the objects on the table in her own hands and rearrange them as she wished. The fortune-teller would then read the message that she placed on the table before him. That appealed to her enormously. She scooped up all of the bits and pieces into a cupped palm, then began to arrange them in a design—a mandala—on the surface of the wood as the old man waited impassively.

There were more seashells than anything else, so she formed a rectangle of them as a frame in which to set the other things. There were four old copper Chinese coins; she put one in each corner. She set the two feathers crosswise in the enclosure and filled the four triangles with pebbles, not separating them by color or size but allowing for a variety in each of the sections. Then she stood back to evaluate the arrangement and smiled at Chester in childish anticipation.

The old man lowered his head toward the table to study the design. His hands remained on his knees, but he swayed slightly from side to side, and began to speak in a singsong drone. "You will live a long time," the guide translated, "and never be exposed to any danger." His litany of good news lingered on through the years of her children's lives and the lives of her grandchildren; promises of purity and prosperity, the love of her family, the loyalty of friends, the peacefulness of her surroundings, the assurance that her ancestors smiled upon her and took their rest after showering her with blessings.

Shelagh remembered suppressing her laughter as Chester paid the fee, and then reveling in the thought she would express to him, in the privacy of their room when they were back at the hotel, that the only "fortune" we want to believe is the best we can wish for ourselves; "how reassuring to be told that our best hopes will come true."

"Especially in a very exotic language," he replied.

"I suppose his ancestors were making the same predictions a thousand years ago."

"Not to American tourists," Chester said.

"There was 'one born every minute' even then."

Even now, she thought, we take reassurance from the words that name our wishes. "You will never be exposed to any danger" had remained with her over the years like an amulet. It didn't matter if the fortune-teller was an old charlatan; the thought remained—someone else had said this of her and it had been true ever since then. The right word spoken may well save us.

Shelagh shifted in bed, pressing the length of her body against her husband's warmth, realizing that she was still wide awake while he was unconscious. But that struck her as exactly the wrong word. He was asleep, which is to be only temporarily unconscious—he could be rallied back into consciousness in a matter of seconds. When one is truly unconscious, it is uncertain when—or whether—consciousness will be regained. The right word reassures us with its accuracy. We are here, this close together and this far apart. We come together and we part; this has been the rhythm of our lives, through varying degrees of closeness and distance. All approximating the ideal, if unrealizable, goal of being One. The Two to be as One. The desire to be saved from living only your own life.

When the children were young, she and Chester had always flown in separate planes on trips of whatever distance. Even ten years ago—when they were in the Far East—they had come and gone on different flights. The Judge was in Japan at his meetings for four days before Shelagh joined him in Kyoto. The next night the banquet was given for the end of the congress. It was held in the great hall and on the grounds of a secular monastery attached to an ancient temple. A keg of sake was cracked open, after a proper ceremonious prayer, and the wine was served, they were told, "country style" in small square wooden boxes instead of porcelain cups; with crude salt to be placed on the tongue before the wine was sipped—like drinking tequila in Mexico—and each guest was urged to smell the pungent fragrance of the pine after it had absorbed some of the sake, and then invited to keep the box as a souvenir of the evening.

The sliding doors on one side of the hall opened to the view of a raked sand garden with three uneven rough rocks stranded in a landscape as strange as the moon. But from the other side of the hall it was possible to step down into a flower garden and wander along mossy paths to the far end, where a group of the guests gathered at the edges of a shallow pool. A rectangle of ice about four feet high was placed on a rock that emerged a few inches above the surface of the water, just off center of the pool. In water over his ankles, a short, sturdy Japanese wearing a colorful bandana around his head, a blue sleeveless jacket, and white trousers rolled up to his knees stood barefoot in the pool. Wielding two knives, one blunt as a hatchet, the other smaller and delicate, he began to cut into the block of ice, bone-white in the moonlight. Even the birds perched on the branches of a tree beyond the pool remained silent watching the craftsman at work.

He cut away from the top down. At first, it appeared as if he might carve a human figure, shaping the top into a head, rounded and fluted; but then four sides were sharply curved outward, slightly flared away from the peak; and he cut away under that first roof to make four walls underneath; and again carved away the winged lightness of another roof below. Gradually, a pagoda emerged from the ice—six stories high, each flared roof slightly larger than the one above—until he had completed a replica of a classic pagoda. The sculptor bowed to the admiration and applause of the audience and withdrew from the pool. During the course of his carving, as the ice began to thaw in the mild evening air of early summer, its opaque cloudiness disappeared; what remained became clear as glass, as shining crystal. And then slowly, inevitably, the pagoda began to melt.

Along the fluted incisions from the top roof beads of water gathered into a tear, slipped down, hovered at the lip of the roof, and then dropped onto the roof below, again and again, dripping from one level to the next one under it until it dropped beyond the rock on which it stood, and vanished into the pool below. The effect was of a diamond pagoda, secure on a sacred island, caught in a gentle rain, viewed as from heaven. In the course of the evening, Shelagh and Chester returned to it time after time, wandering back from the great hall, drinking sake from the wooden boxes, to confirm that out of water ice had been formed, which artistry created into a shining pagoda that by its very nature must yield itself, transformed, and merge again into the pool from whence it came.

❧

Shelagh had not put out place cards. When they all moved into the dining room, Chester suggested the seating: Brita von Bickersdorf on his right, Walter Webster next to her, and Mrs. Rosenblatt next to him. That put Clifford Rostum at Shelagh's right; his wife, Elsie, next to him; and Dr. Rosenblatt at the Judge's left.

"It can't be helped," Shelagh apologized to the Rostums; "you'll have to sit next to each other."

"That's all right," Elsie assured her. "We won't have to look at each other." But she patted her husband on the arm. Shelagh thought of Elsie as not very bright, but at least, willing to exercise some sense of humor. That was more than she could say of Clifford, whom she knew to be brilliant but dour. He and Chester had been roommates in college and close friends ever since. At about the same time that her husband was made a judge, Rostum had become Dean of the Law School, and now, for years, was Provost of the University.

The Provost held her chair for her, and when Shelagh took her place, the others seated themselves. Shelagh smiled her thanks. The Provost was a slender man with a strong, clean-shaven face and silvery white hair, who looked out of place at any table where he wasn't sitting at the head.

Along the length of the table, between the low vases of russet and yellow mums, four tall candles lighted the room as in the golden glow of an autumn sunset. Shelagh spread the napkin across her lap, looked over to the Judge, and asked if he wouldn't say Grace.

He tilted his head back, raised his eyes, and intoned: "If it please the Court. . ." It was an old joke for them all and reconfirmed the tone of their conversations. The Judge rose and moved around the table pouring the first glass of wine. Mrs. Yates, who helped at parties, served the onion soup.

"I suppose," Mrs. Rosenblatt said to Shelagh, "this is a going-away party for yourself. You always go to England about this time of year, don't you?"

Shelagh disliked Priscilla Rosenblatt for her ill-concealed envy, but replied simply, "No. I won't be going until later. In October." Mrs. Rosenblatt had once had the nerve to ask Shelagh where the Jackmans' "extra money" came from to make all their far-flung travels possible; and Shelagh had exaggerated part of the truth by saying, "From my *art*." How her mother had come to possess a great deal of money which she willed to Shelagh and her sister was nobody's business.

Chester said, "It's more like a coming-back party—since our return from Alaska," and then proceeded to describe the snow-covered mountains, the campsites, the lives of the Eskimo—while Shelagh regarded Priscilla Rosenblatt, considering that she was a peculiarly American phenomenon: this gawky, rawboned, blue-eyed blond WASP who had married a Jew to identify herself with a people of suffering. Of course it was an elitist people, and so she hoped that her children would marry blacks. She was a professional champion of the underdog. She had come to the party in a long skirt of camel's hair and a "poor boy" sweater.

As if to take Shelagh's mind off thoughts of his wife, Dr. Rosenblatt began to address the whole table:

"Well, while you were off discovering Alaska, we completed our *ill-starred* experiment as a two-house family."

Brita laughed across the table at him. "I love the idea of a psychiatrist who believes in the stars."

"This certainly was fated; a punishment from heaven."

Priscilla said, "He's going to blame me. I wanted a house in the country, so it's my fault."

"Not at all. We'd both thought it would be great to have a place we could relax in on weekends." Dr. Rosenblatt, heavyset and shaggy-maned, wearing a cashmere turtleneck sweater under his sports jacket, looked like a man who perpetually enjoyed a state of relaxation. "Instead of buying a house, we lucked into renting a beauty—an eighteenth-century saltbox overlooking the river near Old Lyme—for a year."

"I remember," Walter Webster spoke up. "You told me last winter the water pump broke about once a month."

Priscilla added, "And the water heater . . ."

"And the furnace," her husband continued. "The pipes froze; the septic tank backfired . . . In other words, to wrap it up: Everything that could go wrong went wrong."

This time Priscilla was the underdog: "Instead of a hideaway to rest up in, we suffered a year of worries we certainly didn't need."

"Let me get to the point. We paid a hefty rent month after month; we saw to all the repairs that were necessary—month after month; and I hired a boy with a power mower to mow the lawn every few weeks for about a hundred dollars a month."

Elsie asked, "How much land?"

"About an acre. Well, just before the end of August, when our lease was up, the boy became ill and couldn't do it, so when we cleared out, I left a note for the owner explaining what had happened, after seeing that everything else was shipshape; but I didn't leave a check for the August rent because it was the same amount as the security money I'd given him in the first place."

"As for 'shipshape,'" Priscilla interrupted, "I put a lot more work into cleaning that house than I do in my own home."

"Now, the owner got back later than he expected, about a week ago, which means the grass hadn't been cut in a month—and he's written me the most insulting letter I've ever received in my life."

Clifford Rostum muttered, "You're lucky. You ought to see some of the letters I receive every week."

"He accuses me of being 'presumptuous' for not having paid the August rent, because the security money should have covered his hiring somebody to mow the lawn."

Brita chuckled. "Ah, the spirit as against the letter of the law."

"There wasn't one word of thanks for what had been done to take care of the bloody house for a year—not the faintest sign of gratitude; instead, only his outrage, as if after all the thousands of dollars I'd poured into his pocket, I'd deliberately cheat him out of a hundred bucks." Dr. Rosenblatt, who had started his story as if to amuse the group, ended on a note of indignation.

"I know exactly what you're feeling," Walter Webster began. "When I was a senior at Harvard, I rented a small apartment at the back of a large house in Cambridge, and when it came time to leave, I made a gift of my bicycle—a rather expensive one, I should say—to the fourteen-year-old son of the landlady. She knew that, and she thanked me for it, but on my last day she announced herself at my door to check out her property."

Elsie nodded, understandingly. "To see if you'd broken or stolen anything."

"Exactly. In the kitchen she discovered that one fork and one teaspoon were missing from her five-and-ten-cent-store 'silverware.' "

"She charged you for it?" the Provost asked.

"Fifty cents. I remember distinctly. She stood there with her hand out waiting for me to count the coins . . . while my bicycle was already chained up in her garage."

Brita said, "Incredible."

"Not at all," Chester Jackman began.

But Walter Webster said, "I can still sense my disbelief. She came from very Puritan stock, I might add."

"And you don't," the Judge commented.

"I was still a practicing Catholic in those days."

"But practice didn't make perfect," Brita interjected.

Chester said, "It's the difference between justice and mercy."

"The hell it is," Dr. Rosenblatt exclaimed. "It's the difference between a tight, closed, literal mind and any subtle capacity for generosity."

The Provost needled the psychiatrist by asking, "The difference between a Protestant and a Catholic mind?"

"I wouldn't go that far."

Walter suggested, "How about Pascal's distinction between the spirit of *finesse* and the mathematical mind?"

"That's closer to it," Rosenblatt allowed. "An accountant's mind as against the capacity to make adjustments appropriate to individual circumstances."

The Judge tried to sum up: "Everything depends on one's sense of reciprocity, on how to interpret what we owe to each other, in making exchanges or forming partnerships . . . in order to be just."

"But the medieval problem of how to determine 'a just price' never did get resolved, did it?" Walter asked. "A *fair* price."

"Fairness," Cliff Rostum moaned aloud: "That's even vaguer than both. The idea of fairness clouds up the difference between justice and mercy."

"But let's admit," Shelagh urged them all, "that the Yankee landlord in Old Lyme treated the Rosenblatts unfairly."

"Unjustly," Brita suggested.

"Unmercifully," the Judge submitted, at the end of a sequence rounded out with comfortable laughter.

The empty soup bowls were removed; the crown roast of lamb brought to the sideboard by the maid; Chester carved it. Shelagh added the vegetables and the potatoes and served the plates. Chester poured a Pommard into fresh glasses.

Just before she sat down again, a chill shook Shelagh from her shoulders to her waist. She steadied herself against the back of the chair and then left the room to look for a shawl in the front hall closet. It was crocheted of black and pink afghan squares, and although it clashed with the long royal blue and gold embroidered Chinese dress Shelagh wore, she shrugged her shoulders and returned to her guests. As she entered the dining room, Brita thrust out her arm behind Walter's chair to reach for Shelagh's hand. "Are you all right?" she whispered.

"Quite. Don't give it a thought"; and she squeezed Brita's hand in thanks.

Earlier that evening, before most of the others had arrived, Brita had taken Shelagh aside, knowing that she was to have seen Dr. Connolley on Friday, to ask how the examination went. "It didn't take place," Shelagh answered. "His nurse called to say not all the test reports were in, and postponed the appointment into next week." Her manner was casual if not indifferent.

"Don't knock it," Brita insisted. "If something is wrong . . ."

"It's hardly worth mentioning."

"But you must be examined. You know he found a cyst I wasn't the least aware of in the course of a routine examination."

"I will be. I promise to be good."

"It's for your own benefit. . . ."

Brita was barely older than Shelagh, but still she had somehow established a quality of maternal concern in her friendship. At first she had been only Chester's friend. She was a professor of law originally from Sweden, married to a German physicist who had agreed to come to the University on condition that his wife be offered an appointment in the Law School. Clifford Rostum had acquiesced in the arrangement despite his reservations. Although no one could have predicted it, Brita had become a much more influential and popular member of the faculty than her husband; Cliff Rostum had come to believe that it was only what he had anticipated from the beginning. After her husband's suicide, Brita had become a national and international figure as a consultant to the United Nations and a lawyer who argued cases before the World Court. She was a large woman. Shelagh, who had never known her other than plump, could not imagine her a tall *svelte* Swedish beauty; for her, in spite of Brita's graying hair, she seemed an agelessly robust peasant lady, with rosy chubby cheeks without makeup and a readiness to make jokes. The Provost had introduced her to the Judge, and from the first time that Chester brought her home, she and Shelagh had liked each other enormously. Perhaps her larger size, her widowhood, and her public status were conducive to the maternal manner—or perhaps more important was her childlessness.

Now that Shelagh thought of it, Brita treated even Walter Webster, in his sixties, as a big bear of a boy. He didn't drive, and when Brita called for him in her car—as she had this evening—she would send him back to the house if she judged that he needed a scarf or gloves. She would point her head forward at you, pat her nose with a long finger, and wink conspiratorially. She did not say, "I know what's best for you"; she appeared to assume it, and you were merely to take advantage of her thoughtfulness.

Having resumed her place at the dinner table and while cutting into the roast lamb allowed herself these reflections on Brita, Shelagh tried to discover where the conversation had got to in her absence.

Elsie was saying: "I saw something like that happen once. It was early in the evening. I was in a subway station in New York waiting for a train."

"You ride the subways in New York?" Priscilla asked with mock disbelief.

"Some years ago. Nobody takes the subway anymore," Elsie continued. "There were a number of people milling about, including a black man about twenty years old, probably tipsy, weaving back and forth among the people who were standing still . . ."

"Or high on some drug," Dr. Rosenblatt added.

". . . when all of a sudden he stopped next to two teen-aged white girls— very pretty girls, I remember—stood quite close to one of them; no one said anything; and then he simply tilted his head right down to her face and planted a big wet kiss on her cheek—I could hear the 'smack' of it—backed off, and smiled down on her."

"What did she do?" Brita asked.

"She let out the most piercing scream, positively the most horrendous shriek I've ever heard—as if she'd been stabbed and stood there petrified, watching her own blood gushing . . ."

"And then what happened?" her husband said, having heard the story before and wanting to get it over with. He had cleaned his plate, but said nothing to Shelagh about how good the lamb was or that he appreciated her having chosen something he was especially fond of.

"Well, the subway came charging into the station, drowning the scream as it came to a stop; people got off and others got on, and everyone went about their own business as if nothing had happened."

"Nothing did happen," Dr. Rosenblatt said, smiling.

"But the poor girl felt horribly abused," Elsie went on. "That's what I meant by a woman being aware of treatment as a sex object rather than as a human being."

"Hardly *abused*," Brita commented.

"Well, taken unfair advantage of." The Provost came that far in support of his wife's example.

Chester laughed. "It wasn't even a stolen kiss. He didn't steal a kiss of hers that didn't belong to him."

"Or hadn't been earned by him," Walter Webster said.

"No," Chester continued, "he merely placed his kiss on a location to which he had no rights."

"Why are you treating it as something funny?" Priscilla asked.

"It was harmless," the Provost asked.

"Not to the girl," Elsie insisted. "She felt harmed. Her physical integrity had been invaded. . . ."

"Too strong," Brita said.

"All right. Not invaded: compromised. How's that?"

"By a kiss?" Shelagh asked. "Surely there are circumstances when an unexpected kiss would be charming."

"Of course," Priscilla said, "if the boy had been white . . . right? It's the color prejudice that knocked her for a loop. Not the kiss."

"Yes," her husband agreed, and went beyond Mrs. Rosenblatt's remarks: "and the fear of what might be the next event: rape."

Elsie felt that her point had finally been appreciated. "Exactly! Women have to go through life in fear of sexual assault—not because they're especially desirable, not even because they're personable; simply because they are women. Their privacy can be invaded at any moment—even in public, even in broad daylight."

It seemed to Shelagh that the group had tired of the issue. Walter Webster evidently agreed with her and changed the subject by introducing a new topic.

"In Boston last spring I was attacked in broad daylight, and by a woman, but the assault was not amatory, let alone erotic. I wasn't made to feel a sex object; but I was exploited. It was a matter of financial piracy." He had taken a cigarette from his silver case and paused to light it, his audience waiting for the story to unfold.

Shelagh remembered now that she'd known Walter Webster even longer than she'd known Chester; while he had thickened and mellowed and softened with the years, he still struck her as diffident and self-deprecating, content to describe himself as a victim. He had pursued his professional life with single-mindedness and ever-increasing acclaim—as a scholar of Renaissance art—but he was a man of secretiveness; a bachelor who lived with his sister; probably a closet queen. If *his* privacy had been invaded, Shelagh thought, it must have been by an enemy who had breached the exceptionally wide moat in which his seclusion was encircled. Walter Webster took a long puff on his cigarette, and then told his tale.

"I was on Beacon Street. I had just come out of my publisher's office. I was on my way down to a new exhibit of William Blakes at the Public Library when I became aware of a creature approaching from the opposite direction disguised as a clown."

"Disguised?" Priscilla asked.

"Dressed as a clown," he corrected himself. "That is to say, I believed it was a clown. The only reason I say it was a woman is that she wore a long Gypsy skirt and, instead of a blouse, what might have been the top of a black leotard, displaying a very well-shaped bosom."

"It could have been a man in drag," Dr. Rosenblatt supplied.

"Granted. I am only saying why I assumed it was a woman. Nothing about the face could be identified as male or female because it was all painted as a clown's face is made up—with a coat of white. And on that had been painted red stars and blue moons and gold sunbursts. The hair was black and plaited into two large pigtails."

"Probably a wig," Elsie said.

"And she was holding a bouquet of flowers. As she walked along, just as slowly in her direction as I was moving in mine, she would stop a passerby and hand him or her one of the flowers, appear to say something cheerful, and then move on."

Brita sighed. "I know what's going to happen. . . ."

"Then she came right up to me. I stopped willingly, almost eagerly. I thought it very jolly to be handed a flower by a cheerful clown on a lovely spring day in Boston. I remember wondering which one of the flowers would be mine. She stood a little too close to me, and I had started to step back when she followed just as closely, pulling a small revolver out of her skirt, holding it against the flowers in her other hand and saying—the voice was unmistakably feminine—'Give me your wallet.' "

Elsie said, "No!"

"But why not? She had put on a performance and wanted to be paid for it—but not under the usual theatrical circumstances, and so she had to guarantee the payment. She took her time until she found a likely prospect. I was wearing a blue blazer and gray flannel slacks." He looked down at his shirt and said, "And a University tie," as he was wearing now.

"And you gave it to her?" Shelagh asked.

"Of course."

Dr. Rosenblatt wanted to know: "Why didn't you call for help?"

"On Beacon Street at eleven o'clock in the morning? With a pistol three inches from my stomach?"

Brita said, "Then what did she do?"

"She took the cash out of my billfold and handed the wallet back to me."

"Very polite," the Provost concluded.

"At the same instant she spied a taxi at the corner, called for it to wait— and ran off with my money in hand."

Suddenly struck by the cleverness of the thief, Elsie said, "Naturally, you'd never be able to identify her."

"Naturally. I never saw her; only her costume and her makeup." The long gray ash at the end of his cigarette fell onto Walter's jacket and he brushed it away, embarrassed.

"And that was the end of that?" Shelagh asked.

"No, there was one further turn of the screw. After she'd opened the taxi door, she turned to see that I was still staring at her. She raised the pistol over the flowers and shot a thin jet of water into the street between us."

"A *water* pistol?" The Judge shook his head. "How easily we're taken in."

"How easily we're taken advantage of," Dr. Rosenblatt said.

Priscilla said, "When what we crave is universal fairness . . ."

"Wait for heaven," the Provost counseled her.

Priscilla looked offended. Not to be put down, she spoke sharply to the Provost, seated directly opposite her: "What is all this talk about? What are we talking about?"

Shelagh interceded: "There isn't an agenda. We're not holding a meeting."

Priscilla was relentless: "But we're all gabbing away as if there's some purpose."

"The purpose," Judge Jackman announced, "is to entertain each other. Inform and entertain . . ."

"Like how our landlord insulted us," Priscilla insisted. "How women are prey to sexual abuse . . ."

Walter Webster added, "And men are exploited by women."

"That's what we're talking about?" Priscilla was both bewildered and hostile.

Chester summed it up: "The inane, the insane, and the criminal."

Shelagh said, "At least Walter's thief had some imagination, some charm. What she did was more like a hoax." And then added, "Noboby plays a hoax anymore; nobody I know. . . ."

Disapprovingly, Elsie stated with pride, "I can't think of a hoax."

Shelagh regarded her—Elsie of the pompadoured gray hair, Elsie of the white shirtwaist dress, with her grandmotherly bracelets, her need to "speak up" but always in order to put down something. She had considered her the wife of her husband's friend and therefore a social acquaintance to be suffered; but she suddenly thought of Elsie now as inexcusably dull. "A really lively hoax?" Shelagh asked her. "Oh, I can think of some. I remember one my father told me about. It took place in London just before the war. Evelyn Waugh was behind it.

"A group of his friends made a number of junk 'abstract' paintings, and pretended they were by a German nun who had escaped from the Nazis. They rented a fashionable gallery and announced that the income from the sale of the paintings would go to support German refugees. On opening night, one of their friends pretended to be the artist-nun, in a wheelchair, dressed in a habit, and introduced as a deaf-mute. Well, all of the junk was sold at high prices—to prove that judgments of taste can be put in the wrong place, if your charitable heart is in the right place."

"And if you can afford to be fashionable," Brita commented.

"Very unkind" was Walter Webster's opinion.

Dr. Rosenblatt said, "Evelyn Waugh wasn't a kind man."

Elsie said, "I don't think I like hoaxes."

The Provost repeated Chester's list: "The inane, the insane, and the criminal."

The maid removed the dinner plates.

Shelagh addressed Walter Webster: "Your clown/thief in Boston may not have given you a flower, but I have one for you—in the dessert."

Mrs. Yates wheeled in the tea wagon with eight small rust-red flowerpots, each with a bright autumn marigold, yellow with scarlet edges, apparently grown out of potting soil, and delivered a pot to each place, as the diners smiled or chuckled appreciation of chocolate mousse transformed into a floral offering.

Walter proclaimed, "You've just made a visual pun."

Dr. Rosenblatt and Brita applauded.

With her dessert spoon raised in hand, Elsie asked, "What shall we do with the flower?"

Shelagh thought of a vulgar suggestion or two but replied, "Put it on the plate under the pot—although I was hoping that each of you would wear one over your left ear."

When the table had been cleared of all but the plates for fruit and nuts and the Port glasses for the men, Chester brought the decanter from the sideboard, and Shelagh led the women into the living room, closing the doors behind her, separating the two rooms completely.

"You are old-fashioned," Priscilla said.

"Yes," Shelagh snapped back. "Old is basic. Back to basics," she continued. "I love the rhythm of separating and then coming back together again."

"Separate but equal?" Elsie asked, seating herself in one corner of the sofa.

Brita, who stood, arms akimbo, in front of the fireplace, took a deep breath, sighed, and said, "The idea of Equality causes even more trouble than Justice or Mercy."

Priscilla, lowering herself into an armchair, quickly took that remark as a personal affront and asked, "Is there any idea that doesn't cause 'trouble'? We're here to try to resolve troubles."

"Here?" asked Shelagh, seated on the sofa near Elsie, beginning to pour Cointreau into silver liqueur cups.

"Here on earth," Priscilla explained.

"Well, we're not on Duty Call this evening," Shelagh said cheerfully as she handed a liqueur cup to each of the ladies.

As if wondering what she was here for this evening, Priscilla complained, "I still don't understand the drift of that dinner-table conversation."

Elsie said, "People were mentioning things that bother them."

"Or amuse them," Shelagh said.

Brita said, smiling, "We make Progress Reports to each other on how we're getting along."

Irritably, Priscilla insisted, "I still don't see where it gets us."

Shelagh had made herself comfortable in one corner of the sofa; after a pause, she announced: "Columbus didn't know he had discovered America."

Elsie sounded surprised. "Didn't he?"

"Not at all. He thought he'd landed on some islands off the coast of China."

Brita's interpretation was that "He knew he'd discovered something; but it was left to others to find out what it was, the significance of it. He made that possible."

Priscilla asked, "Will someone come along afterward and find out what the small talk at dinner tonight meant?"

"But it was really an end in itself," Shelagh said.

"I wonder," Elsie wondered.

Shelagh proposed that "It's like every other event you're engaged in—you know what it's worth to you while it's going on, but you don't know what any of the consequences will be."

"That almost sounds to me," Brita said, "like the difference between private life and public life."

"We go back and forth," Shelagh enjoyed saying, "from one to the other."

"Perhaps we were free-associating," Priscilla suggested, reminding them all of her husband's profession as a psychoanalyst.

As a member of the Law School faculty, Brita said, "We were acting *in* association."

"But free association," Priscilla persisted pedantically, "demonstrates what you're not free of; what comes out when you're not talking to some purpose."

Judge Jackman's wife said, "The purpose was to enlighten and amuse each other."

"By mentioning what bothers us?" Elsie asked. "I know I told the story about the black boy who kissed the white girl in the subway station because what bothers me is women being taken advantage of as sex objects."

Shelagh had difficulty imagining Elsie as a sex object, but acknowledged no accounting for tastes.

"It works the other way too," Brita began. "Even while you were describing that incident, I was thinking of what I did the last time I pleaded a case before the World Court." She sat down in the other armchair at the side of the fireplace and leaned forward, lowering her voice. "I wore a low-cut dress and an elaborate gold cross on a thin chain"—pointing to the center of her full bosom. "As I spoke before the judges—all men—I occasionally fondled the crucifix, drawing their eyes to an ample exposure of chest. I counted on the *frisson* brought about by the combination of touching the cross and exhibiting the flesh. A kind of invitation to sacrilegious thoughts. . . ."

Elsie said, "You should be ashamed of yourself."

Brita laughed, "Fair advantage! One just doesn't want to be taken *un*fair advantage of."

The Judge's wife said, "So it all comes back to the concern about what is fair," as she stood up with the bottle in hand to refill the cups of her guests.

Brita looked up at the collection of plates that decorated the wall above the fireplace. "I've forgotten what you told me about them." In the soft glow of the lamps that lit the living room, the group of flat plates and shallow bowls shone blue-white, with a raspberry-colored flower and a blue one surrounded by small green leaves in the center. Ovals of the same colors were linked into wreaths within the rims.

"They were made in China for the export trade, in the early nineteenth century. It's what the Chinese thought the barbarians wanted. 'The barbarians' being the feudal lords of Persia."

Elsie said, "How extraordinary," with a faraway look in her eye.

"They are lovely," Priscilla admitted. "Where did you get them?"

"In Isfahan. Chester and I were there many years ago."

Priscilla then turned her back to the fireplace and gestured across to the wall above the sofa. "And those pictures over there, what are they?"

"*The Four Seasons* by Archimboldo." Anticipating Priscilla's next question, she added, "They were a gift from my father."

"What *strange* faces!" Priscilla remarked, with a shrug of her shoulders.

"Faces?" Elsie asked; she had turned around where she sat at one end of the sofa to look up at them just above her head. "They're not faces. They're baskets of fruit and vegetables."

Shelagh said, "They're both."

"From where I sit," Brita commented, "I see the faces."

The profile of *Spring* was constructed out of roses and white wild flowers; the green-and-gold brocaded jacket was made of young strawberry leaves and ivy and cabbage, the ruffled collar of white daisies; from the back of the elaborate hat of flowers, a lily appeared to be a feather. The head of *Summer* was formed of fruits and vegetables: a black cherry the eye, a ripe peach the cheek, a Dijon pear the chin. A cucumber made the nose, an open pea pod the lips and teeth; the hair was a tangle of golden wheat, corn, olives.

"If you focus at them close up," Shelagh explained, "you see the individual fauna and flora; if you move back to focus on the general impression, you see the faces as a whole." She herself moved closer to the paintings and then backed away toward the far corner of the room to demonstrate. "Of course, the point of focus is different for each of us, so you must try it out yourself."

Elsie got up off the sofa in disbelief, walked to the fireplace, and quickly turned around, to be struck by the difference in the effect on her. "Really," she said, disapproving, as if she resented a joke being played on her. "Is it a hoax?"

Priscilla smiled, repeating Walter's comment: "Or 'a visual pun'?"

"His patrons thought they were miraculous—ingenious. They called him Archimboldo the Marvelous, and displayed the paintings as if they were among the Wonders of the World."

"Are they modern?" Priscilla asked.

"Yes. Late sixteenth century."

Priscilla snorted, out of a different sense of time.

Shelagh continued, "Painted for the Hapsburg emperors in Vienna and Prague."

"Are these the *originals?*" Elsie asked.

"Hardly. They're considered Czechoslovakian national treasures today."

Priscilla was then bending forward over the sofa examining one of them closely. "But they look exactly like real oil painting."

"They are oil paintings. 'Handmade' copies. Making replicas like these was considered an honorable craft—before photographic reproductions were possible."

Pressing her knees against the sofa, Brita came close to the head of *Autumn*: the blackberry eye, russet apple cheek, potato nose, mushroom ear, the neck of roots, the hair of ripe purple grapes. But the bright and lively colors were gone from the profile of *Winter*—this face nearly was as dark as the backgrounds of the other three: gnarled, bare, wrinkled bark of a tree formed the lines of an aged face, the grim eye a blackbird in flight. "You have such remarkable things."

"But do you like them?" Elsie asked.

Shelagh laughed. "I find them endlessly instructive."

"How did your father come by them?" Priscilla asked.

"He bought them in Prague about 1900." Shelagh felt wearied and beginning to be bored. "As long as all of us are standing," she began, "why don't you come with me to look at the orchids?"

"I think," Brita responded, as she lowered herself onto the sofa, in front of the Cointreau, "I'll sit this one out."

While the other women were out of the room, Brita poured herself and drank more of the liqueur, closed her eyes and rested for a moment, stood up, stretched her arms, listened to the sudden laughter of the men in the dining room, walked about, gazed out the window at the placid street. Returning to the fireplace, she contemplated the Chinese porcelain plates decorating the wall—to think of tricks, jokes, hoaxes; and then noticed lying on the mantel-piece a book bound in blue leather, without a title or author's name on the spine. Opening it at random, she started to read the handwritten document; then, after no more than a moment, she dropped it back into place as if she had been stung.

The instant Shelagh returned to the living room, Brita chided her. "How can you leave your *diary* lying around just anywhere?"

"I usually forget where I leave it."

Priscilla and Elsie each carried a miniature orchid in hand.

"Well, I find that very unnerving," Brita continued.

Priscilla dropped her orchid into a marble ashtray on an end table; Elsie unsnapped her handbag and placed her orchid inside it.

"I'm sorry, Brita. It wasn't meant as an invitation for anyone to read in it."

"But, darling," Brita said in a whisper, "it is like leaving incriminating evidence around for anyone to find."

"I told my family years ago that they'd better not look into the pages—if they found the diary lying around anywhere—because they'd discover that I'd said things about them that they wouldn't like—and I wouldn't mean later on."

"Still," Brita continued at lowered volume, "we're not only family here to-night; and there's always the chance that an inappropriate person might take a look. . . ."

"I'll be more careful," Shelagh conceded, without giving the matter any serious concern.

Priscilla yawned. "It's really quite boring without the men. No offense meant. But just how long do we have to wait for them?"

"I think I'll invite them to join us now." Shelagh smiled, slid the partitions open, nodded to her husband, and urged the others to join the ladies.

"Very distressing," Brita muttered. "Such an opportunity to invade your privacy. Like looking at you through a keyhole."

"Brita—you have such a formal view of it. I never told my family I would mind; I merely said they might be disturbed by what they read there. As far as I know, none of them has ever taken the risk."

As the gentlemen came into the living room, Elsie asked Clifford Rostum, "Have you ever noticed these paintings, darling? They're not the originals, but they're copies of Archimboldo the Marvelous. Aren't they funny?"

"Yes, my dear," he replied. "Many is the time I have thought of them, when I'm aware of some of my colleagues as a bouquet, a bucket of vegetables, or a basket of fruit."

There was laughter, until some of the guests felt a guilty discomfort in the presence of Walter Webster, who, although he was not effeminate, would have been considered, in an archaic and more slipshod vernacular, a "fruit."

"Let's go into the library," Judge Jackman proposed. As the group walked through the entrance hall, past the two front doors, into the book-lined room, Chester Jackman told a story on himself. "I was thinking about Learned Hand the other day and remembered an incident to my shame. You know his cousin Augustus was also a judge. And when I was clerk to Cardozo, the phone rang once while his secretary wasn't at her desk, so I answered it. A voice said, 'This is Judge Hand'—and full of pride to make it clear that I knew there were two of them, I asked, 'Which one?' Well, after a pause I heard 'Why? Will he speak with only one of us?' "

A cloud of cigar smoke followed over the heads of the group as they moved into the library and made themselves comfortable on the sofas and in the armchairs.

"This is very civilized," Dr. Rosenblatt stated, gesturing toward all the books, the mahogany tables, the collection of brass objects, and the glassed entrance to the orchid greenhouse—but meaning: the pace of the evening, the pleasures of the dinner, and the situation of bringing such people together for social life, which gets them out of themselves. "It's like watching an apple as it grows on the Golden Bough."

"How poetic," his wife said.

"How nice," Elsie agreed.

Brita said, "It's late, and we're all a little high, and I don't think any of us should say anything we might be held accountable for tomorrow."

"Oh, accountability," Walter began: "that's the last thing required of us under the circumstances. When one has been made content . . . Well, it's unforgivable. No one should be accountable for what he says when he's happy!"

Everyone laughed at length, as if nothing said thereafter would be other than the inconsequential remarks of serious people when they actually relax; and then, unexpectedly, Clifford Rostum announced: "By the way, Chester, I've been meaning to tell you about a visit from the 'Silence Lady.' "

"The 'Silence Lady'?" Priscilla echoed him, her voice rising.

"You all know the case: last spring, the business about heroin, and the witness who pleaded the Right to Silence."

Shelagh was the one who said, "No. I don't remember anything about such a case."

"It came before Judge Spencer," her husband said.

"I still don't remember it."

The Provost sighed, preparing to summarize the events, despite being kept from making his point to Chester. "Well, about eight months ago three young women were arrested by the police. They were in possession of a pound of marijuana and a small amount of heroin. They were all militant women's-libbers—"

Priscilla interrupted him quickly: "That's what made them suspect?"

"No; but it didn't help. Anyway . . . two of them live here and work at Chamberlain Electronics. The third girl, who was visiting them from New York, was probably the source of the drugs."

Walter snapped his fingers and said, "I recall it now. They claimed they were framed. That the stuff wasn't theirs. It was planted in their apartment."

"And the police believed the visitor from New York was a lead to some sort of dope ring. What the police wanted was as much information about *her* as possible."

Brita now remembered the details. "One of those girls whose apartment it was refused to cooperate, refused to give any information at all. Insisted on remaining silent."

"In court?" Shelagh asked.

"No. It hadn't gone to trial," the Provost explained. "The case was before the grand jury. What the young lady claimed was her Right to Silence, not under the Fifth Amendment—because she insisted there was no question of incriminating herself—but under the First Amendment, on the grounds of freedom of association."

Priscilla said, "That seems reasonable to me."

"It wasn't desirable to the State's Attorney. He wanted evidence. So he offered her immunity, which she refused. And then he threatened to cite her for contempt of court."

"What's the purpose of that?" Dr. Rosenblatt asked. "He still wouldn't get her to talk."

"In order to intimidate the other witnesses."

"Oh, I see," Dr. Rosenblatt said.

"Well, he carried out the threat. Took her before the presiding judge . . ."

Chester added, "That was Spencer."

". . . who cited her for the charge and put her in jail."

Priscilla asked, "For how long?"

"For the remainder of the time the grand jury sits."

"And how long is that?" Priscilla wanted to know.

Brita stated, "A grand jury sits for eighteen months."

"What?" Priscilla was appalled. "You mean she was jailed for eighteen months for remaining silent?!"

"No," the Provost continued. "The grand jury had been sitting for about a year when this happened; so she spent about six months in jail."

Walter said, "It does seem very unfair."

"That's the way she feels about it. It looks especially unjust because no indictment was brought by that grand jury. Out of the whole affair, she was the only one to go to jail."

"That's appalling," Priscilla said. "Infuriating."

Coming back to the beginning of the story, Shelagh asked Cliff Rostum, "Why did she call on you?"

"Ah, yes. Well, she's infuriated too. She thought I was still Dean of the Law School and wanted my advice—on how she can sue the State's Attorney."

Dr. Rosenblatt asked, "Can you do that?"

"It's not impossible—if you can find a lawyer who'd be willing to take it on."

Chester said thoughtfully, "If you couldn't do it, in theory, it would be tantamount to assuming that a State's Attorney can do no wrong."

Elsie smiled. " 'In theory'? How about in practice?"

Brita leaped in: "He is assumed to act in good faith to execute the duties of his office."

Priscilla persisted, "But he can 'do wrong'?"

"The young lady who visited me believes she has cause to see it that way. She wants to bring suit against him for depriving her of her rights under the First Amendment. She wants to accuse him of abusing the privilege of seeking a contempt-of-court citation."

"Why not?" Walter asked. "And why should a State's Attorney ask a judge to put a witness in jail anyhow?"

Chester answered: "To induce witnesses to talk. When Mr. Thompson, as a State's Attorney in Chicago, puts crooked high-level officials of the government of Illinois in jail by using such means, it is considered a justified legal method. But"—he was thinking out loud—"by making this a common practice, instead of an extreme method, to be used only in instances of extreme danger to society or an emergency, it does seem it will result in abuse."

"Exactly," Priscilla insisted. "Doesn't the First Amendment protect you from having to squeal on your friends? Isn't that what's meant by the Right to Silence?"

The Provost smiled patiently. "There is no law that requires you to 'squeal' on your friends; but under different conditions, there will be different consequences."

"You mean—if you keep your mouth shut, you will be punished."

Chester laughed suddenly. "There is no law explicitly protecting the rights of friendship."

Shelagh interjected, "Well, this wasn't a national emergency; it didn't even result in bringing anyone to trial, while the poor girl—"

Priscilla interrupted: "It was only about some drugs."

Her husband groaned: "You wouldn't take that light tone if one of your children became addicted."

"I think we've lost the thread," Brita said. "Maybe there was some police vindictiveness because of their being in women's lib."

"Anyway, what advice did you give the girl?" Walter asked.

"I gave her the names of four lawyers, and wished her good luck."

"Enough of that," Shelagh commanded, eager to continue the badinage but wanting to change the tone: "It's time we thought of how each of us might change our lives if we unexpectedly inherited a fortune...."

❧

As the cloudy pearl light of dawn dispelled the darkness of their bedroom, Chester pressed his long body against the warmth of Shelagh's back, the roundness of her behind, the smoothness of her thighs. He listened to her steady breathing. Bringing his arm around her shoulder, he cupped her breast in his large hand. She sighed and arched her back, feeling his pressure against her, signaling that she was awake and *sympathique,* moving her head back against his chest, brushing her hair sensuously back and forth against his neck and his chin. He fondled her breast, her shoulder, her earlobe; his fingers retraced his touches and then below her breast, he stroked her stomach, remarked the line where her leg met her hip, ran his hand along the silken surface of the inner thigh.

She turned onto her other side to face him, to share a kiss with him, to embrace him and caress him with both hands. He urged her up onto him; and then she lay against his full length. They made love slowly and tenderly at first, and then he rolled over on top of her and they made love quickly and fiercely until the intensity resolved itself in an ecstatic release in which their separateness was lost; uncertain of the limits of their own bodies, they were as if truly merged with each other and together merged with an inchoate sense of limitless well-being. Afterward, they regained themselves.

He said, "Long time no see."

She said, "Welcome home."

"I have loved you all my life; but only now have I found you."

"Remarkable for a hundred-year-old man," she chuckled. "Go back to sleep."

"Back? I thought this was a dream."

"It was the fulfillment of the dream."

68

Chester did, gradually, return to sleep, although he did not let go of She-lagh; she lay on her back; he lay on his side with one arm around her shoulder, the other hand draped across her waist.

But she did not fall asleep again.

She reveled in the sense of feeling radiant—aglow, shining, burnished, she imagined to herself, with her eyes closed. Her body relaxed; the glow began to subside. She resented the fact that it would fade away—that it was a great joy which they shared but infrequently now; but the value of the intensity was all the more increased as it occurred more rarely. The animal bliss of ecstasy. But that is only sexual. The human bliss of making love with the "one indispensable person"—ah, that is the apogee of love! To escape from the boundaries of yourself in the blind thrill of intercourse, indifferent to your partner, is a self-serving experience more in the imagination than in the flesh—a masturbatory pleasure; but to care about the person as well as the pleasure of your partner, as he cares about yours—that is to be perfectly used. The right use. No unfair use; no unfair advantage taken. No abuse. It is to be well used. No kiss on the cheek from a stranger in a subway station. The enhancement of joy in knowing—each time it comes about—that you had made the right choice.

Albeit hadn't she, at least for a few moments, imagined she was making love with Quentin Connolley? Only a few moments. He was hardly the right person for her—let alone the indispensable one—but the memory of his touch was itself a stimulant. And it had come to mind to excite her further: an additional erotic incentive. Do all human beings share such secret sexual forces with each other? she wondered; unknown to each other? Her desire intensified by Quentin's suggestive stroking; Quentin Connolley stimulated by the sight of a passerby in the street; Chester thinking of some girl in the witness box of his courtroom: the private use of someone else's existence. Such images functioning as arrow-pointed strokes from within one's own psyche. Sources of revitalization that take nothing away from the source.

Unless they cease to be private—images, fantasies—and are acted upon: Quentin stopping the girl on the street to strike up an acquaintance; Chester asking the witness to his chambers after the trial is over. Does Chester have affairs? The question presented itself to Shelagh's mind despite the lack of any wish to ask it. And the answers appeared as passively as if she heard someone else's voice announce them: There are some things better not known. And: It didn't matter anyway. She could not ask to be loved better than he loved her.

But he was a man, and the pattern is, supposedly, well known: women make more private use of the existence of others than men do; and men act out their fantasies.

She had always wondered whether her father had affairs: more so when she was young than recently. But it came to mind now—the thought of Sir Hans Markgraf, that noble and engaging man, powerful with accomplishments and honors: hadn't women thrown themselves at him? Adoring students, wives of colleagues, hostesses at the foreign conferences and symposia he attended. His authority must have been an aphrodisiac.

Even if he had, that wouldn't matter either. No daughter could have been better loved by any father.

She exulted in her gratitude. She turned to face Chester, who half-smiled in his sleep, and pressed her cheek against his in thankful benediction.

LETTER FROM SHELAGH JACKMAN TO HER SON IN NEW YORK

Dear Morgan:

I forgot to ask you when we were together last whether you have anything in mind for Thanksgiving. Last year Dad and I drove into Manhattan and took you and Claire to a restaurant, but that did seem rather forbidding, rather inhibiting to high spirits. So I wonder what you'd think of coming here. I'll make a great banquet; we'll celebrate together, and end up singing songs around the fireplace before the first fire of autumn. I haven't asked Claire yet. Do you want to bring anyone with you? Girlfriend, I mean. I know you have a number of friends who are girls, but you don't refer to them as girls or as friends; you call them "dates"—which makes me think you pluck them from trees.

I realize this is only the end of September, but if you say "yes" I'll have to start cooking now. No, joking aside, I am already thinking that a few weeks from now I'll be off to London for a visit with Aunt Adrienne for ten days and by the time I get back it will be nearly November & by "Nearly November" one ought to know how to celebrate Thanksgiving. It may not be important to me because I'm a naturalized citizen, but it ought to be very important to you because you're native-born. Think Thanksgiving! and let me know what you decide. (You have a lot to be thankful for.) (I too have a lot to be thankful for. I am thankful. I want to celebrate. I will be thankful for a word from you saying whether you'll come, alone or with a "date.")

Now let me see . . . we gave a dinner party just the other night for a number of people you knew in an earlier life—the Rostums, the Rosenblatts, Walter Webster, and Brita—and I was extremely disappointed by the way it ended. (It went very well, with a good deal of lively conversation, up until then; although your father told that story about the two Judge Hands for the thousandth time.) And then I asked what each of our guests would do if they suddenly came into a fortune, and you know what? they all became maudlin about how satisfied they are with what they're doing—which may well be true—but showed a decided lack of imagination. Of course, they fantasized about servants and vacations; but none of them could conceive of themselves as being something different. They're so identified with what they do. And that made me wonder about you. What you do is entirely involved in making money; but do you identify yourself with that? Rather than with spending it? I realize I don't know what you would do if you came into a (small) fortune. What has become of your desire to write fiction? You've barely spoken of it since college days when you were so prolific in wonderful short stories. As I recall, you ended it then, saying something like you were tired of imagining how people might behave and wanted to learn how actual people do behave.

No doubt I've been led to think about the possibility of your writing again by the fact that the last time we were together you gave me a gift—a novel of Anthony Trollope's, The Way We Live Now—and as I promised you, I read it within the following week. Of course, on the surface it seems clear that you wanted me to learn something about the world you work in, about the stock market and the people who are engaged in it. I take from your inscription, which reads "This was written 142 years ago!" that you imply some degree of awe in the discovery of how little has changed between then and now. There must be as much corruption and swindling and illegal (or at least immoral) behavior now as there was then—and as few decent and sound and sensible people who will not be perverted by the passion for money as there were in those days. I don't doubt that. Most people think you have to be very rich to be moral. But they don't know how to square that with the opposite belief that especially the very rich are immoral. It's really a matter of whether one is only self-serving, at all costs, or if one has an investment in something other than the self which justifies self-sacrifice.

But under the surface of these impressions that reading The Way We Live Now made on me is the deeper satisfaction that comes with the experience of a remarkably good novel. (I can see how Tolstoy learned from him.) It is the discovery of dealing with a variety of people on their own terms, through the sympathy they feel with themselves, without ever losing the capacity to judge them against a standard of what would be better for them and for their society. And I'm reminded that all good fiction exercises one's capacity for such human sympathy for possible people which, much more often than not, we do not exercise toward the actual people we come to "know" in real life. So I thought again of how marvelous it is to be a writer who can do that and I wished, for your sake, that you might return to fiction.

I've stopped and reread what I'd written so far and confess I had to burst out laughing. I do sound like a Know It All Mother writing at excessive length to her prep-school fledgling. And I'm sorry. I can't help that. I want to write you. I don't feel in the least like a Know It All, even if these words appear that way. I don't know anything down to its "All"; but I don't see why I can't give advice to my son or my daughter. It's like passing on family recipes; at least, growing up in the family you already know what the dish is supposed to taste like. Not the same as taking instructions from a cookbook, when you don't have any background in whether something should be tart of sweet or runny or firm. (Oh, well; is there an analogy here with learning from sex manuals too?)

Anyway, I've been thinking that you have to develop a formula for your life: not just for how you earn a living, but for a way of living (that the earning pays for), and a little advice from your mother has a right to be introduced into the process of formulating the formula. The course you are set on is planned to bring in more and more money for you; and that money means you can be well housed, fed, dressed—and can afford a lot of "dates." But thinking about your writing again makes me wonder if the "course" has thrown you off balance because there isn't any time for distance, reflection, imagining: for making something money can't buy. Think of how some of your money can buy you time for that. For balance you need a chance not only to make a way for yourself in the world but to remake the world within yourself.

Good Lord: this sounds like low-church preaching, or as if I'm in a senti-mental mood. But neither is true. All I can do now is act like the proper lec-turer at the school I went to and tell you at the end of the lecture what it is that I have told you, namely:

(1) I thank you for the Trollope.

(2) Because I enjoyed it so much, I thought of your own writing and want to urge you to take it up again.

(3) Because I am being thankful and thoughtful, I became forethoughtful about Thanksgiving and I invite you(s) to come and celebrate it here.

I must stop writing now before trying to guess how long ago you might have stopped reading this; but unlike the proper lecturer at my school, I shall end by sending you my most heartfelt Love.

LETTER FROM SHELAGH JACKMAN TO HER DAUGHTER IN NEW YORK

Darling Claire:

Is your telephone working? Do I have the correct number? Or are you never in? Don't mind me—just my way of saying I've tried reaching you oc-casionally during the past few days but without luck. I like to imagine it means you are thoroughly busy with the pleasures of work—and the work of pleasures. I just want you to know that I think of you.

The dinner party is over; and I thought of you most affectionately in con-nection with the menu. I served your creation for dessert. Remember how

you once pulled a carnation out of a centerpiece, stuck it into a bowl of chocolate pudding, and announced: "A flowerpot!" Well, they were marigolds
this time, and a mousse spiked with rum, but the idea was the same. How old
could you have been when you did that? Ten or eleven, I suppose; you still
braided your hair and refused to wear a dress. You must have gone through
three dozen pairs of blue jeans by that age.

Power of association: I see you most vividly stretched out on the living-
room rug in blue jeans and a cowboy shirt, along with Morgan, Dad and me
playing Chinese checkers on a wintry Sunday afternoon. (How competitive
we all were—[are?]!) I loved the clash of colors in the middle ground. You
were always gold, Morgan green, Dad blue, and I white. How we used to
make ladders to jump toward the opposite triangle and then get in each
other's way or take advantage of each other's moves. I had never played Chinese checkers in my childhood, so for me it came along as a benefit of moth-
erhood. I was always looking for new games to play in those days. Shall I confess something to you? Whenever I come upon a toy store I instinctually
pause to window-shop, feeling that I ought to go in and find something new
for the children—before I do a "double take" and realize that I am no longer
the mother of children. I am a middle-aged lady with two grown-up offspring.
Disconcerting, I'll tell you.

What shall I tell you about the dinner party? Brita is both as sharp and as
warmhearted as ever. Walter Webster was robbed in Boston by a girl in a
clown's makeup; Priscilla Rosenblatt is still the world's greastest Do Gooder;
Elsie Rostum becomes more of a stick as time goes on. Cliff Rostum becomes
more of a stick as time goes on. It is said that husbands and wives come to
resemble each other the longer they live together. (Can anyone say that about
your father and me? Would there be any truth to it? I don't think so; it's the
differences between us that I most appreciate.) Anyway ... this passel,
mainly of your father's friends, makes me think of how you used to bring
home stray cats when you were young. (That's cute, but it's unkind. I take it
back. "The jury is instructed to disregard that remark.") I often think of the
one stray cat we kept—for seven years!—and I do miss him; but I wouldn't
want another one.

Power of association: the dinner party was like a game of Chinese checkers.
Each of us maneuvered the colorful balls of our conversational gambits before
the others, crisscrossing the dinner table, making unplanned, haphazard designs, until finally we each safely arrived at the goal, reconstructed in our own
triangles, all of our own colors (meaning what?), ending by withdrawing into
ourselves. (I feel there might be a clever analogy about social life lodged in
this somewhere, but it would take work to carve it out. . . .)

Before I forget: do think about coming home for Thanksgiving, will you? I
don't believe any of us was very pleased with last year's experience, even

73

though the restaurant was fine. But it was open to the public! Would you like to bring a friend with you? You have lots of friends. How will you choose? (Does anyone use the word "beau" anymore? I suppose it's evaporated—the way laws about "breach of promise" did. . . .)

Conclusion: I'm feeling very cheerful. I hope the same is true of you. We'll talk again soon. Dream the dream onward!

Your adoring mother

LETTER FROM SHELAGH JACKMAN TO HER SISTER IN LONDON

Dear Adrienne:

Our letters have crossed again. The latest I received from you was written before the last I sent to you. This feels like talking with you on a transatlantic telephone call: I hear the echo of what I said a few moments ago while I'm answering your next question.

Of course I'm still planning to visit in October; don't think that because I didn't mention it in my last letter I have any reservation about it. Is that a pun? Actually I don't have my flight reservations; but I have no reservations about making them. I'll be with you on the 18th or 19th of October. Start weaving the red carpet.

What I recall about the letter I sent you last week is: the problem of what the serpent looked like before it was cursed; my thanks for your gift of the Port; and some mention that I was about to see a doctor because of vague and unspecified "complaints." I did see him, and I have, so far, only a vague and unspecific result. Tests were taken; I am still waiting for the results; but all I'm aware of now is that the doctor doesn't know any more of what's going on than I do. It's probably all related to the phases of the moon—hormonal and menopausal (although I must say, it seems the pause for me is taking forever to reach cessation).

Chester is in good form and in good spirits, and truly regrets that he is not able to come along with me on this next visit to you. So does Claire—who hasn't been in England for over a year (and wonders what became of a friend of hers who went to the Royal Academy of Dramatic Art—Caroline Taylor; I remember she called on you once when she first arrived. Conrad Taylor's daughter. Do you see anything of her?) Claire is working with great concentration on her career: as well as taking classes, now she's rehearsing for a play to open after I return. Morgan is determined to do the right thing by himself (to say nothing of the rest of the world) in the stock market. Odd that he should have inherited that from Mother. . . .

I gave a dinner party the other night, mainly for friends of Chester's; I count Walter and Brita more as friends of mine. I think I've come to know them all too well. They wear thin. Well (making exceptions for Walter an Brita), it seems to me that the others feel they're so intellectually or morally good that they don't have any obligation to be charming. What I'm disappointed by was the low-level charge of vivacity or the intention to be engaging. Maybe I'm getting old. Maybe they're getting old?! But it is obvious to me that there are different voltages in the electricity of a gathering among any number of people—I suppose it's the social equivalent of a sexual charge between any two people (and everybody knows how degrees of that fluctuate). The truth of knowing anyone too well would be that they've become so predictable or repetitive as to be boring; while I do know these people well enough to predict what they care about and how they'll express it—they are not repetitive. Wait; let me think this through. . . . They're not boring because they always introduce something new from their current experience, but their investment in engaging anyone else's interest (my interest) is not charged with concern—the concern for making a good impression, as you would in meeting someone for the first time. Ah, I understand it now! It's the condition of being taken for granted. Damn.

I don't like seeing evidence that I am taken for granted. Shouldn't one always have the right to withdraw approval or goodwill—or friendship, for that matter—if the other person goes too far? (Being really boring would be going too far.) Or if he or she doesn't go far enough? (Not doing anything to engage my interest would be an example of that.) Yes, that's it. There are both upper and lower limits to the range of good relations with other people; and I was feeling that these "old friends" were approaching the lower limit. I had gone out of my way to present them with an excellent dinner and good company; but it felt as though none of them would go out of his way to become acquainted with any of the others if they weren't already familiars. It's not that I feel as if I ought to be courted or "won" anew each time I reencounter someone I've known over many years; I'm neither that insecure nor that egocentric. But I resist the status of "old shoe." I don't want anyone to be so "comfortable" with me as to forget that I too need to be "stroked." That's what was missing.

Thank God for Chester! Who needs friends?

Good grief. Why am I saying all this to you? Answer: Because I can think out loud in your presence.

And also I suppose because I'm anticipating a party in your flat, and other parties I expect to go to while I'm in London, where there'll be a mixture of old acquaintances and new faces. Not any "old shoe" friends as at home. Who was it who wrote, "Superficially is the best way to know people"? (I.e., people who aren't your husband or your sister.)

Conclusion: Never take anyone for granted; it's bad manners.

My love to you, dear girl.

75

Dear Freddy Tiejens:

I much appreciate receiving my copy of the signed contract for the illustrations to your edition of the Old Testament which arrived in the mail the other day, along with the check for the advance. I am well into work on it, and as "an old pro," if I say so myself, I have no reason to think I won't finish on schedule.

Therefore, the note that came with the contract about "take your time" and "no hurry" disconcerted me. Are you having second thoughts about the project?

I have tried phoning you three times now; have given up; and write this letter instead. I'll grant that you don't have to be at your desk every minute of a nine-to-five day. But do you get messages? Does the same person ever answer your phone twice? I've spoken to a different one each time I've called—and, of course, have to start from scratch: who am I? what is it about? does he have your number? I realize there is a great delusion in this country—where bigger is assumed to mean better—about the relationship between size and how well a business is run. Must I assume that your publishing firm has become too big to be efficient?

I'm only partly teasing. Do, please, let me hear from you when you can.
Fondly,
Shelagh Jackman

❦

On the day Shelagh was to see Quentin Connolley again, she worked at her drawings all morning in her bathrobe, and dressed only after lunch when she prepared to leave. Puddles on the streets and sidewalks remained from the rainstorm of the night before, but the sky was the almost-cerulean blue of almost-October.

This time Shelagh entered Dr. Connolley's office without trepidation over the pain in her side, but with apprehensiveness, an uncertainty of how she might feel if he resumed his flirtation. She was no longer bothered by discomfort in her side, and therefore, "strictly speaking," told herself she need not keep this appointment but for curiosity to learn the results of the tests that had been made. Still, when it occurred to her that she could learn those results in a telephone conversation, she realized that the desire to visit Quentin's office again was sparked by a different curiosity. She wanted to enjoy his harmless flattery.

She was surprised, then, to find him only professionally businesslike. She-lagh sat in the armchair at the side of his desk; wearing his luxurious white jacket, he leaned forward over the documents in front of him, apparently reading aloud. "No complications in the standard blood chemistry. That's all right," he announced. "Your heart, lungs, and blood pressure are normal. The urinalysis shows no bacteria; clear; concentrates well—which means the kidneys are fine. They're doing their job."

Shelagh interrupted: "The truth is that the pain has hardly recurred since I saw you last. . . ."

He looked up at her briskly. "Recurred at all?"

"I don't think so." She chuckled. "I should tell you that when I was twelve or thirteen years old, I woke up one morning with an excruciating pain in my abdomen. I was doubled over with pain—literally. My mother was already in Harley Street."

"Was she a doctor?"

"An ophthalmologist. My father phoned her and she arranged for a friend of hers to see me immediately. Father bundled me up and drove me into town. Throughout the drive I lay on the back seat of the car, with my knees up to my chin, moaning and groaning—until we came to within one block of the doctor's office. And then it was gone. Disappeared. I sat up. I felt per-fectly healthy. I walked into the office without any support. It was over."

Quentin Connolley said, "Medical magic."

"It was some form of food poisoning. But I suppose proximity to a doctor was enough to cure me. The only consequence I recall was that I lived on rice pudding for twenty-four hours."

"Do you suppose I cured you ten days ago?"

"By being in your presence?"

"By the laying on of hands. Doctors may have inherited that power from kings. . . ."

With the reference to having touched her, he appeared to relax, though Shelagh didn't realize she had given him that opening to take advantage of. He leaned back in his leather desk chair; he surveyed her with his bright blue eyes. Her coat and hat were in the closet of the waiting room. She wore a gray cashmere sweater and a Black Watch pleated skirt; her legs were crossed at the knee and she sat with her hands at either end of the envelope handbag on her lap.

He stroked the short beard along his jaw, fondling her with his eyes.

"Well, then," she said, "perhaps I should thank you for the miraculous cure—and leave now."

"Hardly." Again, his tone was clearly professional. "The routine tests so far don't display any malfunction. But that doesn't mean there's nothing organi-cally wrong. Only that we haven't found it yet."

77

"Oh."

"I must examine you further."

"What will you be looking for?"

"From where you say it hurt, there might be a problem with an indolent appendix. Possibly an inflammation causing an adhesion—if it's in contact with the small bowel. The fact that you're not feeling pain at the moment may mean it's artificially stabilized."

Shelagh laughed. "If there's no pain, why call the stability 'artificial'?"

"Because it can't last," he replied. "I must examine you. But there's no hurry. I have no one else coming in after you. Are you in a hurry?"

"No."

"Fine. Why don't we have a cup of tea? Would you like that?"

"Yes."

"We can chat." And then he added, "I like being with you."

As Quentin rose and walked to the door, Shelagh gazed through the office window to the leaves of the trees beyond, just beginning to hint at their coming change into autumn colors. She smiled to herself with the thought that he meant to continue the flirtation, but more cautiously now, in a more mature and sophisticated manner. Behind her back, she heard him give instructions to his nurse.

To make conversation, she began by asking, "Do you know a Dr. Lyman?"

"The gerontologist? You won't have need of him for a long while."

"I wasn't asking for myself. He came by my house by mistake last night. During the downpour. He was looking for the people next door—a very elderly couple. I don't know what will become of them."

"What *has* become of them?"

"The old man either had a stroke and fell down a flight of stairs, or fell down the stairs and that brought about the stroke. His wife is so infirm, she couldn't help him at all. It's so pathetic. He was taken away in an ambulance later, while the rain still teemed down." Momentarily her eyes were wet with the possibility of tears. But she contained herself. She remained seated in the armchair.

Quentin stared down at her from where he stood near her side. "You are," he declared slowly, with admiration, "a very compassionate person."

"I suppose so," she said cheerfully, but to lessen the value of that, went on: "However, in this case I'm afraid I was feeling how awful it would be to happen to me—paralysis, decay . . ."

"If we live long enough, everything awful will happen to us." And therefore, he added, *"Carpe diem."*

The nurse appeared with tea on a round teak tray and set it down on the low table before the sofa, as if it were part of the doctor's daily routine. That seemed perfectly ordinary to Shelagh, but not that Quentin accompanied the nurse to the door and said, "You really can take off the rest of the day." Then he returned to Shelagh's side and with one hand under her elbow urged her up, saying, "Come, sit on the sofa. Drink tea. Let me bask in your presence."

It was the novelty of his intrigue that delighted her.

With teacups and saucers in hand, they sat side by side contemplating each other.

"Do you make all of your patients so comfortable?"

"Not in the least. Usually I'm not much aware of them as human beings—just as cases."

"Like a case of Port."

"A case of pneumonia. A case of diabetes . . ."

"So you deal with one form or another of suffering all the time."

"More or less. But it feels very good to be able to help people."

Shelagh thought that such suffering was passive, never one's own fault, for diseases are never invited. But Chester as a judge dealt with self-inflicted sufferings: the criminal, the inane, or the insane. But she did not want to mention Chester in this situation. "What do you do to relax, to put all this out of your mind? To 'recreate' yourself, as they used to say?"

Quentin put his teacup down on the tray. "I play golf. I read a lot."

"What do you read?"

"Novels. Nineteenth-century novels. Balzac. George Eliot. Dickens. Tolstoy. I can go through them again and again."

"No contemporary fiction?"

"I can't make 'em out. I've tried Graham Greene, for example. Can't figure out what all the suffering is *for*."

"You want your authors to make clear what it's all *for*."

"Right."

"I've just read Trollope's *The Way We Live Now*. It's full of such clear-cut purpose. Full of unequivocal judgments—like: 'She was false through and through, but there was some good in her. . . .' "

He laughed. "Yes, I confess that's what I like."

She toyed with him: "In literature, but not in life . . . ?"

"You can't have it in life. You can never know any other living person the way an author can presume to know a character."

"Is it true that we never can, or that we just don't choose to concentrate enough on anyone else to appreciate them from the inside?"

"Love is supposed to give us that kind of appreciation," he said, suggesting a smile.

"Oh, that danger," Shelagh replied quickly. "Well, that explains why so few of us come to know much about anybody else." Yes, *danger*, she thought. One love is all a person can handle. Otherwise, you are always overwhelmed, overthrown, in turmoil. If you have a life, you can't forever be re-creating it.

"Danger?" Quentin asked. "Why, I thought it was the Christian ideal—thy neighbor as thyself. . . ."

"Then why does it seem possible only in books and not in lived experience?"

He looked away from her but said in a clear, steady voice: "Most people don't have the determination to go after what they want."

She sighed. "I think we're talking at cross-purposes."

He threw up his hands and chuckled: "That goes to prove it. . . ."

Neither of them wanted another cup of tea. He took her hands in his, slipped his fingers under the cuffs of her sweater sleeves, and stroked the flesh of her wrists.

"You haven't told me about your own work these days."

"I'm illustrating a new edition of the Old Testament," she said happily. "I'm up to David and Goliath."

At that point he only shrugged, stood up, and declared: "Let's get on with it."

He left her alone in the examining room adjoining his office, with directions to undress and put on the hospital gown for the examination. The room was long but not wide, dominated by the examination "table" made comfortable with a thick mattress, covered by a smooth white sheet. A corner near the door was concealed by a folding screen, behind which she removed all her clothes and placed them on hangers or on the low stool. There was a pink porcelain bidet with a towel rack on the wall above it. Shelagh smirked: she had no need for that; she was properly bathed and perfumed.

Wearing the hospital gown loosely tied behind her back, she came into the room from around the folding screen, intensely conscious of the silence, the warmth of her bare feet against the tile floor, and of the clarity of the blue sky through the high window at the opposite end of the room. She stared up, recognizing that it was too high for anyone on the sidewalk along the parking lot to see in, and suddenly discovered that three cut-glass or crystal balls were suspended before the windowpane. They were hung at different heights by invisible wire from little nails in the top of the frame. She walked closer to them and examined each carefully. They were the size of golf balls, crystals cut in hundreds of triangular facets. Just as she studied their appearance of immobility, considering the pale fluidity of rainbows entrapped within each globe, the sun dipped a little farther in the west, striking like flint against steel, and a beacon flash of pure scarlet flicked out of the middle one, and then a shaft of Kelly green out of the surface from the one above, and at last, a blaze of liquid gold from the one below. Then, as the late-afternoon sunlight beamed steadily through the crystal balls, a display of rainbows appeared on the wall to her right: a haphazard array of mini-flags—each red, yellow, green, and purple—no larger than postage stamps, randomly scattered, lifting up her heart with a gift of beauty.

When she heard Quentin enter and close the door behind him, she said, "How charming!"

"They're from Bohemia. A patient of mine gave them to me—in a container for golf balls, no less."

"How thoughtful of you to hang them in here."

"Twist them," he suggested, as he washed his hands at the sink, "and they'll blaze all around the walls, even on the ceiling."

So she gave each of them a turn between two fingers, and thought only of the delight of seeing the little rainbows dance around the room, a trifle mechanically, as if each was a marionette on a string, as she climbed up onto the examination table—smoothing the hospital gown down over her legs, lying back, concentrating on the colorful fireworks, thinking of hypnosis and distractions while she was about to be exposed before Quentin Connolley.

First he listened to her heartbeat. He made her turn on one side in order to untie the gown at the back and then, with his hand under the light fabric, he stroked her abdomen, applying pressure here and there, asking, "No tenderness? Here? Here?" muttering, "No swelling; well, then, good. . . ." He examined her breasts, while he spoke of the possibility of doing X-rays of the digestive tract if the symptoms persisted. His hands played over her body, his words flowed over her mind, her heart beat much faster than usual as she forced herself to focus on the ceiling of square blocks; they reminded her of slices of Muenster cheese. He prepared her for a pelvic examination—setting her bare heels in the two stirrups drawn outward from the table, lifting her knees high and spreading her legs apart. The hospital gown was tented up over her knees and then overlaid with a white sheet, so that while she was naked and vulnerable below it, she could see nothing beyond the wall of fabric that separated them.

His almost-musical droning continued: "Possibility of cysts. Palpate the cervix. Uterus fine. No fibroids." She trembled at his stroking touches. She kept her head immobile, but followed the rainbows with her eyes; as their movement gradually slowed, she tried to teach herself to feel less tense, to relax her body. But her muscles were vibrant with resistance. "Now to check the ovaries. If you relax as completely as possible, Shelagh, I can identify them better." She was aware of a cold thin lubricant, of an insertion of probing—twisted, returned, withdrawn. More lubricant. Two fingers. The drone of the muttering had stopped. The movement of the rainbows was over: they remained stationary on the wall to her right. Quentin Connolley was humming very softly. The probing again. A groan escaped her involuntarily. Then she was shocked with the instant awareness that what she felt was not fingers.

81

She knew exactly what it was. She raised her head to see him looking down below the sheet that concealed the rest of him from her sight. She felt one hand stroking her abdomen, the other trying to lift her up at the edge of the table; then a deeper probing.

A howl of outrage roared up from inside her: "How dare you!" in the same instant that she brought both of her heels out of the stirrups and flung her feet and legs with all their might against his chest; her knees still high, she struck him fast twice below the shoulders, and he fell backward as she shouted, "You fool!"

The worst thing she could imagine happening under these circumstances was exactly what had happened.

Shelagh leaped off the table, drawing the hospital gown close around her, intensely aware of the slimy lubricant dripping down her thighs, disgusted, unable to keep from numbly repeating, "You bloody fool!"

He had staggered back against the wall under the windows, and was awkwardly adjusting his clothes. She felt flushed with fury, and the sight of him zipping up his trousers only lashed her to fiercer anger. She wanted to smash him. She felt her right hand knotted into a fist and raised to the level of her shoulder, and she took two steps forward before she realized what she was doing. In the same instant she knew she could not touch him with her bare hand. She looked for something to beat him with; she wanted to hit him, to hurt him.

She heard herself spit out, "You vulgarian."

Her body was poweful with concentration; vibrating with outrage; all her senses directed toward revenge. She surveyed the room for objects to fling at him. On a low cabinet next to the sink lay a collection of instruments for examining ears and eyes and noses. She picked them up quickly and hurled them at him. He caught one; another hit the wall next to him and fell to the floor; the last one struck him on the shoulder, as she called him "Vile! Contemptible!"

Shelagh felt herself lunge to the window and yank a crystal ball with each hand, snapping the invisible wire away from the nails that held them. But now she was within four feet of the corner where Quentin stood, and he moved forward instantly and grasped her hands in both of his, preventing her from throwing them, arresting her hands around the crystal balls. "Please don't."

"Why not?" She felt naive in her bitterness.

"I'm sorry." She was aware of how much taller and stronger than she he was.

"You're *sorry?*" She made the word sound insultingly inadequate, as the most minimal, the most trivial of possible apologies, unworthy of consideration to attenuate the outrage.

"I'm terribly sorry."

"You're even more of a fool that I thought."

"What else can I say? I thought you wanted—"

"When did you think of what I wanted? You think only of yourself."

"You led me to believe—"

"I led you nowhere." She struggled to free her hands from his, only to discover that he held them as in a vise. "You are as stupid as you are strong."

At that point he let go of her hands and remained still before her, his arms fallen to his sides.

Instead of hitting him, she tossed both of the crystal balls onto the mattress of the examining table. She was conscious of the fact that the hospital gown was untied behind her and pressed her back against the wall under the window. "Get out," she demanded, as if this room were her domain and he an interloper. "Leave me alone."

When he reached the far wall, by turning the latch he demonstrated that the door had been locked. The moment he was gone, she went to the door and locked him out. She pulled the hospital gown off her shoulders and down her arms until it fell to the floor, and she kicked it under the sink, where it caught on the metal foot pedals. Behind the folding screen, Shelagh sat on the bidet and ran the water until it became too hot, and then ran it until it became too cold.

What had she led him to believe? That she liked being paid attention to: yes, she would admit to that, if that had been as far as it went. She had liked his attention; to be admired, to be flattered; not to be made unfair use of, to be abused. He had violated her. When the word actually took form in her mind, she burst out laughing—completely surprised by her automatic reaction. She might just as easily have burst into tears. What was funny about it? That she had lived her whole life, as any woman might, with the dread of being violated as a possibility simply because one is aware of possibilities, just as men are aware that they might come to death in battle, or women of death in childbirth, but never with a sense of imminent danger. Owning to a fortunate life in which being kissed by a black man on the platform of a subway station was unlikely enough, the chance of rape by a stranger in a dangerous situation over which she had no control, in which she hoped for no protection, was so remote, so luckily improbable, she could see it only as funny that she should be violated not by a stranger but by a "friend," and not in a condition of obvious danger: on the contrary, in a situation she had brought about by herself in seeking help from someone who could do her good. She laughed again, acknowledging the relief that came with accepting the absurdity of it.

Her fury passed, but not the resentment. She began to wash herself again, but she recognized she was only postponing the next steps of leaving. She knew she would have to confront him; there was no way out of the complex of rooms except through his office, and he would be standing there, abject, saying, "I'm really terribly sorry. . . ."

She stood up and dried herself with the soft towel, saw her face in the wall mirror: impassively cold, her lips tight, scowling. What if he had heard her laughter? she wondered; what if he misunderstood that to mean it was all right with her, that she forgave him? It was *not* funny, and she was not disposed to excuse him or to pardon the offense. The sense of physical danger still permeated her whole being, although the fear of bodily hurt had subsided, sinking into a coldness through her legs and arms even as she drew on her sweater and wrapped her skirt around her.

She was not hurt in her body, she reassured herself; but she was morally offended by having been forced. Never before in her life had she been made love to against her will. Only twice in the many years of her marriage to Chester had she experienced intercourse with any other man—and both instances had been at her instigation: One afternoon, with Henry Warner, while his wife was in the hospital having delivered their first child. And one night, with Conrad Taylor, after he had divorced his first wife and when his only child had gone abroad. Those encounters were not "affairs"; they were, she told herself, acts of friendship. By what name should this act be called?

Was she at all responsible for bringing it about?

Was it even remotely possible that either Henry or Conrad—or both—had ever said anything, implied or hinted anything, about those solitary incidents to Quentin Connolley? She shivered with resentment at the thought, rubbed her hands up and down her arms and around her shoulders to press away the chill. She was determined to be self-controlled and in self-command again. Her stockinged feet in her firm shoes signaled that she was again on hard ground. Even if anyone else had indicated to Quentin that she could be "made," and if she had unconsciously led him into thinking that that was what she wanted to happen—although she rejected that idea—she would brazen it out. She combed her hair; not to make herself appear attractive but to emphasize that she was self-contained. She looked once again around the room to see if she had forgotten anything and then, impulsively, instinctually, and with no rational motive, scooped up the two crystal balls from the mattress of the examining table and hid them in her handbag.

When Shelagh stood in the doorway of his office, she saw Quentin standing behind his desk, rubbing his shoulder where the instrument had hit him. "Do you want me to feel sorry for you?" she asked.

"I am sorry for everything."

"You have good reason to be. I thought we were sharing an innocent pleasure."

84

"So did I."

"You ruined it."

Plaintively he said, "I could have loved you."

"I could have been an astronaut. But I didn't even try to qualify." Her sang-froid amazed her. She continued to suffer coldness in her arms and legs, but she was determined to show him only her dignity.

"I made a terrible mistake. I'm covered with shame."

"What a cant phrase." She held her handbag tightly under one arm.

"It was very bad judgment. But you see: you came back. . . ."

She smarted at his innuendo, the implication of her complicity. Even across the distance of the room, she could see the sweat smudging down his neck from behind his left ear to the collar of his shirt. Coldly, she said, "It was misjudgment."

"What do you want me to do?"

"Never speak to me again."

"How is that possible? We see each other—"

Shelagh's laughter interrupted him. "Oh, don't be afraid. I won't snub you at cocktail parties. But if you're so sensitive to public appearances—"

She had put her finger on the live nerve. Now he interrupted her. "You won't tell anyone."

The only satisfaction she took away with her at the end of that event, beyond having maintained her self-restraint while she stood in his office eager to escape, was her pleasure in choosing to make him suffer uncertainty by replying: "I don't know. I'll have to think about it."

❧

DIARY ENTRY

Do I tell my husband?

I have waited a day even to "tell" this journal. Not that I have any intention of turning yesterday's event into statements recorded here. There was an unpleasant incident. Doesn't that sound innocuous? Why shouldn't it? Innocuous means producing no harm, no injury, no consequences. What should be the consequences? I am neither damaged nor humiliated. I am angry to have been abused. But am I totally innocent, without any responsibility? I don't know. How can I have certainty about what happens along the border between consciousness and the unconscious?

If unconsciously that is what I wanted to happen, then why did I respond consciously to it with so absolute a rejection, with a refusal of such intensity?

85

What if the answer is that morally and socially I am a prude, but as a body (and what is my unconscious but my body without any instructions from my mind?) I send signals of desire that I can neither control nor condone?

Oh, hell; it isn't all that important. It isn't a catastrophe: children won't die from it.

And yet, I feel insulted. Something had been taken for granted which in fact I had not granted. So the insult is to my pride; to the pride of belief in the extent to which I can influence the action of another person. Or is it that I played like a gambler and lost? I was gambling—with a small investment— on the pleasure of a flirtation; and a more determined gambler wiped me out, eliminated the possibility of pleasant results for me by playing a more dangerous game. I lost. But he lost too. I wiped out his chance of "more" or "ever again."

It all turns on what we can expect of each other; but we keep making mistakes in judging people. (Oh, poor Adrienne and her almost-husband!) How can we ever be discriminating enough to escape unpleasant events? or world-crushing events? (Adrienne doesn't appear to be crushed, but she never has married and I don't believe she ever will marry.) We can't avoid them. We have to live with mistakes.

Of course I hate him. But for what? I could say because he is a bounder, a cad, a vulgarian; but it would be more truthful to say: for spoiling my fun.

He owed me more time . . . and I owed him more warning.

What do I owe Chester?

What should he know of this? Anything? and why? We have been so open and honest with each other. For all practical purposes I have told him everything. Ah, but only for "all practical purposes." There are so many such purposes: to charm him, to entertain him, to unburden myself of a worry, to ask for advice, to help solve a problem, to keep him up to date. That last looks funny to me, but I suppose it means: as we live a separate life apart from the other, we do have to bring news bulletins as we come together.

I don't mean that we have no secrets from each other. It would be naive of me to imagine Chester has never suppressed any information about himself. But then why should he offer me any reason for lowering his estimation in my eyes? That's it, exactly: why should I owe it to him to devaluate myself? I can keep to myself whatever I might be ashamed of, or whatever would not contribute to our good feelings about each other.

Chester has a longtime friendship with a man who offended me—but I admit, probably not without provocation. I don't want to put myself in an unfavorable light any more than I feel the need to poison their relationship. Now that I think of it, that must be why I said, "I won't snub you at cocktail parties. . . ." I want it not to have happened, but despite the fact that it did occur, I shall pretend that it didn't. I don't feel any need, any obligation to *tell Chester. I can't think of any good to come from telling him, but I can see a lot of ill that would result if I did. I can think only of good reasons to protect him from knowing. I take upon myself the right to keep my mouth shut.*

I will not tell my husband.

Early one morning, a week later, the telephone rang even before the Judge had finished his tea and left for the office. Shelagh answered it next to her side of the bed.

Dr. Quentin Connolley repeated her name: "Shelagh? Shelagh?" in a whisper.

"Yes."

"Will you let me have another chance?"

Impassively, Shelagh said, "No" and hung up the receiver.

"What was that?" Chester asked.

"Wrong number."

∾ৎৎৎ∾

On Friday morning Shelagh took the train into Manhattan. If it hadn't been for the opera tickets, she would have driven; or even if Walter Webster had wanted a lift into the city she would have taken the car. But he declined this opportunity, and she and Chester thought it better to stay overnight after a late performance, so she traveled ahead in the morning to spend the day in her own way, and to meet her husband and her children—with their "dates"—over drinks at Claire's apartment after Chester's arrival on a late-afternoon train.

The railroad car was not clean, but also not very crowded. She sat alone on a plush blue-cushioned seat idly staring out the windows as the train approached Stamford, primarily conscious of the fact that she was alone, indulging her sense of privacy. *I do not have to think of anything, if I don't want to,* she said to herself. *I do not have to respond to anyone. I can merely drift. Continue to breathe, behave myself and I will be let alone.* She had thought a great deal about privacy and secrecy in the past few days—since the incident in Dr. Connolley's office: wondering whether one is more oneself in private or in public, in subjective communion or when engaged with others. She felt stuck with the question, a rhetorical question, because she imagined that the answer was sometimes one and sometimes the other, depending on how you come to realize what is most one's self. Shelagh remained stuck with the difficulty of not knowing how to distinguish between one's self at its most typical and what you are at your best, the most intense, profound and

87

uniquely you. It worried her that she was suspicious of secrecy at the same time that she prized her own privacy.

And then it came back to her that at some moment of childhood she had overheard a conversation between her father and a guest that began with the statement "There is no word for 'privacy' in Russian."

"How can that be?"

Her father explained: "In Russian there are words for 'solitude' and for 'secrecy'; but in a country of vast spaces, isolation is a danger, not a source of self-satisfaction. In a country of totalitarian paranoia there is no margin for personal secrets."

"You are talking about the Soviet Union?"

"No, no. The Russian language isn't an invention of the Soviet regime. There has *never* been a word for 'privacy' in Russian."

"Amazing."

"But then, there is no word for 'privacy' in Greek or Latin either."

"Difficult to believe."

"Not at all. Think of it this way: no one in the history of the world ever kept a diary before the Reformation. No individual's daily thoughts or feelings had been considered significant enough to be recorded. Even the chronicles of kings have none of the character of a subjective daily journal. And why should they? Those are not the records of private individuals; they are the histories of public events. No individual had been thought of as important enough in the eyes of God—let alone in his own eyes—to examine everything unto the smallest detail of what he felt or thought. Until the Reformation—and the Counter-Reformation. That is the reason for and the beginning of infinite self-examination."

There was a pause, and then her father's guest had said, "I've lost the point. You were making an analogy . . ."

"Between the writing of diaries and the concept of privacy."

"Yes. Now I remember."

"Privacy is of no importance—it cannot be thought of as a good thing—unless circumstances allow for isolation or being alone that is not threatening to the individual, on the one hand, or secrecy threatening to the state, on the other hand. So you see, the idea of privacy is a child of the Enlightenment, a very recent, newborn concept that is a hybrid offspring of the Rights of Man."

"I can hardly believe it," the guest replied. "I had assumed it was a universal and eternal idea."

Shelagh recalled the good humor of her father's laughter as he ended the conversation.

Marvelous, how marvelous! Shelagh wondered with appreciation that on this early-October day in 1973, on a train moving along the pleasant countryside of southern Connecticut, she should remember with perfect clarity a conversation that took place in her parents' house in London in 1938 or '39, to reinforce that sense she had been keenly aware of during the past few days that her privacy consisted of what she took to be peculiar to herself, that was nobody else's concern, that she had the right to keep secret—for not knowing it would harm no one, and for anyone else to know would only harm her. That was the kind of secrecy that justified privacy, for she had experienced something that she was not necessarily expected to disclose to anyone else.

It amazed her that she could recollect that fragment of a conversation which had taken place some thirty-five years before, drawn out of memory by the word "privacy." She could not remember whether she had been in the room or standing near an open door; who her father's guest was, if it was evening or afternoon, or what she had been wearing; but she could recall even now the stab of surprise she had suffered at the discovery that there are people for whom there is no privacy. She felt appalled for them, for how deprived you must be, who can never feel that what you owe yourself, to protect your own well-being, can ever take precedence over what you owe to others.

Arriving at Grand Central Station was like entering a great theater where an enormously popular spectacle was about to take place. The sudden parade of travelers all hastening from the train in the same direction along the platform was like an audience eagerly marching to their seats in a coliseum. But once they had entered the huge barrel-vaulted central hall, they were dispersed—each to his own performance. Over the years, from the time Shelagh had first seen it, the great station had deteriorated: the advertising placards destroyed the grandeur of the walls, the booths for placing racetrack bets had turned it sleazy, it had been burst open on one side for the escalators leading to the lobby of a new skyscraper grafted onto it. It had fallen into decay. It looked in disarray. But for the ceiling: the radiant night sky on the long dome making vivid the figures of the zodiac. The constellations of stars became the signals of titanic figures. It amused Shelagh to stare up at this remnant, this residue of classical imagery, with its belief that the powers of the whole universe contend or conspire to determine our fates. It's true, of course, Shelagh thought, smiling to herself; and any myth will do that brings it home.

Shelagh loved walking the streets of Manhattan in good weather. She went out of Grand Central along Vanderbilt Avenue and headed north, zigzagging across to Madison, up Madison and then over to Fifth, under a clear autumn sky, in moderate temperature, with a hint of a fresh breeze in the air. Waiting for the traffic light to change at one corner, she caught sight of herself in the tawny light of a brass-colored mirror along the side of a new glass-and-steel office building. In the midst of the pedestrians waiting at the corner around her, she read her reflection in the mirror as that of a middle-sized, middle-aged, middle-class lady; self-possessed; attractive, competent, well disposed; neatly dressed in a rust-colored velvet suit, with a beret made of the same material jauntily tilted over her right ear.

She knew she wanted to spend most of the afternoon at the Museum of Modern Art, but had enough time to drop in on her editor at Harvest House. Its offices were at Fifty-sixth Street and Fifth Avenue, and she would go there first and come back afterward to the Museum.

For all its modernity—the display of books behind a wall of glass, illuminated by hidden lights; the chrome-and-teak desk; the white telephone with two dozen buttons for switching calls; the deep purple carpet in contrast to the silver-papered walls—the reception "area" of Harvest House affected Shelagh with the quality of a fortress. The side doors were locked. You were free to come out of the elevator onto this fifteenth floor above street level, but for you to move from this "landing" to any of the other offices or any of the other floors in this publishing house, it was necessary for the receptionist to call and for someone else to convoy you to the appropriate place. There had been too many robberies, too many "unauthorized" visitors wandering around the halls, too much oppportunity for violence. The receptionist herself was locked out of the office. She had a panic button under the surface of her desk, for she was the exposed and vulnerable guardian of this elaborate and successful outpost of a commercial enterprise in liberal civilization.

Shelagh asked for Freddy Tiejens and was allowed to talk on the phone, standing in front of the receptionist's desk, with an assistant or secretary of his. "No, I don't have an appointment. Doesn't anybody ever just drop in?"

"Not usually" was the petulant reply. Then the voice added, "It's nearly lunchtime. But I'll ask him."

Five minutes later, it was Mr. Tiejens himself who unlocked one of the doors to the receptionist's outpost from the inside and greeted Shelagh warmly, took her by the shoulder, and led her through alleys of more silver-papered walls to his modest office. It was hardly more than a cubicle, but it had purple carpeting on the floor and a large window that yielded a view of other Manhattan skyscrapers all the way west to the Hudson River. Down the corkboard of one wall were tacked Xerox copies of production schedules, proof copies of forthcoming book jackets, clippings of reviews, the paraphernalia of effective publishing. Mr. Tiejens cleared a set of color separations off the armchair opposite his cluttered desk for Shelagh to sit in, and then he nervously bit at his right thumbnail.

"I'm sorry, but I have a lunch date in fifteen minutes."

"Of course," she replied. "It was thoughtless of me to barge in without an appointment. But I hoped you would find it refreshing."

He actually responded to her smile with a shrug of his shoulders that seemed to her a slight sign of having been put at his ease. He remained standing behind his desk as he asked: "You did receive the contract and check for the advance, didn't you?"

"Yes. And I acknowledged them."

"I don't remember . . ."

"I haven't heard from you since, and I wondered about that odd remark in your letter."

"What odd remark?" he asked uncomfortably; he wasn't the kind of man who used the word "odd."

"Well, it seemed peculiar to me that you should send a check and a contract with a specific delivery date in it—April twenty-sixth—and then in the covering letter add the phrase 'Don't hurry.' "

He appeared bewildered for a moment and then explained, "Well, April twenty-sixth just happened to be seven months from the date the contract was drawn up."

"I understand that. What I don't understand is what's implied by 'Don't hurry.' "

Freddy Tiejens ran one hand over his forehead as if to press the proper answer out of his brain. He stood there with his eyes closed, the other hand in a pocket of his tweed trousers, tall and lean, a man unsure of himself, as if he were wearing someone else's white shirt and plaid bow tie, not knowing whether they were right for him. When he opened his eyes, Shelagh was aware that they showed the same pale brown as his hair, touched with amber. He swayed from one foot to the other, lowered his hand from his forehead into the other pants pocket. "I shouldn't have told you that" was all he could say.

"Do sit down," Shelagh requested. And the long length of him flopped into his desk chair wearily. "I'm sure you're trying to tell me something."

"Well—" he blurted out: "I don't know what's going to happen here."

"In the Juvenile Book Division?"

"In the whole goddamn house." He took a deep breath. "I shouldn't have said that."

Shelagh looked to the photographs at the edge of his desk against the wall: pictures of his bride, his son one year old, his daughter in a jumper and bonnet astride a donkey. He may be a hick, she thought, out of his depth, a big overgrown country boy who is making his way in New York, but he is a responsible human being worried about his job and his family's future.

Softly she asked, "What can happen to this great house?" spreading her hands wide to encompass all the offices on all the floors in this bastion where the whole show took place.

"It can go down the drain," he snapped out.

"Impossible."

He snorted. "There's a lot of talk about selling the firm to bankers who own a Hollywood movie studio."

"Ah . . ."

"Bankers," he repeated with contempt.

"Would it be that bad?"

"Maybe. I don't know. They say it won't, but there's no knowing till it hits you."

"Would it change everything?"

"It has elsewhere. They always start by saying, 'There won't be any changes made.' Then about twenty minutes later the efficiency experts—the accountants—come in and start making editorial decisions."

"So you're living under a cloud."

"Exactly. I shouldn't have said anything about it—anything to bother you. *You* don't have to worry."

"Why not?"

"Your contract's sound. The project's terrific. Public-domain material and *your* illustrations. It's a sure thing." He added: "You're a prizewinner."

"You are too. A prizewinning editor."

"Creative director," he corrected her.

"Sometimes you live under a cloud and then the cloud blows away."

"Sometimes . . ."

"Call on me if you need a friend," Shelagh said as she stood up.

Caught by surprise, he looked at her as if it had never occurred to him that she wasn't only someone he made use of but someone who thought they were friends.

The Museum of Modern Art was for Shelagh a twentieth-century maze without a Minotaur at the center, for it had no center. The rooms were but enlarged alcoves along a serpentine corridor, as are the state chambers, the salons, the bedrooms at the Palace of Versailles, for there were no doors to shut, let alone lock, to make for separation, to say nothing of privacy. It was, after all, a public place; a place where the public could come to see works of art: as Versailles had been a palace where the Court would see works of state. The corridors meandered from one floor up to the next and on to one above that—spaces enclosed by partitions of plaster or of glass, a labyrinth of space leading from the entrance uninterruptedly back to the exit. But the glass walls had been scarred with white strips, like cordons, to protect the uninitiated. Shelagh remembered the opening night of the retrospective show of the sculpture of Jacques Lipschitz in the late 1950s or early '60s; a very formal affair with women in evening gowns, the men in black tie—a balmy night, with Champagne served in the open-air garden—when someone (it was rumored at the time to have been Jacques Lipschitz' own teen-aged son) walked right into one of the glass walls, shattering it into a hundred thousand fragments and knocking himself unconscious. How frustrating to the architects—who had wanted a real wall at the same time so perfectly transparent that one would imagine it was as if no wall stood there at all—to discover that there are people who, like birds who don't know what glass is, could not entertain that "as if" but believed no wall did stand in their way. So the cordons came to disfigure the purity of the architects' glass walls and the public was helped to recognize their limits.

Shelagh Jackman had come to see the exhibit entitled "Nineteenth Century People—The Ordinary and the Extraordinary," a traveling show that had been assembled in Paris and brought to New York by way of Rome, Tokyo, San Francisco, and Chicago. It had been on view for six weeks; the Museum was not crowded.

It was an odd exhibition, ranging as it did from Goya's *Lunatic Asylum* of 1800 to Lautrec's *Salon de la rue Moulin* of 1894. There were self-portraits of artists from Louis David through Courbet to Van Gogh and Degas—a curious downhill slide from self-esteem to self-doubt. One room was filled with fashionable ladies, like Ingres's Mme. Rivière with her arrested-adolescent eyes, her velvet and satin, her narrow fur boa like a live eel, all microscopically seen, as though Ingres had studied her inch by inch through a magnifying glass. There was Frau von Cotta by Schick—with a pig face framed by Messalinian tendril curls, dressed in a diaphanous classical robe, as in a Greek garden, but wearing silk shoes with ribbon bows and carrying not a parasol but an umbrella. Shelagh laughed out loud. Nearly nude women and overdressed women staring out from the canvases with almost universal uncertainty, apparently asking: "Am I doing the right thing to allow this picture to be painted? Is there not some dangerous risk to be taken by permitting the appearance of a single instant of my life to be given the status of an eternal object?" Shelagh Jackman did not try to answer them.

There was a room full of laborers: coal miners, laundresses carrying heavy baskets, farmers weary at dusk, women pausing to stretch their aching backs behind the tables on which they ironed clothes. In the end: the blank stare of a barmaid waiting to take orders, and then the decay and despair of an old bawd in *The Drinker of Absinthe.*

On the floor above, in a vast exhibition hall, Shelagh surveyed the series of monumental paintings like Géricault's *Raft of the Medusa,* Delacroix's *Massacre at Chios,* Manet's *Execution of the Emperor Maximilian*—these were the nineteenth century's "news shots." The images of shipwrecks and plagues, earthquakes and political events that had been taken over by candid cameramen and television photographers, losing the chance to be transformed by art into candidates for awe and veneration; the events now re-

93

mained raw material, "unprocessed data," simply experienced in the immediacy of pretending "you are there" without the interpretation that names significance.

But Shelagh was led from there to a small room containing only domestic scenes by Vuillard, small canvases above and below each other around all four sides of the room, making her feel she was standing in the middle of the courtyard of an apartment house in Paris, looking through the open windows on the second and third floors—a voyeur to middle-class domestic life, seen in the evenings by firelight or gas lamps: fathers reading to their children, grandmothers resting in comfortable armchairs, daughters playing the piano. The artist has made us into spies, Shelagh thought; this room in the Museum simulates the courtyard, and I find myself prying into the interiors, the home lives, of people I don't know, can never know—people who died a hundred years ago. Deciphering messages of domestic tranquillity.

There were only two other people in the room, a tall, heavyset couple, carrying their raincoats neatly folded over their arms. They circled the room at the same pace as Shelagh, but half the track away. As they reached the archway leading to the next gallery, the wife concluded perfunctorily, "Beautiful! Beautiful!" and walked on ahead. Her husband glanced once more toward the window-paintings and said in a stage whisper, "Not to me . . ." before he followed her.

Shelagh felt sorry for him. What a bore it must be for him to be forced to look at—what?—somebody else's family album: Aunt Maude watering the rubber plant, Cousin Betty setting the table for dinner. Instead of seeing a picture as a gift from the gods, he resented reminders of his own "family album." Still, he was having his own experience. Whose experience was his wife having?

Shelagh realized that she'd been standing on her two-inch Italian spiked heels for nearly an hour. She bent over to pry her feet out of the shoes and held them in one hand. As she straightened up, she came face to face with a guard who stood in the doorway where the couple had disappeared. He was an elderly black man, stout, in a blue uniform, staring at her stockinged feet with disapproval. She smiled at him and whispered playfully as she walked past him, "Don't you wish *you* could?"

In the next long hall were displayed canvases of circuses and theater events—saltimbanques, actors, audiences, and Lautrec's prostitutes. Then she became aware that the guard was following her, at a not very discreet distance. He looked apprehensive, as if her one irrational action was a signal that worse might follow and he must remain on the alert. She hitched her handbag higher under one arm in order to swing the shoes in her hand more ostentatiously and sauntered to the stairwell wondering if he would follow her up to the next floor—which he did.

94

But in a moment he was forgotten. Shelagh was alone among the glories of the shimmering moment, what in his books her father had called "the earthly paradise"—Manet's *Music at the Tuileries*, Seurat's *Sunday on La Grande Jatte*, Degas's *Carriage at the Races*, Renoir's *Boating Party*, lunch in the fresh air of 1879: the glow of well-being—and what a golden glow it was! The peach-fuzz golden-faced children, the radiantly rosy young women, the self-satisfied virile men. Of course, it wasn't what Renior saw: it was what he felt; he painted his feeling for life, for the firmness and the roundness and the radiance of girls and women, the roundness of breasts and buttocks, of plump arms and fleshy bellies, golden as oranges, as ripe peaches, everything circular, glowingly circular, every feeling within the rectangular space of the canvas rounded, turning back to complete itself, as most of the brushstrokes themselves were worked—in semicircles. Shelagh moved closer to the picture of a nude model, focusing her sight on the details of the colors that created the shoulder and arm: tawny and pink gestures of curvature made up the shimmering roundness. Unconsciously, with the thumb of her clenched right hand she traced in the air, close to the surface of the painting, the arc of the brushstrokes.

"Oh, no you don't!" was shouted at her.

She turned to recognize the guard who had been following her.

"You don't *touch* pictures," he commanded.

"I didn't touch it."

"Looked that way to me."

"You were behind me. It might have seemed that way from where you were standing."

He stared briefly at her feet again in hostile criticism of bad behavior. "What you want to do—poke a hole in it?"

"Don't be silly."

"What did you want, then?" He stood square before her with his hands on his hips.

"I wanted to feel the picture with my whole body, not just with my eyes." Shelagh leaned forward, lifted one foot to slip the shoe on; the guard took a quick step backward, as if afraid she had intended to strike him with the shoe.

"I knew you were going to be trouble," he said.

With both shoes on, Shelagh straightened up to her full height, took a deep breath, and announced imperiously, "You can keep your old pictures," stalking past him and out of the Museum.

Therefore, when she was greeted by Claire with the question "What happened to you today?" she answered: "I was accused of attacking a Renoir."

She and Chester had changed clothes for the evening in their hotel on

Central Park South and taken a cab up Broadway to Claire's apartment in the West Seventies. It was a bed-sitting room with a Pullman kitchen and an adequate bathroom in an ugly white brick building thrown up in the late 1940s, originally advertised as an "Efficiency" and then inexplicably renamed "Studio Apartments." There was no doorman and no elevator operator and no furniture in the lobby. Shortly after Claire moved in, three thieves dressed as moving men parked a large van in front of the building and "ripped off" all the sofas, armchairs, end tables, lamps, and rugs that had been in the lobby and drove away. No one questioned them; and the owners never replaced the stolen goods. The news of that event had chilled Shelagh with anxiety for Claire, but she could not live her daughter's life for her; besides, there was "no hiding place nowhere."

There was nothing of the "studio" about Claire's apartment; "efficiency" was all. And cool whiteness. It made Shelagh think of all the home-decoration articles in the Sunday *New York Times Magazine* that she'd read for two decades—the excess of simplicity praised as neatness: white curtains and white corduroy bedspread, white plastic lamps and white cushions to sit on around the pale parquet floor. White walls with no pictures. The only color was Claire—tonight in a navy blue Empire-style dress; and then there was a rather wide black-green Norfolk pine, standing six feet tall in a corner, which Claire called "George." The sterility of the room pained Shelagh, who loved warm colors and clutter and "collections" of things, for she had thought of it first as a rejection of herself and the atmosphere of the home Claire had grown up in; but gradually she had come to interpret it as a necessary new beginning—a clean slate, a fresh start, which in time Claire would stamp with the images and objects that expressed her experiences, her character, and her taste. It was like a declaration that she reserved the right to make up her own mind.

"Well *did* you attack a Renoir?" Claire asked, laughing.

"No, but it looked that way." She turned to Chester. "There was no eyewitness. Only the plaintiff and the defendant. I'm lucky I got out without even posting bail."

Her husband replied, "You have all of the words but none of the tune." Chester detested museums but had no idea why that was true. Shelagh remembered and said, "Something today made me dislike being in the Museum very strongly. It wasn't just the officious guard or having been misjudged. It was something about the collection."

Claire brought her parents each a glass of Sherry. They sat on the edge of her bed. She curled up like a cat on a low stack of cushions. "It's called People of the Nineteenth Century, isn't it?"

Her mother replied, "Yes. And they're very grand paintings indeed. I'm not gainsaying that. But only a museum could consider making such a 'gath-

96

ering' of great works, or even imagining there's something worthwhile in bringing together such a group on the principle of selection that they're 'people.' No private person would want such a collection. Ah, that's what was wrong with it: There's nothing natural about such a collection. It's a purely intellectual exercise." She paused for a moment and sipped her Sherry. "And then there's a teasing subtitle: The Ordinary and the Extraordinary. I wonder what they meant by that."

Chester asked, "Couldn't you tell which were which?"

"No," Shelagh blurted out with surprise. "Of course, there were the crazies, the whores, the nudes, the rich, the workers, the happy bourgeoisie—but which is extraordinary and which are ordinary?" She sounded genuinely baffled.

"Everyone is extraordinary to himself," Chester suggested, smiling, "and ordinary to everyone else."

"I knew you'd make trouble," Shelagh said to him, and then told her story of the museum guard.

Claire got up to look at the clock on an end table and was wondering what was keeping her boyfriend, Simon, and why Morgan and his date were late, when the buzzer sounded and suddenly all of them were in the room and the evening began.

What disturbed Shelagh about Morgan was that he looked too good to be true. He was as tall as his father, but muscularly slender—all shoulders and arms; he had not yet filled out the frame. His nose was strong, his lips full, his pale blue eyes cool, his brown hair neatly trimmed but fashionably long—it concealed his ears. There he stood in a gray pin-striped suit with a white shirt and a regimental tie. If he were in England, his mother worried, he might find himself beaten up by some Guardsmen who knew he had no right to wear that tie. But in America it was not the emblem of a regiment, it was only a necktie; in America a thing is merely what it appears to be—it does not signify something else. That was what made her afraid for Morgan in general. He was much more comfortable with men than with women, just as he was more at home with his father than with his mother. Despite their rather formal manners, the Judge and their son seemed to communicate in an easygoing speech of "shorthand phrases," whereas Morgan expressed himself with a diffident politeness to his mother—as, in a sense, he behaved to all women she'd seen him with. He doted on his dates, but with a reserved authority, as if always testing to see whether they might break a rule—and implying that he not only knew all the rules but intended to see them upheld.

His date that evening was Christina Greene—"Surely you'll call me Tina," she informed Shelagh when they were introduced. Within their first five minutes together, Shelagh overheard her telling Claire: "Morgan believes we're 'going steady'; neither of us has gone out with anyone else during the past ten days." Christina Greene wore a Gypsy blouse with many gold chains and a floor-length black skirt. Hers was a long, fine face that reminded Shelagh of elegant pedigreed dogs, made to seem longer by the length of her straight honey-blond hair, which touched her shoulders. The heavy gold bracelets she wore were so old-fashioned that they could have been justified only as heirlooms. She worked for *Ms.* magazine, Morgan made clear, out of commitment to "The Movement," not because she needed a job; her mother was a Van Rensselaer.

"I've heard so much about you, Mrs. Jackman," Tina confided when Claire went to the kitchen for more drinks. "I'd love to see some of your illustrations. But Morgan doesn't have any of your books in his apartment."

"Really?" Shelagh replied. "I must sell him some—wholesale, of course." Christina Greene laughed out loud.

Judge Jackman stood in the corner with the Norfolk pine chatting with Claire's boyfriend, Simon Monroy. Like Claire, her young man was small-boned, compact, very fair-complexioned, with crew-cut hair which helped to maintain his youthful appearance, because he had become prematurely gray, being only thirty. Shelagh and Chester had met him several times before, but he remained known to them only as an idealist in his professional life, working for Amnesty International, and a loner in private life; despite the fact that Claire was very much in love with him, he would neither move in and share her apartment with her nor ever let her visit at his "pad," which he shared with two other bachelors on the Lower East Side.

"You'll be interested," she heard the Judge saying to Simon, "because it involves Brita von Bickersdorf, who's written several articles for your magazine. She's taken up the cause; a former student of hers is going to represent the plaintiff . . ." and then went on to describe the "Silence Lady" who was bringing a suit against the State's Attorney for abuse of her civil liberties. Shelagh joined them and interrupted the conversation to ask if Simon had ever attended *Tristan and Isolde* before.

"No. And I've always wanted to," he replied without conviction. "It's awfully nice of you to invite all of us to go along."

"Charity," the Judge explained.

Claire asked smartly, "Are we your charity cases?"

"I didn't mean it that way." Chester stroked his daughter's arm. "It was our contribution to some charitable benefit that we made, months ago, that resulted in these tickets . . ."

"And you wanted to share the benefit," Tina said, smiling.

"Spread the wealth," Morgan declared.

"We always have done," Shelagh concluded.

Claire, who had been serving hors d'oeuvre of salami and cream cheese, egg rolls she had defrosted, and raw vegetables and a garlic dip, brought out another trayful, saying, "You know, of course, there won't be time to go to dinner before the opera. Some of you were late—and the curtain is early. Just eat up more of these and we'll be all right."

"We can go out to supper after the performance," Shelagh suggested.

Simon was obviously disappointed. He pressed Claire with "But your folks wanted to take us out to dinner."

It struck Shelagh that he was willing to sit through the opera only with a full stomach; the dinner had been what he had looked forward to.

"But there isn't enough time now," Claire explained.

Morgan announced: "I'm thinking of joining the Episcopal Church." Tina and Shelagh were seated on the bed. The Judge rested back against a window jamb. Morgan squatted on one of the cushions. Simon was flattened against the wall next to the pine tree. In the middle of the suddenly silent room Claire stood still with the tray balanced on both hands.

"Why?" asked the Judge.

"I think it would be the right thing to do."

"Is it because," Tina asked, "*I* was raised as an Episcopalian?"

"No. I began thinking about it before I met you." He smiled sweetly. "Maybe that's why I came to meet you."

"You met me at a party of extremely uninteresting people. The reason we left it together is that you and I were the only people there who were not boring."

Shelagh deliberately kept her mouth shut. It was not as bad as if he'd confessed to taking heroin, or that he'd abandoned a mistress and two children. Still, there was something indecent about both the idea and the way he'd sprung it on them all.

"Are you being serious?" Claire asked.

"Perfectly," he replied.

That's the way he likes to do everything, his mother thought. He was raised free of mumbo jumbo, free of false assumptions, unbelievable fantasies, the unfair authority of priests, the distorting demands of unsatisfiable standards, and now that is what he will freely choose to inflict upon himself. She looked at Chester Jackman, remembering that his English ancestors had come to America in the late seventeenth century, Puritans all, who had been Congregationalists until the Civil War. That was the turning point. Nationalism had proved to be the greater commitment. Since then his family had been noble atheists. Shelagh's own ancestors had been Middle European Roman Catholics until the revolutions of the 1870s. There had come a point at which their religion baroqued itself to death; it was all display and no substance. The hopes and aspirations of social justice in this life, as against the dreams of salvation in any afterlife, broke the bubble of that make-believe. They became agnostics who strove to achieve socialism for the well-being of all. But did it ever work well for any unit larger than a close-knit family? To each according to his needs; from each according to his ability. Isn't that a family?—until the children graduate from college, and surprise everyone. There was Morgan announcing his plan to join the Episcopal Church, propped up on cushions on the floor of his sister's apartment, as casual as if he said he'd decided to buy an imported automobile. He had become a mystery to her. Did he have a spiritual life: a need for the metaphor and symbolism of a life of the spirit? Or did such a plan signify only that he meant to continue enriching his social status? He was already a member of the New York Athletic Club. But what was *she* doing?—illustrating a new edition of the Old Testament.

"You feel a calling to religion?" his father asked without irony.

Morgan replied, "I'd rather not talk about it."

"Then why did you mention it?" Claire asked.

"Just one of those things. Like telling your family you've moved into a new apartment."

Shelagh said, "Yes, it's always reassuring to have the current address where your children can be found." She caught her husband's eye with the expression of postponement, implying: This is not something to discuss here and now.

Simon Monroy apparently felt called upon to pick up the lagging conversation; he sighed and then said: "A number of Episcopal clergymen have been active in the Amnesty movement."

"Surely," Tina agreed. "They're not just otherworldly, you know."

Shelagh tried not to stare at Morgan, but as she scanned the people in the room, her eyes kept returning to his face: to the cornflower-blue eyes, the strong nose, and the full lips. At the moment she fixed her gaze upon him, he was as still as a piece of sculpture. This is my son, she thought, who is building a fortress around himself. There will be those he lets in, and those he keeps out; how can I not feel that he means to make me one of those he will protect himself against? He is digging a moat around his fortress, and entry across the drawbridge will be by invitation only.

Entering into the Opera House was to receive a cymbal clash for their eyes: the bright light splintered away from the chandeliers onto the gold and the cushioned seats, the varicolored crowd of people, the uniformed ushers, the crackling of programs. In the taxi, Tina had sat on Morgan's lap on one side of Shelagh and Claire had sat on Simon's on the other side. Chester took the seat in front next to the driver. The mood was cheerfully carefree in the course of the drive—a tone that had been missing during the time spent in Claire's apartment. But their seating arrangements, close to center of the orchestra floor, separated them again. Shelagh and Chester went first into the long row, Claire and Simon sat next to the Judge, and they were followed by Tina and Morgan. Shelagh was disappointed to find herself at the far end of the "lineup," with a heavy woman in an African caftan spotted with silvery mirrors seated at her left. She was trapped by the large lady's sickly-sweet perfume, as though a bouquet of gardenias had been pushed up to her nose, and turned abruptly toward Chester, kissing him on the cheek and squeezing him for reassurance as she slipped her hand into his.

The opera, she felt, was an interruption; it would kill conversation—converse—the chance to commune. It had been an occasion to get together: that was what she had looked forward to; but now it would separate them. She had no love of opera; she loved her family. She wished, rather, that all of them were back in Claire's apartment seated cross-legged on the floor in a circle, holding each other's hands. . . . She shook her head and told herself she was being ridiculous, a throwback to archaic times, a cavewoman wanting to hover over her brood. She stifled a snort. In the course of an hour Morgan had informed them that he intended to become a practicing Christian and Shelagh had felt the urge to behave like an Earth Mother. Not that either was egregiously out of character; we have so many characters secreted within ourselves, she imagined. But there is the difference between the urges we act on and those we suppress. Shelagh realized she wasn't even free enough to tell them she felt like doing this. The world had gone beyond such behavior: certainly the world all of them lived in. They were seemly, they were well behaved, they abided by sophisticated rules of etiquette. How could she have got them to sit in a circle to communicate love and to protect them against all comers? Yet that was what Morgan could gain by joining the Church. Besides, what were Christina Greene and Simon Monroy doing here anyway? She wanted only her own children. Should she be unable to have anything to do with them now unless she also took on their current "affairs"? She sighed heavily as the house lights dimmed, the applause rose at the appearance of the conductor, the overture began, and then the curtain was lifted. Tristan and Isolde were about to relive their tragic glory.

Shelagh thought she was indifferent to that medieval fable, and Wagner's bellows-music had not enchanted her since her adolescent years. She wanted to be loving and to be loved; she wanted the active pleasures of her children's company; but for the sake of propriety and decorum she sat becalmed between her husband and a fat matron who reeked of gardenias, in a huge hall full of strangers, dark but for the sparks coming out of the orchestra pit and the stage setting gradually becoming more visible as the ship of fate. Ah, well, she thought, we will have more time together later.

As the opera proceeded, Shelagh gradually withdrew from engagement with her children, just as her hand was unselfconsciously withdrawn from Chester's hand, and her awareness became focused on the performance: the immediacy of stage set and actors, the colors of the shifting lights, the lyrics—pervaded by the insistently seductive music. She had heard *Tristan and Isolde* at intervals over the past forty years, in London, Vienna, Salzburg, Paris, and New York. At first some memories of those previous experiences protruded into her thought; but, slowly, increasingly, she was taken up by the insistent tide of the sensuous, hypnotic, serpentine lines of music, repetitive, continually building to climaxes that never let go to catch a breath but unraveled only to ravel the listener up again in a new variation on the same theme, until she ceased thinking of other performances, ceased thinking of her children, of her husband, of herself, and became exclusively a participant in the immediacy of this performance, the spectator-listener absorbed by this particular sequence of sights and sounds and thoughts. She was embodying the opera as it was absorbing her.

Even the intermissions barely broke the spell; the succession of acts gathered up in new beginnings all that had gone before through repetition and made connections; so smooth and insistent was the recapitulation through new variations that she was caught in the warm stream and her spirit swam with the current effortlessly, as passive as the lovers were passive to their passion. Only as the end approached, the end of life for the lovers, the end of the story, the end of the performance in the long death duet was Shelagh struck by the knowledge that she understood the lyrics, that she was aware of the meaning of what was being sung, that none of the rest of her family understood German, and that it was even possible that no one else in the entire audience comprehended the significance of what had been expressed throughout the opera. For them it might be only the musical appearance without any significance. The music itself was one long, slow, deliberate sexual stroking, the insistence on a certain languorous determination to incite desire; all within the confines of magic and mystery. The lovers do not fall in love, they are thrust into love, they are plunged into love—the choice is totally out of their hands, for they are drugged; and in the end they are plunged into death by a drug. All this is a promotion of the single-minded and simpleminded belief that erotic fulfillment, being more desirable than anything else in the world—honor, honesty, loyalty, duty—is worthy of purchase at the expense of everything else in the world, quite literally including life itself. This is, Shelagh thought, the apogee of Romanticism for the masses: the idea that the best in life is erotic passion so overwhelming that no other value is to be taken into consideration: to couple and to die—like insects. To die for love. To commit suicide rather than to live apart, for to be separated is worse than to die together. To die for love. Shelagh turned her eyes away from the stage to look at Chester, and from his face to Claire and Simon, to Morgan and Tina. Which of them would choose to die for love? Which of them would knowingly end his or her life rather than suffer separation; who is so closely interwoven with another that to exist without the other is not possible? There is still no rational explanation of love. A drug, a magic potion, is as good a metaphor as any for the mystery. But who inflicts it upon us? She thought of the signs of the zodiac on the barrel vaulting of Grand Central Station and believed for a second time this day that all the powers of the universe *do* conspire or contend to determine our destinies.

The long, slow dying came to an end, the curtain fell, the applause boomed, the opera stars took their curtain calls and their bouquets of roses. The very heavy lady on Shelagh's left wiped the tears from her eyes and blew her nose in sorrow. What passion has she survived or is she enduring? Shelagh wondered, realizing that it is possible to be sympathetic with anyone human, no matter how unattractive. She almost wanted to console her, but thought better of it.

She wanted more to console her children. She wanted—what?—to take joy from all the beauty of the sadness. She wanted to cheer them on, to be rewarded by them with their interest in what she felt, so in the lobby as they put on their coats, jostled by the crowd, eager to leave, she asked: "Where shall we have a late supper?" assuming it had been agreed to.

Instead, she was told by Morgan, "We really can't. It's much too late."

"But it's the beginning of the weekend," she replied.

"*I* have to *work* tomorrow," Simon said. "But I'll see Claire home."

They were among the hundreds of the audience on the sidewalk now hoping to locate an available taxi.

Tina had an apartment on the East Side between Park and Madison on Seventy-fifth Street, and Morgan lived in a new high-rise in Kip's Bay. "We have to go our separate ways," Morgan said, meaning that he and Simon should take different cabs.

"What a pity!" Shelagh complained. "I was so hoping we could continue. . . ."

Chester explained that he and Shelagh did not need a ride; the reason they stayed in a hotel on Central Park South was so that they could walk there from Lincoln Center when the opera was over. He wished them well and saw each couple into its own taxi. Shelagh's cheeks were kissed good-night four times.

When they were alone, Shelagh said to Chester: "Damn it!"

"Don't take it so hard," he responded. "Can't you see they want to go to bed?"

"I wanted to be with them."

"In bed?"

Shelagh pretended to box his ear. "I simply wished to enjoy them longer."

"That would be greedy," he said.

"I resent that."

"*I* will take you for a later supper. Wouldn't you like to enjoy me longer?"

They had begun walking away from the crowd toward Central Park. The night air was almost balmy, more like a spring night than autumn; the dark sky was clear, and a bright half-moon could be seen. They walked along separately, upright, until Chester lifted her arm and placed it over his. "Let us go arm and arm into that good night."

Shelagh relented; she squeezed his arm affectionately and said, "You are still my best friend. But"—and then she took a deep breath—"why the devil did you call me 'greedy'?"

"You wanted more than your fair share."

Shelagh stopped in her tracks, as if she'd been slapped in the face. "You're so smart," she said softly, "you always know what one's fair share should be?" She took her arm away from Chester's and stared at him defensively.

He took her by the hand and urged her to continue walking along with him; they were nearly at Columbus Circle. "I don't always know." He was not patronizing, he was thinking out loud. "But I'm made to feel it soon enough, if I want more than others are willing to give. It's others who tell you what their limit is. Or, if they give in to your will despite their own desires or their better judgment, they'll make you pay for it later. The 'fair share' has to be, somehow, for the common good, a mutual benefit. I see it from the bench all the time."

"If I seemed greedy, it wasn't for myself alone. I felt that prolonging the evening would be good for all of us. We hadn't even discussed the opera. . . ."

"Of course it might have been good—it would certainly have been worthwhile. Surely. But there are other goods too. And different people want to realize different goods. They have to choose. They make preferences. Did you know the word 'decision' comes from 'cutting off'?"

"You've never called me 'greedy' before."

"All of us—always—want to have our own way." Chester suddenly laughed. "It's just that you've had your own way so much of the time, it never occurred to you that you've been successfully greedy." He put his arm around her shoulder and hugged her.

"Are you insulting me?"

"Hardly." He refused to take his hand from her shoulder. "You are a very forceful, not to say willful, person. And *now* so are your children."

"*Our* children."

"Indeed."

"We're all greedy."

Chester said, cautiously, "Some of the time."

"What are *you* greedy for?"

"My fair share!"

They laughed together, dispelling Shelagh's self-righteous tension, her offended self-esteem. She could relax now. She could link her arm through his again. The breeze was cool as they walked along Central Park South. They kept close to each other. Just short of their hotel, they came to Rumpelmayer's and stopped to look in. The lights were still on; people were seated at tables.

"You remember?" Shelagh asked.

"Morgan," he replied. " 'I think I'm in heaven.' "

"I'll never forget it. That was one of the happiest moments of my life. What ever became of Morgan?"

"This is where we should have our midnight snack."

"Of course, my darling. We may have lost our children, but we haven't lost our—"

"Nostalgia," he said.

"Our sense of humor."

"Our money."

Chester held the door open. "After you, Isolde."

Shelagh nodded and curtsied. "My Tristan."

So, smiling broadly at having regained their good spirits, they entered the child's ideal of a Konditorei.

✆❧

DIARY ENTRY

"Successfully greedy"—?—what a peculiar idea of Chester's. To think that I've persistently wanted more than my fair share—and been able to get it. I've certainly never thought of it that way. Of course, that must be because I got what I wanted, I had things my way; but then, that's what I thought was "right"—i.e., fair. Unsettling. Why do I feel it unsettles me? It challenges the rhythms and the patterns of my life. I've felt myself to be "settled" for a long time now. Not in the sense of settling for less than I'd hoped for; no, not that at all. Rather, settled in the way a colonist having left the Mother Country establishes a settlement: builds a home; farms, feeds, weaves; celebrates the seasons, repeats the ceremonies, the rituals; isn't upset all over again and again by having to learn a new language, a new landscape, new ceremonies, new rituals. On the contrary, all the rhythms of my patterns seemed well founded, secure, comfortable to repeat. And they include expectations about being with my children, being together for certain stretches of time. And here's Chester telling me that I'd expected to have too much of their time, more than they wanted to give me.

105

I'm being put down.

I'm being put in my place.

I really don't like that at all.

Still, there must be some truth to it. Chester is a very perceptive and accurate judge of such matters. I suppose all of my desires are endless or limitless and I can find out how far they can be satisfied only by others saying, "No more from me."

All of my patterns seem so well established: my work, my caring for Chester, my taking care of the house, my friendships, my acquaintances—a sort of schedule of habitual good behavior for worthwhile rewards. The rhythm of work and play. Even at the moment, as I prepare to leave for ten days in London, I don't have to ask myself: why am I going on holiday? It's a good habit. It restores me, refreshes me to be away, to commune with Adrienne, to see other people and other sights; to have nothing to do for a little while. I come back the better for it.

And now Chester's telling me to "adjust" my desires, to alter my expectations, to want for less—so as to reckon with other people's wishes, accommodate to their needs. But to "lower my sights" is to change the rhythm, the pattern I'm accustomed to. It's like being told to live on a reduced income! I've been wishing beyond my means!

LETTER TO HER SON

Dear Morgan:

When we were together last, the night of Tristan and Isolde, I forgot to ask about Thanksgiving. At the risk of being a bore, I repeat the invitation, but without "greed." I'd love to have you and Tina here for that celebration, but please believe that I'm not trying to pressure you into accepting. If you wish to come—fine; if not, I'll understand. (I'll weep a little, but I'll understand— truly.) Perhaps I'll find a note from you about it when I return in two weeks.

Enclosed here are three of the books I've illustrated. Will you show them to Tina, who seemed interested—but had no evidence . . . ? Too bad books for adults are no longer illustrated as they were in the 19th century. It would be such fun (I mean an honor) to do the illustrations for a novel by you. I suppose that's pressure; scratch it out.

You will do what you wish to do.

I will do what I can.

I do love you.

Mother

Claire, Darling:

You were such a gracious hostess the night of the opera! If it hadn't been for your thoughtfulness, and your hors d'oeuvre, all of us would have fainted from hunger during the second act. Thank you so much.

I forgot to tell you how beautiful you looked that night. I will now: you looked beautiful that night.

I forgot to ask you about Thanksgiving. How about it? You and Simon, both? Just a thought, a whim, a hope. But your choice—truly.

I forgot to ask you if there's anything you especially want me to bring back from London for you this time. Is there? How about a cashmere sweater—gray and salmon pink? Or a clutch of potpourri pillows from Culpepper the Herbalist? Or some Rajistani jewelry from one of the Indian shops. I'm feeling generous; I've just finished my sketch for Moses' fury on descending from Mount Sinai to discover his people worshiping a Golden Calf. They were so impatient. He'd been gone only a couple of days, and they were ready for another god. Do you realize he had three thousand of them slain? But you must see my drawing. I think I have the fierce fury. Golden Calf indeed; with a Lord like theirs? They wanted more than their fair share!

My dearest love to you,

As ever,

Mother

❧

It was a dry autumn, and the leaves of the maples, the elm trees, and the oak began to fall early. Before the middle of October, when Shelagh would be off to England, she suggested that the cleaning man spend an hour raking the leaves around the house. Burning them was prohibited now; if he'd gather them up into mounds in the backyard, she proposed to help him press them into large plastic bags. Garbage collectors would remove them the next day. After he'd raked them around from the front, along the narrow margins of grass on both sides of the double house, the scarlet, the tan, the saffron leaves rose into piles around the blue spruce in back, as Shelagh watched from the kitchen window. The sky was a pale blue lightly veiled here and there by thin white clouds. All but the evergreens were becoming skeletal, bare outlines of themselves, revealing more of the buildings beyond. The gilded dome on the college tower gleamed; the white shutters of the windows looked freshly scrubbed against the rust-colored brick walls.

Shelagh put on a topcoat and gloves and, carrying the plastic bags, crossed the back porch and went down the stairs to where the cleaning man continued his raking. She let the breeze billow out one of the bags, turned back its edge on itself to form a collar, and held it open for him to begin filling it up with leaves.

From the corner of her eye, she perceived that Virginia McGrath was approaching from her own backyard next door, moving an inch at a time, pressing against the aluminum walker in front of her. Shelagh let go of the plastic bag and hastened to her neighbor, to shorten the distance the elderly lady would have to walk.

"How nice to see you," Shelagh said. "It's mild for this time of year, isn't it?"

She'd intercepted Mrs. McGrath before the old woman had reached the driveway separating the two backyards.

"My husband's in a nursing home." Her voice was hardly more than a whisper.

"I'm so sorry to hear that."

The old lady's eyes were rimmed in red, the white eyelashes like icicles; her pink scalp showed through the wispy white hair of her head. "That's all right. Good as can be expected." She wore her husband's black raincoat, which fell down to her sneakers. There was an object in a brown paper bag clutched in her right hand. "I'm gonna go too."

"Go?"

"Into the nursing home. My son's gonna sell the house to pay for it all. That's all right. Good as can be expected."

"I am sorry," Shelagh said limply. "What a shame." She barely knew the woman—older than her mother, if her mother were still alive—but they had lived next door to each other for nearly two decades.

"I wanted to say goodbye."

"Will you be going soon?"

"In a couple of days."

"Oh, my . . ."

"This might be the last time we see each other."

The old woman handed the weighted paper bag to Shelagh with the words "Here. For you."

"Well, that's not necessary. I should be giving *you* a present. But how very thoughtful of you."

"We've been neighbors for a long time. It's been very nice knowing you."

Shelagh felt slightly unnerved by the thought that Virginia McGrath imagined she "knew" her. "We've been good neighbors, haven't we?" she said.

"I didn't want to go away without giving you something."

"How kind you are."

"Now, you take this," she urged, pointing to her gift. "You can make use of it next summer." She paused. "Don't know where I'll be next summer."

"It's a long time off."

"Yes. But the nursing home's comfortable. I've visited there. Twenty acres, about. Outside Middletown. Some gardens; mostly woods and lawns. Lots of lawn chairs." And then, sprightly—vivaciously—she said, "They've got wheelchairs with motor-power. Just flick the switch and you're off and running." Her dry laugh was a cackle, hollow and frightening. Then suddenly she said, "I'm gonna miss you."

"But, we barely . . ." Shelagh corrected herself. "Believe me, it won't be the same without you here. I can't imagine how different it will be."

"I always thought we ought to get together more. But in those days my husband was still here. We never did get together much. Oh, well, later on, maybe. Do you think you can visit the nursing home?" Fortunately, Shelagh was kept from answering by Mrs. McGrath's adding: "I'll send you a postcard with the address on it."

After the leaves had filled up five of the plastic bags, and they were stacked in front of the house for the next day's garbage collection, Shelagh went back into the kitchen with the brown paper bag.

Virginia McGrath's goodbye present was a citronella candle in a glass jar, still carrying a sticker reading "69¢" from a local five-and-ten-cent store. Shelagh Jackman told herself: It serves you right. You never meant anything to her; you never gave her anything of yourself, and vice versa; it was always a matter of being as carefully noncommittal and noninterfering as possible. Not to be bothersome or snoopy or prying. The result of twenty years' worth of caution and consideration is to "earn" only a sixty-nine-cent superfluous citronella candle for keeping mosquitoes away on summer nights. Too true; too rich, she thought. No one will believe me when I tell this story. It's too American. It probably didn't happen, they will say.

During the evening before Shelagh was to take the plane to England, she and Chester surveyed the orchids in the greenhouse, snipping off the dried brown leaves, checking the humidifier, making a selection of thin branches of flowers—buds, actually, just in anticipation of flowering into yellow and white and pink petals—to be packed in moist cotton in a long flat cardboard box for the trip to London, as a present for Adrienne. Their temperaments were subdued, befitting the night before parting, their manner tender with each other, without being sentimental.

"Do you have any other gift for your sister?" Chester asked.

"As a matter of fact, I was in Warner's store the other day and sorely tempted by a statuette I looked at. It was called *Flaunting*—a darling object about five inches high on an ebony square base, which seemed at first a ballerina balanced on one foot with her arms up above her head and her hair flying out behind her. But up close it turned out to be a young girl in a feathery outfit with a great smile on her face, her head flung back: the quintessence of joy."

"Why didn't you buy it?"

"I thought it was brass, but it turned out to be cast in gold and cost a small fortune. I wished I could have it for myself. Besides, you know, Adrienne is unsatisfiable. I never take her things to keep. It's best to give her presents that get used up, like liquor and flowers. This time I'm taking her a 'CARE package' of cosmetics—eye shadow and lipsticks, things like that."

Chester said, "Yes, of course," as he closed the doors to the greenhouse behind them.

And just as casually, Shelagh said, "But I have a present for you that I don't think you'll want to throw out."

With mock surprise, he asked, "A present for me?" as she always gave him a gift when she went off without him.

"To remind you of me while I'm gone."

They were standing on opposite sides of the table with her collection of brass objects displayed between them. "Wait here, and I'll get it."

Chester walked to the fireplace and then lowered himself into one of the armchairs. He looked up at the walls covered from floor to ceiling with his books, and said loudly enough so that his wife could hear him elsewhere in the house: "Don't think I'll be alone. I'm surrounded by friends."

"Yes," she agreed, returning to him with a package in hand, "the room is teeming with your friends. But just remember—I'm your best friend."

"That's true." She seated herself in the chair facing him while he removed the tissue paper from a clear plastic rectangle that framed a photograph of Shelagh he had taken in Alaska.

His first words were "When did you have it enlarged?"

"Immediately after we looked over all the snapshots from that trip and you said this was one of the best pictures ever taken of me."

"I love it!" He stared at the brightly colored glossy print: the sky was azure, and the landscape of snow-covered mountains made it clear that Shelagh, in a pale green parka with a white-lined hood about her head, stood alone for an instant at the top of the globe radiant as the first human explorer to brave the uninhabitable. The late sunset of the long summer afternoon in Alaska set a roseate glow to her cheeks, and though her head was turned to one side, her eyes staring from their corners caught the eyes of the viewer whichever way he moved, and the hint of a conspiratorial smile on her lips made them intimates.

"It's just beautiful!" he nearly shouted. He stood up and planted a great loving kiss on each of her warm cheeks. "I can't thank you enough. It's so thoughtful. So wonderful of you . . ." He placed it on the mantelpiece over the fireplace between them, seated himself to stare at it, then got up and angled it so he could see it even better. "I do adore you."

Quietly, Shelagh said, "I cherish you."

"It's such a strange thing," he began, "about *gifts* . . ."

Shelagh remembered that all of *Tristan and Isolde* turns on the gift of the mother who gave her daughter's servant the magic potion to bring about eternal love, to be shared by King Mark and his bride on their wedding night, and how it was used by mistake. She said: "I'd thought of giving you a sixty-nine-cent citronella candle."

"That really bothered you the other day, didn't it?" Chester had been barely conscious of the McGraths' existence.

"Well, it was all I deserved."

"You believe people should be given what they deserve."

"Naturally . . . but it's very subtle: they shouldn't know what they deserve until it's given."

They fell silent. He seated himself again opposite her, and they smiled at each other.

Finally she asked, "What are you thinking?"

"At least two thoughts at once. One was about the social nature of reality; the other is that you're so beautiful!"

"I much prefer the other, my darling."

"I'm grateful for both," he replied.

Shelagh rose, patted his cheek, went away to the kitchen, and returned with two snifters of brandy. "Will you play some Vivaldi?" she asked.

"Will you knit?"

"Will we grow old, old, old together—and be to each other what we deserve?"

"Finding out what that is as we go along?"

"Yes," she responded.

"Yes," he reaffirmed. He was staring at her again as if he had suddenly become aware of what she was wearing. He looked at her brown pleated skirt and the white mohair sweater buttoned only at the waist; she wore it over a blouse of autumn leaves and flowers against a golden-beige background. "What a lovely blouse," he said.

She looked down at it and said, "It's from Liberty of London."

"I wish I had a shirt made of that."

"Oh?" she sounded on a note of doubtfulness. "Will you become a dandy in your old age?" But she knew instantaneously that when she left for England, she would take with her one of his old shirts.

DIARY ENTRY

The pilot has announced that we are now flying at 23,000 feet; I find it very difficult to believe. It feels more likely to me that I'm in a movie theater, one where lunch is served. On the narrow tray before me a glass of Dubonnet stands perfectly still. There isn't the trace of a ripple on the surface of the liquid. I can't feel any vibration through the cushioned seat I'm tucked into. No sense of motion at all—let alone the thrill of flying. It's all become so safe; the passion for comfort conquers all. This is some sort of magic carpet indeed. I can read a book or write a letter, watch a film, or call the stewardess for cigarettes, perfume, wine—a flying resort hotel. It offers all those pleasures, with one exception: the thrill of flying.

But I experienced that once at its purest, most intense, when I was a child. It must have been very soon after my family settled in England. I can't recall how it came about. I know I was alone with my father at a small airport near Oxford. The plane had a single propeller at its blunt nose, the wings were covered with canvas, there were two open cockpits. The pilot sat in front and I sat on my father's lap behind the pilot. Father wore spectacles and the pilot had goggles on. It seemed to take no time revving up; the wings trembled, we hobbled along the ground a little way, and then we rose into the sky—up, up, but not too high: well above the treetops, but not so high that people became only specks of color. We could see farmers clearly, little people who waved at us, and I waved back. That was the thrill of flying! being inside a bird, with a bird's view of the meadows and roads, horses, houses. The propeller sounded a constant whirring buzz, and I vibrated along with the whole body of the bird in flight, the wind streaming across my face and fingering my hair. I kept one arm around my father's neck and leaned out just enough to see how far above the earth we flew.

I remember that we went on a route over the downs as far as Stonehenge and I saw the circle of mammoth stones from above—as eagles see it—and then we turned in the sky over Blenheim and returned, looking down on the medieval towers of Oxford, back to the runway out in a field. I never loved my father more than I did that day. I wonder what that says for me? I was so grateful to him: to realize he had fulfilled my wish for an experience I barely knew I longed for.

Lunch is now being served on this flight.

Adrienne looked older to her; she was beginning to show her age. It was the shadowed lines and the puffiness under her eyes that did it, and a thickening of flesh in her cheeks, making just perceptible the tendency toward jowls. She will look more like Mother every year, Shelagh thought. Her figure is still trim; she will always be good-looking, with her rich dark hair, her deep-set agate eyes, and her high cheekbones, but she is older than I, and that has become obvious now. The knowledge pleased Shelagh; it enabled her to feel more compassionate.

There was nothing ceremonial about Shelagh's arrival in England. Adrienne never met her plane at Heathrow. But Shelagh enjoyed the taxi drive by herself. She felt that riding in a London cab, up high on the dark firm seat in the roomy carriage, was like being carried along in one of the royal coaches that appear on state occasions. From the airport, she watched the scenery change along the modern highway from fields to factories, past a Tudor estate, preserved on a few acres, before the land was blighted by miles of low, narrow dull-gray row houses, as the cab drove closer to the city. Past the rooming houses and hotels that now bore Pakistani and Indian and Caribbean names, in the outer reaches of Kensington; past Harrods and a new high-rise hotel, and then through the streets where Georgian houses had recently been painted creamy white. London is always becoming brighter: the buildings are lighter, the brass is shinier, the streets are cleaner. Hyde Park was still green in mid-autumn as the cab rode between the gates; paralleled the bridle path; rounded the turn near Wellington's mansion, past the monstrous monument to the memory of Byron, past the lone deck chairs on the lawn, the Milles fountain, toward Brook Street—to the center.

Adrienne lived in an apartment on Brook Street halfway between Grosvenor Square and Bond Street. The mid-Victorian red brick building had been damaged during the war but gradually repaired. The ground floor was now the salon of a fashionable hairdresser. The first and second stories were offices. Adrienne's flat consisted of a series of rooms on the third floor, with a small stone balcony facing Brook Street beyond her sitting room and a large balustraded terrace off her bedroom at the other end of the floor.

The moment of arrival for Shelagh was the instant when she stood with her luggage on the sidewalk, the cardboard box of orchids under her arm, and the taxi drove away. In the evening light, she looked in one direction to the handsome square that ended in the American Embassy, and then in the opposite direction past Claridge's to the house in which Handel had lived his last years in England. She checked to see if the window in the elegant gentlemen's club across the street was crowded with freshly colored asters and Sweet William *as ever* and felt content, finding that all was well. She mounted the few front steps and rang the bell.

Adrienne appeared in a burgundy bathrobe as if fresh from a bath, slightly out of breath from running down the three flights of stairs, and embraced her sister in the foyer. "Let me take one of the bags," she said. "You look wonderful."

"I look dead after a flight that long."

Shelagh was shocked to see a priest in Adrienne's sitting room, but it turned out to be a man wearing a white turtleneck sweater. Shelagh instantly labeled him: her latest lover. One floor lamp glowed in the comfortable room; two partly filled glasses stood on the occasional table. The man came forward vigorously, extending his arm to shake her hand—smiling, no taller than she, slender, balding, with a pert brindled mustache, cheerful, pink-cheeked. Has he just taken a bath too? she wondered.

Adrienne introduced them, explaining, "Hugh is one of our leading columnists."

The column of flesh, Shelagh thought.

"I've heard so much about you," he announced, and then, looking at his wristwatch, added, "It's a pity I must be leaving."

"Just wait to see the orchids," Adrienne said as she began to lift the lid from the box.

Shelagh drank in the familiar room in a glance: the low cushioned chairs splashed with colorful flowers in glazed cotton, the collection of books and pictures mostly inherited from their father, the Chinese jade bowls, the Persian carpet. "Which is your column?" she asked Hugh.

"About French politics. The one signed 'Vercingetorix.' "

"Oh, yes. I've read it. It's very clever." She thought, How immediately I revert to type: the one compliment an Englishman would never mistake for flattery is to be called "clever." Hugh beamed gratefully, brought a package of cigarettes out of his blue blazer, obviously decided to stay a little longer.

The column appeared in *Dialogue*, the monthly journal for which Adrienne was Managing Editor. It was a review of cultural and political affairs whose *raison d'être* was to publish at least two different views of whatever event it covered. The Frenchman who always wrote in contrast to the Vercingetorix articles used the pseudonym "Lutetia." For a dozen years now *Dialogue* was established as a journal of significance among the intelligentsia both in the English-speaking countries and on the Continent, but it had never been self-supporting, and Adrienne herself often helped to bail it out financially.

"Aren't they exquisite!" Adrienne exclaimed, carefully raising one of the branches out of the box of orchids. "So exotic."

Hugh pointed toward one of the jade vases. "Shall I get some water?" He was entirely at home in Adrienne's flat.

"They don't need water," Shelagh said gently.

"I have a long pewter asparagus dish. That's what I'll lay them out on."

She threw an affectionate glance at Hugh as she went out of the room to fetch it.

I am going to cramp Adrienne's style by being here, Shelagh told herself. Why hadn't she written to me about a new affair? Hugh? Had he ever been mentioned in one of her letters? There had been so many affairs. It was when Adrienne returned that Shelagh realized she looked older.

"I have some Bourbon for my American. Hugh, would you pour Shelagh a drink? I apologize. You must be desperate after that flight. Hugh, will you have another?"

"No. No. Bless you, but I really must be going. I'm so glad to have met you. I'm sure to see something of you while you're over here." Then he kissed Adrienne's hand and left the room.

With the hall door closed behind him, Shelagh looked at her sister, her bathrobe, the hand that had been kissed, and asked, "Won't I get in your way?"

Adrienne smirked slyly, and answered, "He has a house of his own."

"Isn't it tiresome having to dress again and leave afterward?" Shelagh chuckled but instantly regretted that remark. It was meant to be amusing; Adrienne would take it as a personal criticism.

"Not as tiresome as being married." Adrienne had never married. Her parents were dead, her sister lived in the States, she had a different set of friends from decades ago; Shelagh was the only person she ever saw who knew that Adrienne had been jilted. She had been rejected and abandoned at the last minute. She was literally getting into her wedding dress, Shelagh and their mother in her bedroom with her, when the maid brought her the fateful letter. A messenger had delivered it to the door in Golders Green. Her fiancé couldn't go through with it. He would not appear at the Registry Office if she showed up. He was going away. He was profoundly sorry, but it would be better so. Trevor Cartwright was his name; he was ten years older than she, a civil servant in the Colonial Office, with a lust for adventure in faraway places. Adrienne never saw him again. He became a game hunter in Kenya and was murdered by Mau Mau in the 1950s. Adrienne had been publicly humiliated by Trevor Cartwright, and in revenge, she rejected marriage.

"This is no way to begin a visit," Adrienne said, making herself smile. She reached out, drawing Shelagh into an embrace, and said, "Welcome to kinky England, darling."

The warmth of her hug was reassuring. She smelled of a delicate rose-based perfume. Over Adrienne's shoulder, Shelagh saw, on the wall next to the balcony, the set of watercolors—scenes of the sea and the mountains in Greece—painted by their great-aunt Greta. Two of them were off-center, tipped in opposite directions. Breaking away from the warm embrace, Shelagh put down her drink on an end table and straightened the pictures with both hands, adjusting them on their concealed wires until the balance was right.

"You caught me off-balance." Adrienne chuckled; but she was indifferent.

"That sort of thing doesn't bother you."

"No. I must have a different sense of balance."

"You always did."

She tightened the cord of her bathrobe around her waist, dropped herself into the nearest armchair, and demanded: "Now tell me everything—about Chester and Morgan and Claire and yourself. . . ."

"From the mountain of my experience"—Shelagh paraphrased a line from one of Virginia Woolf's novels—"which stone shall I break off and present to you?" It had become an old joke between them to start off this way.

They talked for hours, in the sitting room and then in the kitchen over cold cuts and cheese with French bread and Bavarian beer; they talked of Adrienne's plans for a party; of which concerts and plays they would have to see together while Shelagh was there, and which galleries had interesting exhibits; of Shelagh's having been accused of attacking a Renoir; of Claire's "beau" and Morgan's "dates"; of Adrienne's holiday in the Hebrides and Shelagh's vacation in Alaska; of corruption in American politics and apathy in England; of how Hugh had fallen into Adrienne's life; of the *Dialogue* crowd; of illustrations for the Old Testament.

"That reminds me," Shelagh said: "you never gave me a suggestion for what the serpent should look like."

"Serpent?"

"In the Garden of Eden. Before it was cursed."

"I can't imagine." Adrienne paused and added coyly, "I have no taste for evil."

"Ho, ho!"

"Actually that's not it. It's just that I'm verbal; you're the visual one."

"I'm not at a loss for words."

"But you think in images; I think in words. I'm the journalist; you're the artist."

"Did we agree to divide the world between us like that?"

"We didn't have to. It was determined by the genes. You inherited Father's eyes and I inherited Mother's—"

"Money."

"Don't be mean. I was going to say—her scientific mind." Because their mother feared that Adrienne would never marry, she had left two-thirds of the family fortune to her and one-third to Shelagh.

"You know it doesn't matter to me. I have more than enough." Shelagh felt that was a mistake too. Adrienne would take it for smugness.

"What you can't forgive," she said sharply, "is how she made the money."

"It's not a question of forgiving. I just never understood it."

"Perfectly simple," Adrienne started slowly. It was the middle of the night and she had drunk too much; she began to slur her words. "When we settled in England, we lived off only what Father earned. Mother saved all the money she made from her practice." Having escasped from Vienna and the fear of being made destitute by the Nazis, their mother had lived as if she must always be prepared to escape again. "And then right after the war she invested all of it in stock."

"But the choice of stock—what she invested in—never ceases to astonish me."

"Why? She bought cheap what became more and more valuable."

"And more so!"

Lady Markgraf, wife of a director of the Cortauld and the Warburg Institutes, daughter of a nineteenth-century schoolteacher in Innsbruck, with a thriving practice in ophthalmology in Harley Street, had invested nearly a quarter of a million dollars in 1946 in German stocks which, at that time, were not worth more than the paper they were printed on: Mercedes and Krupp and I. G. Farben, BMW and Zeiss, the names of bombed-out factories, of heavy industries leveled to the ground.

"She was very, very clever."

"It was shameful," Shelagh said.

"You are unbearable." Adrienne got up to wash the dishes but changed her mind, poured them each one more drink, and sat down again at the kitchen table. "You simply will not see it from her point of view."

"She abominated the Nazis. She might have been a victim of the Nazis herself. And yet the minute they're defeated she turns around and pours her life's savings into Germany. Unimaginable!"

"Compassionate! She felt for the German people, not the Nazis. She knew they had to rebuild, they had to start over again—to recover."

"So they might do it all over again."

"That's what you're afraid of."

"Of course. Why let them succeed, grow fat and self-important and try to rule the world again?"

"You are a throwback. Would you have left the German people to starve?"

"Yes."

"Well, your precious Americans didn't. They sent them food."

"And Mother sent them money."

"This is so tedious."

"I can still hear the air-raid sirens."

"That's the trouble: arrested development. You're still living during the war, hoping the Germans will burn in hellfire forever."

"Right."

"You married Chester, took off for the States, and turned your back on reality. Mother knew better—understood more—and you're a rich woman because of it."

"You're richer."

"Oh, God, give me sleep—that I might survive this visitation."

This conversation had become a ritual between them. It occurred, with variations on the theme, whenever they were together. It served the purpose, Shelagh realized, not of exchanging ideas, let alone persuading one or the other to change her mind, but of affirming that each of them remained the same. It was their way of confirming their distinct identities.

The second bedroom, which Adrienne used as her study, between the small dining room and a large bedroom, became the guest room for Shelagh's visits. The daybed had been made up and the covers turned back. There were electric lights in the room, but Adrienne preferred to light a pair of candles on her desk, and kissed her sister good-night. Adrienne liked to do things her way.

She had decorated the wide wall above her desk with a collection of mirrors side by side—large and small, silvery or opalescent, antique and modern, metal-framed or bevel-edged: a gallery of mirrors, each slightly angled toward the surface of the desk, so that when she worked there, editing or correcting the galley proof of articles for *Dialogue,* whether about a famine in West Africa or a new ballet at Sadler's Wells, at any moment when she raised her eyes from the pages, she could see a hundred different reflections of herself; a different aspect of her face appeared on each of the mirrors, as if it were the design on every petal of a giant flower.

Shelagh began to unpack her bag but felt too tired to go on. There was a chest of drawers, of olive wood and inlaid ivory, an Italian Renaissance museum piece, which Adrienne insisted she use for her clothes, but when Shelagh found her nightgown and took off her dress, she decided to leave the rest of the unpacking for the next day. She contemplated the tall, thin chest of drawers. Over the surface of its dark top, Adrienne had draped a white lace mantilla. It had been a present their father brought back from one of his trips to Spain; but their mother had never worn it. She had preserved it. She had kept it carefully folded away in tissue paper for "the right time"—which never came. Adrienne's attitude was just the opposite; she wanted to make use of whatever she possessed, here and now. The alabaster dish from Sumer that rested on top of the lace mantilla was now used as an ashtray. Their mother's silver service, once employed only for special guests, had become Adrienne's daily silverware. Her principle was that nothing should exist For

Special Occasions Only, any more than good behavior was only company manners. She was a "consumer."

It occurred to Shelagh that there are Occasions which *should* be recognized as Special, and if you have held nothing back to celebrate them as out of the ordinary, then how do you distinguish them? She was too tired to stand on her feet any longer. She took a brief glance at the hundred reflections of her face in the wall of tilted mirrors as she bent over the desk to blow out the candles, thinking: I'd rather not look at myself until tomorrow. She got into the bed, covered herself, and felt limp, although her mind was still awake.

Adrienne is the only person alive whom I have known all my life, she thought; and still I barely understand her. We are children of the same parents, we had similar childhoods, but we have gone our separate ways. Whatever degree of closeness we once felt with each other has been diminished by repetition and distance. The bonding has been diluted. Shelagh recalled the watercolors of Greece off-center on the sitting-room wall and all the mirrors tilted at odd angles. Of course, she has a different sense of balance; she restores herself from different shocks of fate than have thrown me off-balance.

Do I really think in images? she wondered. If only I could stop thinking now and fall asleep.

I am woven into life in this world more tightly than Adrienne because I am a wife and a mother. Adrienne is only loosely connected through the lives of others. My best self is half of an entity called "our marriage." This is the first night in months that I will sleep without Chester close to me. What image of him will come to mind and console me?

She saw him then, as at their last dinner party, at the opposite end of their table, about to invoke Grace, with a playful smile on his lips; and she could hear him say, as his eyes looked to the above: "If it please the Court . . ."

In the middle of the morning, Shelagh began to walk about the city alone, doing again the things she loved to do in London.

Along Brook Street she window-shopped, past the florists' and the interior decorators' displays, pausing to take in the new replicas of Battersea boxes at a jewelry store and the high leather boots in a women's shop; she strolled through Hanover Square past the statue of Robert Peel—noticing for the first time that a Japanese bank and travel agency had taken offices in the square; along Regent Street to Liberty of London. The air was clear and bracing. The sky was divided diagonally between light gray clouds and a baby-blue that shaded into turquoise. She raised her face to feel the warmth of the sun.

At Liberty's Shelagh bought a cashmere sweater for Claire and two neckties befitting her Wall Street son before asking for the fabric department, where she found the printed cotton that Chester admired, the golden-brown leaves and flowers on a beige background, and bought more than enough yardage for a large man's shirt. Then she walked along to Savile Row, where she remembered a shirtmaker. She took her husband's white shirt out of her large handbag and asked if he'd use that as the model for neck size and arm length. But he wanted to know if the cuffs should be made for links or buttons and whether they should be square, rounded, or angled; and if the collar should have buttons, stays, or holes for a pin; whether the buttons down the front should be visible or concealed; and if she'd like initials embroidered in one of the seven designs of monograms and a dozen colors he showed her—or if she preferred a pocket on the left side of the front panels. It could be readied in five days.

"What a lot of decisions to make on the spur of the moment," she concluded.

The shirtmaker approved. "You did very well, madam," he said, implying a fraternity among people who get things done.

She took a light late lunch at the fountain on the ground floor of Fortnum & Mason's and then went up to the stationery section. It was there, once a year, for what seemed to her most of her life, that she picked out the book of blank pages to use as her diary in the coming year. This time she chose a volume slightly thicker than usual, bound in leather on the spine, the color of burnt sienna, and covered on the front and back with hand-printed patterned paper from Florence. The four corners were protected by triangles of the same leather as on the spine. It was both handsome and eminently durable. She riffled through the blank pages and wondered idly what the future would bring. One of her minds responded complacently: "Repetition."

She would have the pleasure of doing again what she liked to do. Shelagh walked out of the store, along Piccadilly toward the Ritz, beside the thick traffic of buses and automobiles and bicycles, past the bookshops, the courtyard of the Academy of Art, the airline offices and porcelain shops, and then up Bond Street back to Adrienne's flat: feeling that she had completed her tour of The Golden Circle.

But not quite. There was something more she wanted to do. The cloudy gray half of the sky had traveled away, and the afternoon light was mellow. She wanted to pay homage to her father. Even as she stood in front of Adrienne's building, she replaced the keys in her handbag and continued to walk up Brook Street, then turned right, went through the traffic across Oxford Street, and continued to Portman Square, unexpectedly quiet at that hour.

There was no grave. The bodies of both her parents had been cremated. But at the Cortauld there was a memorial to Sir Hans Markgraf.

All the squares of London have such neatness, she thought; are so reasonably proportioned, on a decently human scale. Even the trees and bushes in the center of the square are of a modest size. Nothing overwhelming. No gaudy facades. The mouse-brown bricks of the houses with white trim around the windows and doorways seemed well tempered and unpretentious. If returning to London brought Shelagh the reward of going "home," it was not because their old family house was to be visited, but because the Cortauld, which remained in a building on Portman Square, was where she could commune with the spirit of her father—although she had no foreknowledge of that when she was a girl visiting in her father's office or tracking him down in the library or eavesdropping on his seminars in the classrooms. It had once been a very grand mansion, designed and decorated by the architect Robert Adam in the eighteenth century, one of those treasures concealed in a brown paper wrapping, and now it was a seat for the study of art treasures of the world.

Shelagh turned the knob of the front door, to find it locked. She rang the bell and waited. She rapped on the glass panel and waited.

A young woman with tight curls of bleached blond hair all over her head came to the door, opened it a crack, pursed her pink lips, and condescendingly gave out the information that "We're not open to the public today."

"I'm not here on public business. It's a private matter."

"We're not open for private matters either," the receptionist announced smartly.

"Is Mr. Lettcome in?"

"You know the Director?"

Shelagh noticed how the young woman looked her up and down. "Yes. And I'd appreciate it if you'd tell him that Shelagh Markgraf Jackman is here. From America."

The blonde looked at the purple shopping bag from Liberty's suspended from Shelagh's wrist, raised her eyebrows as a questioning expression, and repeated "From America?"

"Are you familiar with the name of Sir Hans Markgraf?"

"I've heard of it."

The poor girl probably wasn't born before he died, Shelagh thought. "Tell Mr. Lettcome that Sir Hans's daughter would like to come in."

"Yes, ma'am." But she closed the door and left Shelagh outside.

The sun was beginning to set. The glow of scarlet clouds in the west sent rays of warmth into the sky above the low buildings in the distance. Birds chirped in the trees of quiet Portman Square. She stared at the gilded treetops.

"How wonderful you look," she heard nearly shouted at her when Peter Lettcome opened the door behind her.

"Oh, Peter. I hadn't meant to disturb you at all."

He was a warmhearted enthusiast, a burly man in his sixties, who kissed her on both cheeks with the assurance of a beloved family friend. He had been one of her father's premier students. She had known him since childhood. "Come in, come in, my dear. I knew you were due here any day. Adrienne rang me up. About her party. I hadn't expected to see you till then. Would you like some tea?"

He ushered her through the receptionist's office to the beautiful cylindrical stairway. She stopped him then, with a hand on his arm, as he began to mount the stairs. "Peter," she said softly, "forgive me. I didn't mean this to be a visit. I'll tell you all about Chester and the children and what I'm illustrating these days when you come to Adrienne's. I don't want to interrupt you. I just wanted a few minutes—by myself—in the garden. You do understand. You won't mind, will you?"

"Of course, of course." He came down two steps to the parquet floor and led her, arm in arm, to the glass-paneled double doors at the rear of the building. "The garden is yours," he said gently, "but this vision of you is mine." She shook his hand affectionately in both of hers. "Until Tuesday evening, then," he said, leaving her alone.

The garden was darker than the square. Surrounded by four- and five-story buildings that cut off the light from the sunset beyond, it seemed a cool, hidden, secreted place of shadows—green and gray. In her childhood, Shelagh recalled, it was nothing but a rectangle of grass and moss with a gravel walk around the four sides, edged about with yew trees and bushes that no one had to pay any attention to. But now the linden tree grew tall in the center of it, and the gravel path had been extended to lead the way to a low bench built in a circle around the base of that tree. This particular linden was a lime tree of the variety native to Austria, the tree that predominates in the Vienna Woods. Shelagh's mother had decided against a funeral when her father died, but the directors of the Cortauld and the Warburg had persuaded her to agree to a memorial service in the garden and to attend the planting of the linden tree in memory of Sir Hans Markgraf. He had been transplanted from Austria to England, flourished in that land, grown great in his chosen soil, and sheltered others in the shadow of his branches. The devoted colleagues and disciples who conceived of this memorial had fervently wished that the symbol would flourish likewise.

They were rewarded. The elegant tree of mottled bark and delicate leaves had taken to the earth of this garden, had grown high and strong, and cast the relief of shade in the heat of summer.

Shelagh sat on the bench that encircled it and stroked the bark of the thickening trunk; it was as if the memory of her father had been transformed into this tree so that others could easily focus on the meaning of his life. She looked up and saw Peter Lettcome watching her from the window of his office—which had once been her father's office. He withdrew as soon as he saw her looking at him.

Shelagh Markgraf Jackman had flown in from the United States to attend the memorial service. The Austrian Ambassador had read three of her father's favorite poems by Goethe; Peter Lettcome had delivered the eulogy; Sir Kenneth Clark had evaluated the significance of her father's life's work. As the tree was planted, Lady Markgraf had stood erect, stolid and steadfast, dry-eyed, holding the hands of her grown-up daughters, Adrienne and Shelagh, on either side of her. Shelagh had never loved her mother as much, and never loved her more, than at that moment, silent, with the pressure of their bare hands held together, sharing the awareness that death had robbed them of The Excellent Man; that eventually, all of them would be metamorphosed into trees or bushes or flowers. If they were to be memorialized. The burlap that surrounded the roots in the Austrian earth was cut away, the bulb of ground to be transplanted was set into British soil, the shovels brought the two lands together; the tree was righted, the earth made firm; the young leaves danced, shimmering in the bright London noon light. Lady Markgraf let go of her daughters' hands, moved forward, reached out to take the trunk of the tree in both her hands, and *smiled,* her eyes closed, as though she too were already dead.

Adrienne never went shopping or to the museums or galleries with Shelagh; but they spent every evening together dining out—at the Savoy Grille or Rules or Simpson's in the Strand for old Old Times' Sake, or in the newly fashionable restaurants, or at the homes of friends. On Tuesday the party took place at her flat.

It wasn't easy to get in. There was no automatic release button that Adrienne could press on the third floor to open the street door when the buzzer sounded. She could have installed that system; but it amused her to maintain the practice she had initiated on moving in here. When the buzzer was heard, Adrienne went out onto the balcony beyond the sitting room and looked down to see who had rung the bell. All of her familiars, accustomed to the procedure, stepped down from the front door back to the sidewalk and looked up, usually calling out their names. Adrienne then threw down the entrance key, in a small brown velvet sack with yellow-threaded ties; the gift of a cigarette lighter (long since lost) had been given to her wrapped in that string bag. She prided herself on never hitting any of her guests with the missile. Some of them caught it in their cupped hands. Others had to light matches before they could find it at their feet. And after they'd let themselves in and climbed the three flights of stairs, caught their breath, even before they'd taken off their coats, in the moment of kissing their hostess's cheek, they would slip into her waiting palm the short pipe of a key in the little velvet bag so that Adrienne would be ready to fling it outside as soon as the sound of the buzzer was heard again. Adrienne called the practice "Dickensian."

People had been invited to come after nine P.M.

Seeing Adrienne lean over the balcony and throw down the key frightened Shelagh. Her sister seemed so close to falling over, Shelagh's heart jumped to her throat; she reassured herself with the thought that her fright must be caused by her point of view. She was seated in a low armchair, and therefore Adrienne only seemed higher above the balcony railing than she actually stood; when she leaned over, it appeared that she might easily tilt out of control and fling herself down. Shelagh turned her gaze away to the watercolors of Greece. The two that had been off-balance were that way again. She pointed to them as Adrienne returned to the room, said, "I think it happens when the hall door is closed," got up, and centered them.

Adrienne shrugged, as if to say, "I'm not the one who does it." Shelagh thought her especially smart-looking in a silver-gray hostess gown, just as she was more than a little pleased with the brown leather skirt and boots she had bought herself that morning at Burberry's and the tan silk blouse from Harrods.

The editor of *Dialogue* and his mistress were the first to arrive. In fact, it was she who kept him. This small milk-faced lady with long black hair was the widow of a Bolivian millionaire, something of a displaced person in London. "I wake up every morning," she confessed later during the party, "with the same terrible dread: will I be bored today?"

Harold Sissgull, the editor, also was small but rotund, with the inexhaustible cheerfulness of an inveterate partygoer. Originally from the Bronx, he had lived in England for a quarter of a century and become a British citizen. "Following the example of Henry James," he said often—and harboring a dream of buying the house in Rye. The receding dark hair of his brow was compensated for by a bushy, pepper Van Dyck beard, and he sailed in like a tireless tugboat blowing before him puffs of smoke from an ever-present Dutch cigar. Shelagh had known him for years. He was a polymath, an optimist, a Burkeian conservative, a marvelous raconteur in love with the sound of his own voice, an entertaining manipulator, who truly believed *Dialogue* to be the ultimate criterion of sanity and critical judgment in a maddeningly depraved and dangerous world. The Bolivian widow comforted him in the security of her house in Belgravia.

A waiter in a white Nehru jacket asked for their orders and quickly brought them drinks from the dining room.

"Adrienne, my darling," Harold Sissgull began, "I have an idea for two articles we must plan but I forgot my pen and my diary. I have nothing to make notes on." He showed her his empty hands. He looked pitiful.

"I'll take care of you," she assured him.

He smiled. "Like Einstein—all I need is a pencil and a piece of paper."

Adrienne led him away by the hand toward the desk in her study.

Shelagh expressed her admiration for the colorfully patterned paisley shawl that covered the Bolivian lady's shoulders and ran down her back in a triangle that nearly touched the floor. She clutched it closer over her arms, saying, "This is not one of those imitations from Paisley, Scotland." She pronounced it *Shotland*. "It is an original. From the Kashmir. About 1850. In those days, this was the equivalent of a mink coat . . . did you know?"

"No."

Peter Lettcome and his wife arrived.

Then Hugh appeared, without having sounded the buzzer.

Within an hour both the sitting room and the dining room were crowded with writers, one of them a Member of Parliament; painters whom Shelagh had known since her days at the Slade; motion-picture people; an opera singer—with spouses or "dates" or with the spouse of someone else—all of whom were familiar with each other. The life of *Dialogue* had given Adrienne access to the acquaintance of anyone of whatever importance who interested her, and her endless curiosity was perpetually rewarded.

The silent waiter refilled the drinks of the guests constantly, so that not one of the people seated, standing, or moving about in the flat ever had a glass only half-full. Shelagh had the impression that all of them knew everything and had been everywhere. In snatches of conversations she listened to, someone was saying he had just come back from Abu Dhabi or Sri Lanka, or she was just off to Nepal or Borneo. Shelagh stepped out onto the balcony for a breath of fresh air and a view of the night sky. Immediately behind her she heard the question "And what did you enjoy today?" Hugh had followed her out onto the balcony, where they stood alone together. He wore a blue pin-striped suit like a banker in the City; one hand pulled at the hairs in his mustache as if to make them stand out straight.

"You're *assuming* that I *enjoyed* something."

"Naturally; you're on holiday. Your business is to have pleasure. Your purpose is to be gratified."

"Well, I went to Buckingham Palace."

"To visit the Queen? And what did you there?"

"I frightened a little mouse under the chair."

"I believe you."

She was not sure how to be serious with Hugh. He was easy to talk with, but then, everyone was—as long as he could be clever about something. "Actually," she said, "I went to see the Queen's Pictures."

"Oh, yes. I've never been there myself."

"It had a curious effect on me. I was looking at a family album. Do you remember as a child—long before television—how an evening's entertainment of a visitor might begin by looking through the pictures in a family album?"

"I think I recall suffering such a pleasure once or twice. Grandfather in his Crimean War uniform. The seven cousins on the beach at Trouville, August, 1907. That sort of thing."

"Exactly. Well, here you have five hundred years' worth of the royal family's paintings. Generation after generation. The ancestors and their cousins, the battles, the castles, babies and banquets, each painted by the choicest artists of their day. It's not an impersonal collection of masterworks—the history of England being haphazardly the history of the crown—and there I was, as a visitor, allowed to look through the privately accumulated family album."

"What a charming thought."

Bluntly, she asked, "Are you happy with Adrienne?"

"Frightfully."

"She seems quite content to me."

"That's because she knows it won't last."

"It mustn't?"

"That's her way. I tell myself it intensifies the pleasures knowing that someday soon I'll get the boot."

"She made all this clear—in advance . . . ?"

"Adrienne believes she can explain it scientifically. Her hypothesis is that love's opposed to nature. In nature—en gros—living or inanimate, everything changes; all interplaying forces bring about transformations, metamorphoses. All actions in nature are means to ends which become new means to other ends. Everything in nature is propelled by the inescapable requirement to change. Transiency is the one permanent principle."

Shelagh asked, "Isn't love in nature?"

"Well, no. Love is experienced as desire fulfilled in such an intensely satisfying way as to make you long for permanence, to resist any possible change. 'May it always be like this!' lovers plead with each other. 'May we never feel anything less perfect than this! May it last forever!' they pray. That sense of completeness at being in love is an end in itself. But it must be self-consuming. Either it burns itself out or, if it becomes institutionalized, it changes anyhow, it becomes a means to another end—the continuity of the marriage, the maintenance of a family; in either case, it's transformed. In that sense Adrienne believes love is unnatural."

Shelagh snorted a short disapproving laugh.

"Well—antinatural. Adrienne likes being in love occasionally, and natural the rest of the time."

"I think that's appalling."

"What's this man done to appall you, my dear?" They turned to find Peter Lettcome behind them on the balcony. He took Shelagh by the shoulders and kissed her on both cheeks, as was his custom, by the right of decades of affection. She knew that once, when he was a student of her father's, he had wanted to be her suitor, but in those days he had been unable to declare himself. Then he shook hands with Hugh. "Vercingetorix, I believe."

"Warburg, isn't it?"

"What's appalled you?" he repeated to Shelagh.

Hugh answered for her: "It's the Arabs. The presence of Arabs all over London."

"Yes, it is a bit much," Peter agreed. "But we're becoming accustomed to the sight of them. Each time we see another woman in purdah—all wrapped up in those sand-colored sheets with only a slit for her to peep through—the shock is lessened. We're reassuring ourselves we haven't been transported to the desert; it's they who are out of place. Soon we'll be habituated. Then they'll start wearing our garb."

"They can afford it, God knows. They're buying up everything else. Have you heard they've just purchased the Dorchester Hotel?" Hugh asked. "In Paris last week there was a wild sight. Some practical joker paraded a camel in the streets around the Stock Exchange."

Shelagh smiled. "I like the thought of a camel in Paris."

"Well, he carried a placard on either side of his humps—one in Arabic, one in French—which read: 'Your Europe interests me. I'll buy it.' "

Shelagh said, "It's become too chilly out here. Let's return and benefit from all the body warmth inside."

Just inside the room, an aging philosopher from Oxford was being courted by the wife of the journalist/Member of Parliament. He stuttered, and she was literally stroking his long neck, from his chin over the Adam's apple to the collar of his shirt, as if her sensuous massage would make him more articulate.

Hugh excused himself; Adrienne had signaled to him for help in the kitchen—to lay out on platters the catered food that would be served as the midnight supper.

Peter Lettcome and Shelagh found a sofa suddenly vacant and made themselves comfortable, side by side, ignoring the others. She gave him the latest news of her family and of her life in New Haven; she described her work at illustrating a new edition of the Old Testament.

"It situates you firmly in the line of a great tradition," he said.

"Ah, 'great traditions' ..." Shelagh repeated the words slowly. "You know, my father used to say something about the word 'tradition' having the emotional charge for an intellectual that the word 'fashion' has for the ordinary man."

"Yes, yes, indeed. I remember. And that scholarship has no predictive value except to reflect the layman's belief that what falls out of fashion in one man's generation will be revived by his grandchildren."

"Exactly. Who could have imagined thirty years ago the re-emergence of Art Nouveau, let alone Art Deco? They were either a desecration or a joke to our generation, but our children have discovered them and resurrected them with the kind of intense joy that thinkers must have felt in the Italian Renaissance, when Plato was found again."

Peter laughed. "Cycles of fashion. Definitely. The next to be revived will be Victorian Gothic."

Shelagh frowned with distaste.

"The Albert Memorial will become an aesthetic Holy Grail."

Shelagh burst out in laughter.

"Of course, there are some fashions that might never be recovered—at least, I hope not. Think on this: it is a fact that throughout the nineteenth century, thousands upon thousands of volumes of the sermons of English, Scottish, and Irish *divines* were published. Sermons. Yes, yes. Two-volume, six-volume, ten-volume collections. Subscribed to or sold over the counter. Of course, one can't believe anybody read them. But they bought the books. They were the backbone of nineteenth-century British publishing. They were the fashion then. I simply can't imagine their ever being revived now or in the future."

Shelagh decided to say nothing of her son's announcement about joining the Church. "Well, at least, it was a genuine taste of the times. Or the taste of the leaders of the times; fashion is a game of Follow the Leader."

"In any case, illustrating the Old Testament must make you feel very important. Doesn't it?"

"Once can have pretensions. I don't."

"That, my dear, is a pretension."

Lettcome appeared preoccupied. He meditated. "There is a passage in one of Ortega's books—I can't remember where, at the moment—when he plays on the word 'pretension' as an admirable way of understanding how our hopes draw us into our own future: the tension of feeling the aspiration to bring about something that does not yet exist. It is a lyrical tribute to pretension as the means for raising us up into the future—our future accomplishments."

"Didn't he mean ambition?"

"No. I think he was trying to explain how ambition comes about. By imagining in advance of the fact what we might achieve in the future—and if we do not feel that, nothing draws us forward into becoming anything that we are not already."

Shelagh was quietly reflective for a moment and then admitted: "I never feel that kind of tension; I suppose I'm simply not ambitious for what might become of me in the future."

"I know. I know. You are one of those *rarae aves* who are actually content to live in the here and now. I think you have always been like that. It's what makes you a calm pool, that one comes to refresh himself at, while the rest of us are racing brooks."

"You haven't told me anything about yourself." She could see in the adjoining room Mrs. Lettcome chatting with a young Cambridge don. Peter spoke of his son's work-study trip on an oceanographic voyage; of his daughter's engagement to a French banker; of his purchase of a country house in Dorset.

"But what are you writing? What are you thinking about?"

"I'll tell you. I'm trying to solve a puzzle I've posed for myself." He described a recent trip to Portugal, where at the fishing village of Nazaré, the murals on the walls of cafés or hotels were of the local scene along the beach—the very fishing boats one saw as one looked across the road to the harbor and the ocean; and in the mountain village of Sintra, the murals in the public buildings were of the mountain view beyond the windows of Sintra; just as in Lisbon itself the murals in bars and stores were of the cityscape and maplike layout of the city that stood beyond the walls they were painted on. "I have noticed this before," he said: "the primitive paintings of Alps which is verily the view of Alps in Switzerland, in Austria, in Italy—where the picture you see is what you look at in nature when you turn your back on the painting. Think of Oberammergau, or Seefeld . . . it is more akin to portraiture for preservation within a family—"

"I was just referring to a family album to Hugh . . ."

"—than it is to any of the purposes of High Art."

"Ah, those we know are all compensation or inspiration or titillation."

"Quite right. Compensation satisfies an understandable need. If you are trapped in the Alps, your need for the Mediterranean would be satisfied by a picture of Capri or Sicily. If you live in the fog of Lübeck it would be understandable for you to have murals of China imagined under a brilliant sun. But why should the fishermen of Nazaré want to look at a picture of the beach and the boats of Nazaré itself?"

"The ordinary and the extraordinary," Shelagh said without thinking. "Perhaps there is a point in trying to assimilate experience when human beings feel that even what they take for granted, what they know best and are most at home with, must be reckoned as 'extraordinary' and only through the mediation of a painting re-presenting it are they able to learn to live with it again."

Peter Lettcome stared at her for a long moment. "How like your father" was all he said.

Mrs. Lettcome, who looked as though she thought her husband had been talking alone with Shelagh long enough, brought the Cambridge don along with her and they pulled up two low side chairs to sit nearly knee to knee opposite them.

"Mr. Putnam," she said, "has just agreed to do an essay for *Dialogue* on Anthony Powell's series *A Dance to the Music of Time,* now that it's finished. That's why Adrienne pinned the orchid on his lapel."

It was a tiny greenish-yellow flower freckled with brown spots. Shelagh called it a ripe banana. It appeared almost iridescent against Mr. Putnam's black jacket. A youngish man, he wore an open pale blue shirt with a foulard ascot at his neck. His face was clean-shaven, his eyes enlarged by horn-rimmed spectacles; a shock of blond hair fell over the right half of his forehead. "I've only just finished Powell's twelve volumes . . . in the past twenty-four days."

"How fortunate you are," Peter Lettcome said. "I read them as they came out—one book biannually. It took me twenty-four years!"

"I don't know what I shall say about it yet."

Joining the conversation momentarily, Harold Sissgull came up to rest his hand on Putnam's shoulder. "You'd better let me know, when you decide— so I can arrange for someone else to do it from an opposite point of view." He then lit a new cigar and meandered into a different conversation.

"I see you're staring at my orchid, Mrs. Jackman," Putnam said.

"It was my orchid once. I brought some of them with me from home."

"Really? Do you know the etymology of the name?"

Shelagh paused for an instant. "If I ever did, I can't recall it."

"Testicle," Putnam supplied. "From the Greek, *orchis.* Because of the similarity between them and the usual shape of the tuber. From the same root as the word 'orchitis' meaning inflammation of the testicles, and 'orchiectomy,' the surgical excision of the testicles—that is, castration."

Shelagh smiled. "Are you putting me on?"

"No, no. I assure you. Not at all. You'll find it in the O.E.D.—between 'orchestrina,' a mechanical instrument resembling a barrel organ, and 'ordain,' meaning to put in order, arrange, prepare, equip, appoint, decree, or destine."

His audience laughed. Mrs. Lettcome applauded.

With mock modesty, Mr. Putnam explained, "I have a photographic memory."

Peter asked, "Have you photographed the *O.E.D.?*"

He answered, "One needs all the words one can get, don't you think?"

Shelagh said, "It depends on what you want to do with them."

"I want to write a novel. For the past fifteen years I've been teaching literary history and literary criticism, evolving my own theory of the nature of fictional creation, on the one hand, and considering the sociology of literary taste on the other, and I believe I'm now in a position to start a popular success."

Mrs. Lettcome asked, "Do you have a title? I mean, what are you going to call it?"

"*Filet d'Amour.* You see, two-word titles are the most successful of all—*vide* Dickens, Tolstoy, Flaubert, *et alii.* And in the British and American popular mind the mere sight of a French word is the signal for expectation of erotic sophistication. Of course, most people don't know French. But there isn't anyone who reads a novel who wouldn't recognize 'amour'; and the second French word best known in the English-speaking world is 'filet'—as in filet of sole or *filet mignon.*"

"Charming," Peter opined. "Charming. But what does it mean—*Filet d'Amour?*"

"I haven't decided yet. But now that I have the provocative title I feel I can begin."

Adrienne appeared, and urged Shelagh to move closer to Peter on the sofa, making room for her to join them. Shelagh summarized: "Mr. Putnam is proposing to write an erotic novel with a title implying 'The best cut of love.' "

Adrienne needled him. "What do you know about love, darling?"

"It's what I know about novels that matters." He crossed one leg over the other, removed his spectacles, and swung them like a pendulum back and forth from his extended forefinger pointed at Shelagh in the middle of the sofa. "One reads a novel judging everything as you go along in the light of wondering: 'Why is the author telling me this?' That is because a novel is a very lengthy and elaborate answer to a question that is not fully understood until you have read the whole answer. For example, what is *Anna Karenina* about? If you say, It is an answer to the question 'What would happen if a woman like Anna fell in love with a man like Vronsky?'—while that appears deceptively simple, it takes hundreds and hundreds of pages to appreciate. You need the beginning to show what they are 'like' in general, and the world they live in; the middle to have a temporary solution—which, it turns out, cannot last; and an end to realize the consequences of the choices made—no longer because of what they're 'like,' but only, by the very end, as you have come to know fully what they are in all their particulars."

Mr. Putnam than replaced his spectacles, swept back the hair from his forehead, and folded his arms over his chest. He seemed to await his students' response.

Peter Lettcome asked, "So what question will be asked by *Filet d'Amour?*"

"You'll have to wait for the answer."

The Bolivian widow approached the group, the original Kashmiri shawl, about 1850, more casually, loosely draped about her shoulders now. "Have you seen the *Macbeth?*" she asked Shelagh. "*Macbeth* in Zulu?"

Adrienne responded for her. "We went to it the second night Shelagh was here."

"Isn't it marvelous?"

"What are you talking about?" an advertising executive asked.

"The rage of the season," Sissgull's mistress replied.

"The Zulus?" he said. "They're here for only a month or so."

"What difference does that make?" she asked. "They've perked up everybody."

Mr. Putnam looked at her milk-white face. "With their happy killings?"

"Yes. They make the murders such an affirmation of life."

"It's just that they look so sexy," Adrienne added.

"Of course," Mrs. Lettcome said, "they're so big and—"

"Black," Peter supplied. "So very black. Blue-black."

"Some of them are bronzed-black," Shelagh said. "All very tall, muscular."

"Nearly naked," the advertising executive said. "Thin. And strong. Very flat and long-legged, with big, powerful buttocks: black melons. Romping around with spears."

"Zulu sounds like 'click-click, bomb-boo, clack-clack,'" Mrs. Lettcome said.

"It doesn't matter. Everybody knows *Macbeth*." Mr. Putnam made it sound comfortable.

Peter said, "Revitalizing. I found it very refreshing. The Zulus play *Macbeth* with conviction. Totally identified with their roles. No one is separated from what he's doing by any self-consciousness. No one understands regret or remorse or guilt. They play it as if the Zulus have no self-judgment."

"They don't understand Shakespeare at all," Mrs. Lettcome criticized.

The Bolivian lady was their protector. "But they understand themselves," she said magisterially.

"They're a lot easier to take than all the Arabs in London." The advertising executive was blunt.

"They're not staying as long," Mr. Putnam said.

Peter asked Shelagh, "Have you seen *The Philanthropist?*"

"We're going tomorrow night, as a matter of fact."

"You'll enjoy that. Terribly British, of course. Prizewinning comedy. A clean remedy for *Macbeth* in Zulu."

"Why does one need a remedy from it?" the Bolivian asked. "You yourself just said it's refreshing, revitalizing. The beautiful blacks at their happy killing."

She knew nothing about Trevor Cartwright and the Mau Mau, Shelagh realized.

"It's refreshing," Peter replied, slowly, "as spring water is after a hike in the mountains. But if you've a taste for vintage wines, my dear, you wouldn't be interested in spring water as a steady diet."

"You talk in metaphors." She shrugged her shoulders. "I liked the Zulus. Their happy killing." And strolled away toward the dining room.

Mr. Putnam quietly said, "You must know—the Bolivians aren't all that different from the Zulus. . . ."

Shelagh left to make use of the bathroom.

When the platters of food were served, they were very elegant indeed. There were smoked eel and horseradish sauce, artichoke bottoms stuffed with curried shrimp, gray caviar from Iran with minced sweet onion, and Scotch smoked salmon on black bread.

Shelagh returned to the party as an eavesdropper listening to one clutch of conversation after another.

"The current situation in 'Communist' China," she heard an interminably tall fellow saying to Harold Sissgull, "is not just a contradiction in terms, it's a contradiction in fact. The most obvious facts. You *cannot* have a central government that gives orders when you have local authorities who do not *have to* carry them out. 'Local *authority*' means you do not have central *government.*"

"I know, I know," Sissgull said, insinuating that it is bad form to tell your grandmother how to suck eggs. "But what story do you have in mind?"

"My trip to the west. I should call it my trip to the past. The farther west you go from Beijing, the clearer it becomes that China is in the control of local army commandants who wield the only power in those provinces. It is as if the central government does not exist. They are the territorial rulers. Warlords. No different from the situation under the Empress a hundred years ago." His voice rose: "No different whatsoever."

"Three generations—four generations—different," Sissgull suggested.

"It's not the substance I'm referring to. It's the form."

The waiter refilled her wineglass. Shelagh wandered toward the table in the dining room and ate a slice of bread with smoked salmon and capers.

She overheard from a corner of the room behind her: "My husband needn't know."

"But my wife would."

"You give her too much credit."

"All the charge cards are in her name. . . ."

Hugh reappeared. "Are you enjoying yourself?"

"And everyone else," she replied. "Who's the terribly tall fellow over there talking about China?"

"Which one? Oh, yes, Lord Byrne, erstwhile Ambassador to India. He was supposed to be a great scholar, but an early Labour government elevated him to the House of Lords and he's been a Pooh-Bah pundit ever since."

"He writes for *Dialogue?*"

"He writes for everyone. Makes you think of Lord Curzon. Did you know that when Curzon was Viceroy of India, and his wife invalided in England, he'd write her a letter every day—sometimes a hundred pages? A day? No sense of proportion."

Laughingly, Shelagh said, "He should have kept a diary instead. Do you think many people keep diaries anymore?"

"I doubt it. I don't. It doesn't pay. People do work for hire." He paused. "On the other hand, now that all those letters and diaries and biographies of the Bloomsbury group suddenly have been published upon us, it gives one pause. Perhaps I'm wrong. Who knows? Maybe keeping a diary is the last secret vice, and a generation from now the unborn will be able to read what Sissgull and Lettcome, and the advertising executive over there, and Lord Byrne thought of this evening."

"Perhaps. . . ."

"Fortunately, I don't think it's a disturbing idea, for the simple reason that I shan't be here to read them. But then—one's lived experience is only 'history' to those who come after. Isn't it?"

"Quite right. And we all know—so much of history is fiction."

"What do you think of Mr. Putnam?"

"I suspect his fiction will be history."

"That's very sharp. I like that. I do wish you lived here. It's such a pleasure seeing you. . . ."

"How very kind. This is how I will remember you. Thank you."

Peter Lettcome approached them at the table with the accusation "Hoarders. Let me at that caviar."

"Be my guest," Hugh said, stepping aside and then leaving the room.

"Peter, my dear," Shelagh began in a whisper. "I'm not able to remember the lady standing alone in the corner, behind me to my right. No—you look to your left. She's in a brocaded jacket, with a long black skirt. Rather gray hair. A thin line for a mouth."

"Yes. I see her now."

"You know who she is?"

"Of course; so do you. It's just that she's aged more than you have. Evelyn Knops—the Abstract Expressionist."

"Good lord, we were students together."

134

"Her parents came from Belgium during the first war."

"We're the same age."

"But you haven't lived the same life."

"I must talk with her. You will excuse me, won't you?"

"Do I have any choice?"

Shelagh turned around slowly where she stood, regarded the guests in the room, focused in on Evelyn Knops, and let her face be suffused with the pleasures of surprise. She moved directly to her old friend. "Evelyn!" She took her hand in both of hers. "I didn't see you come in."

"I'm the sort who lives in fear she won't find the key when Adrienne throws it down." She smiled. Her teeth were capped with an egregious uniformity. She wore no makeup, and a network of red lines seemed scratched across her nostrils and up into the cheeks of her otherwise pleasant face. She was always reserved, Shelagh remembered; but her youthful good spirits had long since been ground down, eroded. She now appeared to live by a strenuous will to overcome frustration and dissatisfaction; but it was a daily battle. She proffered Shelagh her gift in its totality, all at once: "How I envy you."

"Me? Envy me?"

"You look all of a piece. As the children say today: together. I'm just a bundle of fragments. 'Bundle' is putting it flatteringly. A 'dustpanful' is more like it."

Shelagh did not let go of Evelyn's hand. "But you look so well."

"Compared with you?" She snorted. "I'm a mess."

"How is David?"

"Gone. Gone. You realize we never were married. Each of us was free to leave if we wanted to. He finally wanted to. Oh, waiter, let me have another drink, will you?"

"I'm terribly sorry."

"Don't be. It would have been worse if he'd stayed. It's just . . ." She threw back her head and took a deep breath. "It's not that I miss him. I just loathe being alone."

"It must be terrible."

"Don't patronize. I can see that you're all right; and I know that I'm not. I wish I were, and that's why I envy you. Well, that's one of the reasons. But you can't know. You simply can't know. . . ."

"I don't pretend to; but I feel with you."

"You're still illustrating books, aren't you?"

"Yes."

"That's the other difference. Do you remember conversations years ago—about a thousand years ago—when we were happy that painters no longer suffered under patronage? Didn't have to do the bidding of the piper. 'I want a seascape in the living room. Give me more pink in the clouds on the ceil-

135

ing.' No more commissions. The artist was free to paint anything—everything—he wanted to; and the world would come begging for a chance, fighting with each other for a chance, to buy what in the privacy of his genius he would deign to create. Remember?"

"Yes. I do."

"Well, in the solitary confinement of my genius, I paint what I alone want to create, and you know what?—no one wants a chance to buy it."

"But you have a gallery that represents you. You have shows . . ."

"No one, Shelagh. No one buys. You have a patron. A publisher. Your illustrations get used. I am free to paint whatever I choose. But I'm of no use. No one makes use of what I do."

"But you."

"Even I don't. I don't care anymore. At first you paint because it's a miracle that it is any good at all. And then you paint and go on painting because you are a Painter: there are no miracles anymore, no ecstasy of wonder and joy. You just don't know how to do anything else. Sometimes, I think I'll bore myself to death."

"What if next Thursday Ben Nicholson writes an article in the *Burlington* 'discovering' you? Praising you. Recognizing your uniqueness. Attracting the world's attention to your work."

"I'll shoot him. It's too late."

Shelagh tried to laugh. "You don't mean that."

"I don't mean anything," Evelyn Knops said decisively.

Shelagh felt thrown off balance by this onslaught of bitterness. Evelyn had never raised her voice; there was nothing shrill or rude in her tone; but the message of her embitterment was overpowering. Shelagh received it like a slap in the face. She let go of her old friend's hand. "When we were girls," she began, uncertainly, "we imagined it best to be as free as possible."

"We're aging women now. And I'm without a man who says, 'I'd like corned beef and cabbage for dinner.' And I'm without a patron who says, 'Paint me a ceiling full of pink clouds showing the ascent of Lord Byrne into heaven, carried on the wings of angels.' "

"People who make things are happier than people who don't."

"Only people who make things for somebody else."

Shelagh gestured about the dining room and the flat in general. "Everyone here makes things for somebody else."

"But if nobody wants them . . . ?" Evelyn squared her shoulders, as if pulling herself up. "I'm glad I came. I'm glad I saw you again. It's good that some people are well off. I don't begrudge it you. But we're not girls anymore. . . ." She looked as if she wished to go on talking but what she had in mind was unspeakable. "I'll have to go. Perhaps, another time . . ."

Shelagh embraced her and kissed her cheek. Evelyn was unyielding.

"Goodbye, now," was all she said, and headed for the door.

Shelagh felt bereft, standing immobile where she had been left, following Evelyn with her eyes. We believe our reality is in our own hands—when we get what we want—but it is mostly a matter of luck: of destiny, she thought. Our reality is created between what we bring to life and what the rest of the world does to us. It's what Chester means by "the social nature of reality"; and when the going is good, we think we've earned it. Only when it's not do we recognize *bad* luck. Does Evelyn deserve that? We don't "deserve" our good luck any more than she "earned" her demeaning destiny. No one can ever, not *ever* answer the question "Why me?"

"You left me," Peter Lettcome began, "to talk with Evelyn, and now you're alone—brooding."

"Yes. She sent a chill through me."

"There's warm soup on the table now. Come, have a cup. It's a pheasant soup."

Adrienne ladled the soup out of a silver punch bowl into pottery mugs.

"Isn't there a chance, Adrienne, that *Dialogue* could commission Evelyn Knops to do illustrations or decorations for some of its issues?"

Adrienne raised her eyebrows. "She doesn't draw, you know. Her work looks like smudges. Splotches. Drippings. We don't use color. In black and white in our pages they'd look as if the printer had spilled a bucket of ink."

"She is a victim of Mathieu," Peter explained. "When she went to Paris after the war, he was the rage. Action painting. What you see is the energy, the physicality of the painter as he made the picture. That is the picture. Nothing else." After a pause, he added: "It doesn't seem to be enough. It doesn't wear well."

Shelagh sipped the soup and then came to the conclusion "She had bad luck with everything she fell in love with."

Adrienne, who saw Evelyn infrequently, nevertheless felt well disposed toward her. "Perhaps," she said, "that style will become fashionable again in the future."

"Peter and I were talking earlier this evening about cycles of fashion."

"But I said some styles are unlikely ever to become popular again."

"The sermons of divines. But in the graphic arts it appears there's nothing that can't be revived."

"Well . . . that seems to me a function of market values, not intrinsic interest. There are investors in painting with their own financial layaway plans. Art for investment has nothing to do with taste, wishes, or needs. It's impersonal. Perhaps they'll latch on to Evelyn's sort of thing and store it in an attic until the art dealers need a new thrill. Some people can afford to gamble on anything. It's conceivable. But they won't buy in order to look at the pictures and cherish them." He chuckled. "They're not good for the eyes."

Shelagh said, "It's as difficult to find those who'll love your pictures as it is to find those who'll love you."

Adrienne said, "That assumes you are lovable."

"That was delicious." Shelagh put her soup mug down on the table. "Too bad there are some things that just can't be rectified."

The opera singer confessed, "I've been eavesdropping. All of you sound like critics. Terrible thing: critics."

Peter was not disturbed. "Everyone is a critic by nature."

"But some are good; the rest abominations." She was of the new breed in opera, svelte as a ballerina, in a black outfit with gold and scarlet trim, and a white ruff of a collar that reminded Shelagh of a portrait of Queen Elizabeth's Walter Devereux, Earl of Essex, in the sixteenth century. "If a critic dislikes what you do, he should be disqualified. Negative criticism is just a form of revenge."

Adrienne laughed. "Only those who applaud you, Vanessa, should be allowed to speak?"

"Basically, yes. The only value of a critic is to help you appreciate something better—not point out why you shouldn't like it."

"That's totalitarian, my dear." Peter continued: "Different police states impose different kinds of censorship. I prefer a free market in ideas as well as other goods. At least, there's a chance for everyone to be properly appreciated."

Shelagh became gradually aware of an ugly odor—a rather acrid, metallic scent. It couldn't possibly be Vanessa's perfume, which was sweet. She looked about her. No one was smoking. Even the ashtray on the dining-room table was empty. Peter took off with a mug of the soup for his wife. Vanessa turned her back and then launched herself after Mr. Putnam, who stood in the hall.

Shelagh whispered to Adrienne, "What is that terrible smell?"

Her sister inhaled. Paused. "I don't smell anything odd."

"But I certainly do."

"It must be your imagination."

"What an unpleasant thing to imagine."

"No. There definitely is not any bad smell. . . ."

Shelagh said no more and made her way slowly through the hall and the sitting room, testing the odor as she moved. It remained constant, neither increasing nor decreasing, and she was at a loss to identify the source. Certainly no other person there appeared to perceive it. A faint cloud of smoke hovered in the sitting room. Shelagh made for the fresh air on the balcony—but even the late-night breeze did nothing to alleviate it. Determined to take her mind off the irritating mystery, she returned to the main room as guests began to take their departure. She felt herself to be the victim of some strange hallucination.

In the end, no one but Hugh and Harold Sissgull remained in the sitting room. The Bolivian lady was napping in the study. Adrienne suggested to Hugh that they talk about something privately on the terrace, but Shelagh presumed they would not get all the way through the bedroom to the terrace door. She sat alone with the editor of *Dialogue,* who smiled contentedly through his bristly Van Dyck and puffed on his cigar.

"I really don't understand . . ." Shelagh said to herself out loud.

"What don't you understand?" Harold Sissgull asked, ready to be of help.

She had no intention of mentioning the bad smell. It seemed a cruel trick of her imagination. What she said was "People. I find it more and more baffling as I grow older: why people behave the way they do. Whereas one should expect to grow wiser, I find myself growing more puzzled."

"Ah, well." Harold Sissgull made himself even more comfortable in the armchair facing the sofa on which she sat, prepared to lecture. "You suffer from a conflict between human understanding and intellectual comprehension," he announced. "It is a common impasse which most people find themselves in most of the time."

"Really?" Shelagh was only half-listening, admiring how silent it had become in the rest of the flat.

"Human understanding is an emotional experience. It allows us to know another person by feeling with him or her; it results in the wisdom of sympathy. It enables us to say, 'I know what you feel.' But it is not rational: that is to say, it supplies no causes, no explanation for how or why that person is what he is."

"Yes, yes."

"When we seek for reasons we are usually baffled because there are so many principles of explanation available: God's will, the Devil's doing, socioeconomic factors, the id . . . you see what I mean? Anyway: the intellectual understanding of a person, as of any other kind of event, is not another instance of the complex phenomenon to be understood, it is a rational formula."

"You've lost me."

"I could appeal to Plato for the example you need, but—anyway: consider this paradigm. There are round things in nature and there are round things that are man-made and both of them fall into the class of things we call 'circles.' One may have human understanding of that class of things—in a sympathetic way. But when we ask, What is a Circle? as an intellectual question, we find that the answer is a mathematical formula—pi equals, et cetera—not itself an instance of the class of things, but something radically different.

Thus, the definition of a circle has nothing in common with a circle; it has no roundness, no dimensions, occupies no space. It is not a circle; it is a formula."

"Very well," Shelagh said sleepily. "I see."

"Aha. Then we are getting somewhere. Intellectual comprehension of a human being requires the same kind of understanding—and we call that sort of formula 'the pattern,' the key to the repeated ways of doing things that explains most, if not all, of the behavior of that person. If we can discover the source of the pattern, the event, or sequence of events, that established the essential pattern—the kind of action we see repeated over and over again in that person's behavior—then we have arrived at intellectual, rational understanding of that person." He smoked his cigar with a gesture of unqualified self-approval.

Shelagh wondered how many times before this he had made the same speech, and whether he had originated the thought himself or borrowed it from someone else. If I apply the idea to my sister, for example, she told herself, then the fact that Adrienne had been jilted might be the cause of the essential pattern of brief affairs—the minimal investment in important private relationships. But how far did that go toward making her "understandable"? And how often can one find out even that much about others? "Well, at least you're not saying the rational understanding of a human being is a mathematical formula."

"Right. I'm not saying that. It's analogous, however. A circle cannot have understanding of itself. But if we understand it by our intellects, the explanation is a definition as well as a description in terms quite different from any actual circle."

"A person can't understand herself?"

"I'm not saying that, although it's a rare person who does. There is sympathy and there is intellect; there is understanding from within and rational explanation from without. Whitehead's 'self-enjoyment' and 'significance.' " He took a long sip of his watered Scotch. "Would you like another drink, Shelagh?"

"I've been drinking for . . . days."

"Well, there you have it. Incidentally, you can see how the theory applies perfectly to the editorial policy of Dialogue."

"I suppose so," she replied uncertainly.

"At least two views of any event are necessary for a sense of its reality: the complexity of its reality."

"Harold, Harold, my dear—the key to the pattern," Shelagh echoed. "It sounds so Freudian."

"Of course it is."

"No one knows enough about anyone else's life to understand him that

140

way. I mean: we can't pretend to be God, let alone each other's psychoanalysts."

"Well, then, we can't understand them."

"But that's not understanding. That's the Procrustean bed—making them fit into a model of what's assumed to be understandable."

"Quite right. I'm a little tired now. But I think, if you want a rational explanation, you have to settle for the Freudian dirty secret."

"You mean: everyone's had some rotten experience that justifies his rotten behavior?"

"No. The lucky ones have had some good reason for becoming achievers; and the unlucky ones have good reason for being revengers."

"That's so disappointing, Harold. I had thought Freud's discovery—that we all have our little dirty secret—would have enhanced human sympathy."

"So did he, I believe. But Freud was wrong. Compassion isn't increased by thinking this, because self-interest is always stronger than sympathy. There's so much more pleasure to be taken from thinking someone else a victim and an asshole than by suffering with him that the Freudian view hasn't expanded human generosity . . . it's given us license to feel superior to everyone less lucky than we."

"A kind of elitist depravity."

"You could put it that way."

"We're both quite drunk, aren't we, Harold?"

"You could put it that way."

"I don't think you know what you're talking about."

"Possibly, possibly, my dear. I thought I was talking about the intellectual understanding of human beings."

"But you veered off into a therapeutic concept of people. I'm not interested in what one has to know to change them; only in what one has to know to live with them."

"Oh, that," Harold Sissgull said with aplomb, "merely takes the ability to be indifferent."

"No. That's not what I'm talking about. If I were indifferent, I wouldn't care to understand."

"You're very foolish. It's the only human protection."

Adrienne and Hugh strolled lazily into the room. The waiter had finished cleaning up and left. Adrienne said, "One knows the end of the evening has been reached when Harold starts on 'the only human protection.' Really, Harold, have you no mercy?"

"I shower people with mercy," he said, hoisting himself up from the deep chair; "I offer them the benefit of my thought. But now I shall retire. I'll wake my Sleeping Beauty and take her to her bed. Can we drop you on our way, Hugh?"

"No, thanks. I have my own car."

"It was a most agreeable party, Adrienne. Excellent food! If you visited here more often, Shelagh, we'd enjoy ourselves more frequently."

I'm afraid, Shelagh told herself, that from this moment forward I will always associate Harold Sissgull with a disagreeable metallic odor, an unpleasant smell that no one else notices.

After saying good night to her sister, Shelagh wearily took off her clothes and put on a nightgown, stretched, yawned, felt aches throughout her body as if she'd been standing on her feet for five hours. She straightened the covers of the daybed where the Bolivian lady had napped, and turned down the sheet and blanket. The bad smell evaporated; but in its place, she now became conscious of a different odor, the stale fragrance of a burn somewhere in the space of the study. She sniffed. She raised a candle, throwing the gilded light from one mirror to another across the breadth of wall above the desk, cautiously examining the things in the room—the wastebasket, the windowsills, the carpet—until she found the burned-out cigar on the top of the Renaissance chest of drawers. One of Harold Sissgull's endless series of long, thin Dutch cigars. A live cigar he had forgotten there. It had slipped off the alabaster dish and burned through the white lace, burned into the top of the inlaid olive-wood dresser. Burned itself out. She gasped at the dark gap in the antique lace and the bruised black gouge in the polished surface of the museum piece. Then she knocked on Adrienne's door and asked her to see something dreadful.

Sleepily, Adrienne followed her in her burgundy bathrobe.

Shelagh showed her the damage. "It's simply horrible," she said. She felt outrage for Adrienne, compassionate with her, and contemptuous of Sissgull.

But Adrienne was perfectly calm. "If you're going to make use of things, darling," she said, "you must be willing to risk their getting used up."

DIARY ENTRY

The difficulty is: how to start "the morning after." What a difference there is between feeling that I enjoyed Adrienne's party of last night and that I survived last night's party. I woke up feeling both elated and exhausted. I suppose the elation—the memory of elation—comes from having been called upon to exercise powers I'm not ordinarily (otherwise) required to call into play. To respond to the character of people, to the ideas and feelings of others, which are unusual, novel, unexpected. And by the rules of this game, the standard is cleverness, ingenuity, originality. What a drain on one's resources! The demands come so thick and fast, the pace is so accelerated, the changing of partners in such a minuet so unpredictable—the challenge is to be equal to the risk of how the dice fall out. Placing each bet immediately and instinctually. The classic situation of not knowing what you think until you hear what you say.

And still: it is such adult entertainment. The conversation of adults. Perhaps the form is not so different from that of a twelve-year-old's birthday party: jockeying for position in the pecking order, for status, for location in a hierarchy of influence and authority—no, no different from that manipulation of the childhood search for "place" in the group. But the substance really is different. It's not a matter of hockey scores or the number of dates, school grades or vacation plans; it is a play of ideas—not all of which must be believed in, only tried out for size. Original ideas, played with, fondled, put on the platform to see whether they can perform. One mind communing with another, through all the complexity of telling the truth (as one see it) or telling a make-believe (for the fun of it): that is adult conversation.

Pervasive, throughout the evening, were statements of certainty: everyone was so bloody convinced of what they said, so firm, so self-assured. It truly didn't matter whether the British Commonwealth is about to sink beneath the waves or not—it didn't matter at all; these people—these heirs of the British Empire, living on reduced rations of power and prestige—still behave (think of themselves) as the leaders of the world, and they don't really give a damn if they're proved wrong. It's a remarkable performance. It is the juggernaut of self-confidence in disregard of fact. Their self-assurance is not to be undercut by anything.

Their decisiveness flows from indifference to being proved wrong. They're all so decisive—whether bitter, or speculative, or manipulating, or authoritarian. Each one just "knows it all," as far as he's concerned.

But at the same time, they are willing to entertain—nay: determined to entertain. They see that as the social obligation they're competent to fulfill. I think they're determined to entertain because they fear being boring as the only crime deserving grim punishment; being a bore is quite explicitly thought of as the only sin left for which one should be made to suffer.

A man does not simply say: "I'd like a pencil and a piece of paper." That's merely a declaration of his wishes. Here he says: "Like Einstein, all I need is a pencil and a piece of paper." That's a three-act drama. Is that all Einstein needed? Is that all you need? Just how like Einstein are you? A whole tragicomedy is instigated by one subordinate clause. The range of audience response is unpredictable. There are those who will affirm that given the same modest requirements, you are indeed like Einstein; those whose sense of outrage will ridicule the vanity by which he presumes to compare himself to a certified public genius; and those who will find the comparison amusing by its absurdity. He has contributed to the engagement of their feelings in one way or another. No one is left alone with the bare question of whether he's going to get a pencil and a piece of paper. They've been forced into wondering, *Just how much* like Einstein *is he?* That's what's very entertaining.

And debilitating.

I found it enervating, trying to keep up with all the wit, and the charm, and the indiscriminate cleverness. But what fun!

LETTER TO CHESTER JACKMAN

My dear heart:

I have survived another of Adrienne's parties. It was engaging, but I suspect you wouldn't have enjoyed it very much. Adult conversation, good talk—adult entertainment—has the benefit of engaging your mind with the mind of another (an equal or a superior), but more often than not, it results in reassuring you that other people are not preeminently trustworthy. Does that sound patronizing? I don't mean it that way. Can you put much trust in people who believe that to entertain is very much more important than telling the truth? Or is my criticism unfair because of how difficult it is to know—let alone to tell—the truth? Still, when you and I talk, I have the feeling that we care to protect, and cultivate, and improve each other's spirit— mind/soul/heart. The caring is even more important than truth and entertaining. Or perhaps it's in the way one entertains that how much one cares can be discovered. Under these circumstances, however, I suspect that each "performer" is intent on scoring his own points without regard for the particular needs of anyone in the audience. Does that make sense? Probably not. (I'm under their influence.) I come away from the party pleased, but slightly dissatisfied with having been a participant in a group ritual that would have been about exactly the same even if I had not been present. It's not the case that I can't "hold my own"; I can. But that doesn't matter much in this here-and-now. Everyone here is a monologuist, a single (singular?) stand-up comedian who imagines he doesn't need a particularized audience; the idea of eternity will suffice for that.

I just don't want you to think I'm enjoying myself too much.

All love,

> *Your devoted*
> *Shelagh*

She telephoned Evelyn Knops and invited her for lunch three days from then. It was a brief but pleasant conversation. They agreed to meet at an Italian restaurant in Chelsea. Shelagh felt she must try to "make things up" for

Evelyn. Not that she had any idea of how to do that. They could at least be in each other's presence.

During the afternoon, she took in the current exhibitions at the Royal Academy—two contemporary British painters and a collection of monumental bronze sculpture from Venice. And just before five, as Savile Row was so nearby, she asked at the shirtmaker's whether the gift for Chester was ready. To her delight, she was able to carry it off with her, knowing she would keep it a secret until Christmas.

She was resting in an armchair when Adrienne returned to the flat carrying a bunch of asters. "I had to look at these all the way home to get Angola out of my mind. The Cubans in Angola. That's what I spent the day on."

"They're lovely," Shelagh said, taking them into the dining room, rolling them out of the brown paper wrapping on the table. Adrienne fetched a copper vase. The many-petaled round flowers showed an inner center of apricot color surrounded by a circular margin of pale lavender. "At home," Shelagh began, "my next-door neighbor grows asters very much like these. They too will be in bloom right now." She thought of old Mrs. McGrath hobbling one inch at a time. Where was she now?

"Are you homesick?"

"I think I am. Just for this moment I am. I miss Chester."

"How do you feel that?" Adrienne asked, while she placed the long-stemmed asters into the vase one at a time.

Shelagh replied slowly, "It's like looking into a mirror and seeing no reflection of yourself."

"I told you, you think in images."

They ate a late tea of sandwiches and cake, and then dressed for the theater.

"It might rain later," Adrienne called out from her bedroom, "but there's such a pleasant twilight now. If we leave soon, we could walk. Would you like that?"

The two sisters walked together in a relaxed silence, as close as they could be to each other.

The Philanthropist is a three-act play about a man who "loves" everybody and thereby loses the woman who had said she would marry him.

"It's perverse" was Shelagh's judgment. She stood talking to Adrienne at the bar in the lounge of the theater after the last curtain, having ordered Champagne for both of them. They would wait until the rest of the audience had left before trying to find a cab on the street.

"But it was amusing."

"I really don't think so. In fact, I can't imagine why this is considered a comedy."

"It makes you laugh."

Shelagh shrugged her shoulders. "—At the wrong things. The hero's a patsy. The most shocking things happen: a man's brains are blown out by accident—splattered on the wall in front of your eyes; horrendous stories of human abuses are told; stupid mistakes of behavior are made; the most vulgar language is used—all for the purpose of shocking, and no one in the play *feels* anything."

"That's why the audience thought it was funny."

They sipped the refreshingly chilled bubbly champagne.

"But it's actually tragic," Shelagh went on. "It's not that the hero loves everybody. He just doesn't want to hurt anyone's feelings. That's stronger than his desire not to have his own feelings hurt."

"He doesn't have any desire."

"So if you truly love others enough, you can't even take care of yourself."

Adrienne laughed a long chuckling sound before saying, "If you turn the other cheek, that will get slapped too."

"It's really appalling, the more I think of it. What we're shown is a man so refined . . ."

"Overcivilized."

". . . that consideration for everyone else takes precedence over consideration for himself. He doesn't have what it takes to defend his own best interests."

"He doesn't know what they are."

"But it's instinctual. And his instincts have been ground down. Pulverized." Shelagh growled in disbelief.

"Give me the Zulus with their happy killings," Adrienne said in agreement.

They finished their Champagne and left the glasses on the counter. The lounge was empty. They moved slowly toward the lobby. The street was wet but the rain had stopped.

"Well," Shelagh continued, "that's why I think the playwright had his head screwed on wrong. It's as if he took the story of *Macbeth* and played it for laughs: see how the three witches pulled the wool over his eyes; see how Lady Macbeth led him astray—Ha, ha! Watch the poor sucker suffer—Ha, ha! It would be wrongly experienced."

"But this play is a success. It's been running for nine months to full houses, and it won a prize. The author's done something right."

"So did King Midas."

146

Once they were seated in a taxi that began to drive away from the theater, Adrienne, putting an end to the conversation about the play, said, "You have to admit there were some amusing lines."

Shelagh turned to say, "Yes. Let it go at that." Momentarily, once again she sensed the oddly unpleasant odor. Adrienne was looking out the window.

As the cab drove into Upper Brook Street, Shelagh felt a chill that sent a long shiver down her left side, all the way from her face to her foot. It did not stop. It seized her and kept her shaking. She felt her cheek twitch, and her arm and leg quiver, faster and faster—out of control. Watching her left side spasm involuntarily, she thrust her right hand onto her left knee to hold it down. She felt light-headed, but her heart pounded furiously. Her mouth opened, gasping for breath. She saw her left arm convulsively waving before her eyes as if it belonged to someone else; the gold link bracelet she wore vibrated as if to escape from her wrist. It was then that she heard her own deep-throated moan and saw Adrienne turn her head back toward her. She read the horror of astonishment on her sister's face.

"What is it?" Adrienne demanded.

Shelagh could not speak.

"What's happening?!"

Shelagh's head was flung back against the high leather seat, pain squeezing her eyes shut tight, the convulsion at its height. Her right hand fell limply away from her left leg. Her left arm suddenly shot awry and her elbow struck Adrienne on the chin as she moved over to embrace her sister. Shelagh opened her eyes to see her fingers flagging before her face in a blur, the gold bracelet striking and flying away from her wrist. Adrienne, recovered from the jolt, slid next to her and grasped the quivering arm to hold it steady against her middle. Shelagh moaned again, suffering the twitches in the side of her face and down her neck even more intensely now. She felt herself sweating, and her eyes rolled back in her head. She was aware that she was urinating uncontrollably, and she wished she were dead.

The seizure stopped abruptly but two moments before the driver brought the cab to a halt at the address he'd been given. He turned around to discover one woman embracing the other and sneered disapproval. Adrienne snapped: "I'll need your help. She's ill. Do you understand?"

"Yes, madam."

Together they half-carried, half-led Shelagh out of the taxi and up the steps to the door.

Shelagh looked broken and ashamed, but whispered, "I can walk."

"Lean on me," Adrienne urged, after she'd unlocked the door.

"Excuse me, madam—the fare?"

.

Adrienne helped Shelagh undress and throw her soiled clothes into the hamper, while a warm bath ran into the tub. They spoke in subdued tones. "It couldn't have lasted more than three minutes, wouldn't you say?"

Shelagh said she had no awareness of how much time had passed; that nothing like it had ever happened to her before; that it was terrifying; that being helpless is what frightens the most; that she could not remember ever before in her life wishing she were dead.

Wearing Adrienne's warm bathrobe, Shelagh was propped up against an extra pillow and tucked into bed. Adrienne fetched them both tumblers of Scotch and soda, and then sat down at the foot of the bed facing her.

"You'll have to see a doctor, of course."

Adrienne had reacted immediately, instinctively, and compassionately, from the instant she saw what Shelagh was suffering in the taxi to the moment she took a sip of the whiskey. She had been practical, sympathetic, and helpful. But hearing the tone of her voice, when she told her sister that she must see a doctor, Shelagh recognized Adrienne to be distancing herself, to put the danger at arm's length. Adrienne was saying that this was Shelagh's problem, not hers. Adrienne had more than a dislike of any disease; she was repelled. Once she had fulfilled her obligation in such a situation, she allowed herself to recall her more common attitude of distaste. She had never nursed a child through so much as a sore throat.

Shelagh, who had no cause to believe herself a person who was sick, remembered Adrienne's quick statement to the taxi driver: "She's ill." And now she realized that Adrienne was recoiling from that discovery.

"Yes, naturally I'll see a doctor," she said as coolly as possible. "Is there someone you'd recommend?"

"Let me think about it and telephone some friends in the morning. I can pull strings." She stood up and looked about her study. "Perhaps I should leave the candle burning."

"Yes."

"Is there anything else you'd like? A hot-water bottle? A sleeping pill?"

"No, no. Don't trouble yourself. I'll be all right."

Adrienne kissed her on the forehead. "I'm terribly sorry, darling. I hope you sleep well. I'll bring tea at eight-thirty."

Meaning: as usual, Shelagh thought, as if everything will be restored to normal, everything will be its usual self, at its best. She was too exhausted to reply. She lay there with her eyes closed and heard Adrienne leave the room.

What if it happens again during the night? she wondered, recapturing the horror of the convulsion. What if she died during the night? Never to see Chester or Claire or Morgan again. She felt the warm tears run along the sides of her face.

She did not want to lie down in the darkness with the fear of death. Shelagh told herself that was melodramatic. It was not sudden death in her sleep that she believed would happen to her this night. For now it was only fear of another seizure, fear of helplessness, fear of ignorance, of not knowing what was happening. What causes convulsion?

Only once in her life, on a street in New York, had she ever seen anyone suffer an epileptic fit. Some years before, when a "pocket park" had been opened just east of Fifth Avenue, where the Stork Club used to be, Shelagh had gone to see it. She was standing before the gate looking in at the tables and chairs under the trees and listening to the waterfall that curtained the far wall of the oasis when she heard the slap of a briefcase falling onto the cement sidewalk near her. She turned to see that a middle-aged man in a dark business suit and a brown fedora standing next to the briefcase was shaking all over. His hat fell off. He staggered back against the corner of the building next to the little park, and quivered. Other people stopped in their tracks to look, but immobilized as if in fear of contagion. She covered her mouth with one hand, suppressing a scream, while she watched a fearless man approach the victim and put something between his teeth for him to bite on. There's almost always someone able to help, she recalled thinking at the time. There's almost always someone who knows what to do, and she turned her back and walked away from that unnerving incident.

Not all fits are epileptic. Doctors know how to control seizures nowadays, don't they? She would see a doctor. How soon? She opened her eyes to look at the clock on the desk. It was two o'clock in the morning. The candlelight glinted off the gold link bracelet lying next to the clock. She wiped her face dry with the edge of the sheet, thinking, I will never want to wear that bracelet again.

She was instantly aware that she had no desire to sleep, no wish to be unconscious: that consciousness was evidence of life. She knew she was alive because she could identify that desk, those mirrors, the olive-wood dresser from which the lace mantilla had been removed, this bed, the tawny candlelight upon the clear polish of her fingernails. She drew a sigh of relief. She was able to escape from self-consciousness into awareness of other things. Silently, to herself she gave the names of objects. This doorway, that closet, those shoes under the dresser, that silver candlestick, my wedding ring.

Shelagh fingered the plain platinum band on her left hand, remembering Chester. And then, wanting to feel worthy of him, equal to him, she was suddenly saddened by the recollection of the seizure—humiliated by it: not so fearful of the pain or the helplessness as she was of becoming an invalid, of becoming a charge for him to take care of, a burden, an object of pity. Her lips drew down toward her chin in her effort to keep silent, to keep from crying out. She felt herself grimace in the struggle to prevent a moan or a scream blurting out of her. Her body wanted to issue an agonizing sound, but she

149

willed the presence of mind to prevent it. She would rather choke on a howl than make any sound, rather gag than let it be known how fearful she felt.

What is it I'm afraid of? she asked herself. Adrienne is in the next room. I am at one of the great centers of civilization in the world. In ten or twelve hours I'll be in the hands of a medical doctor. I shall learn whatever the bad news is, and then the situation will be under control.

From somewhere in her mind came the simple information that death is never under control, can never be prevented. She was overwhelmed by the self-pity that followed the news that she too could die. It is the last prediction we are ever willing to confront. She had to admit she was not afraid of pain, of helplessness, of humiliation, or of being pitied as much as she feared believing she could die. Not then and there, alone in her sister's study in the middle of this night—but ever. Death happens to other people, but one believes one's own life is endless.

Shelagh could not remember, as long as she had been alive, ever experiencing what is called a "premonition" of death such as she felt at this moment. For it struck her that to cease to exist meant never to know what would become of Morgan and Claire. She sensed that she was fully formed, as were Chester and Adrienne. They had achieved themselves; they had come to be of as great value to others as was possible for them. But Claire and Morgan were still inchoate, nearly shapeless; they could go in any number of directions. Their stories had just begun. And for Shelagh to die—she felt clearly, with a longing that would be eternally unsatisfied—meant she would not know how their stories come out.

The long visit—more than three hours in all, not only in a doctor's consulting rooms but in a "medical center"—reassured Shelagh, even though it was inconclusive. Harold Sissgull's Bolivian lady had discovered the group of specialists who practiced together as "Associates-Limited" with offices in a very modern glass-and-brick building on Russell Square, and Adrienne indeed did pull strings so that Shelagh was given the red-carpet treatment starting at one-thirty the next afternoon.

The neurologist, Dr. Marjorie McNeill, had great natural talent for reassurance. She was beefy and cheerful in a long crisp white doctor's coat with a nosegay of colorful pens sticking out of her breast pocket. Her moon face was freckled, and the no-nonsense cut of her wavy copper-colored hair made her look burnished with competence. A woman of about forty, she had a professionally tactful and humanely sympathetic manner. Shelagh imagined Dr. McNeill must have been a nanny in an earlier incarnation, one who kisses the scrapes and bruises of her charges, takes them on her lap, and tells them "all will be well" with such certainty that the hurt evaporates instantly.

The furniture of the office was neat and unpretentious: a steel-and-chrome desk; firm, thinly upholstered armchairs; a plain examination table covered with a white paper sheet. Large motley-colored anatomy charts of a male and female were the only wall decorations. The wide windows gave onto the view of the chestnut trees in Russell Square.

The doctor asked questions as if they were simply to become acquainted socially. She appeared genuinely interested in why the American woman was visiting in London, wondering how she spent her days; asked her what her life at home was like; was surprised to learn how soon Shelagh intended to fly back to the States. Then she invited the patient to describe the seizure of the night before: all the details she could recall.

Dr. McNeill made notes. She asked for a general medical history. She took down Dr. Connolley's name and address. She could not say whether the pain in Shelagh's side, for which Dr. Connolley had examined her, was in any way related to the convulsion. "There are still medical mysteries," she admitted with a depreciating smile. In another room the doctor's male assistant took a chest X ray and then a blood specimen; a panel in the lavatory wall slid open and a hand removed the urine sample.

Back in Dr. McNeill's office, Shelagh was asked if she'd noticed any other odd symptoms. She wasn't aware of anything peculiar.

"Well, then, we shall have a neurological exam."

Shelagh shivered as if expecting her nerves to be exposed somehow.

"Oh, it's really quite simple," she was told. "Almost jolly—playful. Come. First let me see your gait." They stood up. The doctor watched Shelagh walk about the room; turn quickly; stand still with feet together, with her eyes closed, waiting until she was no longer swaying.

Shelagh then sat on the edge of the examining table, her toes barely touching the footstool. The doctor tested eye movements—"Follow my finger with your eyes." She checked visual fields—"Look at my nose and tell me when you see my finger wiggling as I bring it in from the side." She scanned Shelagh's retinas with a brilliant beam of light. She brought out a pocket watch and tested her hearing of the tick near and far. Clenched arms were pulled, raised knees were pushed, tendons at elbows, wrists, knees and ankles were tapped with a rubber-tipped mallet, and the soles of her feet were sharply stroked. As Shelagh sat with eyes closed, a safety pin was dropped into the palm of her right hand, a coin in the left, and she was asked to feel them and say what they were; fingers and toes were moved up and down, and she was asked to tell the direction. Is it possible some people can't do these things? she wondered. Could she feel the vibration of the tuning fork placed on her wrists and ankles? She was asked to protrude her tongue, hold her hands out steadily in front of her, touch her thumb to various fingers rapidly, say a few tongue-twisters; made to sniff from several aromatic vials. She was asked to smile. "I thought I *was* smiling," she replied.

"Now, lie down on the table. Comfortable? Place the heel of your right foot against the knee of your left leg. Yes. Now slowly slide the heel down the shin to your left foot. Fine. Now the opposite side. Oh, that's lovely. Do sit up again."

The doctor stood back and appraised her with a comforting smile. Casually, she asked, "By the way, did you sense any warning just before the seizure—any feeling that something was wrong?"

"Yes," Shelagh said vigorously. "A very odd smell."

"Metallic?"

"Yes. It lasted only a moment, but it was very strange. I noticed it once before. At a party the other night. No one else smelled it."

"An uncinate fit," the doctor said almost under her breath.

Shelagh snorted. "There's a technical term for that too?"

"Oh, yes. How long did it last at the party?"

"Fifteen minutes? Ten? I'm not sure. Does it matter?"

"I'm trying to find out what does matter. Did it ever occur earlier in life? *Any kind* of seizure? Even the distant past. Did your mother ever tell you of fainting spells? Was there ever a head injury? No . . . No . . . ?"

"Well, if you haven't found anything wrong with me—what caused the convulsions? And will they recur?"

Dr. McNeill resumed her seat at the other side of the desk, saying: "No. They can be controlled by medicine. We don't know yet what caused them, but I can prescribe a treatment that should prevent the seizure from occurring again."

"I'm very grateful for that." She sighed with relief.

Dr. McNeill wrote on a pad as she said to Shelagh, "You will have to take two tablets of phenobarbital at bedtime and one in the morning, as well as one capsule morning and night of phenytoin, which is called Dilantin in your country."

Shelagh's next sigh had the quality of a sob, for she recognized herself in some sense entering the status of invalid, one who must take preventive medicine every day. "For the rest of my life?"

"Possibly. But we have yet to learn more."

"Isn't phenobarbital lethal?"

Dr. McNeill looked up with surprise. "Taken in very large doses, yes; measured in grams. But this prescription is for thirty to sixty milligrams. No cause for worry. It won't do you any harm."

Something else is doing the harm, Shelagh thought.

"Now, how do we find out more?" Dr. McNeill asked, weaving her fingers together, resting her hands on the prescription pad. She is so straightforwardly businesslike, Shelagh thought with respect; of course, this is her business.

"In the old days—and they aren't very long since past—the next thing that would have been done to try discovering the cause of the two fits—"

"Two?"

"The convulsions and the uncinate fit."

"That metallic smell was a symptom too?"

"Yes. Very much so."

"It seemed merely an annoyance."

"But it gives a hint of the cause."

"You were saying—'in the old days . . .' "

"The next thing to do was a test called a 'lumbar puncture,' to see if there was an abnormality in the spinal fluid."

"But what would you be looking for?"

"Evidence of a lesion in the brain."

Startled, Shelagh felt her arms and legs chill with fear. She stiffened visibly. Very slowly she repeated the words: "A lesion in the brain. A break? A split?"

"No. 'Lesion' here means injury, any localized abnormality resulting in malfunction. The seizure and the bad smell are such effects."

"And the cause?"

"The main thing to be decided is whether the cause is something old and stationary, such as a scar from a head injury in the distant past, or something progressive."

"Oh God, when you say 'something progressive' do you mean cancer or a brain tumor?"

"Well, we are getting ahead of ourselves, are we not? Most of the time," Dr. McNeill continued reassuringly, "seizures come from something that never goes on to cause other kinds of difficulty. But we do need to make certain, and as I was about to say, we can do that more simply and precisely than in the past, and with no discomfort to the patient at all. Have you ever heard of a CAT scan?"

"No. Cat?"

"For the initials C, A, and T. They stand for computer-assisted-tomography." Warming to the subject, she assured Shelagh, "It is the most valuable technical advancement in medicine since the invention of the X ray. And it's painless. But you might feel warmth in your head for a little while. No surgery. Only an injection of contrast material."

Shelagh shivered.

"Let me describe it. You lie down with your head inside an opening rather like a short tunnel in a sealed square machine. You see nothing happen, you feel nothing. But inside the big box an X ray on a moving axis is taking pictures at the rate of one each second, and these images are translated by computer onto a cathode-ray screen. They can be kept on film or printed out. By moving around the brain at different angles it is possible to see pictures as three-dimensional. It won't take as much time as half an hour. And we'll know exactly what's going on."

Barely audibly, Shelagh asked, "How soon?"

"I'll see if the scanner is in use. For you, Mrs. Jackman, everything can be arranged quickly." She telephoned the neurological technicians, and smiled for Shelagh's benefit even before telling her that all would be readied.

"I mean—and *then* how soon will you know . . . whatever is found out?"

"Ah," Dr. McNeill considered. "I will consult with two other neurologists on the staff—Dr. Reed and Dr. Dyrud—within the next forty-eight hours. Would you be able to come back at this time two days from now?"

"Yes."

The CAT scanner made Shelagh think of the entrance to a bank vault, but without a great steel plug to fill the hole at the center with an elaborate combination to lock it. Rather her head would lie in that hole and the X-rays would decipher the combination in her brain that had brought about the two fits. Dr. McNeill had accompanied her in the elevator down three flights to the laboratory floor and then turned her over to a woman who led her to a dressing room and presented her with a paper dress and slippers.

Lying on a high stretcher, she was wheeled no more than a dozen yards from the dressing room into the presence of the scanner. From the corner of her eye, she saw Dr. McNeill through a window in the adjoining room, and behind her an array of twenty-first-century machinery. A male attendant adjusted the wheels so that the stretcher was aligned with the center of the opening in the scanning machine and then slid the moving narrow bed forward so that Shelagh's head lay in the middle of the opening. He placed a small white pillow that felt like a bean bag on either side of her head and asked her to remain still. Her eyes were open and she saw only the pale yellow metal arch above her head. If it should cave in, she wondered, how much does it weigh? I wouldn't be able to escape in time, would I? It would crush my face. "It won't cave in on me?" she asked the attendant.

"It can't, Mrs. Jackman," he replied with aplomb.

"Does everyone ask you that?"

"Some people do. It's natural. Don't be afraid."

"Afraid? No. I'm numb."

He smiled. "You won't feel a thing." He then left the room.

She did not feel a thing, or hear a thing, or smell a thing. She lay there immobile, her eyes closed, one hand resting on the other on her abdomen, feeling only the crinkliness of the paper dress and slippers—imagining herself the dead Cleopatra being prepared for mummification: they will wrap me, and wind me, and swaddle me in gauze and strips of linen, place me in an enameled coffin, and ship me back to New Haven, where even now a pyramid is under construction.

Shelagh ordinarily enjoyed solitude—the self-refreshing isolation of her work during the day, while she was alone in the house, or alone at a gallery or a museum; but she recognized this event as a unique experience, for while she lay isolated in this room, she was being watched through a window in the next room, and all the while a computer was sending electronic messages from inside the scanning machine to build up one picture after another of the inside of her skull on a screen before the eyes of people she had never met in her life. They will then learn something about my existence that I do not know. And with a profound wish for self-protection, she hoped that they would not tell her what they learned. I don't want to know, she said to herself like a willful child. And then laughed at herself, recognizing the most important fact: I am not a child.

I am, rather, all grown up. I shall pass the time by counting my blessings. I am healthy; I am happily married; I am the mother of two fine human beings; well, two potentially fine human beings; I am rich in friends and acquaintances; I do worthwhile work that is appreciated; I have both good looks and money; I affirm my fate. I am a European-American, and I am happy for that. I am not a Zulu or an Eskimo or a Trobriand Islander. Not that I am incapable of imagining what it would be like to live such a different life; but I am free of any desire to exchange my life for one of those. It is amusing to hear nowadays the new use of the word "lifestyle"—as if one could change the style of one's life as one changes her clothes. One's *lifestyle* is one's destiny. It is that which cannot be changed. Pity those who do not know it. Gradually, it is what becomes more and more true about each person. I wait to see it clear in Claire and Morgan. I already know my own. I know Chester's. It is what we cannot choose but to enact.

"Done!" announced the attendant. "Now, that wasn't bad at all, was it, Mrs. Jackman?"

No, that wasn't bad, but what will it lead to? Shelagh left the building of the medical center on Russell Square without any thought of where she should go. It was midafternoon, too early for tea; she had eaten nothing all day but felt no hunger. There were very few days left before she should be returning to the States, and she felt completely at loose ends: her life had been attacked—quite literally shaken. The prescriptions to prevent convulsions were in her handbag. She got into a taxi and went to the Boot's pharmacy near Oxford Circus and waited to have them filled; then she walked the few blocks from there to Adrienne's apartment.

Adrienne was both solicitous of me and pleased with her own part in arranging for the medical examination. We sat opposite each other—she on the small sofa, I in one of the armchairs—and I knew she would rather not hear any of the details. I didn't volunteer any. I had been delivered not only into the hands of competent doctors but into the care of experts. We drank the Scotch and soda she prepared and brought into the sitting room. "Merely a muscle spasm," I said to ease her mind. "Controlled by a 'relaxant.' I had the prescription filled a few hours ago." I wanted to say: You're free to forget all about it now. But I didn't go that far. "I'll see them again the day after tomorrow."

"Cutting it rather close," Adrienne said.

"I'll cable Chester, about getting back a day or two later than expected."

Adrienne nodded, indifferently acquiescent. "As for this evening, we don't have to go out, if you're not up to it."

"But you were looking forward to it. Why don't you go without me? Go with someone else."

"You don't mind?"

"Not at all."

We had had enough of each other.

After eight, when Adrienne left, I spent the evening alone in her flat in the luxury of silence. I had to keep suppressing the desire to pack up my things, take a cab to Heathrow, and get on the next plane leaving for New York. I wanted to hug Chester. I wanted to feel safe in his arms. A childish longing for escape and immediate gratification.

But I reminded myself for the second time yesterday that I am not a child. I must learn what the doctors think of my "pictures." Odd to realize that there are now images on film that show the contents of my skull, which I have not seen, and that will reveal something or other which I know nothing about.

I wandered through Adrienne's books, reading a passage here and there, trying to forget myself, trying not to worry. Drinking too much of the Scotch. Falling asleep early.

Last night I dreamed what I suppose should be considered the dream of a lifetime—if I put much store in dreams. It was a dream of golden peace; a dream of painless death. I was aware that I had said goodbye to everyone, without tears, even without sorrow. I had said farewell contentedly. Then I lay in a shallow pool of turquoise-blue water, like a rock pool on a Caribbean island. The water was soothingly tepid, the sunlight warm, the sky a cloudless, azure blue. All around the pool, tall palm trees and giant delicate ferns grew in Edenic profusion, fresh and firm and proud as in the first flush of the

Creation. I felt myself to be a Special Creation, as fully formed from the moment of birth as Athena was from the mind of Zeus. I understood that all this beauty came to me much more as a gift than as anything I had earned, yet something of both. This idyllic place existed and I was in it under the idea "providential." I had trouble with the word: it was provided; I was fortunate; this was the opportune time—all of these seemed implied.

And then that whole world, that dream world, dissolved into atoms of jewel-like splendor: emerald and sapphire, topaz and diamond—the blue sky and the palm fronds, the sunlight glinting off the surfaces of the pool, the ferns, as well as myself all were fragmented into their precious elements and suddenly scooped up anew into another arrangement: the whole scene was reconstituted, kaleidoscopically—the warm water, the glowing heaven, the flourishing flora, the body resting half-immersed in the pool, half-exposed to the balmy breeze. I knew that all the elements had been interchanged. It was no longer possible to separate myself from the tree or the rocks or the ferns or the blue sky or the soothing water. They and I were in and of each other; we were each other. We were at peace, for as if then as never before, we saw that we were each other.

I drifted and glided all morning in the comforting aftereffect of that dream—letting time pass, needing a day, and then half of another day, before I would know "the verdict," but calmed by the dream, awaiting it with a kind of equanimity in a nearly hypnotic doze of cosmic reassurance that all things sustain each other, interpenetrate each other, are transformed into each other. And then the telephone rang.

"Shelagh? Is that you?"

"Yes." I didn't recognize the voice.

"This is Evelyn Knops. I'm at the restaurant. I've been here since noon. It's twelve-thirty."

"What?"

"Aren't you coming? Why are you still at Adrienne's?"

"But—I completely forgot."

There was a pause; then: "You forgot our appointment?"

"Yes. I'm so sorry. You see—"

"You forgot about me."

"No. It's just that—"

"I'm forgettable."

". . . Evelyn, listen. I had a—an accident. . . ."

"No. Don't make up lies! I can't stand lies. You just forgot about me. That's bad enough."

"But that isn't what happened." I felt my face burning with embarrassment.

Evelyn said, "Don't get in touch with me again."

"You don't understand."

"I don't want to 'understand,' " she mimicked. "You can just go to hell!"
And then she slammed down the phone hard.

I have failed her. I had wanted to do her some good—but not strongly
enough to remember about her in the midst of worrying over myself. So I
have earned her curse.

By God, the world is full of other people . . . but I have no time (no heart)
for them right now. Well, then, she can go to hell too.

I must get through the afternoon, get through the day, Shelagh told herself—dressing in the new leather skirt and boots, the new sand-colored
blouse, throwing Adrienne's white Moroccan cape over her shoulders and
planning to stride out of the flat—to walk somewhere, anywhere. In New
Haven she would have walked to the Green and back, picked up a jar of *mar-*
rons glacé's at Henri's, bought a new novel at the Co-op. In London, she
found herself homing toward Trafalgar Square, knowing she would come to
rest in the National Gallery.

Yet it was not restful. There were too many people, to begin with: tourists,
students, art "lovers." There were too many rooms, too many pictures, too
many floors. It struck her, as never before, that the museum constituted a
shameless glut, an ostentatious excess of riches—an endless smorgasbord for
the variegated tastes of millions, the citizenry of the world, "open to the public." She had no need for the vast majority of the paintings and absolutely no
need for the presence of all the other people in the building. What are they
doing here, she thought, when I want to be alone? Striding from one familiar
room to the next, she rejected the Italians from Pisanello to Bellini. Their
sanctimoniousness bored her: their visions of holiness—whether fierce drag-
ons or pious prettiness. "Commissions," she said under her breath, contemp-
tuously. With Correggio and Titian, they became fleshy, sensuous—the
motifs of antiquity gave them license to become titillating; Tintoretto obscene; Veronese pornographic.

The endless Flemish and Dutch portraits of uncertainty or self-satisfaction,
which once had exalted her as images of eternal truth, now settled like the
smell of low tide on her soul, as fatuous as the bland landscapes of Holland.
With Rubens, the motifs of antiquity gave license to become obscene. Only
the Vermeers coupled sensuousness with dignity.

The Germans' pictures were unspeakable.

She hurried on to the French collections. But stopped short, suddenly
aware that she knew them all—the French, the Spanish, the English paintings; was as familiar with them as she was with relatives or family friends
since her childhood—and she didn't want to see any of them again. She

knew them as well as she could—as well as she knew Adrienne. What she wanted was a mystery: something to ponder with uncertainty; something to meditate on.

She came to rest, seated on a bench before Bronzino's *Allegory of Time and Love.*

Here is a genuine painting, Shelagh thought: not a window onto the Dutch landscape or a keyhole view into someone's bedroom. This never existed anywhere else in the world, in any way. This is an imaginative vision. Bronzino's meditative vision: a supreme make-believe. Within the frame, the figures themselves frame the central view of Venus and Cupid embracing. The long, powerful arm of Time and the strong hands of Truth that hold back a blue veil place a limit to the top of the scene; the horizontal naked legs of Venus, with one foot against the masks of an old man and a young woman, draw the limit to the bottom of the scene. Naked Venus, the mature, worldly, glamorous goddess of love, is embraced by Cupid, a naked youth with golden-red curls, one hand upon one breast of Venus, the other hand against the back of her head, against her hair entwined with strings of pearls: their lips touching—no, just about to touch. They might yield to each other, but that is not their destiny, not their role. Cupid is the servant of Venus, not her lover. She may incite him with the implications of license, but she will not deliver on the false promise. She holds a golden apple in one hand and an arrow in the other. She originates the dangers of love and controls the rewards. Behind Cupid the face of Jealousy is contorted by miserable suffering; she tears her hair. Behind Venus stands first Pleasure, a naked child, hands filled with rose petals, smiling, ready to pelt the mutually adoring pair with the fragrances of joy, and behind him lurks Deceit, sweet-faced, with the body of a gryphon, offering a honeycomb in one hand while holding in her other the end of her tail, which has a sting in it. The pretty-boy Pleasure is but an even more youthful Cupid, to the symmetry of the curly blond hair. And Deceit is a more withdrawn, plainer version of Venus, full-faced rather than in profile, with a simpler strand of pearls in her hair.

Shelagh had always felt the *Allegory* to be mysterious, elusive, and singularly sexless despite all the naked flesh and the provocative pose. But it had never struck her before that the childlike smile of Pleasure was unselfconsciously simpleminded, blatantly naive; and that the face of Deceit was a slight variation on the face of Venus herself: without maturity or glamour. There were the feathered wing of Time and the wing of Cupid and the winged dove in the left corner below Cupid's foot. Everything was captured in an instant of motion but for the stationary masks, which any one of them might pick up at any moment. *Time* and *Love*, Shelagh thought. Love and Time. Life and Death. I wish I could understand it. If I owned it, possessed it, lived with it day in and day out, perhaps its meaning would be illuminated for me. Idle thought. It is now public property. Cosimo the First, Grand Duke of Tuscany, who commissioned it of the chief portrait painter of the Medicean court, gave it as a gift to the King of France four hundred years ago; and now it is available to the world: so that no one has it long enough to comprehend it. Glorious mystery. Those *almost*-kissing lips without intimacy; the agony of Jealousy; the mindlessly bright-eyed, smiling childishness of Pleasure; the insistently hovering, complex, nearly central figure of Deceit.

Shelagh got up from the black-cushioned bench on which she was sitting; but just before leaving the gallery, on a last-minute whim, she moved slowly toward the painting as if coming within three feet of the surface she might discover why the alabaster whiteness of all that naked flesh left her cold, why it seemed more like a Laocoön of marble sculpture than like the living flesh of any breast or shoulder in a Renoir. She was shocked by the discovery that only at very close range could be seen Venus' tongue licking into Cupid's mouth. So it was a dirty picture after all. An erotic stimulant; cryptopornography. The gift of one horny fellow to another. And the King of France could display it in a royal chamber of stately proportions with the assumption that he alone would be likely to stand within three feet of it, and no one else could see what he saw there. The secret French kiss in that otherwise chaste tableau of Mannerist symbolism was as unexpected and obscene as being groped under the table by the man sitting next to you, in the ignorance of everyone else, at a dinner party.

❧

She was punctual for the consultation with the medical doctors, but Shelagh was kept waiting for half an hour. She stared out the window at the chestnut trees in Russell Square; uneasily she readjusted her velvet suit, she checked her wristwatch. She was alone in the waiting room, but decided not to smoke a cigarette nevertheless. They would call for her soon enough. She calmed herself.

Ushered into Dr. McNeill's office to find her standing upright behind her desk alongside Dr. Reed, whom she introduced in simple formal terms, Shelagh sensed instantly that only bad news could follow. She looked from one to the other of their solemn faces, feeling called upon to put them at ease. "In the world I live in," she said, "there is only one message that is always expected, namely: everything is going to be all right."

"What world is that, Mrs. Jackman?" Dr. Reed asked in a flat-footed way.

"The world of the safe and sound," she answered. "But you have a different message for me today, haven't you?" She felt as if she might have to pry it out of them.

160

Dr. McNeill gestured to the chair on the other side of her desk; Shelagh sat down, and then the two doctors took seats opposite her. On the desk between them lay the results of the CAT scan—the images and the analyses: the "evidence." Dr. Reed wore the same kind of white jacket as his colleague; he peered at her through steel-rimmed glasses. He was clean-shaven and balding. His nose was long and strong, reminding her of Chester, which she took heart in. He was younger than Chester, though, and stroked his chin nervously. Dr. McNeill was self-possessed. She spoke clearly and firmly. "It's a terrible pity that your husband isn't here with you. Is there any chance he'll join you before you leave?"

"No."

"And Mrs. Jackman, you're departing almost immediately?" Dr. Reed asked.

"Yes."

"Perhaps," he suggested, "we might communicate with Judge Jackman." He looked at a pad with notes on his lap. "Or with your sister, Miss Markgraf."

Shelagh had the distinct impression that the doctors were trying to protect themselves as well as her. Were they afraid of making a mistake? "Is what you have to tell me," she asked, "so dreadful that I mustn't hear it by myself?"

Dr. Reed answered, "It would be preferable if we could talk with your husband first."

Yes, Shelagh felt, I would be much happier to have him with me here, in a moment of panic which she struggled to suppress; oh, how I wish I were wrapped up in the safety of Chester's presence! But what she forced herself to say was "I think it is offensive—patronizing of you—to treat me as a child."

Dr. McNeill folded her hands together on the desk and responded to that graciously: "You are right, Mrs. Jackman. We must be straightforward. Yours is a very serious situation."

Dr. Reed interrupted. "You may have to be under the care of a neurologist for an indefinite period of time."

Shelagh remained calm. "Yes."

Dr. McNeill said, "There is an abnormality in the brain . . ."

"What kind?" Shelagh asked.

"A glioma. Localized in one lobe. A silent lesion in the right temporal lobe." Dr. Reed raised one of the computer pictures to show her.

"Why 'silent'?" Shelagh asked with a smile, knowing that all the technical terms were incomprehensible to her.

"It does not ordinarily affect the motor—muscular—or sensory nervous system. That's why it has advanced to this extent without there having been a seizure before."

Only then did she look at the X-ray–like image he held up for her. A thick gray spot appeared in the lower-left quarter of the walnut-shaped skull frame.

"That is my 'lesion,' " she started, still thinking of it impersonally as if they were speaking of someone else, or of an item she *might* want to buy or decide to turn down.

"As seen from one angle," Dr. Reed supplied. "Now, with this sequence of impressions you can see it from all four directions." He was taking refuge in "data." Slowly she looked at one image after another. She did so quietly, objectively. She felt no pain, and therefore she did not know to what degree she should feel endangered.

She broke the silence to ask: "Is it destroying something?"

Dr. Reed said, "Well, not exactly." He looked to Dr. McNeill and then continued. "It is displacing other structures."

"And will it get worse?"

"It will cause increasing local pressure. . . ."

"I'm about to go home. Could it be dangerous for me to travel?"

"Not at all."

It struck Shelagh that her question about the risk of travel was disproportionally trivial. The doctors were indirectly, vaguely trying to tell her something infinitely more important.

"Just a moment. I feel a little faint. May I have a glass of water?"

"Of course."

Her face and neck were clammy with cold sweat. Her body had learned something fearful before her mind had comprehended it. She got a grip on herself. If she must infer the consequence of what the doctors were implying, she must do so one step at a time. "That is a tumor," she began—pointing to the picture, not to her head. "Isn't it?"

"Yes."

"Can it be removed?"

Dr. McNeill replied, "It would be extremely dangerous to attempt that."

"And it cannot be arrested? Halted? Treated in any way?"

One doctor looked at the other. "No. It cannot," Dr. Reed admitted.

"Why not?" Shelagh demanded. She felt fearless. She had survived the bombing of Britain, she had survived the delivery of two children, she knew herself to be strong. She could recover.

"Because it is too deep in the substance of the brain itself." Dr. Reed was now tutorial. "Such tumors expand at different rates, and they may be external to the substance of the brain or embedded in it. It used to be much more difficult to find out. A biopsy used to be made to learn if the growth was dense or loose, and to try to find out the rate of growth. But now, all that is perfectly clear. These results are not 'educated guesses'; the scanning determines all those unknowns."

Dr. McNeill summarized: "Dense. Embedded. Rapid growth."

Shelagh asked: "You are certain that it cannot be removed by surgery?"

Dr. Reed deferred to Dr. McNeill, who haltingly explained: "When a tumor is that deep into the substance of the brain itself, surgery is a very risky procedure. If it fails—the patient dies. Even if it succeeds—that is, *even if* the surgeon is able to get *all* of it out, which is highly questionable—there is a terrible price to pay: paralysis, blindness, or speechlessness. But the chance of such success is fantastically slim."

Shelagh echoed, disbelievingly: " 'Such success.' "

"I deeply regret having to tell you this, Mrs. Jackman."

"Do not be distressed, Dr. McNeill. Are you familiar with Bronzino's *Allegory of Time and Love* at the National Gallery? I went back to see it only yesterday. Would you believe that of all the figures in it, like Love and Time, Jealousy, Pleasure, Deceit—only Truth shows no emotion."

The doctors regarded her self-possession with amazement.

Compassionately, Dr. Reed said, "This must be terrible for you to learn."

"But what am I to learn?" Still feeling as if they were talking about someone else, she asked, "That I must die of it?" and in the same instant Shelagh saw not herself but Adrienne fall off the balcony of her flat and disappear into thin air.

Neither of them responded immediately.

Shelagh continued. "Forgive me, but I am trying to make sure of what is going on. We are seated here in this room on this overcast cool day in October, in the presence of the images your CAT scanner delivers to you, and on the basis of your reading them, you want me to believe that something terrible has happened to me and that nothing can be done about it."

There was no reply.

Shelagh asked, "Is that right? Am I doomed to die of it?"

Dr. McNeill said, "That is the eventuality."

"When? How soon?" Shelagh demanded.

"That's very difficult to say."

"But possible? I insist."

They caught each other's eye and then, in the same instant that Dr. Reed said, "Six months," Dr. McNeill said, "Nine months."

Shelagh asked: "One year?"

"No"—Dr. Reed shook his head sadly—"the rate of expansion is too rapid in this case. By my calculations, six to nine months would be the maximum . . ."

Shelagh had to complete the thought ". . . amount of time that I have left."

"Yes."

While part of her spirit wished to rush to the window and hurl herself out onto the pavement below, the rest of her remained in a sense perversely calm, self-controlled enough to ask, "And how will it happen? How will this thing kill me?"

Dr. McNeill began very slowly: "There may come a time when the pheno-barbital and the Dilantin will no longer be able to prevent seizures. Some weakness may develop in your left limbs, so that you will not be able to hold things firmly in your left hand. A teacup and saucer, for instance, might tend to rattle in your hand."

"My drawing pencils and my colors. I will no longer be able to hold them. No longer make them do what I want." She thought of crippled Renoir with the paintbrush strapped to his wrist.

Dr. Reed continued: "And then your field of vision may be constricted. It will be gradual, but you will become aware of a narrowing—from the left side." He held up his left hand as a blinder and moved it gradually inward toward his nose.

Dr. McNeill said, "You may come to have difficulty with spatial relations—such as an uncertainty whether to turn left or right. You might not have your usual powers of concentration."

It was then that Shelagh felt the tears well in her eyes.

"Why has this happened?" she asked. "To me?"

One doctor looked at the other. Dr. McNeill volunteered, with the tone of apology, "What causes cancer is not known. But it is not personal to you," she reassured her.

"My death will be," Shelagh replied.

<hr/>

How or when she left the medical center she could not recall with certainty later on. She remembered her tears and the readily offered box of oversized Kleenex; that the disposable paper handkerchiefs were "giant-sized" for giant grief and immediately available—prepared in advance—put some things in perspective for her. She was not the first to hear such news. This was not the first time those doctors had had to convey such news. The situation was not unique; there was a method for carrying it out. The handy Kleenex was part of the routine. She controlled herself.

She asked to see the pictures again. Then she said, "You have no doubt about what you've told me." It was meant to be a question but came out as a conclusion.

"There is the highest probability . . . " Dr. Reed conceded.

Dr. McNeill suggested, "You might want to have these findings confirmed . . ."

"In my own country . . . ?"

"Yes."

"I suppose I should."

"You're being very brave." This was Dr. Reed's comment.

"No," Shelagh said softly. "I should very much like to run screaming through the streets, blasting out 'God damn it! God damn it to hell!' . . . but I probably won't. Not brave . . . incredulous."

"Of course," Dr. McNeill reassured her.

When she regained consciousness of where she was, Shelagh found herself on a wooden bench in front of the British Museum. She must have walked the few blocks from Russell Square to where she found herself now, but she was unaware of having done so; she must have passed through some minutes of such blinding rage or terror that her memory refused to admit them.

How could she live with such news that she would be dead in six to nine months?

Of course, it might be preposterous. Those could have been the pictures of someone else's brain.

She *felt well.* That made it easy to disbelieve.

She felt resentment at being unfairly treated. *If* it is true, it is completely unfair: the prediction of an *untimely* death. But then, is a *timely* death so much easier to accept?

She thought of the doctors rather than of herself. McNeill and Reed. Professionals diagnose. Prognosticate. Inform. Two medical experts have read me a sentence of death. What can they feel? Both so apparently healthy. Shelagh groped for an analogy. In *Out of Africa*, Isak Dinesen's lyrical memoir of life on a coffee plantation in British East Africa, she described how she taught French cuisine to one of her native black servants. He came to master soufflés and éclairs and other French delicacies, despite the fact that he had no taste for them, had never eaten anything like such food in his life. Actually, he spurned them, but he re-created those dishes in his kitchen to the satisfaction of the Danish Baroness and the joy of her English guests. His name was Kamante.

Doctors McNeill and Reed were like Kamante. They had never been told of having a tumor growing intractably—irreversible and irremediable—in their brains. Yet they could relay such information to Shelagh. They had "no taste" for it themselves—no idea how it tasted!—and yet they could carry out their roles as messengers. An imperfect analogy.

Must she tell Adrienne? But it was not to be believed. Must she tell anyone? She was about to go home. . . .

Shelagh looked up at the classical columns of the stone facade of the British Museum, thinking: Both of us have survived the bombing of Britain—and the delivery of my two children—and you are one of the greatest repositories of knowledge and wisdom in the world. Or what has passed for knowledge and served as wisdom across the eons and around the globe. How will you help me now? I shall never learn anything more than I know at this moment. I'm too old. But I'm a repository like you. And out of the vast collection, I'll be able to choose something to make use of.

"*Poor* Shelagh!"

She half-bounded up from the bench to see who had said that, before realizing it was a voice within her own mind. She slumped back into her sitting position and echoed the thought: Poor Shelagh. It is all to come to an end, if I am to believe the doctors. Come to an end—soon. Am I to believe them? Or do I return to the States and go through the exercise again—pretending I am in New York to serve some other purpose, while my head is being scanned again. Returning from another "consultation," to have the American counterparts of McNeill and Reed—probably O'Connor and Goldblatt—tell me the same sad tale: irremediable. It cannot be cured, cannot even be arrested. It is fatal.

If Morgan has joined the Church, she wondered, should I ask him to pray for me? It was a flippant thought. She did not believe in the efficacy of prayer. Even if she did, what would she ask him to beseech God for: a postponement? eternal life? rebirth? She believed in neither an eternal return nor a resurrection. Death was the end, with nothing beyond it to hope for or to fear. Only dying was fearful, painful; but it must be endured. Not God but doctors made it less painful.

She thought of the death of her grandmother: the only person she had actually seen die. Her father's mother, who died shortly after the family emigrated from Austria to England. A small, very old woman, over eighty, she remembered, a lady of dignity and strength as well as charm. She saw her against two large pillows in bed, waxen-pale, tired, but clear-headed. She gave Shelagh her blessing; she wished her a long and happy life. Shelagh kissed her on the forehead, aware that her lips touched a film of cool sweat. Her mother and father stood behind her alongside the bed. She heard the death rattle—the slow filling up of the lungs—like a gurgling for breath in her grandmother's chest and looked startled into the old lady's eyes. In the most gently consoling manner possible, her grandmother said, "It won't be long now. . . ."

At this moment, Shelagh could not recall whether that conversation had taken place in German or in English. Her grandmother died and the world went on without her in it. That was what death meant to others: we continue; you do not. Neither the fear of a painful dying nor the future blankness of extinction was credible to Shelagh. But if the doctors were right, within a year she would no longer exist. The world would go on without her in it. *That* is possible, she realized. In imagining the lives of others going on without her, anticipating that the world would continue without her in it, she received the meaning of the doctors' message. She was going to die. With her eyes closed, she threw up.

Just as the need to vomit was irrepressible and instantaneous, so was her doubling-up movement over the edge to her left side, her hands pressed flat on the surface of the bench. Her stomach emptied a pale coral puddle onto the surface of the chipped gray stones and black asphalt of the macadam. She let out a moan.

"May I help you, madam?"

She looked up to see a large, elderly uniformed and helmeted policeman standing in front of her. No one else approached or embarrassed her by appearing to have noticed what had happened or stopped to express curiosity.

She took her hand away from covering her mouth to say, "What a shame. I'm frightfully ashamed."

"Think nothing of it. It'll be taken care of."

"I've made such a nuisance of myself."

"Not at all, madam." He made it sound like an everyday occurrence.

He lifted her handbag up from the pavement where it had fallen before her feet and handed it to her. She took out a handkerchief, dabbed it about her face, and pressed it to her lips. As if in answer to a request she had not yet made, another police officer—or a museum guard—appeared with a paper cup full of water.

"How good of you!" Shelagh said gratefully, and then began to sip the drink.

"You're ill?" the first policeman asked.

"Is it that obvious?"

"Your complexion is a shade peculiar."

"Oh? Yes, I suppose it would be." She took a deep breath. "But I'm feeling better now."

"Is there anything I can do? Get you a taxi?"

"You've been very kind. Yes. I'd like that."

Shelagh stood up and pulled herself together. If she had been alone in a private room anywhere, she would have let herself scream with tears pouring down her face, would have pounded her fists against a pillow and wailed; but she had vomited in a public place and wanted to be composed now. A taxi drew in through one of the gates, the black-speared and golden-tipped fence and gates, of the British Museum and halted just before where she stood. The elderly policeman got out and held the car door open for her. It was like leaving a well-run hotel. Shelagh thought of giving him a tip, but that would have been improper. She simply thanked him again and did not look back at the mess she had made. Then the taxi turned and drove out through the other gate.

She told the driver to take her to the corner of Bond Street and Brook

Street, from where she walked toward Adrienne's flat with the slow pace of the overburdened. What would she tell Adrienne?

When, across the street from Claridge's, she saw flowers in the windows of their florist shop, she waited for the traffic to stop so that she could cross the street. Inside the flower store she asked whether they had a telephone book and if they could find an address for Miss Evelyn Knops, which a saleswoman did with dispatch. She then chose a wicker basket with a bouquet of straw flowers to be sent with a card that read:

EVELYN:

PEACE . . .

SHELAGH

The incident filled her with purpose. Giving a rationale to what she had done instinctively, as she walked out of the store, she said to herself, That is what I have time left to do: to make peace.

She had not walked half a block past the hotel to the corner, half the way from the florist's to Adrienne's, when she felt illuminated as by a revelation. Standing still, waiting for the light to change, she said to herself: I have been given the answer to the question that everyone must ask and almost no one ever learns: *When am I going to die?* We imagine that if we knew, we would transform ourselves: misers would become spendthrifts, virgins voluptuaries, workhorses beachcombers. What do we *not* think—if we knew how little time we had left—we would make of ourselves: heroic, virtuous, or happy, or irresponsible; we would become in the days of that last chance what we are not, now, but have always dreamed of being, once we abandoned all hope of living forever. I am one of the few who know when they are going to die. She felt herself smiling, relieved, freed. Free of what? Of endlessness. She actually believed that her life would come to an end, that she knew it would be six, nine, or twelve months from this day. And that promised somehow to glorify the time she had left. But how?

What should she tell Adrienne? A lesion in the silent area of the brain. That wiped the smile off her face. The light changed and she walked along Brook Street to her sister's home.

She climbed the stairs, unlocked the door, placed the keys next to her handbag on the narrow table in the foyer, thinking, From now on, must I calculate the end of each repeated action? Must I say to myself, "This is the last time I will use those keys"? "The next-to-last time I will climb those stairs"? "The second-from-the-last time I shall see Adrienne"? Will that

168

heighten the experience—and console—or only increase self-pity? She knew none of the answers.

Shelagh made a cup of tea and carried it from the kitchen into the sitting room. From the armchair in which she was seated, she looked out in the graying twilight to the balcony from which she'd imagined her sister—not herself—falling away and disappearing. That was what she had to look forward to: disappearing. It was the universal fate, the end of each destiny— and still, inconceivable. She got up out of the chair and straightened the frames of Great-aunt Greta's watercolors of Greece. While we live, she thought, we must regain balance; no matter how severe the blow that knocks us off-balance, without getting back on an even keel—what then?—we'd topple off the balcony. How am I to regain my balance now?

My body has betrayed me. The cause of my death is growing in my brain, inside my skull. I neither see it nor feel it. No one in the world but McNeill and Reed and I know about it. Its effect on the rest of my body can be controlled. My body can perform all its functions as if I were entirely healthy, and yet I'm told it is for a specifically limited period of time. My body, the stranger, is now the enemy of my length of time.

What claim does anyone have on me to share that information?

She shivered, drank more of the warm tea, got up and walked around the rooms, coming to rest at the desk in Adrienne's study, the guest room. She sat in the desk chair at just the right angle to see the reflection of her face in the dozens of mirrors tilted toward her: her face repeated again and again as on each facet of a huge diamond. It made her feel the reassurance of the familiar; there was nothing with which she was more familiar than her own face, and yet she could never see it too many times. It calmed her. It made her feel that nothing was changed, that no one could *see* anything different. And if it was *not* obvious, then why should it be made known?

She would not tell Adrienne that anything was wrong. The many mirrored reflections of her face urged her to keep that resolve. There was nothing good to be gained by telling her sister. There was everything to be lost. She would become an object of pity—that self-abusing emotion, for it takes your sorrow to the point of frustration in knowing there is nothing you can do and then throws the sorrow back on yourself. Because you can no longer act effectively with or for the other person, your feelings change from compassion toward the person who is the object of your pity to feeling that the person has become an object: it cannot be influenced, cannot be affected—it must live out its time now on an unalterable course. I will not let myself become an object of pity! Shelagh said to herself; all those reflections of her face in the mirrors before her confirmed her determination to protect her feeling that she must be treated as a person and not as an object.

It was not that she would mislead anyone by saying anything dishonest, but she would not reveal anything about the doctors' truth. What she would lose in genuine intimacy, sympathy, compassion, the shared grief, the sad support, she would gain by protecting her sense of being fully alive. Even in that instant of determination she knew it was impossible to separate self-protection from self-serving; it could not be carried off without some degree of deceit.

That thought brought back to her mind Bronzino's Venus and Cupid embracing and the nearby presence of Deceit as a pale, smaller version of Venus herself. The face of Deceit: those self-absorbed eyes, the self-concerned face, and the complex, cunning figure. It was the word "cunning" that made Shelagh think of Eve and the serpent in the Garden of Eden. What could the animal have looked like before it was cursed? *How* was it the most cunning of the beasts? By being a paler, smaller version of Eve herself. If Eve knew what her own face looked like, would she not trust, more than anyone else, the creature who looked most like her?

Shelagh reveled in the thought: as baroque a conceit as Adrienne's arrangement of all those mirrors so that she could see herself again and again. What the serpent looked like before it was cursed—was Eve.

❧❧❧

DIARY ENTRY

Given the verdict of the doctors here, and given my sense of self-protection, I have just perpetrated an act of deception: the pretense that all is well.

I had bathed and dressed for the evening before Adrienne's return. The first words out of her mouth were "Did you learn the results of the tests? What does the doctor say?"

"Nothing serious," I lied. "Just something I'll have to live with." I liked that!

"I'm glad."

"Adrienne, will you promise to do a favor for me?"

"Certainly."

"Would you never mention the seizure, or my visits to the medical center—to anyone, please."

"Of course, I won't tell a soul." It was not that she was easily sworn to discretion; her tone implied it was beneath her dignity to talk about someone else's health.

"Then let us forget all about it and have an enjoyable 'Last Supper' together."

"Last?"

"You forget: I'm leaving tomorrow."

"Yes. We'll have a good time."

Adrienne is now changing in her bedroom.

It was as easy as that, not to offer the information, not to blurt out the truth. And now she won't even send a "sisterly" note of concern to Chester or say anything to Claire or Morgan. I must keep them all from knowing as long as possible.

How else could we have "a good time"?

For dinner on that last night of this visit to London, Shelagh had booked a table at the Savoy.

Their taxi drove up to the entrance of the hotel, and when they'd stepped out of it, Shelagh turned to watch the cab go around on the circle in that cul-de-sac in order to drive back out to the main street.

"You know," she confided to her sister, "when I was about fifteen, I thought this circle must be the hub of the universe."

"Where do you think it is now?"

She laughed. "Wherever I happen to be."

In the softly lit, handsome dining room, their table was on the first level raised above the central dance floor. The orchestra played fox-trots of the nineteen-thirties. Shelagh ran her fingertips along the surface of the pink tablecloth, regarded the white rose in the bud vase at the middle of the table, touched the heavy silverware, fondled the crystal water glass. "It's like entering a living fossil. So unchanged from our childhood. Isn't it amazing? Look at that couple dancing there: the short bald man, and the tall woman with the henna-colored hair up in a pompadour—those smooth, neat ballroom-dancing steps; look at her chiffon dress, the pattern of lavender wisteria flowers on a brown background. My God, it's 1937. Nothing's changed. You can believe they've danced here together, just like that, wearing those very clothes, every night for the past forty years."

Their cocktails had arrived. Adrienne proposed the toast: "To preservation."

"Hear, hear." She sipped her Russian vodka and then began, "On the other hand, I had a bad time about preservation at the National Gallery."

"One of the curators try to put you on display?"

"No. I became increasingly angry about the fact that to preserve things—the paintings and the sculpture—and exhibit them to the public is to take them out of circulation. They become impersonal. No one can ever own them again. That gives even the smallest portrait or the most imitative icon a monumentality that it doesn't deserve."

"I *never* liked museums."

"It makes them public monuments, rather than private pleasures. Without a human, useful context. The portrait was painted so that a family could remember what Pietro looked like at twenty-one; and the icon was to be prayed before in the privacy of one's bedroom. But a museum 'collection' is without a collector—there's no need of any living human's being satisfied by keeping them together there like that, cheek by jowl: out of use. Not in the real world they were made for."

"On the shelf, so to speak."

"Yes. I would make a terrible Communist; I can't even imagine sharing everything. I think I shall come to hate museums."

"That would be quite a switch—considering how you and Father—"

"—always haunted them? Yes. That's true. I'm grateful for what I'd never have seen otherwise. But this overwhelming effect—after a lifetime of 'brief encounters'—is that if I can't have it, I don't want it."

"Very odd, coming from you."

"I surprise myself."

"My own complaint against museums is more metaphysical." Adrienne smiled coyly to deprecate in advance a possible plunge into pomposity, but she continued: "They mislead people into thinking that some things can last forever. A silver cup from the tomb of Alexander, two thousand years old, is a travesty against nature. Nothing in nature remains—or remains unchanged—for that long."

"Yes . . ." Shelagh meditated. "Hugh mentioned how you identify what's natural with change."

"Oh. Did he?"

"But with a warm understanding. He's very admiring of you."

"He has good taste."

That made both of them chuckle.

Then Adrienne said, seriously, "It's important to know that nothing lasts forever."

Shelagh took a great swelling of breath into her lungs, as a barrier against tears that threatened to fill her eyes, and swallowed hard. She forced herself to smile and to say, "Even this dinner," raising the menu from her lap. "We'll have to order. You are my guest."

The musicians left the stage for intermission; couples returned to their tables from the dance floor; a waiter took their orders.

Suddenly Shelagh said, "I'm eager to get back to work—illustrating the Old Testament. I have a new idea to try out."

She saw the face of Deceit in the shadow behind Bronzino's Venus, the myriad reflections of her own face on the mirrored wall in Adrienne's study—the face of her need to protect her pride—and thought of her scheme to represent the serpent as a younger, paler, self-absorbed Eve in the Garden of Eden: remembering that her drawing of Eve looked like Claire and, therefore, somewhat like Adrienne.

"I can't imagine rereading the Bible." Adrienne laughed. "It would be like reliving my childhood. Who could go through that again?"

"But for centuries it was the only book that anyone read, so people saw how they changed as the stories meant different things to them at different times of their lives. Nobody rereads anything these days; they don't know how they've changed. . . ."

"But the Bible's so gory—like the Iliad: full of barbaric violence."

"And heroism."

"Happy killings . . ."

"I'll never forget *Macbeth* in Zulu."

"You have had a pleasant visit, haven't you?"

Shelagh ran through her clotted feelings for a moment before smiling the reply "As your friend Sissgull would say: there are at least two points of view on any topic."

"Oh, at least. But you have enjoyed yourself, haven't you?"

Shelagh sensed that her sister wanted praise as a hostess, needed gratitude to bring the visit to completion, to round out the experience. "I've had a marvelous time," she said slowly, adding: "most of my life." And then quickly said, "I do thank you—sincerely—for your hospitality, your kindness, and your company!" She raised her wineglass in Adrienne's honor.

"I think well of you too."

They fell into silence for a few minutes, then remarked on the lamb, the mint sauce, and the salad.

"Isak Dinesen came to mind earlier today," Shelagh began. "You remember how we adored her *Seven Gothic Tales* and *Out of Africa.*"

"A scratchy lady . . ." Adrienne commented.

"But a wonderful writer."

"I suppose so. But such *intensity* . . ." It sounded like criticism for lack of social grace.

"Well, I can't remember where I heard this or read it, but it seems that she hired a young girl to work as her secretary who, over the years—some twenty years or so—became her assistant in a number of valuable ways, maybe even her intimate. They were devoted to each other. One winter night, one of those stormy, cold Danish nights, when Isak Dinesen was very old and frail, about to go upstairs to her bedroom, she asked the woman who'd been close to her for more than half her young lifetime: 'If you knew that I might die in my sleep tonight, is there something you would want to tell me, that you wouldn't say otherwise?' Do you know how the younger woman answered?"

"I can't imagine."

"She thought about it, and then she said: 'No, there isn't.' "

"Oh, those neurotic Danes!"

Shelagh paused before saying, "I used to think, 'How awful!' too, but today I have a different impression of it. If two people have meant as much to each other as those two, can have been as appreciative and significant as they can be for each other—then it is only a tribute to or the measure of their value to each other that no last-minute word needs to be added. Isn't that really preferable to some 'deathbed' revelation or confession or song of praise?"

"If you know everything you can know, as you go along . . ."

Shelagh agreed but corrected her, "Everything you need to know. . . ."

"Then yes, it is enough."

"I think it's much better than not knowing until the very last moment."

"Very well, yes," Adrienne agreed.

"Despite that!—" Shelagh started, cheerfully: "If you knew that this might be the very last time we are to see each other, is there something you'd say that you wouldn't tell me otherwise?"

"Yes," Adrienne answered, pensively. Then she whispered, "Fix your face. You've eaten off all of your lipstick."

Because the traffic was not heavy the next morning driving out of London, Shelagh arrived at the airport two hours before her flight was scheduled to depart. She checked her luggage through to New York and wandered about aimlessly. She drank a coffee in the large lounge, vaguely aware of the numerous families from India surrounding her: slender grandfathers with toothless smiles in their wrinkled brown faces, gauzy white dhotis hanging shapelessly about them below new British tennis pullovers; large women in orange and pink saris—toasted-almond–complexioned—with many rings on the fingers of each hand; hearty but quiet fathers of families and children of all ages, untrammeled, irrepressible. Where were they going? Around the world to return to homes in Madras or Bombay or Calcutta? or to a new life somewhere in between? in Boston or St. Louis or Tulsa? How odd these colorful parties will look at a McDonald's in Cleveland trying to order a vegetarian meal.

Shelagh did not want to think about them; she wanted to think about herself. She climbed the stairs to the duty-free shops to look without sharp focus at shelves of liquor and cigarettes, perfume, wristwatches, jewelry, without any personal engagement. In a maudlin moment she felt: My days for buying things are over. But if she acted like this, she told herself, she would give away the truth. Therefore, she forced herself to buy perfume for Claire and then eau de cologne for Chester and for Morgan. And yet—when the number of her flight and her seat had been written down, the prices added up, the bill

174

paid, and the clear plastic bag handed to her across the counter with the purchases safely taped inside, she had no heart for it. She was not ready for the part she had to play: to arrive home, with gifts in hand, as usual, and pretend that all was well, everything as before, nothing changed. She was not ready. She felt she must postpone it.

She asked the saleswoman behind the counter to hold on to her package for a few minutes.

Determined by her insecurity, she strode decisively down the stairs and back through Passport Control to the airline's ticket station. She wanted to fly to Paris instead; she wanted a flight from Paris to New York the next day. Could that be arranged? But of course; just, "Let's see." The agent began to strike at the keyboard of a computer behind the counter, half-hidden from her view. To the extent that Shelagh felt cowardly for this attempt to put off her reunion with Chester even for one more day, she imagined that her craven wish would be refused. She would be forced to see him, to confront him in what? ten hours? twelve hours? even if she wasn't ready. She now prepared herself for word that this whim, this escapist hope could not be satisfied, that they could not change her flight. Steeling herself for the refusal, she was unprepared when the attendant looked up from the computer to say that everything had been arranged: the next flight to Paris left in forty minutes and would she like a seat in the smoking or nonsmoking section?

The unexpectedness of her wish being fulfilled made her laugh out loud. The agent was resentful, and looked surly while drawing up the new ticket, as if she had been toying with him. Shelagh, meanwhile, felt oddly giddy at the realization that she could just as easily have said, "Madras, Bombay, or Calcutta," and the obliging attendant and the quietly whirring computer would have granted her a much longer reprieve with comparable equanimity. She felt a truant, an escapee—passing through Passport Control for a second time, heading for a different destination, with only her light raincoat over her left arm, her handbag swinging freely from her right hand, and a plastic bag of perfumes waiting for her in the duty-free shop.

❦

Up into the overcast sky the plane rose rapidly, reducing the huge extent of the city of London to miniature status in a matter of minutes, and then it flew upward again, through a thousand feet of clouds, until it leveled off in an azure sphere golden with sunlight from which Shelagh could see no sign of the earth below. Despite the guilty freedom she enjoyed in anticipating one day of postponement before returning home, she was resolved to cable Chester as soon as she arrived in Paris—there was a six-hour difference—so that he would receive a message before he left for his office, telling him of her delay. He would not begrudge it to her, would he? She needed to calm herself before she could meet him again. She needed to prepare herself.

What would she tell him? That given all the genteel niceties of the most advanced medical technology and professionally trained practitioners, she had benefited from this trip to London to the extent of being informed of her promised death in six to nine months. Preposterous! Impossible to imagine the conversation that began with her saying to Chester, "Guess what . . ." She gagged at the thought of it. Yet how could she keep secret from him what promised to change his life irredeemably? Her life would be over; and his way of life would be lost with her. They had kept so few secrets from each other—they told each other their dreams!—how could she not tell him?

This is maddening, she thought. It is enough to drive me mad. Twisting, contorted where she sat, she felt the sun on her face through the window of the plane, closed her eyes, and rested her head against the back of the cushioned seat. I need time to think. I will think about Chester in Paris. She felt her face go slack. There was nothing amusing to find in the situation. She had thought it would seem funny to conceive of herself "playing hooky" in Paris like a child—escaping to heaven for a day—to think about one's homework later, something to put off while enjoying oneself; but what was there to enjoy now? She wasn't so much a truant as she was in hiding. No one knew where she was. If she should be killed or kidnapped, no one would ever know what had become of her. She would simply have disappeared. As she was doomed to disappear! That shook her up. She choked up and wiped the tears from her eyes. The plane descended toward its landing at Charles de Gaulle Airport.

In that futuristic terminal, a surrealistic version of Piranesi's prisons, she found her way along the moving platforms, down through the Lucite tunnels under the open sky in the central amphitheater, to a desk from which she sent the cable to her husband; she exchanged her remaining English pounds for French francs, and then went outside to wait for a taxi. Seated in a German car with smooth upholstery and plastic flowers, she listened to the meter ticking while the elderly driver waited for an answer to his question. Where did she want to go? She would have to stay overnight someplace; she had no intention of getting in touch with friends or acquaintances. "The Hilton Hotel," she said. "The one near the Eiffel Tower."

"There is only one," the pedantic driver replied.

Perhaps there is something to the legend of French precision and lucidity, she thought, after all.

In the lobby there it occurred to Shelagh that she had chosen the American hotel in Paris instinctively as a halfway house, a decompression chamber making easier the transition from Europe to the States. She asked for a single room for one night "at least" and said that her luggage had been misplaced by the airline, but she expected it to be delivered during the course of the day—realizing how easy it is to lie, wondering how many people do it all the time. She was shown to a room on a floor high enough in the hotel so that when she stepped out onto the narrow balcony, she could look over the tops of trees toward the Seine and across to the Right Bank. The sky was clear and bright, a perfect autumn day; it was quiet; she had arranged for her solitude. Leaving the raincoat and the bag of perfumes on the bed, she locked the door behind her, thinking: If I disappear, that is as it should be—gifts for my family, left behind, is all that will be found.

She took a taxi to the Place St.-Germain-des-Prés, grateful to be wearing sensible low-heeled shoes, for she wanted to walk for hours, comfortable in a boxy Chanel-like light wool suit—but she suddenly felt hungry, crossed the cobblestone of the square past the short block of Les Deux Magots, the art bookstore, and the kiosk to seat herself at one of the outdoor tables under the awning of the Café Flore. Eventually a waiter took her order for a *sandwich jambon* with Campari and soda. She smiled at the thought of arriving at the Savoy the night before. If Adrienne were with me now, she reflected, I should have to say, "When I was twenty-three, I thought *this* was the center of the world." In that first year after the war, just before her marriage to Chester, on each of her visits to Paris, this was where she came to rest: the Café Flore.

Boulevard St.-Germain had been widened into a broad avenue now glutted with swiftly moving traffic. But in those days there had been an island down the center of the street at the end of which stood a monumental statue of Diderot, his feather pen poised in the air, ready to capture in words each new rational thought. Shelagh had sat at an outdoor table of the Café Flore nearly thirty years before and watched as Diderot was displaced, carried away with ropes and pulleys on rolling logs along the boulevard and relegated to a cove before the Hôtel Madison from which he looked across to the apse of l'Église St.-Germain-des-Prés, where Descartes is buried. Rationalism was displaced; Jean Paul Sartre was the new idol in the *quartier Latin* during those days. Eventually the island had disappeared from the avenue as well. In that first winter after the war there was not much heat, and people drank coffee all day long in the inner room upstairs at the Flore. Whenever Shelagh had dropped in for a hot drink, at whatever hour of the morning or afternoon, she had seen a handsome woman, always at the same table, writing, writing away at a manuscript, intensely preoccupied and productive. Later she learned that this was Simone de Beauvoir; the book she was writing then was *The Second Sex*. At the same time, Shelagh had been buying her trousseau. By the end of that first year after the war, good cloth was available again, and the fashion of long skirts with many pleats—abundance, amplitude—was reinvented. It was in such a skirt that Shelagh was married: pale peach with a lizard-skin belt.

Now to eat a slice of ham with butter on French bread in the balmy air of an autumn day a generation later was not to have a new experience—not to go on as if life must consist only of one additional event after another—but to re-enter the past, to savor again a simple joy of nearly thirty years before, to taste once more the happiness of her own youth. Was this not why she had to come to Paris?

Yes. It was because, when you are told you are going to die, you want to feel again what had made life worthwhile, joyous once before. There is no more time for new experiences. And yet she did not have to hide in Paris in order to remember visits to Paris when she was a young woman. The past was all there, somehow, within her psyche—like a family album. She had only to turn the pages, and although she sat at an outdoor table before the Café Flore, with the traffic moving before her on the Boulevard St.-Germain, sipping iced Campari and soda, she could see the snowcapped mountains of Alaska, a moonlit night at a temple in Kyoto, a fortune-teller near the pier in Hong Kong, and all the more homely images of her life: the orchids in their humid greenhouse; Chester's cello in the corner of the library; Morgan standing in his crib, one year old, zipped up in a sleeping bag decorated like a tiger—her baby tiger—bouncing in his crib, cheerfully singsonging, "Night-night." And now he soberly says things like "Anthony Trollope," or "Tax-exempt utilities dividends." Shelagh smiled, sadly, thinking: They do not know. I know. And I am here to get my new self settled so that I can confront them all again as if the verdict had not been delivered or as if I hadn't heard it or comprehended it. I will not inflict it on them. She smashed her fist down on the small round metal table before her. The white plate with the green border circling it which had held the ham sandwich fell to the sidewalk and broke.

"What is the trouble?" the waiter asked.

I am going to die soon, Shelagh wanted to reply—sensing that she would want to smash other things in the future and that this mistaken loss of control was ample warning. "I'll pay for it," she said. "I'm sorry. It was an accident."

"No, no." The waiter smiled now. "I remember you well. Think nothing of it."

Remembered? Then he was one of the same waiters she had seen at the Café Flore on and off, again and again, on visits no matter how brief, the past thirty years?—growing old in his calling, as she was in hers. "That is very nice of you," she said appreciatively. They "knew" each other in an anonymous way.

"Nothing. Think nothing of it." He picked up the broken pieces of the plate from under the wicker chair in front of her. When she prepared to leave, Shelagh left him a tip larger than the bill itself. She would be more generous now—with a shorter time in which to "share the wealth."

She walked back through the square in front of the church and then along the rue de Seine toward the river, more or less unaware of other people on the sidewalks, as there seemed to be so few about. It was two o'clock in the afternoon of a weekday toward the end of October. The tourist season was over. Children were in school. But the work of the world went on—in the best sense of "life goes on"—and that thought slowed Shelagh's pace as she realized that her life would not go "on" in that former insouciant way of "on and on. . . ." Her time was no longer indefinite. It amazed her that she was not frightened, but she was uncertain of how to live with it: there was an anxiety altogether unanticipated—oddly as if, once again, she would have to learn an unfamiliar language.

She turned left along the quay and then stood resting with her palms flat against the stone parapet, before approaching the nearest bridge. Being condemned, she realized, it was not enough to *recall* the joyous events of her life, to remember Paris, Alaska, Kyoto: what she wanted, passionately, with an unsatisfiable lust, was to *relive* what she had loved best. Of course, that would be impossible. Memory was all that would be allowed her. The snapshots in the family album: not the weight of Chester upon her in the moment after their first intercourse; not that honey-sweet smell of the infant Claire prepared to splash in her bath; not the triumph she had felt with the first copy of a book she had illustrated, materialized, held firmly in both hands. Still— such were the joys she could not but remember and wish to relive. What, Shelagh wondered, do people who have lived unhappy lives wish for when they learn they are going to die—if there has been little or nothing in their experience they would choose to relive? They are the ones who want to gamble away their savings at Monte Carlo, have an affair with a gigolo, or fly off to become a beachcomber on Tahiti. Whereas I would have nothing different! Shelagh assured herself: I affirm my luck and my life.

She felt an enormous sense of relief, realizing that she could keep her secret precisely because she need not rush off to do something extraordinary, something unheard of before, something outside of the patterns and routines of her accustomed life, in order to make living worthwhile at last. She had not been deprived: so she was not in need of "compensation" or consolation. She had been *successfully greedy*, she reminded herself, getting even more than her fair share of satisfaction, of reward. And now if she were to admit what she had been told by "professionally trained practitioners"—by experts—she would be asking her family and her friends for something even more unfair: to be treated as an invalid, a "terminally" doomed creature when in fact she did not need to be taken care of, for there was no evidence, no symptom, no outward sign that made public the news she had been given privately—of the growth of her death in the silent area of her brain. Taking heart from the name of that place, she believed she could keep her mouth shut as well. It should be the easiest thing in the world: to say nothing about it. Take her pills twice a day. Later, much later on, when the medicine no longer worked, when the seizures could no longer be controlled, when the range of her vision narrowed, and the teacup fell out of her hand—then it would be obvious and she would become an object of pity because there would be nothing to be done to make things better, ever to make things "all right" again. She could live with the warning that she was to die in six to nine months only if she could keep it secret and pretend that it was not so. She had told Adrienne nothing in the first instance, when she was freshly appalled by the word, had vomited, felt chilled to the bone. She had kept her own counsel then; couldn't she go on doing so: for everyone's sake? Especially her own. She knew it would be even more self-serving than a kindness to others, but hadn't she earned the right to protect her integrity? She heard herself moan with the burden of it, and still she felt it would be the best thing for her to do.

Shelagh took a deep breath, straightened up, and continued to walk along the quay and then across the bridge toward the Louvre. She had no intention of going into the museum. She washed her hands of museums now. She wanted only what she could make use of in her own life. I am becoming like Adrienne, she thought: if you want to make use of things, you must be prepared for them to be "used up." But what use should she make of one day in Paris, in the last October of her life?

"Last" was a concept that echoed through her soul. This is probably the last time I will see Paris, and from now on, I shall be judging: this is the last time I'll watch snow fall, this is the last time I'll see tulips bloom; and so I will experience each "last" event with a different heart from Claire or Morgan or even Chester, who will continue to think of going "on and on . . . again and again." For if they were here with me now, they would imagine it is only *this time* in Paris and assume there will be other times, again and again; but how many times does one have to see Paris in order to let go of it, to say, "This is *enough*"? One does not have to relive experiences if they have been lived fully. The insatiable lust for more-and-more is demeaning. It is more dignified to conclude: I have had enough. It is better to recognize satisfaction and to be grateful in bidding "Farewell."

Beautiful! How beautiful is Paris, she said to herself. In the midafternoon sunlight of a cerulean sky, a splendid autumn day, she stood with her back to the Louvre gazing beyond the carousel up the length of the Champs Élysées, from the Place de la Concorde all the way to the Arc de Triomphe, thinking: Here man imposes his skill upon nature until it yields Glory. At the same time, she felt: This is how man impresses his will on other men and says, "I wish to see my plans carried out." Paris had been a chaotic medieval city until Louis XIV transformed it. And Napoleon III had revised it again two centuries later. Here, as she entered the Tuileries Garden, Shelagh realized gardens had been cultivated for nearly four hundred years. The wide gravel path separated large rectangles of lawn bordered by bright red geraniums. On both sides beyond the lawns stood alleys of chestnut trees. Amply spaced along the avenue rose the white marble copies of antique sculpture—the images of Greek myths. Why were they imitated? Is it that mankind as a whole tries to relive the happy events of an earlier life? As if to "return" were always more reassuring than to risk a new experience.

Under the trees on one side of the promenade, small children played in a large sandbox; others watched a Punch-and-Judy puppet show in an open-air theater. A pair of lovers in the fullness of youth sat side by side on a bench at the edge of the gravel. They were kissing passionately. The girl's hands were hidden under the boy's jacket. He held her with one arm around her lower back and the other hand pressed against the back of her head as though to keep her from escaping. It was the man's hand in the hair of the girl's head that pierced Shelagh poignantly: that instinctive hold on love; that assertion of possession. "You must never leave me. You will never get away"—the denial of change. She forced herself to continue strolling along the walk so as not to stare at them. She was not jealous; she had known such possessiveness. She was happy for them. "Life goes on." She wished for Claire and Morgan such passion, freshness, intensity. It was what she had known in her youth in Paris on that first weekend with Chester.

Feeling momentarily fatigued, Shelagh sat down in one of the wrought-iron armchairs at the edge of the lawn, found the change in her purse, and paid the custodian who instantly appeared from nowhere. She neatly placed the receipt in her handbag and then leaned back with closed eyes to let the sunlight warm her face. The silence was broken by the twang of a guitar and the counterpoint of a piccolo and a banjo playing an American "spiritual."

Until then she had not noticed the trio seated in the shade on the grass just beyond where she had happened to sit down; but now she followed the sounds to where they came from. The guitarist sat cross-legged, looking like a Gypsy with long black hair, gold hoop earrings; a thin woman probably in her mid-twenties, she wore black tights under a colorful skirt, and leather sandals. On either side of her was a black man. The tall, heavy one, who played the piccolo, decorated his head with a red bandana like a pirate's. The slender, wiry fellow plinking the banjo wore a sleazy white blouse and puffed on a Gauloise drooping from his lips. There was nothing French-looking about the group at all, which made Shelagh imagine that they might be refugees from Algeria: an impoverished planter's daughter with two inherited family retainers. Their second song sounded like old jazz from New Orleans, but choppy, irregular. The larger man used a tambourine in place of his piccolo. The girl scat-sang along with her own playing.

A gendarme came by on the graveled avenue, frowning uncomfortably, as if unsure whether to let them remain, but he said nothing and walked on, his hands behind his back. Shelagh followed him with her eyes and then saw the young lovers again on the bench across the way: still locked in their embrace. How many minutes could have passed? she asked herself. Five? Seven? The gendarme walked past them as well without a word.

Of course, young lovers don't need Paris; young lovers don't need anything but each other. Still—to be young, in love, and in Paris is to have the best of the world. As the Germans say for perfection: to live *wie Gott—in Frankreich*. Shelagh had known such joys, the first time she spent a weekend here with Chester, in the summer of 1945, shortly before they were married. He had reserved a room in what had been a luxurious hotel between the rue de Rivoli and Place Vendôme. The electricity went off for four hours every day, the elevator didn't always work, Champagne was brought to their room by an aging bellman who panted asthmatically from climbing the stairs—but they made love in the morning when they woke up, in the afternoon before dressing for dinner, and in the evening before they fell asleep. "You make me so happy," she had said. "I am happier with you than I have ever been in my life." And Chester had replied, seriously, "*Our* life is just beginning." As if swearing his oath to her for the decades to come, he promised: "I will make you very, very happy."

There were croissants and brioche with honey and café-au-lait for break-fast, cathedrals and museums and gardens for sight-seeing, nightclubs along the winding streets at the top of Montmartre for entertainment. They strolled together arm in arm—young and in love and in Paris.

The odd trio on the grass had played another song to which Shelagh paid no attention and then the three musicians got up to see if they could collect some money. Holding the tambourine before her, the Gypsy girl approached Shelagh. Her hair covered her forehead in long bangs; unkempt and probably unwashed. Her eyes narrowed accusingly as she came closer; she lowered the begging bowl to her side and asked, "Aren't you Claire's mother?"

Shelagh wanted to say No—mostly because she felt herself young, on a weekend with her lover, thirty years ago; how could she be the mother of any-one? And partly because she was disconcerted to hear American English spo-ken when she expected this *gamine* in a bohemian outfit to speak French with an Algerian accent. But she said, "Well . . . yes, I am."

"Claire Jackman's mother! What do you know. I'll be damned."

Shelagh stood up, hoping to edge her way around the chair so that it would put distance between them. The young woman stood too close to her.

"What a coincidence," the girl went on, and slapped the tambourine.

"I'm sorry. I can't seem to place you. Of course, I know you, but—"

"Caroline. Caroline Taylor."

"Conrad Taylor's daughter."

"Of New Haven, Connecticut, fame," she added with a sneer.

"How embarrassing not to recognize you. I am so sorry." Shelagh looked at her more carefully now. She was no longer the fresh-faced child, a few years younger than Claire—the girl who used to trail along behind her daughter like a puppy. Her face had grown longer and thinner, which the lank hair accentuated, but her figure was somehow lumpy.

"Oh, that's all right. I didn't recognize you at first either."

On her black blouse, wrinkled as if she slept in it, the girl wore a silvery necklace with filigreed amulets and cheap brown beads—the kind of decorations you see on camels in North Africa, Shelagh thought. "What are you doing here?"

"Isn't that obvious?" she asked with a snort—pointing to the spot where her guitar remained on the grass. "Earning some bread."

"I thought you were studying acting in London. I remember suggesting that you call on my sister there."

"Sure. I met her once. Very high-tone. She invited me over to tea and when I got there she asked, 'Chinese or Indian?' I didn't know what to say." She laughed. "We didn't have *anything* to say to each other."

"But she's such an interesting person . . ."

"So am I," Caroline retorted. Impertinence was her trademark. And impatience, too. Because of Claire's love of the theater, the younger Caroline Taylor also wanted to become an actress. But she would not stomach four years in college. Her father had given up, and sent her to the Royal Academy of Dramatic Art. In the meanwhile, Claire had graduated well from Brown and gone to New York to pursue her career.

"And your career . . . ?" Shelagh asked.

"That's a laugh. I decided to give up acting. There's no future in it. I've been in East Africa for the past half-year." There was a pause. She looked at her friend's mother; knowing she was expected to offer conventional explanations, she added, "Studying ethnomusicology."

"I see." Shelagh looked about her to the formal gardens of the Tuileries in the late-afternoon light and back to Caroline Taylor's face with imperfectly concealed disbelief.

"We've been here for ten days. There was a real cheap excursion flight from Nairobi to Luxembourg for ten days. Too good to miss. So we're here, for a change."

To escape from the escape—in Shelagh's mind.

"What are you doing here?" She added, "Mrs. Jackman."

"I?" she asked on the high note of surprise of one who is almost never questioned about her behavior. "What am I *doing* here? Why—I'm reminiscing. I was on my way home, but I thought I'd take one day more: to wallow in nostalgia."

"Sure," the young woman acknowledged with indifference. "And Claire? How's she?"

"I'm not certain. She has a number of irons in the fire. . . ." Caroline chuckled at the quaint expression. "She's rehearsing for an Off Broadway production that's going to open sometime in November." Then, just to rub it in, she actually said: "She has a beau."

That made Caroline laugh. "Well, we have gone our separate ways, haven't we." The large black pirate whistled to her as he returned to her guitar on the grass. "Can you let me have some money?"

Shelagh was relieved to see the conversation coming to an end. "Yes. Just let me look. . . ." She opened her handbag and brought out a wad of francs. At the bottom of the bag lay the gold link bracelet she never wanted to wear again. She thought of giving that also to Caroline, but presumed that if she tried to sell it, she'd be accused of having stolen it; and so Shelagh did not fish it out. Without counting to see how much the handful of money amounted to, she urged it on Caroline, who held out the upturned tambourine. Shelagh dropped the bills into it.

Caroline didn't thank her; she said, "Have a good trip." And turned back to her buddies. When she was very young, and her mother abandoned Conrad Taylor and the girl, Shelagh had consoled and comforted him. It was a long time ago. Conrad's life had much improved since then. He was married to a new wife. But this girl of his, this arrogant, spoiled girl—what would she do with herself if she knew she had only six to nine months to live?

She has ruined my mood! Shelagh realized. I was reminiscing—if not "wallowing in nostalgia"—when Caroline appeared to impose upon me. I was here as it was thirty years ago, but Caroline spoiled it for me. She looked back to see once more the couple embracing—but their bench was empty now. She said, *"Merde"* under her breath.

There was no point in sitting down in the rented chair again. She would have to walk. Caroline Taylor and her two black companions were lying prone on the grass when she passed them, headed toward the Place de la Concorde.

How extraordinary, Shelagh thought, to be confronted in that way, and by Caroline Taylor, of all people. She felt she had escaped from her own escape—had been on leave in the past—only to be brought back to the present, and with an irritating rub, by someone who hardly knew her and did not wish her well. It pained her to consider that Caroline Taylor would go on living long after she was dead. *Why me and not her?* Shelagh knew immediately that that was an unanswerable and, therefore, a make-believe question. Only the rhetoric of despair. It was the kind of feeling she must suppress; otherwise she would end up hating nearly everyone: the feeling of bitterness. Better to think of nursery rhymes, grade-school poems, the periodic table—anything rather than the vocabulary of self-pity.

At the Jeu de Paume she went down the wide stairway to the street. She did not move sidewise fast enough to avoid inclusion in a photograph taken by a Japanese tourist.

Waiting for the traffic to stop so that she could cross the rue de Rivoli, she read the plaques along the wall where she stood. White marble rectangles like tombstones naming the men who had died on that spot fighting the Nazis for the liberation of Paris. For possession of Paris. Wars are fought for the possession of things, for the ownership of farmland and coal mines and railroads and cities like Paris. The issue was: Who would Own them? People as things—as slaves. The ownership of people. But most obviously things like the paintings Goering had commandeered from all over Europe. Things like fur coats and automobiles, jewelry, furniture, porcelain, royal treasures, fresh vegetables, wine, cheese. And Paris. Generations come and go. Invaders come and go—sometimes as vandals who destroy, but mostly to take possession of things for themselves: as if, over the centuries, it is the things that make use of people. To be possessed, they must be prepared for the people who own them to be used up—and replaced by other people. Many people live lives in the service of "their" things. Perhaps the history of civilization should be written from the point of view of things that endure, as the story of the sequence of people who had been temporarily in charge of them. For all their loyalty to Hitler, the German generals in Paris had refused to carry out his order to burn the city to the ground. That "thing" was more important than their duty to obey his command.

That beautiful thing: this city! Shelagh remembered one night, when she and Chester were here together for the first time, strolling through the streets at night. Not all of the monumental buildings were lighted up again at that time. Under a dark sky and a pale moon they found themselves on one of the bridges over the Seine, looking toward the Île de la Cité, to see only Notre Dame and the Sainte-Chapelle lighted up in the distance. The rest of Paris lay in darkness. It was as if they had come upon the city in the twelfth century.

Nothing lasts forever, she thought, with a nod of acquiescence to Adrienne; but nine hundred years is a nice piece of change.

The taxi Shelagh had taken from the Place de la Concorde was prevented from driving right up to the entrance of the Hilton Hotel. A demonstration filled the driveway: about a hundred youthful males in blue jeans and T-shirts, carrying placards in French, English and Arabic, chanting in a language she did not understand, marched in an endless loop through the length of the driveway. French policemen stood guard, but there was no indication of violence or any attempt to remove them. She left the cab at the far end of the square before the hotel and, circling around the demonstrators, made her way into the lobby.

The signs she could read as she walked in said: "SELF-DETERMINATION FOR IRAN. AMERICANS OUT!" and "DEATH TO THE SHAH-MURDERER."

A concierge explained: "Iranian students. Ingrates, you know. It's on scholarships from the Shah that they are studying here."

Shelagh quoted: " 'You taught me a language and my profit on't is I know how to curse.' "

The concierge looked at her blankly, but said, "Indeed."

"Why are they demonstrating here?"

"Ah—the American Secretary of State and his party arrived this afternoon."

"I thought he was shuttling between Egypt and Israel."

"He returns home from time to time." The world-weary fellow smiled. "They'll be leaving the day after tomorrow. You won't be inconvenienced."

"No Molotov cocktails? No bricks through the upstairs windows?" she asked.

"This is a peaceful demonstration," he assured her.

Shelagh rode the elevator to the top floor of the hotel and took a window table in the nearly empty elegant lounge, where she ordered a whiskey sour. How dramatically it would simplify life, she thought, if I were killed by an Iranian bomb while sipping a cocktail in the Paris Hilton.

How different from the life she had married and earned as Chester's wife. In New Haven, Connecticut—as throughout the United States—one feels safely away from militant demonstrators, international spies, political intrigue. "The inane, the insane, and the criminal," as Chester frequently pointed out, "are always with us," but not as agents of conspiracy, subversion, chaos. Free-lance nuts, yes; conspirators, no.

"This is a curious moment for a beautiful woman to be alone—with the wolves of revolution howling at the door." That French sentence Shelagh heard was lightly enameled by an Italian accent. She looked up to find a white-haired gentleman of about sixty, good-looking in a swarthy Mediterranean way, almost as tall as Chester, but not as broad-shouldered. He was dressed in a handsome dark suit with a woven silver-and-black silk tie against his white shirt—very much *comme il faut*—holding a tumbler of what might be ouzo in one hand. She smiled at his lordly phrases. "If you would like, I'll sit out the siege with you."

"That ought to be very agreeable." She gestured to the chair at the other side of her table. "We could tell stories to each other—as in Boccaccio."

"Carlo Ferrari," he announced with a nod of his head, as he prepared to seat himself.

"Shelagh Jackman."

He kissed her hand. "This is a great pleasure. I dislike drinking alone. The cocktail hour is for sociability, not for solitary drinking. Don't you agree?"

"Quite right." She thought him engaging.

"Are you expecting someone?"

"No."

"Neither am I. Then let us raise our glasses in honor of the gods who have seen fit to bring us together. No unexpected encounter," he announced in a half-whisper, "is accidental. The gods have their purposes for us."

"You find that myth useful?"

Momentarily silent, as if discovering she might be more than he had bargained for, he looked at her thoughtfully before saying: "I consider it a fact of life confirmed by my own experience. The most important encounters of my life—those which have led to my profession, my marriage, my house in Torino, and many other valuable events—appeared as accidental at first."

"But you made the most of them." Then, she corrected herself: "You made the best of them and, subsequently, think of them as fated—necessary."

"Perhaps so. But if there is no intervention of the gods, then I alone should be responsible for the peculiar history of my life. And what a burden that would be!" He laughed.

Shelagh considered that all of his beautifully matched, polished white teeth must be capped.

"Madam," he continued, "would you not allow me to share the congratulations—as well as the blame—with the gods?"

"Of course. I know what you mean, after all . . . you did not plan to meet me here just now. And I did not come here to meet you. Still—here we are. Let us agree that the gods make opportunities. What we choose to do with them is our only responsibility." Then she added: "When we are happy with our choices, we feel our 'fate' has been fulfilled."

"And if we are unhappy?"

"Then we feel our fate must be endured—with resentment."

Without ever taking his warm eyes away from her face, he swallowed the rest of his drink as a toast to her; then he ordered another round for both of them.

In their shared silence, over and above the soft playing of dance music from a tape behind the bar, they could hear the faint rhythmic chanting of the Iranian students from outside the hotel.

"They want self-determination," Shelagh said. "They want to make their own fate."

"Well, politically—yes." His hands made a gesture of modesty as if smoothing down the air above the surface of the table. "Which is not too much to ask. It is the wave of the future. All peoples want to rid themselves of outside rulers. To be only for their own kind."

"Even in England I read in the newspapers about self-determination for Wales and for Scotland."

"Pakistan and Bangladesh were carved out of India." He was nodding his head in affirmation. "The next wave is away from large centralized units to smaller and more homogeneous ones: the Basques want their independence; so do the Kurds. The Palestinian Arabs crave a country of their own. It may be that if the huge nations are broken up into feudal principalities again, we will all be the safer for it. With each one ruling itself for its own purposes, no two will agree to become a threat to any of the others." He smiled with appreciation of his ingenuity.

"If you carry it far enough," Shelagh suggested, "each person wants self-determination for himself. Isn't that the argument for anarchy?"

"Yes, of course. However, it cannot come to pass. No person is self-determining in the sense that a political unit can be. The human animal is entirely dependent on others—so that by the time we wake up from the sleep of childhood, we find ourselves fully determined."

"You don't believe much in free will, in freedom of choice, do you?"

He brought his hands toward each other so that his palms were no more than an inch apart. "About that much," he said.

"It is nearly all in the hands of the gods?"

"In human societies, the gods are everybody else."

Shelagh chuckled nervously.

"We will see, now, how much freedom of choice you and I can exercise." He sipped his drink and took a deep breath. "What I perceive is that you are a handsome woman in the splendor of your maturity. You are married but you are also, somehow, independent; here you are alone. I know you to have charm and intelligence—which I appreciate—but most of all I am struck by how attractive you are: how desirable. Shall I say nothing? Should I pretend I do not wish to make love to you?

"I have been formed by a culture that encourages me to demonstrate my manliness by being gallant to a lady, by showing my admiration to the extent of wooing her and winning—her favors. Is it true that I am free to keep silent? To give no indication of my desire to have you in my arms, in my bed? You yourself are the one who said, 'The gods create our opportunities.' How free are we to choose what we make of them? You have not once put me off—given me any sign of disfavor. You have accepted my presence, my drink, my conversation. Should I restrain myself now when I see only encouragement in your eyes? Or even if I wanted to go against my nature, could I refuse to offer this proposal? I do not think I am free to be silent. That I choose to speak to you in this way does not seem to me my own choice at all. It was determined eons ago. From the first Romans who took Etruscan women, down through the centuries, it has been borne in the blood of my ancestors, set in the formation of every virile male child of my race for two thousand years, so that it comes to me as a necessity, an obligation, the very opposite of a free choice. I am compelled to speak to you thus not as a free man whose self-determination allows him any alternative, but as the instrument of an ancient compulsion, an impersonal force of nature and the cumulative style of my culture. I am but a passive agent of that great power. It is not I alone who, here and now, am luring you into my embrace, for I am only fulfilling the requirements for being a man as all of the history of my origins has predetermined them. Even if, by some misfortune, you should rebuke me and refuse me, I shall be comforted by the fact that it is not I alone who has been rejected but the ingrained tradition of duty to my race. I was not free to choose silence; therefore, I am without personal guilt if you should not be free to say 'Yes.' "

Shelagh Jackman burst into laughter and clapped her hands in applause. The few other patrons of the lounge, at the bar and the widely scattered tables, turned to look in her direction, but only for a moment, and then turned their backs again.

Shelagh caught her breath, paused, smiled, and said: "That it is not you who are trying to seduce me, but a two-thousand-year-old compulsion, leaves me speechless."

Carlo Ferrari ordered another round of drinks.

"I am flattered. I am, truly," Shelagh said. "I have not been feeling at all desirable lately. You restore my faith in myself, for which I thank you sincerely."

"You are not taking me seriously. I offer you pleasure. That we should both feel good is the end; but the means is my challenge to your idea of freedom. You think it is you who can choose. What we shall see is how you have been determined."

"You take all the fun out of it."

"Will you have dinner with me? Remember, we are besieged by the rabble-demonstrators. My room is on the fifth floor. We can order dinner to be served in the room."

"Would you make love to a dying woman?"

"I beg your pardon?"

"We can perceive a good deal of each other; but there is much that remains invisible. There is a malignant tumor in my brain. I do not know exactly when it will kill me. But it will be sudden. Would you run the risk of my being found dead in your room?"

His features remained impassive, but Shelagh watched the beads of sweat appear along his hairline and the flesh of his nose begin to glisten.

"Now, what are you to choose?" she asked. "And how much difference does it make if you ask yourself whether you're 'free' to choose or your choice is 'predetermined'?"

Gradually he appeared to regain his voice and said, "We do what we have to."

"We do, my friend, what we think we can get away with."

"You have told me the truth?"

"Yes."

"No one has ever said anything like that to me before."

Shelagh could see him withdrawing from her—his soul slipping away before any limb of his body was able to make a move. He is frightened, she realized, as if I had told him I carried a virulent contagious disease. Was he regretting that he had kissed her hand? She would release him now. She stood up. "I must leave. But, Carlo Ferrari, believe me—I am deeply grateful to you. You have helped me more than I can tell you. Please don't get up. Have another drink. Relax. I'm sorry to have disappointed the ingrained tradition of your race. Nothing personal, of course. But then, there was nothing personal to me in your invitation either. It's just that our two traditions weren't meant for each other."

Benefiting from Carlo Ferrari's suggestion, Shelagh looked through the menu on the desk in her room and then telephoned to order dinner from Room Service. While she waited for it to be wheeled in, she ran a hot bath. She hung up the jacket of her suit and kicked off her shoes. She sat on the stool before the dressing table and studied her face. She would not live to see all her hair gray and thin, her sagging flesh caught in a net of deep lines, a hearing aid in one ear and thick lenses before watery eyes. She would disappear before any of that could happen to her. She would die while a stranger might still call her attractive, desirable. That was a mercy.

But that the gods have their purposes for us, she thought—that's malarkey. We would like to believe the accidents of nature and of human society are, in the long run, purposeful because that would conform to what gives human beings their greatest satisfaction: to make a plan and then to carry it out. To set a goal and then achieve it. Therefore, we impose human psychology on the impersonal; we would humanize nature.

It is difficult enough to humanize ourselves.

Now I have a plan and I will carry it out. She felt that she had steeled her resolve. She would keep silent. It did not matter to her in the least whether she was "free" to make that choice or if everything that had contributed to determining her character had so narrowed and channeled her capacity to think and feel that she was left "unfree" to make any alternative choice. Either way: it was hers.

She had said it once—only once: she had called herself "a dying woman"; she had told a stranger what she had been told by doctors. And she had learned her lesson. She would never forget the sight of the sudden sweat on his brow. He could not have spoken; he did not need to say a word. She had perceived his desire for instant escape. She had seen how he withdrew from her. She had made him afraid for himself. She was a reminder of his own death. That was enough of a lesson. She would never have to give that message to anyone else; she would never wish to give it to anyone she loved. She did not want anyone else in the world to retreat from her. She wanted to remain an equal in life.

Shelagh opened the door to a waiter who brought her an omelette, a green salad, a bottle of Montrachet and caramel custard. He answered her question about the demonstrators by saying all of them had gone away. She signed the bill, thanked him, and locked the door after he had left. She would be alone for the rest of the evening. She ate her meal slowly, savoring it, then luxuriated in the bath. Having no nightclothes with her, she draped a soft, lightweight blanket about her like a toga. Beyond the glass doors to the balcony, she watched the pale gray clouds move against the black-and-blue sky. She put out the lights in the room, made herself comfortable in an armchair, rested her feet upon the edge of one of the twin beds, and stared out at the calm view, waiting for stars to appear.

❦

DIARY ENTRY

Home!

Everything has worked out remarkably well. Even my luggage—miraculous to say—was waiting for me in New York. When I checked out of the Hilton, I was handed one red rose wrapped in cellophane with a note attached reading, "May you be happy, gracious lady" from Carlo Ferrari, and I wore it through the flight pinned on my jacket like a medal.

But best of all, most unexpected, was to walk into the house and find Chester sick—wearing his bathrobe and slippers at five in the afternoon, drinking a hot toddy. He had been at home for two days with a strep throat. And he was cross with me for staying away longer than I had originally planned to. It was wonderful. He is almost never ill. He wasn't so much worried about me as he was sorry for himself, wanting me to take care of him. He

191

wasn't concerned about what might have happened to me at all. And then he was so grateful that I was back.

So for the past day and a half I have been coddling him like a child who is angry because he can't go out to play. Poor darling. He is sleeping now. His temperature is normal again. Being caught up in real life, I haven't given myself a thought. Until now, when I emptied out my handbag. The gold bracelet was there and the receipt from the custodian of chairs in the Tuileries gardens, a few francs, and the card from Signore Ferrari. My talismans from Paris. When I feel hurt and violent, I will remember the broken dish at the Café Flore and I will calm myself. When I am resentful and wish it were happening to someone else, I will think of Caroline Taylor and put foolish thoughts out of my mind. If I feel I shall gag if I don't tell someone, I will recall the cold sweat of fear on Ferrari's face—and hold my tongue.

I am determined to live as though I had never been told the prognosis or as if I did not believe it is true.

LETTER FROM SHELAGH JACKMAN TO HER SON, MORGAN

Dear-to-my-heart:

It was so pleasant to find waiting for my return your welcome-home letter, for which I thank you mightily—and naturally, what delights me most is your saying that yes, you will come here for Thanksgiving. I long to see you. I have a few (modest) presents for you from London. Aunt Adrienne sends you her love. Do you still read Dialogue? She has the most engaging friends. I must tell you about people at her party—like a Cambridge don who wants to write a novel because he has the title for it, and a lord who's just back from a visit to China. There were a Bolivian millionairess who fell asleep, and a journalist—and reflections on the Arabs all over the place. But of course, we'll talk and talk. What's a Thanksgiving dinner for if not good talk? Well, yes, I do know the answer to that: for giving thanks.

What good luck—that the conference you have to attend is to take place in Bermuda. And for a whole week, so you will have two free weekends there. Enjoy yourself.

I certainly enjoyed my "holiday." I must tell you about a dirty joke I discovered in a painting by Bronzino in the National Gallery. And about a woman I know who has been painting for years, but no one wants to buy her pictures. Isn't there a germ of a short story or a novel in that? What would Henry James have made of it?

Your devoted
Mother

LETTER FROM SHELAGH JACKMAN TO HER DAUGHTER, CLAIRE

Dearest girl:

How sweet of you to have a welcome-home letter waiting for me, and with such happy news in it—that you'll be here for Thanksgiving. I'm absolutely delighted. But, of course, I'll see you before then. Your father and I wouldn't miss opening night for the world. Isn't it a shame that Morgan can't be there: having to attend that awful conference will take him away. (Did you know? I'm not sure how often you two are in touch with each other.)

I'm so happy to be home. I love going away to stay at Adrienne's or in a hotel, seeing new sights and meeting new people, but coming home is even better: knowing where the toenail clipper is, and being able to find the bathroom in the dark.

Your father has been ill—nothing serious—with a strep throat, and I am playing Florence Nightingale. He will be fine in a day or so and then I shall get back to my work. I had an inspiration in London for one of the illustrations I must do, and I'm eager to try it out.

And there's so much to show you and tell you about. (I think you'll love the presents I brought you.) The theater was exceptional—have you heard of the production of Macbeth in Zulu? Do you know of a play called The Philanthropist? I disliked it intensely. It reassures me to discover I can still be outraged. Don't believe that to understand all is to forgive all. Balderdash. I understood that play a great deal better than the playwright did—and I don't forgive him. On the other hand, the British think it's a comedy and gave it a prize. They're so perverse.

And funny. Yes, they are entertaining and amusing. Aunt Adrienne has an endless supply of charming people at her beck and call. That kind of social life is entirely superficial—but what a refreshing change from the American "heavies." The intention is to make light of everything, while being as smart as possible.

Adrienne herself is very "smart" indeed—and has a most amiable new lover. I'll tell you about him, too. She sends you great hugs full of love. She longs for you to visit with her again.

You can't imagine what's become of Caroline Taylor. I ran into her in Paris by the wildest coincidence. And then a very elegant Italian gentleman tried to pick me up. So I don't feel entirely decrepit.

It was, to put it mildly, a memorable trip. But I'm glad to be home now; I had to cut my toenails.

Your doting
Mother

•

193

On the day Chester went to his office again, Shelagh prepared a "reunion" dinner. Having done the planning, the shopping, the baking, the cooking, the cleaning up, and set the table, she was prepared, when he let himself in and called "She—la" through the house, to greet her husband with the following news:

"Darling, I know the answer to Freud's question 'What do women want?' It's *servants!*"

Knowingly, he said, "You could have all the servants you want."

"I couldn't bear people hovering around in the house."

"Then, what *do* women want?"

"Invisible servants!"

At dinner Chester said, "You may not have noticed, but I went to a new barber."

"He did very well by you," she said admiringly.

"He gave me five years."

"For what? Baldness?"

"No. He gave me back five years. He trimmed my eyebrows."

"You're joking."

"Perfectly serious. He asked me how long I've had such bushy eyebrows and I said about ten years. 'I was sure of it,' he said. 'No one has bushy eyebrows until he's in his fifties. If I trim them for you, you'll look at least five years younger.' "

Shelagh laughed with approval. "So he did?"

"Yes. Don't you think I look five years younger?"

"You look ageless to me. You look eternal, my darling. If I had to fall in love all over again, it would certainly be with you."

After the end of the meal, in the mellow candlelight, they remained at the table, sipping the last of the Port Adrienne had sent as a gift. Shelagh said of her sister, "She continues to be the most independent person I know."

"Pity she never married."

"I don't believe so. She's very strong."

"Do you think marriage is a concession to weakness?"

Shelagh thought about it. "Not so much as a gamble on stability. I mean—some people want that security even more than they need novelty; and vice versa. Adrienne opted for variety. Of course, she might have had a totally different life. She was jilted, you know."

"I remember."

"There is no perfect stability . . ." Shelagh began, recalling Adrienne's dictum that nothing lasts forever. "Everything gradually changes."

"We're going to have new neighbors. The McGrath house was sold last week."

"Who bought it?"

"I don't know. Heard the name but didn't recognize it."

"Those poor old people. So they'll never come back to the house next door. Mrs. McGrath in a nursing home; and her husband . . . ?"

"You don't know. Well, how could you? You were away. He died in a hospital about ten days ago."

With the word "died," Shelagh felt the flame burn up through her—like Mrs. Dalloway at the end of that novel—at the news of death. "You mean that after a century of living together, they were separated when he died?"

"Yes."

"I think that's horrible."

"You don't even know if they still liked each other."

"After all those years . . ." She saw them hobbling about their little garden together. "She wasn't there to hold his hand."

"I doubt that she understands . . ."

"Oh, that makes it worse." Her eyes filled with tears.

Chester stood up, came around the table, took her head in his hands and rested it against his chest. "I had no idea you cared so much."

Shelagh felt the comfort of one hand against the back of her head, his other hand on her cheek; she could see the young lovers on their bench in the Tuileries Garden, and she sobbed, brought her arms up under his jacket, and held him tight.

"My darling, they were very, very old."

"I'm not crying for them," she whispered in a choked voice against his warm chest.

DIARY ENTRY

I will not be here to hold Chester's hand. Unless he dies before I do. But I do not wish that. I can imagine it; but I don't believe it for a moment.

It's hard to believe anything.

After dinner last night, when I learned about Mr. McGrath, Chester comforted me and cuddled me on the living-room sofa, and we made love then and there with the intensity of adolescents. Amazing. I have been given the death sentence and yet everything else is the same. The plates above the fireplace, the Archimboldos above the sofa, lettuce in the refrigerator; the telephone works; I remember how to broil chicken, unpack my bags, iron the creases out of a dress.

Like a man who went out to buy a newspaper and was not killed but knows how very narrowly he escaped a violent death in an automobile accident while crossing a street absentmindedly, and returns home to a wife spoon-feeding an infant in a high chair—just exactly as he had left it a few minutes before—I come back to find everything familiar and personal to me in place; habits still functional, good intentions still effective. Amazing. Nothing the worse for despair. All systems "Go"!

The only difference is: I am to believe it will end soon. No; everything else will go on. I am to end. And no one else knows.

Chester has left for work. I am alone in the quiet of my house: with the rhythm of life. I lose myself and I regain myself. In the end I will lose myself completely. Those are pearls that were his eyes. But every thought of death becomes a meditation on life. It is impossible to contemplate nothingness. Every time I try to stretch beyond the enclosing limit, I touch on only what is this side of the limit. I am in life. The pictures that come to my mind when I recall my experiences—summer cottages when the children were young, flying in and out of screen doors slamming, building sand castles at the edge of beaches, sea gulls whistling over their heads, one summer vacation after another—all, all of those are more real to me than the picture of a walnut growing in my brain. Correction: It's not a question of what's real. It's a matter of belief and feeling related, connected. I believe in the slamming screen door of twenty years ago. I am related to the plates over the fireplace. I feel no such connection with the object I am told will gradually become larger inside the finite space of my skull. No connection whatsoever. It is as foreign to me as the Black Holes of the most imaginative astronomers. They can imagine Black Holes; I cannot. Dr. McNeill can believe in a glioma; I cannot. I feel nothing for it or about it—or its relationship to me.

And I'll be goddamned if I'll let it interfere with my life.

During the afternoon, in the amber light of her studio, Shelagh completed her first sketch of the serpent before it was damned. The serpent so cunning as to look like Eve in the Garden of Eden. Like an older sister, perhaps; more experienced; shorter, and much more self-conscious; who could always imply that she knew better than Eve.

The idea satisfied her enormously, although she took no pleasure in it. By then, she understood that successful deception springs from the most self-serving motives.

The next morning, one week after returning home, Shelagh received a telephone call from Dr. Quentin Connolley.

"What do you want?" she asked curtly.

"Your indulgence," he replied.

"You should not call me."

"I have to. And you will have to allow it. This is a professional matter."

She repeated his phrase: "What 'professional matter'?"

"Your doctor in London—Dr. McNeill, isn't it?—sent me the records of your CAT scan, the diagnosis, and so on."

Shelagh was dumbfounded with fear of disclosure.

"Are you there?"

"Yes." Then she added quietly, "She had no business doing that."

"That is her business."

"Why?"

"When the supply of Dilantin and phenobarbital that you got in England is used up, how did you expect to get the prescriptions refilled?"

"I haven't thought about it."

"How much of a supply did you get?"

"I don't know."

"It says here: one month's worth. How many days have you been taking them?"

"Nine or ten."

"Then you must come to my office within the next few weeks to—"

"No. I'd rather see you as soon as possible."

"Today?"

"All right."

There was a pause and then he suggested, "Three-thirty."

In the outer office, Shelagh waited, sitting opposite a young black girl whose mother was in the examining room. The child's pigtails came down to the shoulder straps of her woolen jumper, in the tartan of the MacLean clan. She read a comic book and her jaws moved as if angrily clenching her teeth. Suddenly a green egg appeared between her brown lips; it grew larger and larger, ballooning out to hide her chin and nose. Unfazed, the child turned a page of the comic book, and then the green bubble burst, the debris adhering to the girl's cheeks. She licked it off, tonguing the gum back into her mouth without ever taking a hand off the comic book. Shelagh stared at her with amazement, thinking: She has seventy or eighty years to live. She will hold great-grandchildren on her lap.

When she was ushered into the inner office, Shelagh shivered with nervousness. Quentin Connolley stood behind his desk exactly as he had the last time she saw him, as though time had stood still for him, while so much had happened to her. The Viking beard, the white cuffs beyond the raw-silk jacket. A man whose son was a freshman in college.

"Please sit down," he said.

197

She saw the folder open on the surface of his neat desk. He had "cleared the deck" for her. Both the black-and-white and the color pictures lay between them. Now they both sat, separated by the desk.

He said, "I'm terribly sorry."

She found it difficult to speak. There was only one thing she needed to say, but she would restrain herself. She would come to it indirectly. She swallowed and then brought out the question: "Should I get a second opinion?"

"If you'd like to, but . . ."

"There can't be a different conclusion?"

"No."

"That is a second opinion," Shelagh stated bluntly.

"Were the consequences all explained to you?" he asked.

"Consequences? Ah, you mean what will . . . eventually . . . happen. Yes, I think they were made quite clear." She could see the teacup falling out of her hand. She stretched both arms before her, holding her hands palms down toward the desktop to show no tremor. "But not yet."

"No. Not for a while. These prescriptions will have to be renewed monthly." After a pause, he began, "Look, Shelagh, you would be better off if you had an internist or neurologist taking care of you."

"Taking care?"

"Checking up on your symptoms."

"Oh, no. I insist on your care."

Until then he had not ventured a smile; now he was unable to restrain himself from asking, "Why did you want to see me immediately?"

This was what she had come for. It poured out in a rush. "Because I must have your word, your promise, that under no circumstance will you ever tell anyone."

"I am sworn to confidentiality in my practice."

"Have you always kept your pledges?"

"You can shame me, I understand that, but I assure you . . ."

"Chester does not know! My children do not know. There is no human being who needs to know. It is a secret. It is my secret, and I want it to—I must have it—stay that way. How good is your assurance?"

"What can I tell you? The confidentiality of the patient–doctor relationship is inviolable."

She echoed the word with contempt.

"I never discuss a patient with anyone else."

"Never? Not with her husband while playing golf? Not with your own wife—looking for something to make conversation about during a dull Sunday brunch? So she can have something to spread around during a bridge game with the 'girls.' " She was afraid she was going to shriek.

Obviously unnerved, he said, "You are getting carried away."

Shelagh sat silently, composing herself, her hands clasped on her lap. "I will begin again—calmly."

"It would be good for both of us."

"That's what I'm coming to: what's good for you as well as for me."

"Good for me?"

"My silence for yours." She faced him steadily, believing she was right to take the look in his eyes as realization that she could ruin his reputation, his marriage, his career. She could take him to court.

Slowly he asked, "Why do you threaten me?"

"Because I don't trust you. Because this secret is the most important thing in my life. If I have my way, nobody will know it."

"But you deprive them—Chester, your children . . . why would you keep them from knowing?"

She said only, "I want to remain an equal in life." Then, suddenly, she asked, "Does your secretary know? Your nurse?"

"They don't read my mail."

"Have you discussed me with them?"

"No."

She remembered the ceiling in his examining room, the white sheet, his probing, the pressure, her kick against his chest, the crystal balls hanging before the high window. "How can I trust you?" she said, more to herself than to him.

"I take it Chester doesn't know about us."

"About 'us'? You mean: about you."

"About me."

"No. He doesn't."

"I'm grateful to you for that. You have my word: I will not tell a soul."

"Swear it."

"I swear it to you on all that is holy to me."

"What is holy to you?"

After a silence, he answered: "Being an equal in life."

"Perhaps we understand each other."

"I will be as helpful to you as I can."

"I need something more from you." She stood up, feeling that she was fighting for her right to life.

He stood up, with his hands on the documents before him.

"Give me those papers," she commanded. "Give me the X rays and the reports—everything that was sent to you from London. Even if you dared to say something about me to anyone—there'd be no evidence. You would be considered insane."

"You are incredible."

"Believe! Believe!" she urged him.

"It would be completely improper for me to give you—"

"Something else to hold against you."

He gathered all the papers together with the pictures, inserted them into the folder, and handed them over to her.

"If you don't keep an absolute silence about me—I will betray you."

"You make it sound as if we're accomplices."

"We are. Only I am for a good reason."

It took fifteen minutes, between four forty-five and five o'clock that afternoon, for Shelagh to burn each and every one of the documents and flush them down the toilet in the downstairs washroom.

❧

DIARY ENTRY

"Deprive" Chester and my children?

That's sentimental blarney. That's cliché thinking. By what obligation, what imperative, ought they to know? What requirement am I failing? Where is it written . . . ? Am I compelled to speak not as a free woman but as "the instrument of an ancient compulsion . . . the cumulative style of my culture"—?

I did not know it when either my father or my mother was close to dying. Both deaths were surprises. My grief came after the facts. Why should my family know anything in anticipation of the fact?

Now that it is November—they will know soon enough. May? June? July? When it can no longer be concealed from them. Time enough. I'm in no hurry.

I walk through the rooms in this house when I'm alone, touching objects as if to say, "You too will have to get along without me." The humidifier in the orchid greenhouse, the collection of brass on the library table, the curtains in my bedroom. Everything chosen and cared for will soon enough become bereft. Meanwhile, there is time to stroke them. I feel tenderness for the paperweights, lampshades, cups and saucers. I feel sorrow for the drawings that will not be made next year.

I must get on with my job.

But yesterday I took time off to drop in on Chester. I entered and sat down at the back of the courtroom before he appeared, and I don't think he noticed me. I simply wanted to watch him at work, as he has sometimes come up to the studio and stood in the doorway while I was revising a sketch or making color separations. He was presiding over a complex case of possible embezzlement. The courtroom in the new building is modern, sterile, streamlined.

200

Nothing at all like the old Court House on the Green—a white marble Greek temple on the outside with a Romanesque interior. All those symbols of grandeur given way to sleek efficiency. Only the robes are the same: the black robes of the presiding judge. The black disguise over all of his body: to obscure him as this particular person. Only his head is uncovered. How long ago was it that even the judge's head was veiled in black? So that impersonality would prevail: not I alone but the cumulative style of my culture. That fairness and justice should come with the greatest degree of impersonality and impartiality. Thinking with the minds of generations past as well as with your own. Every new interpretation, combination of ideas, "opinion" a possible precedent. Oh, Chester, you dear man, you wise man, you kind man: having to sit in judgment of your fellowman.

Even in that relatively small courtroom there was a microphone, a public-address system. When Chester spoke his voice boomed. He concentrated on the arguments of the defense attorney and the prosecutor. The accused man said nothing. Chester's concentration was palpable to me. He was listening to what they meant through what they said: evaluating, formulating, calculating degrees of credibility, culpability. I was aware that as judgment narrowed in on him, the accused man stood the chance of being sentenced to jail: to the loss of his freedom; and that everyone's life is continually involved in gambles regarding the loss or extension of freedom. Bargains, arrangements, trade-offs, agreements fulfilled or taken unfair advantage of: the endless jockeying for more freedom to exercise one's will—to fulfill one's desires. A profound exhaustion overcame me. I did not feel I could "bargain" anymore. I was afraid I didn't have the strength to get up and leave.

My desire is to be taken—like everyone else—as one who expects to live indefinitely. Why is this so important to me?

The reception at the Provost's house in honor of a visiting scholar was so clearly a formal University function, Shelagh took in at a glance, that for the Jackmans and the Warners, and a few others who were not members of the faculty, to be present meant Elsie and Clifford Rostum were taking advantage of the opportunity to pay off some social obligations at the same time. The reciprocal relations of being your host for I have been your guest. The exchange that makes for balance. Shelagh thought of straightening her great-aunt's watercolors of Greece in Adrienne's flat. The continual effort to keep things on the level.

As Provost, Clifford Rostum was given the use of a handsome house on Hillhouse Avenue, between that of the President of the University and Conrad Taylor's house. But for all the formality—the receiving line, the white-jacketed waiters, the long buffet table—the Rostums remained plain people. They had no flair for ceremony. They did what was required of them by tradition, without adding their own colors to it. They were dutiful but uninspired.

The visiting scholar turned out to be a geologist from Switzerland, extolling the autumn leaves in Vermont. "*Nothing* like it on the Continent," he assured the Jackmans. He had just completed a week's walking tour from Rutland to Manchester and returned to New Haven with examples of "thirty-seven shades of red from blushing orange to burgundy scarlet." He was a robust man said to be much in demand by international oil companies. Petroleum winching.

Shelagh asked Chester, in a whisper, at the bar: "Can you get a Nobel Prize as the Linnaeus of maple leaves?"

"Perhaps there's oil in them."

She felt the reassurance that Chester was her comrade, her colleague, her collaborator. As if he had said, "We're in this together—remember." It enabled her to move around in the crowd by herself. There was much talk of the imminent Presidential election, about which Shelagh found herself totally uninterested.

At the French windows in the dining room she found Marvin Flower, a professor of English literature, a dour man who took unconcealed enjoyment from his pessimistic view of life. "Pity it's too cool to walk around in the garden," he said, pointing to the large backyard in the twilight beyond the house. "There are so many nice dying things to look at."

"Why does it please you to consider them dying?"

His reply was prepared. "Without the Crucifixion there is no Resurrection. Nothing easier to understand in human psychology. As our ancestors watched the seasons change, and saw that what died in the fall was reborn in the spring, it came to them early on that individuals buried at the end of one life would re-emerge in another life soon enough—like daffodils, or rhubarb and other perennials."

"Like bleeding hearts." Shelagh smiled disingenuously.

"So to speak . . ." he said, nonplussed.

Shelagh asked Clifford Rostum about Brita von Bickersdorf, whom she had not been able to reach on the telephone since her return. "She's either in The Hague on World Court business or in New York at the U.N. I'm not sure. She's turned over a case that's going to Chester to one of her graduates."

Isabel Taylor appeared, nearly overwhelming in her youthful beauty, with blond hair and milk-white skin. Shelagh thought that the statue of Pallas Athena in the Parthenon must have looked like this when it was freshly completed: ivory for flesh and waves of heavy gold for hair, eyes like beacons of flashing blue light. She immediately thought of her father saying, years before: "Exceptionally beautiful women run the danger of not being courted, because men are frightened by perfection." Perfect Isabel was, but only in her beauty. Shelagh told her about encountering Caroline in Paris.

"That little bitch" was all Isabel said.

"I suppose I must tell Conrad."

"He's still in the receiving line."

"I'll wait."

"You haven't come for a ride with me in months." Isabel kept her own horse at a stable in Bethany, where there were also horses to rent. "Not since early in the summer. You ride well. . . ."

"I love to canter, but not gallop."

"Come with me again soon, will you? We'll make a date."

"Yes." Shelagh thought herself old enough to be Isabel's mother; the second Mrs. Taylor was too beautiful to have many friends her own age.

Then Walter Webster welcomed Shelagh home. "You travel almost as much as an academic does these days," he said. "I'm glad you're here. Shall we see more of each other?" Meaning: When will you drive me to Manhattan and back again?

"What do you think of the pictures here?" she asked.

The paintings belonged to the collection of the University and came with the house.

"They're all American. From Gilbert Stuart through Remington and Catlin to the Hudson Valley School. Not my field at all." As if he had said, I know a great deal about art, but I don't know what I like.

"I can't say yet how soon I'll be going to New York. But I'll call you. I promise."

"You are very sweet." He kissed her cheek. A eunuch's devotion.

I am not "sweet," she thought; I am not sure what it is I am. I am not certain what any of you are . . . looking around the living room . . . after all this time.

The receiving line broke up, and she ran into Conrad Taylor sipping a drink in the wide hallway. He was another officer, a man of authority, at the University. She told him about being in Paris "unexpectedly," wandering in the Tuileries, hearing the trio, talking with Caroline, who "looked well, if thin." She heard herself describe the girl as "her old self," not aware why she chose that phrase. She had wanted to be a neutral, between warring camps. But it was not the combativeness she saw in Conrad, it was the shock and then the deflation of disappointment that came to him from discovering that someone—another person—knew something about his daughter he did not know and felt he ought to know.

"She hadn't told me anything about a trip to Europe," he said.

"A brief tourist excursion. Too good to miss," Shelagh supplied. The implication was: spur of the moment, no time to inform Dad. "She is on her own now," Shelagh said encouragingly.

Conrad said, "Somewhat . . ." with ambiguity.

They too had been accomplices, once.

Difficult to think of a strong man as needing support. But they all do. Everyone does.

Shelagh turned her attention to Elsie Rostum. "Do you enjoy your own parties?" she asked.

"One hardly gets a chance to. . . ."

"But so pleasant. Have you heard about the thirty-seven shades of red in the maple leaves of Vermont?"

Kate Warner joined them, disconcerting her. Shelagh felt instantly apologetic, but couldn't remember for what reason. Something about their last visit: Kate in her house, her two younger children drawing in the studio. Kate Warner clearly etched before her: a woman of character, with anxieties about her offspring; a handsome woman afloat in the world.

"How nice to see you again," she said. A woman with pride, in Kelly green chiffon, her chin tilted up, her wavy dark hair parted in the middle, unafraid.

"That time you came to my house in September . . . I'm afraid there was something . . ." Shelagh began, with a hopeless gesture.

"Not at all. You were generous and hospitable. The children remember that visit—mention it often—with a certain marvel."

"The orchids, I suppose. But there was something I said to you that must have been wrong."

"You're too sensitive."

Shelagh withdrew. She realized it was what she had thought about the woman after they'd left, not something she had said to her. "Will you come again?" she asked, recognizing that her voice sounded weak.

"I'd love to."

"I'll look forward to it, then. I'll call you."

Chester rescued her and they drove home in silence like two athletes gradually recovering from an intramural meet.

DIARY ENTRY

It is different. I can feel the difference. Something to do with the degree of participation. At the Provost's reception I was not entirely "with it." I begin to feel I am watching it all from a slight distance. Their antics rather than mine, when in fact it should be just as much mine. Despite myself, I begin to

*feel I am taking leave of them. But no one should find out. We will continue
to make appointments, make dates, make plans.*

*In the midst of that gathering it occurred to me to imagine an adult mind
in the body of a young child, "successfully disguised as a child," listening to
how grown-ups talk to it and about it. "Would you like a cook-eee?" "Do you
need to go to the pot-eee?" The assumption being that they know more than
the child, are superior in every way, when in fact the child sees through them,
but must maintain the pretense. Maybe this is how my mind leads me to the
other side of that coin: to be the only grown-up, the superior in such a gathering. Knowing something none of them knows. Not letting on. Keeping
them in ignorance in order to play my part "correctly." To keep the story
going. If the child who saw that the Emperor's "new clothes" did not exist
had kept its mouth shut, there would have been a different story. Everything
depends on what story you want to be part of.*

Beginning to see everything from a different point of view, Shelagh Jackman sometimes found herself doing nothing, uninterested in getting up out
of bed in the morning after Chester had left, sitting back idly in an armchair
in the library, abstractly wondering if there were any book on those shelves
that she wanted to reread or if there might be a book she had never read but
ought to, now. She saw the whole leather-bound set of Sir Walter Scott's
Waverley novels which had belonged to Chester's grandfather. She had never
read Sir Walter Scott; she knew then that she never would. She would never
travel in Uganda. She would never learn Chinese or make pottery, or caress a
grandchild. She thought of Walter Webster's disclaimer: "Not my field at
all." Of Kate Warner's calling her "too sensitive." Of Chester's accusation of
"greed." She felt she must put things *in order*; but not yet, not yet.

She must cultivate her own field.

She forced herself back to her studio. She was working on an illustration
for the story of Ruth. "Orphah kissed her mother-in-law good-bye, and returned to her childhood home; but Ruth insisted on staying with Naomi . . .
'I want to go wherever you go, and to live wherever you live; your people shall
be my people, and your God shall be my God. I want to die where you
die . . .' " She moaned Chester's name aloud; burst into tears; wept against
her arms crossed over the drawing board, in the empty house.

She forced herself to go riding with Isabel Taylor. In the open country,
crisp autumn air alone was refreshing, but cantering along paths in the ever-
green wood or across the stubble of cornfields filled her with vigor. The heaving of the stallion under her thrilled her with the gift of his vitality.

Leading their horses back into the stable, they watched a ten-year-old girl on a small horse being led about the ring by her instructor. She wore a black velvet peaked cap, cashmere sweaters, beige riding breeches, and high leather boots. Her mother, in a similar outfit, stood at the edge of the ring taking one Polaroid photograph after another.

"Poor child," Isabel said, "I know what it's like. Having your every sneeze recorded . . ."

Preserved, Shelagh thought. With pictures, and tape recordings, and home movies, mementos, souvenirs, you can watch the children grow up again and again. You can relive it: the eternal return made practicable, during one lifetime.

Isabel had picked up Shelagh in her car and now drove them back to her home on Hillhouse Avenue for a cocktail. She wore riding clothes as handsome as the young girl's and her mother's. Shelagh was dressed in corduroy slacks and a tan windbreaker that Morgan had discarded after college. They lounged on the sofas in the room Isabel called the bar. Shelagh drank a brandy and soda. Isabel made herself a very strong gin Martini.

"Do you have all the photographs of your own childhood?" Shelagh asked.

"Somewhere," Isabel answered vaguely. "Packed away."

"Biographies used to be written in words, but now they can be constructed with pictures."

"I don't want to know everything about myself."

That sent a chill through Shelagh. "But if you don't know . . ." she began to ask.

"You don't suffer."

Shelagh made herself laugh. "And if you don't suffer, you don't know."

DIARY ENTRY

If you don't know everything about yourself, who can?

"What are you thinking about?" Chester asked.

"Pictures," Shelagh replied. "Pictures. Pictures. All those flickering images on the wall in Plato's cave."

They sat together, quiet, in the library, Chester leafing through cello music on his lap, Shelagh knitting a scarf for him.

"The ride in the country was wonderfully refreshing. But I suspect Isabel Taylor might be a sort of depressive type. Because she's so good-looking, she's probably never been treated as a human being. More as a work of art."

"Is that what makes you think of pictures?"

" 'Pretty as a picture,' " she snorted. "Something like that. And then the mistake of thinking we 'know' things because we've seen photographs of them—Machu Picchu, or Leningrad, or Katmandu."

"We know more than we would have known without the photographs."

"Darling . . ." she began slowly, "when I spent that day alone in Paris, there was a Japanese who took a picture—not of me, but of a view that I happened to be in. What I'm thinking of now is that somewhere in Japan, at this moment, there is a picture, developed and printed, probably neatly catalogued in an album, dated on the label, that shows me on the stairs between rue de Rivoli and the Jeu de Paume, being shown around to family and friends: 'Occidental in place.' Do they know anything about me?"

"Only what you looked like at that moment."

"Ah, just a flicker of phenomenon; no, *noumenon*."

"See what self-protection there is in German Idealism?"

They both laughed.

"Do *you* know the *noumenon*?" she asked him.

He looked up from the music, drew the reading glasses down the length of his nose, and stared at her. "I know where we touch each other," he said: "usually to shore each other up."

Shelagh changed the subject. "Do you remember, from years ago, the photographs—I think they were in *Life* magazine—of French aristocrats, perhaps a count and countess, who decided to settle their worldly goods on their children and enter holy orders—he went into a monastery and she went into a convent?"

"Yes. They let go of the things of this world before this world let go of them."

"We wouldn't know how to do that . . . would we?" she asked.

"Are you ready to let go?" he wondered with surprise.

"No. No, I'm not. I just wish I knew what it takes—when the time comes. It must be better to be magnanimous than to be robbed. I wonder how long they lived in the convent and the monastery."

"Who?"

"The French count and countess. They were only about sixty years old, as I remember."

"Maybe they're still alive."

"And free of this world."

"It's entirely possible."

"Strange—that we've never talked about what we might do when you retire."

"Yes. We don't believe it will happen, do we?"

"I hardly remember how old you are."

"I have difficulty with that myself."

"Do you want to leave here? Go somewhere forever warm like St. Croix or Key West?"

"I'd rather go to London, and die in the Reading Room at the British Museum."

"You mean in the bar at the Garrick."

"Aren't you being morbid tonight!"

"Am I? I won't let it happen again."

❦

The visit to New York for Claire's opening night in an Off Broadway play did not turn out to be the kind of pleasant experience Shelagh had looked forward to. Instead, it was deeply unsettling. The play opened on a Friday evening, and by the end of Saturday afternoon, when she and Chester met Brita von Bickersdorf for a drink, her emotions were even more mixed by the critics' opinions of the show and Shelagh's confusion over loyalty to Claire against loyalty to her own judgments.

Brita was participating in a conference at the United Nations during the day, so the Jackmans met her at the hotel across the street from the Secretariat building, in a bar called the Ambassador Grill: all mirrors, with walls and ceiling decorations out of a geometry textbook, plush seats, black glass tables, and dim lights. Shelagh sought safety in silence. Chester commented that no one within earshot was speaking English and that he couldn't even name half the languages to be heard. Shelagh was uninterested. She picked at her fingernails. Chester appropriated one of her hands into both of his, saying, "You must not take it so hard."

Shelagh's look at him read: Please do not ask me for something impossible.

Brita arrived in a flush of satisfaction; hard work always seemed to invigorate her. Her very plumpness radiated accomplishment. Shelagh made room for her on the cushioned bench and Chester ordered a cocktail for her from the waitress. "Isn't it bizarre," Brita said, "our having to meet in New York?"

"But you're almost never at home in New Haven these days," Chester replied.

"And I miss you," Shelagh added quietly.

Brita instantly took in the vulnerable tone of Shelagh's voice and, studying her face, ventured, "It didn't go well?"

Chester simply said, "No, it didn't."

"I'd call it a catastrophe" was Shelagh's opinion.

"I haven't had a chance to read the reviews yet."

Shelagh said, "Don't bother. The play itself is a crock of vulgarity."

"It's really quite simpleminded," Chester explained. "It's written by a woman whose 'point' is that promiscuity for wives should now be as appropriate for husbands to live with as extramarital affairs have always been the condoned behavior that wives have had to live with."

"Being 'independent' justifies being undependable," Shelagh added to the description. "As if human beings could be independent of each other. Propaganda for sheer self-indulgence and willfulness disguised as the only worthwhile goals—self-fulfillment and, forgive me, she actually calls it 'self-happiness.' " Shelagh sighed. "The last play I saw in London was supposed to be about a man who couldn't love anyone because he liked everybody too much. Of course, that isn't what it was about. It was about a man who couldn't feel anything at all. And this play is supposed to be about a woman who is so determined to be 'herself' that she won't say no to any opportunity to shack up with anyone who catches her eye; but it's actually about the pleasures of impersonal sex. That's what it extols."

"A sort of women's-lib *Picture of Dorian Gray*," Chester said, "with the opposite moral of the story: you grow more beautiful over time if you satisfy every sexual whim."

"Fantasies. . . ." Brita smiled. "Fantasies. . . . Was it done with wit?"

Shelagh groaned.

Chester said, "College humor. Somebody describes a pederast as a 'Fundamentalist' and one of the other characters asks why she called him that. The answer is, 'He'd rather have intercourse with a male's fundament than with a female's vagina.' "

Shelagh remembered: "There was a whole scene devoted to trying to recall what the arguments are in favor of being an honest woman rather than a prostitute—but none of the characters could think of a good reason."

Chester added: "And there was that old chestnut about a married woman being a prostitute for only one man. Mind you, I think eighty percent of the audience consisted of married couples."

"No one has a good word for marriage these days," Brita said.

"No one seems to be conscious of what it's worth," Shelagh said.

"Well, it sounds dreadful," Brita concluded. "What part did Claire play?"

Chester and Shelagh appeared equally embarrassed. "She was," her father began, "the leading lady's maid—who ends up consoling the husband."

Shelagh blurted out: "She is half-naked in one scene."

Into the silence of Shelagh's sense of shock and distress Brita brought the solace of "That's become a commonplace on the stage today."

"Not as far as Claire is concerned," her mother remarked in a voice full of sorrow.

Chester explained: "There was a scene when the wife, showing how egalitarian she is, says to the maid, on a hot day, 'Have a cool drink, take your shoes off, make yourself as comfortable as you'd like.' And the maid takes off her blouse and sits there on the sofa—bare from the waist up. That's when the husband comes in."

Shelagh said: "Claire. Half-naked on the stage. Five hundred people in the audience."

Brita tried to make light of it: "They didn't jump up on the stage and rape her, now, did they?"

"They didn't have to. They went home with the image of her bare breasts lodged in their psyches—to make love with each other, and with the memory of what they had seen. That's the function of pornography."

Chester said, "It wasn't a pornographic play."

Shelagh, suddenly vehement, said, "It was an insultingly stupid play—which included more than one scene meant to be sexually stimulating. And its 'redeeming social value' consisted of the wonderful argument that since we can't expect to achieve social justice for all during this generation, then at least each of us who has the guts for it should see to our own 'self-happiness' during our own lifetime. Some message!"

"But don't you agree?" Brita asked.

"Salvation by promiscuity?" Shelagh replied.

"No, but—moral man in an immoral society . . ."

"This play makes the case for immoral woman because of an immoral society."

"Shelagh," Brita answered, "we are each trying to find a path out of the jungle. . . . Did you see Claire afterward?"

"Only briefly," Chester said, "for a few minutes backstage, and then we drove her in a cab to the cast party. She was exultant—and exhausted."

Shelagh said, "All I can remember is repeating—with a certain disbelief—'Are you all right?' and her saying, 'It was wonderful, wonderful!' " She was measuring the distance between her distress and Claire's ebullience. They were on different wavelengths.

"Have you spoken with her since?" Brita asked.

"Yes," Chester said. "We were supposed to take her to lunch but she begged out. The disappointment was so intense. The reviewers have—unanimously—panned the play, and although they put on the Saturday matinee, it's going to close tonight."

Shelagh said, "And that's simply the doing of the theater critic for *The New York Times*. If he thinks well of a play, it runs; if he knocks it—it's dead. Don't you think it's amazing that the judgment of one person should have such a life-or-death effect on the efforts of dozens of people? Authors, actors, directors, investors—everybody involved. Just one man's split-second opinion?"

"Are you defending the play, now?" Chester asked.

"No! I'm just unhappy for Claire that her chance of doing what she wants to do—to act in a play that runs for a while—is taken away from her primarily by one man's judgment." It suddenly struck her that Chester's "one man's opinion" often determined whether someone went to jail or not; that degrees of freedom for people to do what they want to do are determined all the time by the power of such judgments. And the fact that she agreed with the critic's opinion of the play did not make it easier for her to accept the consequence that Claire would be out of a job, when having an acting job was Claire's way of finding her path out of the jungle.

"Think, now," Brita urged, calmly, "why are you so upset? Is it the bad play? or Claire's bare breasts? or the loss of her job?"

"All of the above," Shelagh answered.

"It is real life," Chester said.

"I don't like it," Shelagh responded.

DIARY ENTRY

How am I to understand why I felt so distressed?

One thing I know is that for the first time since I returned from London, I forgot to take my pills with me. Two days in New York without the five pills I'm supposed to take each day—worrying about whether I'd suffer another seizure because of not taking them. I felt stretched tight as a drum all of the time, sensitive to every twitch of my body. I hardly slept that night. I had a miserable headache. But I was spared. There was no seizure. That mistake must never be made again. Chester once gave me, as a St. Valentine's Day present, a Battersea box with the lines "More than yesterday, less than tomorrow" on the lid. What I'll do is put five pills in it every morning and see that I take them when I'm supposed to. Not that I understand anything of the chemistry of it. Why not all five at one time? What difference would that make? Why not thirty-five pills once a week? This is boring.

I feel so ashamed for Claire. For having to appear half-naked on the stage. I know that many people would say that it means nothing; there is no shame involved. But if that is true, then why ask a young woman, an actress, to do it at all? There is some mistaken concept of "honesty" involved here. Presumably the playwright is being "honest" to the imagined situation. That is what might actually have happened. Given a maid without scruples or a sense of decorum or given a young woman who is an opportunist, able to seduce the wife but willing to settle for the husband. Unsavory either way. And for Claire to play that part! I don't believe that it means nothing. The actress is asked to give up the distinction between what is private and what is public; to break down the limits of what is "mine" and not at the disposal of a public, an audience; to invite complete strangers—with no claim on intimacy—to indulge in the sight of what should remain exclusively a reward for earned intimacy. It's so phony—the experience of phony intimacy. One has only to buy a theater ticket to see Claire's breasts. It's shameful. To betray oneself and to titillate the unknown audience.

It is that betrayal of herself on Claire's part which bothers me the most. It is one thing to act the part of someone entirely different from and superior to yourself—as when she played Antigone in high school or Mary Stuart in college. I saw her once at acting class in the role of the Madwoman of Chaillot. She has the ability to make one believe in nobler personalities. What does it do to a young woman to act the part of a vulgarian? To pretend to be crass and cheap, to sell herself short? To debase herself?

It strikes me that I have never thought of other actors as having lives of their own, off the stage, when I have seen others play; actors playing parts that must be inferior to the persons that they are offstage. When I was in London and saw The Philanthropist it never occurred to me that the actors were actual human beings with lives to live independent of the parts they played in the show. I did not think of them as persons who were debasing themselves. But how can I not think this way about Claire? What is terrible is the thought that she might not be debasing or betraying herself; that she likes showing the world that she is a sex-tease, that she is available, for rent if not for sale. How great a leap is it from the price of a theater ticket to the price for a night with Claire? This is a disgusting line of thought. But how can I avoid it?

How much of these ideas is concerned with Claire and how much concerned with myself? Am I worried about what playing such a part means for her—her conception of herself and what she will make of herself—or how much this means to me? To be the mother of a daughter who will "offer" herself in this way in public? Is this an end in itself or does it represent merely a means to an end, a better purpose, a chance to play better parts—in worthwhile plays, rather than in a piece of junk like this one? Or is it of value to be good at a part that shows how someone merely uses her body—her sexual availability—to get ahead in the world?

I am unnerved by it all.

Chester could not help. He must feel it all through different associations. He is her father. Perhaps the sight of her half-naked pleases some latent desire for incest. So his pose of being nonjudgmental is not to be trusted. He says he wishes her well in her career and this kind of vulgarity is part of the general condition in which she has to make a career for herself. He says he understands it as a stepping-stone. But what if it is a millstone around her neck?

I feel so naive about having encouraged her to become an actress. It is what she wanted; I want her to be happy. I thought of all those sweet ingenue parts

I've seen her play. We are in a position to pay for acting classes and to see that she lives in a comfortable apartment. Why have I been blind to everything else? All the unscrupulous people who will try to make use of her? The oppressive competition for every possible job? The sexual favors as the "marginal difference" when, "all else being equal" . . . ?

What can I possibly do to make Claire's life better for her?

What else am I here for, as far as she is concerned?

LETTER TO ADRIENNE MARKGRAF IN LONDON

Dear heart:

We have seen Claire triumphant in a lousy play. Her acting was excellent. The play was despicable. I suppose that in London it would run for six weeks or three months, but in New York the kiss of death—negative critical reviews—meant that it closed the next day. You know what was wrong with it?—the attempt to treat a profound condition of human unhappiness (absolute fidelity within marriage as against willful promiscuity) as if it were a situation comedy susceptible to a simple single solution. It is interesting how the word "problem" has oversimplified the American's approach to difficulties in life. The assumption is that if you can identify a problem, you can find a satisfactory solution. It obscures the greater awareness that there are some conditions that are not "solvable." Americans don't like to believe that unhappiness is inescapable. They are such idealists. But they don't know the difference between smart talk and wisdom.

Do I? Do you?

I want Claire to be safe. And that's understandable on my part but not very appreciative of the world she lives in—wants to make a career in. The pressures to be un-safe—to risk too much—must be tremendous. I can't say, "Get thee to a nunnery, go!"—nor would I be listened to. But I fear for her. Don't we all fear for each other?

The fact is—I might as well tell you the whole truth—that in one scene, Claire appeared on stage naked from the waist up. I felt—I'm not sure how to put this—I suppose I felt as if I'd been kicked in the stomach, hurled out through the back wall of the theater, and flung flat on my rump in the gutter of the street outside. What does this mean? That I can't accept her as an adult? She is older than I was when I married Chester. Or that I can't acknowledge her as a sexual being—and a sex object? It's true that I don't think of her as enjoying an active sex life—but then, I never think about anyone else's sex life. (Well, almost never.) It's not that I would deny it to her, or deprive her of it if that were in my power to do. I wouldn't. But I don't want to be made conscious of it—especially as the member of an impersonal audi-

213

ence. It's complicated: I was a member of that public audience, but I was not impersonal—I know the person playing that part. There's the trouble: I couldn't separate Claire, the private person, from the part she was playing onstage. I didn't like the person she was pretending to be. I forgot that she was acting; I was shocked by her having become such a person. I wanted to snatch her up and carry her home to safety.

It's the thought that she is just not safe in that world of the theater that oppresses me. It is a vulgar and debasing world much more of the time and to a much higher degree than I ever let myself think of it as being. But how safe can I hope for her to be? To take no risks, make no mistakes, refuse all dangers? No. It's not that I don't trust her—to come out all right, to make the best decisions for herself in the long run. But oh, how I fear for the suffering that goes with making mistakes, and having to live with them, in the short run: taking a risk not worth the dangers involved.

She is not a child; and I am not her nanny.

She is an adult—and I am an older adult.

What can I do to help her? I can't buy her a good career in the theater; it isn't for sale.

—Later:

You may not believe this, but writing you was interrupted by a telephone call from Claire. We must have talked for close to an hour. She is doubly miserable—over the fact that the play was a flop and feeling relieved that she no longer has to act that vulgar role. Very tangled emotions. She wants to be loyal to the group that put on that play—and she was very much a member of that group; but she disliked the part she played. She took pride in acting it well, but she did not admire the role. And there I was consoling her and supporting her and assuring her that it's not likely that one is able to do—in the course of a lifetime—only that which is admirable in itself. Each event is an end in itself, but some are of value only as means to other ends. It was a long, weepy, loving conversation. (It came out that her boyfriend, Simon, had chosen not to see her in that part. I'd give him very good marks for that, wouldn't you?—not to see in public the breasts one lusts to see in private. . . .)

And what also was said was that she had not told Chester or me that she would be half-nude onstage because she felt instinctively there was something depraved about it and she couldn't bring herself to forewarn us, fearing we might persuade her to drop out of the part. Touching!—as if we could still influence her in such a way; but recognizing that we don't have the right. An extraordinary conversation: she was at the same time both proud and ashamed. But that goes with taking a risk that isn't worth the dangers involved. I'm rather close to becoming an old lady, but I think I have the same kind of guts myself. If there were something outrageous I thought was worth *doing, I believe I'd have the courage to risk it. And that's all I'll reveal to you about myself this morning.*

Be happy!

❧❧❧

The Thanksgiving Day celebration did not get off to a good start.

Morgan had rented a car and driven up with Claire—who apparently had described the play to him in detail. But she was unprepared for him to surprise everyone, over Sherry in the living room, by saying how sorry he was that, having had to attend a meeting in Bermuda, he was prevented from "watching Claire air her tits in public."

There was a pained silence into which Chester suggested only that Morgan's remark fell flat; Claire hissed like an asp at both of them; and Shelagh—aware that this was the last time the four of them could enjoy the holiday together—acknowledged that one of the charms of such a family reunion is the opportunity for young adults to behave like adolescents again. But her suggestion did not relieve the tension.

Morgan said, "I can't believe you felt no sense of responsibility about disgracing the rest of us, if not yourself."

"Disgrace?" Claire's voice exaggerated the word into a wail. "What disgrace?"

"The shame of showing off private parts in public."

"There are some societies where women never cover their breasts. Like the Balinese . . . Polynesians . . ."

"Of which we are not members," Morgan retorted.

"Besides, even if you find *what I did* shameful, how does that affect you?"

" 'No man is an island, entire of itself,' " he quoted, "and no sister either. It was the first thing I heard about when I got back to the office on Monday."

"With a lustful smirk, no doubt. Did your buddies ask if you could arrange assignations with me for them? During lunchtime, of course, because they have to be at home with Wifey by six. Isn't everyone on Wall Street made horny by the idea of your sister's breasts?"

"Yes; except those who feel disgrace."

Chester stood up and refilled each of the Sherry glasses as he said: "I've given this some thought myself and I'd like to make a few remarks. First of all, Morgan told us recently that he's thinking of joining the Church. Well, then, he may be more sensitive than the rest of us to judging behavior in terms of grace or disgrace—and with the other assumptions, secular, if you will, of decent or indecent actions. All 'Western' ideas—but our culture is our fate. However, allow me to point out that your sister did not bare her breasts in public."

He resumed his seat and sipped the wine, while the other three eagerly awaited his next statement.

"Your sister is an actress," he continued. "It was not that Claire showed an unspecified 'public' her breasts, as it were, in her own name. She was playing a part, and everyone in that 'public' shared the same understanding—that they were watching a play. The role she was impersonating required that the actress appear naked from the waist up to be true to the nature of the character in the play. The audience was not responding to Claire's personal behavior; they were affected by how well she pretended to be someone else."

Shelagh clapped her hands and laughed: "Bravo!"

Morgan muttered, "Sophistry."

Claire, grateful and serious, said, "Wait, Dad. There's another distinction to make. The very difference between acting and pretending is that the audience knows you're not—as you put it—behaving in your own name."

Morgan said, "You mean—when you're pretending in real life, no one else knows you're being false."

"Exactly," Claire agreed, vivacious now. "If Wifey tells Hubby that she doesn't want to make love because she has a headache, when she doesn't have, she's lying; that's a pretense; she's pretending."

"But if he believes she's lying, then as far as he's concerned she's playing a part—she's acting," Morgan concluded.

Shelagh drew it out slowly: "So half depends on whether it is true that you feel what you say you're feeling; and half depends on whether your 'audience' believes you—all the time."

"Of course," said the Judge. "I see it in court every day. It's the struggle between subjective uncertainty of integrity, on the one hand, and objective interpretation, on the other hand. One tries to convince or deceive; the other wants to determine the truth."

Returning to her thoughts of the theater, Claire said, "But every audience grants in advance that the actor does not mean what he says. He's pretending to something and the audience knows it, accepts it as acting. Except for children and bumpkins who haven't yet learned the rules of the game. They're the ones who think the dagger and the blood are real—and scream out; or the grown-ups who get so caught up in the action, forget a play is being performed and shout 'No!' to the speech about 'Hitler would have loved you, too . . .' in that play about the unregenerate Nazi. What was the name of that play?"

Chester asked, "Does anyone know when 'role-playing' was introduced into the vocabulary of normal psychology?"

Thinking out loud, Shelagh wondered, "But the other person can never know for certain, if I say I have a headache, whether that is true—any more than he can know that I have a headache if I don't mention it."

Chester leaned forward and grabbed her wrist roughly, declaring in a stern voice: "For a long time, it was believed that torture would bring out the truth." He released his grasp, patted her wrist, and smiled. "But most people have given up that method."

Shelagh sighed. "I'm very glad we've had this discussion. I admit I was upset seeing Claire 'exposed' on stage—but I wasn't feeling well, and I over-reacted. Now I know it wasn't Claire."

Everyone laughed and called for another round of Sherry.

I am not acting, Shelagh told herself, except in the eyes of Quentin Con-nolley, who knows the facts. But before everyone else, I am pretending. And I am unashamed. I would not have it otherwise. I would have everything ex-actly as it is: Everything in Place, as it is now. At five in the afternoon it had grown dark. She stood up to switch on the four lamps in the living room. She closed the draperies. She turned to survey her home, her family: the Chinese plates over the fireplace, the Archimboldos on the opposite wall. After re-placing the Sherry decanter on the teak trunk, Chester leaned back again on the sofa. Claire and Morgan sat opposite in the armchairs drawn up to the trunk. Shelagh said, "You know, we can eat whenever you'd like now."

"One more drink," Chester said.

Shelagh sat near him again on the sofa. "Everything's in place."

"Are you happy with your lot?" Chester asked. "Satisfied with your brood?"

She said, "Yes. I think this is heaven." And leaned close to her husband, kissed him on the cheek, and then got up and kissed Claire and Morgan in the same way.

"Is this," Chester asked, as she came back to sit close to him, "the best your imagination can grasp of Paradise?"

"It'll do!"

"Did I ever tell you Judge Learned Hand's description of Paradise?" Ches-ter asked.

"Yes," Shelagh replied. "But tell it again."

"He said it would be to wake up in the morning feeling refreshed, healthy and strong. Eat a hearty breakfast and then play polo all morning. He would score one goal after another and be the rage of the crowd, applauding him and shouting his praise. Then for lunch there would be chilled Martinis first; the food would be delicious, and the conversation intelligent and entertain-ing. After a revitalizing nap, he would play football—star in the football game, during which he'd make one touchdown after another, one end run more spectacular than the last, until the spectators were crazy with admira-tion for him, shouting his name endlessly in chants of adoration.

"At dinner the Martinis would be even drier and chillier than those at lunch, the food even more excellent; and over the long, leisurely meal, the conversation would be brilliant with the most interesting and charming people who have ever lived. The ultimate moment would come when the voice of God would be heard commanding: "Quiet, Voltaire. I want to hear more of what Judge Hand has to say.""

Shelagh laughed heartily; Claire applauded; Morgan chuckled and stroked the smooth skin of his long jaw reflectively.

"Was the best of his imagined Paradise," Morgan asked, "for it to be like that *every* day?"

Judge Jackman suggested, "I suppose he should have built in the condition that he would never tire of it."

"That," Shelagh said, "is beyond my imagination."

"Was he really so competitive?" Claire asked.

"He did have a humble desire to be the best at everything," her father answered.

"And how close did he come to realizing his ideal?" Shelagh wondered.

Chester calculated for a moment and then proposed, "About eight on a scale of zero to ten. But, you know, ideals are to be aspired to, aimed at, not necessarily achieved."

Morgan thought, "There must be a point when you get so tired of the effort—even in Paradise—that you want to chuck the whole thing."

Shelagh was suddenly pierced by the profound sadness in Morgan's remark. "Oh . . . my darling . . ." she barely whispered with compassion. "With a little good luck, it becomes worth all the effort."

" 'Getting and spending,' " he quoted in response, " 'we lay waste our powers. Little we see in Nature that is ours . . .' All the work that goes into making a living and then making a way of life. Trying things on for size. Yourself as well as other people . . ."

"How is What's-her-name?" Claire asked Morgan.

His mother wanted to know: "Have you been doing any writing?"

Morgan looked above the heads of his parents to the four panels of the Archimboldo paintings, slowly moving his gaze across the images of fauna and flora contrived to create the impressions of human faces, with variations on the four seasons of the year and the four ages of man. "Nothing ever is what it appears to be," he said.

Judge Jackman offered a gloss: "Nothing is *only* what it appears to be."

"Those pictures," Morgan, who had seen them as long as he had been alive, continued, "aren't even genuine: I mean, the originals. They're copies. So there are about five levels of appearances visible—an imitation pretending to be an Archimboldo, animals and vegetables and fruit and flowers pretending to be faces, people pretending to be seasons . . . Need I go on?"

Shelagh said, "They're not pretending. Since we know what they're not, they're acting."

Everyone laughed with her but Morgan, who said, "What's so tiresome is trying to separate the false from the true."

Claire said, "The healthy from the sick."

Chester added, "The authentic from the insincere."

Shelagh smiled. "The wheat from the chaff. Which reminds me, dinner is about to be served."

And then it was all present: between the place settings of china, crystal, silver, and large white linen napkins, the platters and bowls contained the crisp turkey, the cranberry sauce, stuffing with oysters and chestnuts, sweet potatoes, a tossed green salad, warm croissants on the butter dish; the claret stood in decanters on the sideboard. Shelagh waved her family toward the dining-room table with an arm gesture of introduction, proudly announcing: "America."

Seated at the table, Chester solemnly spoke for all of them. "We have much to be thankful for."

From the time that their children were young teen-agers, it had been the habit of the Jackmans for each of them around the table to name what he or she was thankful for. It had been done at first awkwardly, self-consciously; but as the ritual became established they had done so without reserve. Shelagh remembered that the year Claire adopted a stray beige-striped cat, she had fervently said, "I'm thankful that Mr. Peanut Butter chose me, and our house to live in, rather than anyone else in the world." She remembered her surprise when Morgan, home from his first semester at college, said, "I give thanks that we're not poor." There were similarities in the litany from one year to the next, but many differences as well. Shelagh believed all of them had become grateful people. She said, "Giving thanks is such a grown-up thing to do."

Morgan commented, "There's an injunction to give thanks in the Bible."

Claire asked, "How are the illustrations coming along?"

"Let me show you some later."

"But if you don't believe in God," Morgan asked in a seriously measured tone, "then who is it you're giving thanks to?"

"In human societies," Shelagh quoted, "God is everybody else." She did not remember at the moment who had said that to her, but she felt the truth of it.

And Chester, sensing the separateness of each from the others at the moment, especially the degree of uncertainty that his son and his daughter felt about their futures, made an unusual suggestion. "This year—let us each give

219

thanks in silence. Let us know what we are grateful for, without parading it, but appreciating that 'everybody else' will know it too by the kind of lives we live."

At the end of the minute of silence, Shelagh's eyes had filled with tears. She wiped them away on her napkin and said, "We love each other."

DIARY ENTRY

Letdown! Of course, it was bound to come. I had worked for days—making all the arrangements, the preparations for Thanksgiving; cooking for two days—and then it seemed over in an hour. It wasn't really; but I was doomed to be let down simply because it couldn't go on forever.

I would have wanted it to go on forever.

Still, there were wonderful moments: and in the end, Claire and Morgan drove off late in the evening with the gifts I had brought back from London for them, and boxes of orchids they had chosen for their own apartments.

Even after all these years, I find it almost incredible—the sensitivity with which Chester responds to me and supports me. The way he picked up and used the phrase "everybody else" filled me with awe. Thus, I was exalted on my last Thanksgiving Day.

My sorrow was neither for myself nor for Chester, but for the children. What will become of them? On the surface, they appear to be "all together," able to cope with whatever luck throws their way. But "nothing is only what it appears to be." They are worried. They are incomplete. Well, as long as we live we are incomplete, but I mean the essential features aren't clear yet.

Could I be wrong about that? If they were to die now, would it not be possible to make a clear judgment about them? To summarize and evaluate them accurately? Yes and no—that is, to the best of my knowledge: and it's that which is incomplete. Even I cannot know everything about them. Or is it that the idea of completeness of knowledge cannot apply to human beings? One of those ideals Chester refers to as worth aiming at without expectation of achievement? Am I thinking in these terms only because I am thinking of a final judgment on my own life? Instinctively, I feel more and more strongly that it is judgment that matters in human relations—not the tipsy answer the editor of Dialogue gave me in that late-night conversation at Adrienne's party about the intellectual understanding of human beings. What he said meant that the abstract comprehension of a person has nothing more in common with that being than the mathematical formula for a circle has in common with any actual circle. But then, what is rationally satisfying in one time and place is radically different from what satisfies the mind in another culture. The more modest aim of sympathetic judgment seems to me more likely to be timeless and universal.

If Morgan is serious about becoming a Believer, could it be because he cannot judge himself well yet, and wants the reassurance that The Omniscient One—the only one who can be imagined to know everything about a person—will be there to make the Last Judgment? Longing for Truth about his own value even more than for his Salvation?

It may well be that his wish for literal truth was behind his sad remarks about "trying things on for size," about wearily trying to understand himself as well as other people. He's not happy with any idea of how much of life must be make-believe—role-playing, in order to create oneself. Just as in works of art. He criticized the Archimboldos as if they were trying to deceive him, when in fact any work of art offers a make-believe as an indirect route, a different chance from the literal, to come closer to a truth. Even the dogmas of the church he might join can be thought of as a superb make-believe, an artifice pretending to show the ultimate truth. It is the story that reassures, for there can be no certainty that it is true. (Everything depends on what story one longs to be a character in.)

Apparently, Morgan suffers from Judge Hand's humble desire to be the best at everything. Maybe that is why he does not write. My guess is that he has considerable talent for fiction. He should go on from the bright, clever, imaginative stories he wrote in college to more ambitious—and more wonderful!—stories and novels. But perhaps he thinks if he can't produce an instantly recognized masterpiece of originality, then it isn't worth the effort. The good is the victim of the idea of the Best.

And there is that hidden fear of his about being poor. Ha! If only he knew how much he stands to inherit! On second thought, that probably wouldn't help. It's not being afraid of having no money that makes him so cautious, so wary, so concerned about "disgrace." It is fear of failure. Money must mean for him the visible sign of competence, success, the ability to take care of himself and others. Since he grew up in a family where there never was fear of being poor, what else could it mean? Were the ideals set so high for him that he cannot but fear failure? I think I understand for the first time why he chose to become a stockbroker; he would not risk his luck at making or doing something that might bring in money or not; he went directly into the world where making money is itself what one does. But that should not satisfy him for a lifetime. Either he will come to see that money is only a means, and the ends to which he puts however much he has are much more important than how much he has. Or, if he never understands that, then his only satisfaction will be to accumulate more and more money. Yes. I see. It is because the penny has not yet dropped to determine his formation in this regard that I feel for him as incomplete.

Do I not feel the same about Claire? I was so optimistic and supportive and encouraging about her wish to become an actress, I put out of my mind all the dangers and the drawbacks to the establishment of such a career—though I should have known better. I wanted to forget her being half-nude in a vulgar play because that demonstrates the nasty risks involved. But I didn't forget it. And when she was alone with me in my studio—enjoying my drawings for the Old Testament with her usual freshness of feeling and enthusiasm—I planted in her mind the possibility of considering an alternative; she might teach acting, or teach the history of drama at a university; teach "theater-literature" or whatever it is called now—rather than forever fighting for a job on the stage. She listened. She was not offended or dispirited. She is not afraid of failure. She is only afraid of not enjoying herself. She will think about it.

Chester and Morgan talked politics in the library, while I showed Claire the new clothes I'd bought in London. The four of us love each other—as well as we can.

I feel let down because my expectations are too high, and because I am anxious over the insecurity of my children. That's commonplace enough, I suppose. Probably all my friends with sons and daughters in their middle twenties feel the same way. But they can enjoy the belief that they will have many years more in which to influence them and to help them. I cannot believe that. I have been given only until sometime next summer. That is the "un-commonplace." If my children knew the prediction of my death, I could have no further influence on them. They would begin to separate themselves from me the instant they learned the bad news. To distance themselves. To avoid any contagion. They would pretend the opposite, of course. Pretend to be closer, to solace me. But it would be out of pity: knowing they can do nothing to change the course of events. And that knowledge would steel them against any attempt on my part to change the course of events in their malleable lives. As I can no longer be "influenced," so they would protect themselves against deathbed wishes and pledges, promises made to the dying, because the conditions for reciprocal relations no longer pertain. There will be no future for me in which to be held to my part of any bargain.

I am so glad that the situation allows me to keep this secret.

Thus, I continue to appear to be accountable for anything I might try to do. . . .

I sit here in the library, the day after Thanksgiving, alone in the house of the-fullness-of-my-life: being thankful. I try to remember the events, the remarks, the associations of yesterday's celebration—everything. Remembering Claire's giving thanks that Mr. Peanut Butter chose her brought back to mind that years later, when it came time to die, that cat—who had spent half his waking hours curled up on the lap of one of us—hid himself away in the corner of a closet, went through his death agony all alone. We found him only after rigor mortis had turned him into the statue of an Egyptian cat divinity. Do most animals secrete themselves away from all their kind to die alone? Do only human beings imagine they can offer consolation to the dying?

Claire told us that her boyfriend, Simon, did not see her in the play because he had to make a trip to Canada, not because he knew all about the part she was playing.

Chester, over brandy after dinner, described the suit of the "Silence Lady" that would be coming before him soon. Not so much a trial of whether one had the right to remain silent during a legal investigation as it is directed against the State's Attorney for punishing her for her silence. I do not appreciate the legal issues involved; but I sympathize with her. There is a structure of "rights" in public life which can be interpreted by a judge in court. I am assuming a right to be silent in private life—I am taking that upon myself as if it were my right, although there is no contract that spells out obligations, rewards, and perquisites. How much does one owe to others to tell them? By what right do I not tell them? Answer: the quality of my sense of survival. It all depends on what people expect of one another—and of themselves. No contract can stipulate that.

There is some Hindu or Buddhist axiom (I have a vague recollection of remarks by my father) about the ten thousand things of the world that distract one from the essence of life. . . . And I remember a statement Dr. Rosenblatt made once about psychosis: it is not so much that some one terrible circumstance drives a person mad, but the aggregation of the ten thousand little affronts and insults and debasements that irritate and chafe and rub one raw, until one can stand it no longer and escapes into madness. I recognize what I am thankful for: the ten thousand things that have brought me joy. The warmth of Mr. Peanut Butter on my lap, Claire's appreciation of my illustrations, Morgan's witty short stories, Chester's respect for my thoughts, Chester's attention to my feelings, his appreciation and support . . . Chester! God, how fortunate I have been.

I hear the sound of the screen door slamming in all the summer cottages of my children's childhood.

❧

Light snow was falling on the afternoon in mid-December when Shelagh drove the short distance from her home to keep her appointment at Dr. Connolley's office. Why am I driving carefully? she asked herself. For the same reason I am doing everything else carefully these days: to spare others. . . .

"How have you been since I saw you last?" the doctor asked her. He conveyed professional correctness and concern. She would not remove her coat and tried to think of him as a computer rather than as a human being.

Her voice was steady, but she confessed: "I have been depressed, or angry, or sorrowful much of the time. I'm able to keep it to myself. I can manage those periods . . . but now I'm beginning to suffer insomnia. I lie awake half the night and then get up with a headache that lasts two or three hours."

"That is to be expected," he replied quietly.

"I don't think Dr. McNeill or you had mentioned that."

"Didn't we? What's growing there is getting larger within a finite space, and therefore is bound to exert pressure on—"

"I like that: 'what's growing there.' "

"Would you prefer I use the scientific term?"

"No."

"Well, let's have you take a sedative to overcome that insomnia. I'll prescribe Nembutal. Start by taking one capsule at bedtime a few times a week. If you find you need it every night, that would be all right too."

An involuntary shiver made her whole body twitch. Then, recomposing herself, she said, "So if the tumor doesn't kill me first, the Nembutal will."

"Not at all. This will be a prescription," he said, looking down at the pad on which he wrote, "for a modest dose."

"How many of them would it take to put me out for good?"

Dr. Connolley calculated in silence for a moment. "At this dosage—at least twelve. This prescription is not refillable. I'll have to write a new one for you each month. . . as I do for the other pills."

" 'Each month' . . ." Shelagh echoed. "I suppose such measurements go back to watching the waxing and the waning of the moon. We haven't come very far from our caveman ancestors, have we?"

"I don't believe they had Nembutal."

"But they had gliomas?"

"Very likely."

Bluntly she asked, "Why do I have one 'growing there'?"

"There is no knowing. All that can be said is: the combination of conditions that has made your unique mind and personality possible included the condition that makes the growth . . ."

Shelagh concluded his sentence for him with the phrase ". . . part of the package."

"Yes." He handed her the prescriptions he had finished writing.

She put them into her handbag and sighed. "I should go now."

"No. Wait. Talk with me . . . for a few minutes."

She stared at him, thinking, He needs attention too. My accomplice.

Grasping for something to talk about, Dr. Connolley asked, "Will you and Chester go away for the holidays?"

"Yes. From Christmas through New Year's we'll be in Florida."

"Whereabout?"

"Palm Beach."

"Good. That will do you good"—and then quickly added, "and Chester too. He's become quite a celebrity."

"He's exhausted."

"All that publicity in the papers about the 'Silence Lady' trial."

"Thank God it's over."

"It was just yesterday that I read about the near-riot in the courthouse. The picketers and the shouting. No fun being called a fascist."

"All her buddies came out to protest the decision. She's a sore loser."

"But I'm sure Chester's right. The state has to expect honesty in a witness."

Slowly, Shelagh said, "I'm not so sure."

"That state has to protect itself."

They stared at each other, without speech.

"A family," Shelagh declared, "is not a political state."

"But it functions best on expectations fulfilled."

"The 'lady' in this case cannot get her revenge on the State's Attorney for keeping silent . . . and having spent time in jail for that. I will not be punished for keeping silent."

She thought he looked at her unsympathetically, as if to say: You Ought to Be. She added, "No one else can decide what's best for me. Including you."

❧

For the Jackmans, nothing was left of Christmas but the exchanging of gifts. They no longer mounted the pagan tree in the living room with decorations, tinsel, strings of popcorn. And nothing Christian in ritual or dogma mattered, either; only the occasion for the spirit of celebration and generosity—under the patronage of St. Nicholas—persisted.

From the radio in the library came the sounds of Christmas carols tarted up with jazz rhythms in an attempt to relieve the boredom of hearing them once again.

"Chester, would you please change that station?" Shelagh called down from their bedroom. "It's enough to make you vomit."

"In a minute, darling. I just have to step outside to vomit."

Shelagh laughed, thinking: Man of my heart. We are hand in glove.

Chester had taken the large piece of luggage and the carry-on bag with his things in it down to the front hall. Shelagh finished packing her small valise. They were adept and efficient at readying themselves for a trip. On the twenty-third of December they had packed for the flight south the next morning. She looked over the lightweight clothes, sandals, swimsuits, and toilet articles that remained to go in her bag. The only difference, this time, was the addition of three sets of pills. She secreted them in the plastic pouch with her toothbrush and tweezers. The clothes for the trip were laid out on the armchair for the morning. She carried the light case down the stairs and said, "Ready."

Chester had found a station broadcasting a performance of Vivaldi's *Four Seasons*. He stood at the desk against the wall opposite the fireplace and looked through the sealed and stamped envelopes, greeting cards with checks enclosed: for Claire, Morgan, Mrs. Yates, the cleaning man, the mailman, the garbage collector. Shelagh stoked the fire, gathering the orange glow into the center of the grate, and added a log of birch wood.

"I wouldn't mind staying," she said, warming her hands by the fire. "But I like the idea of going, too. . . ."

"We need a rest."

"You're the one who needs to rest. What I need is a suntan. Pity the children can't come with us."

Chester snorted. "Miss Christina Greene's family has a ski lodge in Vermont—for the pleasures of young Morgan. And Claire is determined to find a way to redeem herself for some audience on The Great White Way."

"It's just as well. I like you best of all."

He came up behind her and embraced her in a bear hug. "You shouldn't give away your favors so easily."

She felt how much larger and stronger than she he was, and yielded herself to the warmth of his caress. "I've thought about it for some twenty-five years now; and in my considered opinion, I made the right choice."

"That makes two of us," he whispered in her ear, and squeezed her in his embrace. "How about some eggnog?"

"Yes, sir. Coming up, sir." She broke away from him and went to the kitchen.

When they were seated opposite each other close to the fire, Chester inhaled the fragrance of the eggnog. "I think freshly grated nutmeg is one of the great gifts of the gods." He raised the glass in a toast to her.

"You are an appreciator," she said. "There are only two kinds of people in the world—the grateful and the resentful."

"William James once said there are only two kinds of people. Those who classify everyone into two kinds; and those who don't."

Shelagh laughed out loud. "You mean, what's so good about being reasonable? rational?"

"It does help disguise the chaos."

"Well, I had a letter today from one of the resentful."

"Who?"

"Mr. Tiejens, my editor at Harvest House. He's been sacked."

"Just in time for Christmas?"

"The company appears to have been bought by Scrooge, in the spirit of Christmas Present. It was a form letter, Xeroxed, addressed to all his authors and illustrators. No salutation, no signature. Nothing personal. No sign of real life. Just the statement that since a large electronics company has taken over the publishing house, it will reorganize everything, and in the meantime, the Juvenile Book Division will be run by the Vice President for Marketing."

"It's not only the personal that's real," Chester suggested.

"Well, it's what's most important."

"How are your illustrations for the Old Testament coming along?"

Shelagh sipped at the eggnog. "Slowly but surely. I have about two-thirds done—in different stages. Some still just sketches, some polished drawings. Others already in color separations."

"What are you up to now?"

"Job. The calamities of Job. Do you remember it?"

"Well, let me see. How do I remember it? . . . Job is the true believer. He has been devoted to God in thought and feeling and obedient to His laws in all his behavior. He has a prosperous and gratifying public and family life and he thinks they are his reward for being holy."

"Yes."

"Then Satan comes along and needles God with a question like If the 'rewards' were taken away, do You think he would still believe in You?"

"And God rises to the bait, saying, Go ahead: test him."

"So much for bargains with the divine."

Shelagh pondered her thoughts in silence before asking, "Are punishments and rewards the only kinds of relations between people?"

"Between people—yes; except for mutual enjoyment. But the burden of Job is the relation between man and God, or nature. The question of whether living according to the rules, whatever you believe them to be, will make you happy—safe, healthy, prosperous. What happens to Job is the opposite. He lives according to the rules and loses everything nevertheless. Because of Satan—and the vanity of God."

"I think it kinder to the universe to eliminate such an idea of God. A myth

227

that 'pays off' only for the happy. No. I'd rather place my bets on believing in you."

"And 'everybody else'?"

"Yes. It's the same thing as recognizing how chancy everything is."

"Certainly. For example, we might not have had any fresh nutmeg to-night. . . ."

"We understand each other." Shelagh reached across to take Chester's hand in hers. She bent forward and kissed his fingertips.

"We don't really want to wait for Christmas to give each other a present, do we?" he asked.

"I don't."

"My present to you is too heavy, too awkward to take down to Florida. I'd rather give it to you tonight."

"What fun! I'll get my present for you."

In a few moments, Shelagh brought her gift out of the large piece of luggage in the hallway. Chester was rising up from the corner behind his cello with an object in his hands. It was wrapped in fuchsia paper and bound with a silver ribbon.

Looking at it, Shelagh said, "Not as big as a bread box. It could be a half-gallon of Scotch. A football?"

"No hints allowed. Open it. Go ahead."

They stood at his desk, and Shelagh unwrapped her package first. It was the gold statuette of the young girl poised on one foot, her arms raised, turned into a bird's wings, her back arched, her face smiling broadly, called *Flaunting*.

"It's what I told you I saw at Warner's a few months ago."

"Yes? Did I get the right one?"

"This is it. I simply said I admired it . . ."

"Wished you could have it."

"But I never thought . . ."

"You don't have to. You have only to wish."

She took his face in both her hands and kissed him passionately on the lips. Then she said, "I adore you."

"Then why don't you give me a present?"

"I will, I will." She offered him the floppy package in Christmas wrapping from the surface of the desk.

He felt its supple limpness and said, "It's a phonograph record."

"Try to play it."

Unwrapped, it was revealed as the shirt Shelagh had had made for him in London out of the autumn pattern of fabric from Liberty's.

"But it was such a wild idea," he said.

"So unlike you."

"There was a moment when I truly wanted it—but only as a fantasy."

"Your fantasies are my commands."

"You are so thoughtful, so considerate. I wish you were God."

❧

DIARY ENTRY

The hotel is like a very grand private mansion, but I had forgotten how uninteresting Palm Beach is to look at: perfectly flat, with nothing growing beyond the artificially cultivated lawns, like throw rugs around the buildings, except for an occasional palmetto—scrubby little plant. Only the ocean, the beach, and the sky matter here. There was oppressive humidity the first day we arrived, but the weather has been glorious for the five days since then. In the morning we swim in the ocean and then lie on the beach. After a shower and cocktails in the lounge, we have lunch out of doors at a table on the terrace near the swimming pool. We read in long chairs under an awning and then swim in the pool. It is all blue and silvery beige: the water, the cloudless sky, the fine beach sand.

I'm rather bored.

I have the feeling there is so much for me to do and so little time left in which to get on with it.

There are almost no young people here—rather geriatric. On the great expanse of tan beach, where the overweight or emaciated elderly lie half-covered-over with towels like victims being treated for shock, if an attractive youth or young woman appears in a bright red swimsuit or a harlequin-colored bikini, it's as if a fresh flower suddenly bloomed up out of the desert.

We do not "socialize." Chester has no more desire to meet anyone than I do. We have danced in the evening and we attended one concert, but we do not become engaged with people. We take long walks along the edge of the shore. We have fragmented, desultory conversations. We have made love twice. We are good for each other.

One afternoon Chester started talking about retirement but, I thought, flippantly, as if even he cannot take it seriously. He suggested we keep the house on Lynwood Court for spring and fall, but spend every winter and summer at a different place, in Europe or in the States. Will he do that after I'm gone? It's not impossible. We were in cool Alaska during the heat spell at home at the end of the summer; and now that a cold spell is starting in New England, we bask in the sunshine in Florida. There's all that money . . .

229

I begin to feel the pressure of needing to put things in order. *To sort things out. To leave everything neat. I suppose I should write a new Will—and Testament* (!). We haven't changed our wills since the children were babies and all we were concerned about was who would take care of them if both of us died.

I marvel at Chester's body. His rugged face shows his age. His hair is gray, there are pouches and lines under his eyes; but his chest, his shoulders, arms and legs are firm, strong, smooth. All that golf, walking, working out at the athletic club have given him a lifetime of "good condition." There is an odd couple staying at the hotel—passing themselves off as father and daughter. A man of about fifty, well built and fairly good-looking; a smashing beauty of a girl about nineteen, with raven-black hair halfway down her back. I have seen how they look at each other, seated close together on the rim of the pool, their feet touching under the water, and I cannot believe they are not lovers. (Whether or not they are father and daughter.) I can imagine Chester here with a handsome woman very much younger than he—next winter. Well . . . the winter after that? I do not begrudge him another life. He could live to be a hundred. There is a family legend that one of his ancestors did.

I should send a note to Virginia McGrath. She sent me a Christmas card from her retirement home.

Spoke to Adrienne on the telephone Christmas Day, as usual. As usual. All the habits that give order to my life . . . Sometimes I imagine the habits will continue to exist after I'm dead. Mad thought. Half-mad. It's only that the habits are impersonal; the same patterns are there for other people as well. Adrienne is still involved with Hugh. This must be a record—more than six months. How different we are. I had one affair after another before I met Chester. Adrienne was a virgin when she expected to marry Trevor. Poor Trevor! Murdered. Dead all these years. And yet I remember him vividly. He has lain buried in Kenya some twenty years; nevertheless, at this moment I can see him, experience the virility of his cocksure walk, his sly smile, his tension. And yet he is dead. Who will remember me twenty-odd years from now? And how? My laughter? My hand gestures? My profile? A caress? Embedded in the lives of others, something of me will be there for them long after I am no more.

I'm so glad I insisted that we arrange to stay here for two days after New Year's. I know Chester would have liked to go to the New Year's Eve party at the Connolleys'—but I'll be damned if I have to see that man anywhere except in his office. And I'm ashamed to see his wife, Ellen. Were she and I ever friends? I don't think of her that way, although she is an art collector. But she's interested only in the Certified Public Artist. She buys names. What is it she wants to look at?—A fashionable reputation. The fashions of social-class ideas really do determine perceptions, don't they? That makes everyone a snob from the point of view of anyone not a member of her "class." What class am I in?

I sit here in the shadow of a pink-and-white-striped beach umbrella, supported by a backrest, my toes tucked under the sand, the diary on my raised knees; a cool breeze blowing over the ocean's surface brings the fragrance of salted air. Chester spends most of the day out on a rented boat, deep-sea fishing. If the boat capsizes and he never comes back ... God! I've spent my whole life worrying about the safety of the people I love—and about my own "security." And now I know it can't last, it won't last. There will be an end. Although I say that to myself—to what extent do I believe it? For me to keep this secret is to go on living as if it were not to be believed. Making plans. Carrying out promises. Short-term plans and long-term plans. It is in the nature of being alive. Before we left the house to fly down here, I placed the golden statuette on the table in the front hall so that it would be the last thing I looked at before departing and it will be the first thing I see on returning. At some point I must stop making projections into the future, knowing I won't be there to fulfill them.

One night—it was after the string-quartet concert in the ballroom—wandering alone around the lighted swimming pool, Chester tried to answer my questions about the trial of the "Silence Lady." The issue was over whether the State's Attorney had abused his powers to grant immunity, using it as a means to force her to give evidence, whereas she believed in a right to remain silent, which she claimed under the First Amendment about association. She claimed that he had deprived her of a constitutional privilege. The State's Attorney argued that her allegations were not specific enough—that's a matter of the technicalities of the legal process; but the "cause for action" was the greater matter—whether in fact a legally cognizable right had been abused. In other words, the decision did not turn on whether a witness has the right to remain silent in a criminal-law proceeding, but on whether the State's Attorney did anything illegal—regardless of whether what he did seemed unfair or unjust. The issue, as he saw it, was one of "misprision" on the part of a government official, not whether the constitutional freedom of association is rendered meaningless if a witness under pressure to speak—to give evidence about her associates—remains silent, knowing she is threatened with punishment if she does so. As judge, Chester was required to allow or to dismiss the action. He did the unpopular thing—by dismissing it. That's what brought out the picketers. The irony is that she did not ask for a jury trial, rather than appeal to the bench, precisely because Chester is not known to be illiberal.

I think I understand all that—but it's too bad that it was not Chester who made a judgment on the larger issue, the one about whether there is a constitutional right to remain silent. He acted as a "strict constructionist" inter-

preting the complaint brought before him. So the case throws no light on the degree to which there might be a right to remain silent. Of course, it's all about criminal actions, whereas what fascinates me is questions of rights in civil life, and in private life. I have no idea what Chester would think of my remaining silent, keeping my secret, in terms of "rights"; I only know that I am acting in accordance with my instincts.

On the last day of the year, the Jackmans went for a stroll after lunch along the flat shoulder of the highway running behind the hotel. Beyond the sandy wasteland, the sun glistened on the lagoon that separated the atoll from the mainland; they could see the low skyline of West Palm Beach in the distance. They walked along hand in hand.

As they approached a one-story cement-block building in the middle of nowhere, they tried to decipher the brightly colored signs in Spanish for fruit and vegetables. A group of people were gathered at the front door of the store. The sound of a siren pierced the warm air, coming at them in breathless pulses. They stopped in their tracks some twenty feet away, as the police car swung right up to the people standing there and came to a halt. The deafening siren went silent. Two policemen jumped out of the patrol car simultaneously. It appeared that everyone started to talk at the same time.

Shelagh and Chester gradually drew closer to the crowd as it made way for the door to be held open. Out of the store came a sad-faced slender black woman in a loose, sacklike dark green dress, her shoulders slumped, her hands bunched into fists at her sides. Behind her came the owner of the store, with a dirtied white apron wound around much of his girth. He pulled along with him a boy of about seventeen whose hands were tied behind his back with a length of clothesline. The boy looked Hispanic, frightened. He was naked but for a pair of cut-off blue jeans; there was the making of a teen-age mustache on his otherwise clear face.

Between fragments of statements in English and the pantomime of the crowd, the Jackmans pieced together the story. The slender black woman with lank graying hair had been approaching the store when this boy grabbed her handbag and started to run away as she called for help. The grocer had come out of the store and tackled him. Other people had gathered around them—from out of the store and across the road—while the older man wrestled him into submission. But in the confusion, another youth, a black boy, had grabbed the handbag and run like hell toward the lagoon. No one realized what had happened before he was out of sight.

The policemen handcuffed the captive and then removed the rope from his wrists and pushed him into the rear seat of the patrol car. One of them wrote down names and addresses in a notebook; with arm gestures and gruff statements they tried to calm the people and assure them that they would attempt to find the second thief and recover the handbag. No one believed them. They muttered and grimaced and turned their backs. No one comforted or consoled the thin, aging black woman who had been robbed.

Within a matter of moments she stood alone in front of the store facing only the Jackmans.

Chester said, "I'm sorry." He reached for his wallet and had begun to say, "Let me give you . . ." when the woman, who looked them up and down, saw how their hands were firmly clasped together; took in Shelagh's white tennis outfit, Chester's Bermuda shorts and sandals; spat her contempt at them; turned; and entered the store.

The oyster of her spit struck Shelagh on her right ankle; she drew up her leg and hit at it as if to knock away a poisonous spider. Then she knelt down and used sand to dry both her leg and her fingers.

There was no need to say anything. Chester put one arm around his wife and they walked back along the opposite side of the road toward their hotel. Finally, he remarked, "In another scenario, that would have been a hand grenade, and we'd both be dead now."

"You shouldn't have offered her money. She hated to be pitied. She has her dignity too. If nothing else."

"I stand corrected."

The incident dampened their spirits for the rest of the day. Before they should have gone down to dinner they decided to take a nap and later to have supper sent up to their room. They would celebrate the arrival of the New Year by themselves rather than at the masked ball of the hotel. On the balcony of their room, looking out to the ocean under the moonlight, they stood alone with a bottle of Champagne shortly before midnight. The sounds of the dance band below reached them through a filter.

"There are two kinds of people," Shelagh began: "those who believe that human beings are fundamentally solitary—as in 'solitary confinement'—and those who think what is fundamental is the traps and cages of interrelationships—child–parent, husband–wife, employee–boss, parent–child bonds—as in 'bondage.' Why does one have to be fundamental and the other secondary? It seems to me that both operate with equal power all of the time."

"The turning of a new calendar makes you meditative."

"I'm very sorry I snapped at you this afternoon. I was wrong. There's no reason you shouldn't have given her money."

"We have more than we need," he said. "She has less than she wants."

"Was there ever a society with social justice for all?"

He thought in silence for a moment, sipped at the wine, and then said,

"I've read about the gentle Tasadai. But there are only a few hundred of them. A tribe in the Philippines; they live like affectionate monkeys in the trees. An extended family."

"Are there any families with social justice for all?"

"You sound so sad."

"The dream of social justice is only a dream, isn't it?"

"It is the hope that makes mankind moral."

"And makes the fantasy of justice in an afterlife understandable."

"I can easily believe in an afterlife—since there are so many different lives in the here-and-now: and each one aspires to realizing a different dream, as prose aspires to become poetry, walking aspires to be dance. Consider the difference between what that black woman who lost her handbag aspires to and what, say, Walter Webster hopes for."

"What does Walter Webster hope for?"

"To become a sixteenth-century miniature by Clouet."

"You're joking."

"Partly. What I mean is that everyone—ultimately—wishes to become what he loves. To be transformed into what he most admires. We are always in process of transformation, unconscious of it as we may be."

I am in process, Shelagh thought, of becoming a memory. "And what would you wish to become, my darling?"

"A learned hand," he replied.

She laughed, set down her Champagne glass on the low table between them, hugged him in a warm embrace, and then kissed his cheek.

"Quick, quick," he urged her, still holding her in his arms, "without thinking, answer the question as spontaneously as possible: What, at this moment, in your wildest imagination would you wish to become?"

Out of her unconscious longing, with nothing but her instinctual voice speaking through her, Shelagh replied, "A figure in one of my Great-aunt Greta's watercolors of Greece."

"Then you will have it!"

The trumpets sounded from the ballroom below. In the fraction of a second, the New Year was initiated. And thus did Chester promise that as soon as the court calendar was over at the end of May or the beginning of June, they would make a trip to Greece.

❧

They returned to New Haven on the day after a heavy snowfall had blanketed the city. The taxi left them, in twilight, in front of their house and drove away. Chester toted up the luggage while Shelagh unlocked the front door.

She switched on the lights in the chandelier and stared at the front-hall table. The gold statuette of *Flaunting* was not there. She stood rigidly in place and pointed to the empty space on the table when Chester had brought in the last of the bags and closed the door behind him.

Chester stamped the snow from his shoes and brushed off his trouser legs. "Why is it so cold?" he asked, hanging up his coat and hat.

Shelagh stood still in her fur coat, pointing. "It's gone," she whispered.

"Are you sure you left it there?"

"You saw me place it there."

"The house is freezing!" He strode into the living room to look at the thermostat—which, it turned out, was on the degree to which Mrs. Yates had been told to raise it if the temperature dropped. He turned on lights as he went through the room. The blast of cold air came from the dining room. He stopped short as soon as he saw that the dining room had been broken into. Both the storm window and the inner glass were gone. Shards of broken glass lay scattered across the floor of the room. Arctic air poured in through the gaping hole.

He gasped; whirled around; rushed back to where Shelagh stood, taking her coat off—and lifted her up in his arms. The coat fell to the floor. He strode up the flight of stairs two at a time, holding her close to him. His strength was coupled with fear for her, and he carried her as securely as if she had been a child hurt or afraid of being hurt. He set her down when they were inside the bathroom on the landing opposite the head of the stairs. "Lock the door behind me," he said. "I'm going to see if there's anyone in the house."

Shelagh did as he said and waited in the bathroom, her heart pounding, thinking of him: He would save me if he could. . . .

Nearly ten minutes passed before he returned and knocked on the door, saying, "It's all right. Come out. I don't think there's anyone here. Come."

She saw the tears on his cheeks before she heard his low panting.

"We've been burglarized. No," he revised it. "We're vandalized." He led her down the stairs. All the lights in the house were on now. "Before you look around," he ordered, "you telephone the police. I'll get something to board up the dining-room window."

He found five unused bookshelves in the basement and, with hammer and nails, covered the broken window, but cold air still streamed in through the cracks. He took a quilt from the guest bedroom and tacked that all around the boards as well. Then he turned up the thermostat even higher.

"We could make a fire in the library," Shelagh called to him from the hall, just as she was about to enter the room, and her call was muffled by a gasp. She had both hands over her mouth when Chester joined her at the entrance to the room.

"I know . . ." he said.

235

Across the books that lined the wall over the fireplace, the word "FASCIST" had been spray-painted. The silver-colored paint had dripped and congealed so that it looked as if there were icicles suspended from the letters.

Shelagh moaned, "The books . . ."

"It's not just the books." His voice broke. He pointed to his cello on the floor, smashed into splinters. He pointed to the table of the inner room from which all the brass objects were missing—for they had been used as baseballs hurled at the French doors to the orchid greenhouse. Not only were all the panels in those glass doors broken, but the skylights had been destroyed as well. It was freezing in the solarium that had to be kept warm and humid. The orchids were dying. "It must have happened a day or two ago."

The gold statuette of the dancing girl whose arms had turned to wings lay on the slatted wooden floor between the racks of overturned pots. It too must have been used as one of the missiles to break through the glass doors.

Chester burst into tears.

"Oh, my darling," Shelagh consoled him. "They're only *things*. We're all right. That's what's important."

"It'll never be the same again," he moaned.

"It doesn't matter." She repeated, stroking the sides of his face, "It doesn't matter. We have each other. They're only things."

"They're our things."

"But, darling . . ."

"We're not the same without them."

"We'll repair the damage. . . ."

The police rang the doorbell at that moment.

Only after they were in the house did it occur to Shelagh to look behind the volumes of Sir Walter Scott's Waverley novels to see whether the crystal balls from Dr. Connolley's office, which she had hidden there, were missing. But they remained where she had concealed them.

The policemen inspected the damage and made their notes. Mrs. Yates had probably not been in the house for three or four days. The window that was broken faced on the side of the McGrath house, which was unoccupied. It was New Year's. There was the snowfall. Easy to understand why no one had noticed, let alone reported, anything odd. But there had been the demonstrators, the picketers who had used the word "Fascist." The police looked for fingerprints, for clues, and said they would call on the neighbors for information the next day. It was getting late. More blankets were brought to cover the broken French windows. Soon enough, Shelagh and Chester were alone again.

Dry-eyed now but despondent, he clutched at her and repeated himself: "It'll never be the same again."

"It must forever become different," she whispered to him.

236

Neither of them spoke of the fact that, in the living room, the four panels of the Archimboldo replicas had been spray-painted as well, each with one capital letter, spelling: "S. H. I. T."

DIARY ENTRY

This is the first time I've written in the new diary since the beginning of the year, and I have to start it with: Hideous Week! Grim. Saddening and gloomy week.

Chester and I consoled each other, that first night back, with the belief that vandals don't strike twice in the same place; that they were making "a political statement" and aren't out to harm us personally—no matter how personally we take the offense. But the house was invaded and our things abused. I have not yet got over the feeling that I was invaded and abused. The books, the cello, the orchids are not literally extensions of ourselves; but they are incorporated into our thought and feeling, and to the extent that they are damaged or destroyed we can no longer be fully ourselves—yes: to that extent, we are abused and diminished.

I feel neither guilt nor shame at being associated with Chester's judgment in court which led to this vulgar act of revenge, as he believes in the rightness of his judicial decision. There is nothing for us to regret about why this came to happen. But the very thought that strangers, filled with hatred and contempt for us, stood here in the library and flung their anger against our lives as they flung the collection of brass objects against the French doors appalls me. I don't feel afraid because they might come back, do worse, or attack us physically; it's enough to be made afraid by the presence of their ill-will, their viciousness, which remains in the house like a disgusting odor that can't be cleared away, can't be aired out. I find myself cringing with distaste and resentment over and over.

The dining-room window is replaced with new glass.

A boarding-up company sent men with great panels of wood and with insulating material to close over the French doors for the time being. We must leave it until spring to determine how the greenhouse might be rebuilt or replaced.

But the orchids are hopelessly lost. It took years to cultivate that collection. All gone.

Chester will try to take a day in New York soon to start looking for a new cello. That was well insured.

I took the gold statuette back to Warner's store and they will try to have it repaired. It broke off its base at the point where the dancer stands on tiptoe.

Walter Webster tells me he will find, through the Art Department here, who might be the best restoration people to take care of the paint on the Archimboldos. But I despair of seeing them hang in the living room again. They're hidden in the front-hall closet.

It is bad enough to see the wall bare above the sofa, but it is terribly wrenching to look up from where I sit here and be shocked to discover all the books gone from the shelves opposite. Instead of trying to remove the paint ourselves, piecemeal and slowly, Chester arranged with a friend at the University's library to take all of them and work on them together as soon as their restorer in the rare-book section is free.

I suppose I am making this inventory of the damage to things to take my mind away from more severe wrenchings. But I must turn to them now.

Two mornings after we returned, Brita phoned us to say Cliff Rostum had had a heart attack while jogging and died a few hours later. He jogged to maintain his good health!

I will write here what I cannot say to anyone: I am not surprised—as I have witnessed surprise among so many of the people I've seen during the past few days, first at Elsie Rostum's house and then at the memorial service. Because I believe that people will die. What passes for surprise in others is their disbelief.

When Chester and I paid respects at the Provost's house, late on the day Brita called, it appeared to me that Elsie was under the influence of tranquilizers, very low-keyed, so that she should not know what she actually was feeling, and reduced to a ritual of repetition, thinking with only two or three self-pitying phrases about "no warning" and "no goodbye." "We had no chance to say goodbye to each other." "There hadn't been any indication that he was in any danger. There was no forewarning. Not the slightest. He went off that morning and just never came back. There was no time to say goodbye to each other."

But in the next room, the friends and colleagues talked of politics and the relief that if you have to go, the quicker the better. . . .

Then Elsie did something remarkable. She asked everyone but her children to leave because it was time for their dinner. She stood at the entrance of the living room saying good night to those of us who had come to call on her, saying, "Life goes on. Life must go on."

I said, "Yes; in my family the expression is 'But, sir, it's time for tea. . . .' "

She either didn't hear me or couldn't grasp what I said. She asked for no explanation. She kept nodding, shaking hands, and repeating, softly, "Life goes on."

In the silence of our drive home together, I was grateful that Chester could not hear my thoughts, for I was suddenly aware how detestable it is—for the one who dies—that Life Must Go On. The rage against the dying of the light is over the enormity of the contrast: my no longer existing at all, while for

238

everyone else it's Business as Usual. It is too much to ask one who loves life passionately to be content with the thought that life must go on without him or her. For a little while, at least, I have let myself enjoy the gloomy thought that it would be easier to go to one's own death if everything else would cease to exist at the same time . . . but that is like saying: The world cannot exist without me. I know it can; it existed before me. And yet, and yet, for a little while my world ought to act as if it could not exist without me; as if, for a short space of time, it is not possible to believe that life must go on. I suppose that is the meaning of grief and mourning.

And what is so important about saying goodbye?

Elsie made it sound as though there'd been a breach of decorum—lack of good form. The social graces hadn't been observed. I'd never thought of it before as a question of good conduct. Elsie didn't make me feel that she is suffering because she did not have the opportunity to make his death easier for him; or that she failed to observe some sacred ceremony; or that she kept some secret she was prepared to present to him as a gift in his last moments. Could she feel deprived of a chance to love him more because there was no goodbye? I have heard of "love at last sight."

We say goodbye all the time.

We wish for the preservation and the peace, the harmony, of those we love every time we separate from them. If this is not the case in every parting, how can it be made up for in a Last Goodbye?

During the time I spent with the boarding-up people, the glazier in the dining room, the packers from the library who crated the books, I felt myself mean to withhold sympathy from Elsie until I realized my feelings are all for the one who died, as if I do not have any left over for those whose Life Must Go On. But at the memorial service I began to see it differently. The very fabric of her life has been invaded by vandals, abused, and diminished. She will look into a mirror and see no reflection. I feel sorry for her. I regret my earlier attitude.

The memorial service was too academic; too big and impersonal. There must have been a thousand people in Woolsey Hall—very few of whom I could identify. The Bach, Verdi, and Bartok on the program were beautifully performed, but I saw no connection between them and the memory of Clifford Rostum. The major eulogy was presented by the President of the University, Gregory Blackburn—that stick; and I wonder who wrote it for him. It was a talk about the ways in which to appreciate the life and work of the "great" Provost. There were the scientific way, in terms of cause and effect; the ethical way of means and ends; the aesthetic method with regard to the relations between part and whole; and then the overall estimation of the "humanity of the human being." It made me feel that no human being knows how to appreciate another or, at least, how to express it. I wish he had been humble enough to say, "I'm so sorry that Cliff is dead." But that wouldn't have had gravitas. (How my father loved that word—to him it meant the seriousness at the core of civil life; but I imagine even he couldn't have loved Cliff Rostum.)

We had not taken the car. Chester and I walked away from Woolsey Hall toward home. The sidewalks are shoveled clean now, although there is still a lot of snow clogging the streets. I wiped my eyes and blew my nose in a handkerchief. Finally, halfway home we began to speak.

"I think, maybe," I ventured, "that the last judgment is whether a life makes a good story or not."

"Blackburn tried to tell four stories."

"Well, then—whether a life makes Four Gospels or not."

"Not bad," Chester said. "But there were twelve Disciples. Each one might have told a different story."

"We are all the stories of everyone who ever knew us."

"And no one can ever put them all together."

I asked: "Do you think Cliff has gone to his reward?"

"I think he's gone from his reward," Chester replied. "Living is its own reward."

"Yes! my love. . . ."

❧

By the end of January there was enough of a thaw; the roads were clear and much of the snow was gone.

Chester, who drove, wore the shirt made of Liberty's autumn floral pattern, open at the collar, over a chocolate-colored turtleneck. "You look positively dashing," Shelagh said, sitting next to him in the front seat. Walter Webster mumbled agreement from where he filled much of the back seat of the car.

"Now," Shelagh began, turning around to address Walter, "you must tell us about your holiday in Paris."

"The same old thing, really. You know—the museums, the theaters." His eyes closed. He dropped cigarette ashes on his pin-striped suit. "That's not the whole truth. Actually, I had a wonderful time. Rather unexpectable things happened." His eyes were open again and, it seemed to Shelagh, misted over. "I was hoping to go back by this time." He sighed heavily. "But it didn't work out."

Chester and Shelagh exchanged a raised-eyebrow look between them.

Shelagh said, "I'm sorry," but did not pry, thinking: Everyone has his secrets. We tell each other what we choose to—short of losing face or losing balance in the other person's eyes. Balance is an absolute requirement, she realized. The Nembutal worked to erase the insomnia, but at the price of a mental fuzziness. When she had been alone in the house the day before this trip to New York, and started to descend the stairs, her sense of balance had given way and she was saved from falling down the flight of stairs only by grasping the handrail and lowering herself slowly to sit on a step until she felt on an even keel again. Being a well-balanced person has more than one significance.

Walter said, "Terrible thing! your house broken into like that . . ."

"I remember you were robbed in Boston by someone made up as a clown."

"Yes. Never could catch her."

"It's a little like that."

Chester added cryptically, "I hope they aren't caught."

It was late morning when they drove into the underground garage of the hotel at which the Jackmans were to stay. Walter planned to go home by train that evening. He meant to spend three or four hours in the library of the Frick museum; Chester was to look for a new cello; Shelagh had a meeting with her publisher. They agreed to rendezvous at the Bemelmans Bar in the Carlyle at three-thirty that afternoon.

The Vice President and Marketing Manager of Harvest House, who had dismissed Mr. Tiejens and taken over responsibility for the Juvenile Book Division, had told Shelagh it would be convenient for him to see her at twelve noon.

"You don't take lunch?" she had asked.

"No," he had replied self-righteously. He did not ask her whether she did.

When she was shown into his office, Shelagh was introduced to a tall, freckle-faced man with a hooked nose and a high-pitched voice. He neither stood up, shook her hand, nor offered her coffee. He said he was "in process" of reviewing all of Freddy Tiejens' projects and was now "up to" the Old Testament.

"What possessed him to want a new illustrated edition of *that?*" he asked her.

Shelagh shrugged. "The text is in the public domain. No royalties."

He didn't even smile.

She continued: "As I remember, he said something about a new wave of spirituality—or taking religion seriously—in the immediate future. He thought you'd cash in on a growing market."

"I don't think it's a children's book. Besides, it's so fucking long!"

Shelagh could feel her face begin to flush. "I understood you to say you wanted to see what progress I'd made"—pointing to the portfolio on the floor next to where she sat.

"Yeah, sure. But I have to review the whole project—for viability."

Shelagh wondered where he'd picked up that word. In some graduate school of business? There were computer printouts of inventory on his desk, a production flow chart on the bulletin board behind him. No book was to be seen in his office. He was evidently one of the New Management types, who believed publishing could be a really great "revenue stream" if you played your cards right. From the height of his skyscraper office he could look way down on all the little people.

"It's been given to children to read for centuries," Shelagh said. "Some indication of viability. . . ."

"Yeah, but will Sunday schools buy our edition through trade outlets? Our salesmen go to wholesalers and bookstores, not to churches."

"I don't know how Mr. Tiejens hoped to sell it."

"He didn't know either." The man barked out a short laugh. "He just hoped I'd figure out a way." She could hear him thinking: That's why we canned him, although he didn't say a word.

She stood up and lifted the portfolio onto a large layout board that stood behind her. Enclosed in plastic covers, the illustrations were ordered in sequence as they would appear in the book, from the most polished to the latest rough drafts.

The Marketing Manager came from around his desk to riffle through the pictures haphazardly, muttering, "Yeah. Yeah."

He stopped, puzzled, at the sight of Eve being tempted, pointed to the smaller female figure, and asked, "Who's that?"

"The serpent before it was cursed. If it was the cleverest of the beasts in the Garden of Eden, I figure it would look like that." She went on to explain how the idea had come to her when she saw Bronzino's *Allegory*—the figure of Deceit, a pale reflection of Venus. So it might have been that the serpent appealed to Eve, suborned her, by appearing to be as like her as possible.

He let out a low whistle and said, "Jesus Christ!"

"No. He's in the *New Testament,*" she snapped.

Either not hearing or disregarding her, he let forth: "What the hell is this? You can't make the serpent into a beautiful young woman. Nobody'd understand it. You can't do something that's never been done before!"

"Maybe *you* can't," she replied. "But I *can.*"

"Not if you're working for me."

Shelagh slammed the portfolio shut. "You want to get out of this project. I understand. Now you've found the pretext. Where do we go from here?" She zipped it closed, crossed her arms over her chest in a street fighter's stance, and looked up directly into his shifty eyes. He turned his back, moved away, leaned one shoulder against the bulletin board, stuck his hands into his pockets.

"A lot of bullshit gets put out as children's books these days. I'm not going to throw this company's money away. It's a dog-eat-dog market. I know what can sell and what isn't worth the paper it's printed on. This project was an asshole idea from the start. If I'd been in charge then, you'd nevera been commissioned to do it."

"But I was. I have a 'viable' contract."

"We'll buy you out." He sat down at his desk and brought the company's copy of her contract from a stack of papers at his left to lie in front of him. Looking at it, rather than at her, he said, "We'll pay you the second half of the advance that would have been paid on completion, and forget the whole deal."

"Who owns the drawings?"

He looked at her now. "I could care less," he said with conviction. "Keep 'em."

"Put that in writing, when you send me the check, and I'll sign the letter of cancellation. Otherwise, I'll take you to court."

He snickered. "Don't be a jackass. Nobody's ever won a case trying to make a publisher bring out a book he doesn't want to publish."

"Has anyone ever wanted to be published by you?"

"Look: I'm saving this company a pisspotful of money by paying you off and not bringing out the book. The composition, paper, printing, and binding would have been a small fortune—for the quantity Tiejens had in mind. And we'd end up with a warehouse full of remainders, or have to pulp it." She thought he was rehearsing a speech to stockholders rather than talking to her. "Smart money goes where it makes more money. For the rest—we cut our losses. This was a shitty idea from before the beginning."

Shelagh retrieved her fur coat from a chair in the corner of the office. As she brought it around her, she declared steadily, in a slightly supercilious voice, "My dear sir—as long as I live, I shall never accept a commission from this house again. Not because I don't like being published. I'm sure you are an astute businessman. It's just that you're a foul-mouthed pig."

For all she knew, Shelagh admitted to herself, a new illustrated edition of the Old Testament was not a good idea. But the people who had broken into her house were not the only vandals around. There is always the trio that Chester characterized as the inane, the insane, and the criminal—the forces that undermine or destroy what is good and desirable. Still, there may be things that are good in themselves but not desirable from a business point of view. She would swallow this now and think about it later. She had no desire to greet Chester and Walter with an announcement that she'd been "fired." She left her portfolio at the hotel and took a taxi uptown.

They had arranged to get together on upper Madison Avenue, close to the galleries where the Jackmans would look for a new painting large enough to cover the vacant space on the living-room wall from which the Archimboldos had been removed.

Chester had considered a number of cellos but not yet decided on buying one of them. Walter and the Jackmans had a drink in the cheerful bar. Shelagh loved the murals by Ludwig Bemelmans, the brisk Manhattan vignettes of ice skaters in winter, the slapdash views in Paris of nuns with their eight-year-old schoolgirls in uniform. When she was asked how things had gone with the publisher, Shelagh lied, "Fine. I have until summer to finish the job." Actually, she was in good spirits when they started on their search because she compared looking for a painting up to ten feet wide and four feet high to buying books by the color of the binding. It was something like a high school prank or philistine simplemindedness. "In a funny way," she said, "it's going back to basics. It's why anyone should want to buy a painting in the first place—because there's a need to satisfy."

Walter Webster never bought paintings.

The pictures in the Jackmans' house—etchings, watercolors, prints, oil paintings—were always bought on the spur of the moment, wherever they happened to be: capturing a mood, engaged by charm, challenged by an extraordinary image, puzzled by an original vision. Only later, at home, would they consider where it might be located or how it might relate to what else hung on the walls. They owned many a picture which had no place on a wall or which had decorated some space but had then been retired into a closet when they'd grown tired of it. Never before had they deliberately sought out a painting of a particular size for a specific location.

Then, in the course of more than an hour, they marched jauntily from Seventy-ninth Street down to Seventieth, from the Perls Gallery to Knoedler—zigzagging back and forth along Madison Avenue, through the exhibition rooms of Sotheby Parke Bernet, Papp's antiquities, the small shops and large—to look for a very big picture. Of the contemporary works, there were airless cityscapes and portraits of human beings inflated with elephantiasis—impersonally or inhumanly oppressive. Among the older canvases they suddenly saw, as through a window, into a Dutch winter landscape in the seventeenth century, or Rubenesque versions of classical myths; and groaning boards with flowers and fowl and jugs of wine—not only still-ed life, but petrified. Nothing suited them. Nothing answered to their hope for just the right thing. In between the paintings they looked at, they saw the flotsam and jetsam of a hundred different cultures, in all the shops they visited—the relics of skill and artistry preserved: Aztec jewelry, French Provincial furniture, Eskimo sculpture, Japanese pottery, African musical instruments, Venetian paperweights, stamps and coins and crystal goblets, the innumerable voices of vanished speakers, saying, "This too is beautiful . . . believe me."

But in the end, they were let down because nothing was irresistible to them. As they left Knoedler's, Shelagh said wistfully, "I wish we could buy one of the walls in the Bemelmans Bar."

From the depth of his private experience, Walter Webster brought out, "Funny how we want just what we can't have."

They walked in silence along the half-block from the gallery to Fifth Avenue and across to the park side of the street. Beyond the low wall of Central Park they were presented with the pleasure of a large new metal sculpture that had been erected on a low hill: brushed steel or aluminum in the shape of a tulip swaying on a long slender stem at least twelve feet high. As they watched, the cool late-afternoon light was reflected from the silvery stem and flower at different angles, making it look as if the sculpture moved, until Shelagh exclaimed with delight, "It does move!" The tube of the stem was cantilevered and swayed easily with any breeze, and the petals moved gently back and forth without ever striking against each other. "How graceful. What playfulness. Wonderful!" she shouted. Turning first to Chester and then Walter, "Don't you love it?"

"I don't know," Walter replied. "It's like a toy. A giant toy."

"It's ingenious," Chester said. "It does something that's never been done before." He inhaled the pleasure of it.

Shelagh looked at him quickly as if to see whether he had read her mind or had some extrasensory perception of the Marketing Manager's remark about her illustration of Eve and the serpent; but realized it was a coincidence. She looked again at the great swaying silvery tulip. "It fills me with joy."

Walter asked, "But is it art? or a sort of decorative engineering?"

"Would the answer determine whether you like it or not?" Shelagh replied.

Walter was embarrassed. "I really don't know. . . ."

"You don't like it?" Shelagh persisted, with incredulity.

"I didn't say that."

"But it's charming."

Walter looked down at the stones of the sidewalk, almost like a horse chafing his hoof in place, impatient. "You know, my dears, if I don't get a taxi in the next few minutes, I'll miss my train. May I drop you at your hotel?"

"I'd rather walk," Chester answered. "Wouldn't you?" Shelagh agreed.

At seven-thirty that evening, Claire stood waiting for them in the lobby of the Tavern on the Green as they entered it.

"You still have your radiant suntans," she was happy to say, and she greeted each of them with a kiss.

Chester looked at his hands. "I'd forgotten about that."

Shelagh stroked her own cheek. "Twenty percent suntan, eighty percent makeup."

Morgan's tan was remarked on also, as soon as he joined them, but he considered it a permanent windburn from skiing. Still, it was not only the high color of his complexion that pleased his mother; he appeared to be in singularly good spirits.

They were seated comfortably around a table in a quiet corner. Over cocktails, Morgan said, "I'm looking forward to a splendid meal for a change." He took a very deep breath and flexed his shoulder and arm muscles as if preparing to tear food apart with both hands. "The way I live now reminds me of an old joke about two construction workers who take their lunch break together. Every day one of them opens his brown bag and says: 'Damn it. Peanut butter and jelly again.' Finally the other man says, 'Tell your wife to make you something else for a change.' The first man looks at him with surprise. 'Who has a wife? I fix my own lunch.' "

Claire was instantly on her high horse. "That's a male-chauvinist joke," she said over the laughter of her parents. "That's why men want to get married—to have a cook full time at home, among other unpaid services. And that's why women no longer want to get married."

"You take it too seriously," her father said.

Morgan asked, "Does Simon want you to marry him?"

"No. He knows I'm not interested in marriage—at least, not now."

"Frankly, I don't think he's the marrying kind."

"I hadn't imagined you thought of him at all. Are *you* the marrying 'kind'?"

"I'm trying to be. God knows, I'm trying."

"You mean—Tina's turned you down again?"

"Children," Shelagh interrupted them: "the words may be different, but the melody of the duet you're playing has been the same for decades."

Chester smiled. "Let's try a different song."

Soberly, Morgan and then Claire commiserated with their father and mother over the break-in and vandalism of the house; but there was an odd glint in his eye when Morgan asked: "Do you suppose the spray-painted letters on the Archimboldos can ever be completely removed?"

Sadly, Shelagh admitted, "I doubt it. My impression is that even after the paint has been dissolved, the effect on the varnish, which is in more than one layer, is bound to leave an indelible 'ghost' of the letters—forever."

"So they're ruined?" Claire asked.

"No," Morgan suggested. "Just transformed. They've become American kitsch—works of the New York School of Junk-fun—or camp! Something Robert Rauschenberg might have painted from scratch. As an object lesson, it might be entitled *Clash of Cultures,* or something like that."

"Yes," Chester said. "*Clash of Cultures.* I like that."

Morgan reached across the table and stroked his mother's hand. "May I have them?"

Claire said, "Morgan to the rescue."

"Would you hang them? Defaced as they are now? In your apartment?" Shelagh asked.

"Certainly. I've been looking for something unusual for the hallway. And with four letters, there are twelve possible combinations. I could keep rearranging them, so sometimes they will read 'Shit' and sometimes 'Tish' or 'Hits.' I'll pass them off as an original Larry Rivers or Andy Warhol."

Shelagh bent forward and kissed his fingers. "How imaginative!" she said with awe. He did not withdraw his hand from the touch of hers.

Claire admitted, "Anyone who can make 'Hits' out of a 'Shit' can't be all bad."

"The next time I drive to New York," Shelagh said, "I'll bring them to you." She beamed at her son with a sigh of relief, enjoying a resurgence of trust and satisfaction. During the past six months, on the occasions when they had been together, and even during telephone conversations, she had felt his reserve and self-absorption. There were his courtship of Christina Greene; the cultivation of his career; his consideration of joining the Church; his lack of response to her encouragement of his writing. But here this evening, she felt their closeness to each other restored, and her belief in his promise reaffirmed. He had been wary of the Archimboldos in their proper condition, but once they were abused, his ingenuity promised to transform a loss into a gain.

So the history of transformations would continue. In Prague in the sixteenth century, out of his unique sense of visual humor, Archimboldo had painted four panels with images of people created in a mosaic of animals, flowers, and fruit and vegetables; early in the nineteenth century, a copyist had made the four reproductions in all seriousness; her father had bought them about 1900 for his own amusement and taken them along with him among the family's things when they emigrated to England in the 1930s; he wrote a book about graphic symbols in which they were used as examples. They had been one of Sir Hans's wedding gifts to her when she joined Chester in New Haven; and now in the 1970s they were transformed again, first by vandals, and then by the wit of her son, so that they would have a new lease on life. The vandals were forces of destruction; her son was life-giving. For he had different values, associations, attitudes; the capacity to envision a different arrangement; and therefore, another purpose could be served. She felt his worth confirmed, her confidence in him justified.

She then turned her attention to Claire. "And for your apartment, would you like some of the illustrations for the Old Testament, when I've finished them?"

"I'd adore that. Especially the scenes in the Garden of Eden."

"They'll be yours."

Chester said, "Now we must order dinner."

They ate smoked trout, then *petite marmite,* lobster, *pêche Melba.*

Chester described their holiday in Florida, omitting the incident with the police and the black woman who had been robbed; and announced their plan to travel to Greece in June. Claire gave an account of the teachers and classes in the new semester at her acting school, and of her auditions, all unsuccessful so far. But she was undaunted.

Unexpectedly, with a sly smile Morgan began, "I have an idea for a story. Well, not exactly. A condition or a situation that might be worked up in a story. It came to me in the shower room at the Athetic Club the other day. You know that amputees, who've lost a hand, a leg, or an arm, feel sensations in the limbs no longer there? Well, men are either circumcised or not. And I was fantasizing that . . . no one ever talks about it, but . . . a circumcised man experiences erotic feelings in the foreskin he no longer has."

Shelagh laughed. "No doubt you'll couple him with a flat-chested girl—for the mating of imaginations."

Chester asked, "Plan to call it 'The Case of the Missing Prepuce'?"

"I think this is tasteless," Claire declared. "You're just putting me on because you didn't like my being half-dressed onstage."

"Tasteless?" Morgan mocked her. "Unsavory? A piece of penis—tasteless?"

Looking about at the other people in the restaurant, Chester said, "You're going too far."

Shelagh deflected the conversation. "There's another sense of the word 'tasteless'—and your father and I just had occasion to see evidence of it. Do you remember Walter Webster? He's a professor of art history. An authority on Poussin . . ."

Chester added, "And Clouet."

"Well, we were together this afternoon when we discovered a new sculpture in Central Park. A mobile. It's in the shape of a giant tulip—shining stainless steel."

"Or aluminum," Chester said.

"Swaying in the breeze. Pivoting on a long stem. Its petals wavering out and closing together gently—as if it lived and breathed. Perfectly glorious! A wondrous thing." Shelagh paused. No one spoke. "I can hardly believe what I'm going to say now. I asked Walter whether he liked it; and he didn't know."

Morgan chuckled. "Oh, *tasteless* in the sense of not having taste."

Shelagh repeated the point: "He didn't know if he liked it or not. He had no feel for it."

Claire asked, "Is it a matter of knowing?"

"For him, yes. He has stunted feelings."

Chester said, "He is a scholar, an intellectual, an 'authority.' "

"But he has to know what to think before he can exercise his feelings. He wanted to be sure of the category it fell into, first: is it 'art,' a 'decoration,' or a 'toy'?—he wanted to *know*." Shelagh continued, "He needed the assurance of concepts; he couldn't trust his instincts. He wanted judgment first."

Morgan suggested, "Doesn't taste mean educated instincts?"

Shelagh replied, "Yes, but you mustn't be afraid of being wrong in someone else's eyes. You don't become educated by never making a mistake."

Claire laughed. "Then one has to have the courage of his own bad taste."

"At least it's your own," Chester said.

"Well, then, Claire," Morgan said, smiling, "I take it you'll come around to liking my idea about circumcised men as your taste improves."

They all laughed. Dessert was being served.

Chester asked his son, "Do you know what accounts for your own good spirits this evening?"

"As a matter of fact, I do. During the month of January there's an annual review of performance at the office. I've just received not only handsome praise—but a hefty raise in salary as well."

Shelagh chimed, *"Hurray!"*

Chester raised his wineglass. "Let's all drink to that."

"What a lot of difference," Claire remarked, "a little money makes."

Slowly, Shelagh asked, "How much difference would a *lot* of money make? I mean: how would you do things differently if the windfall of a small fortune came to each of you?" She looked back and forth from her daughter to her son. "Not *too* small, of course. Large enough for an unearned income so that you could live at least as well as you do now without working."

"What a lovely question," Claire said.

Morgan sighed. "What a challenge."

Judge Jackman said, "It's an old conversational ploy of your mother's."

"Do we have to answer right now?" Claire asked.

Morgan said, "I'd take early retirement—extremely early retirement—and meditate. Who knows? Maybe I could write something worthwhile."

"Meditate?" Claire echoed with disdain. "I'd have a ball. Of course, I'd travel, especially to the Continent, alternating between the fleshpots of the jet-setters and the new European theaters—to study acting methods there. Could I afford to buy a little-theater group of my own?"

"Imagine . . ." Morgan whispered.

Alone in their hotel room, Shelagh and Chester embraced in bed in the dark.

"It was a splendid evening," he said. "What a pleasure to see both of them in such good form."

"Claire was a little prickly."

"Morgan is still very unsure of himself—for all his well-being."

"Darling, all of my money is willed to go to them when I die."

"Yes."

"Would you have any objection if I changed that—and gave them the money now? Immediately? When they can get the most advantage out of it for themselves: at just this stage in their lives."

"You and I don't need the money."

"Then you wouldn't mind?"

"Not at all. I think it is a nobly generous gesture. If you're not afraid of being treated like King Lear."

"He was senile."

"It is what Aristotle would have called 'magnificent.' Or was it 'magnanimous'?"

She poked him with her elbow. "I want to do it to make it easier for them to grow up, to become themselves . . ."

". . .more quickly," he concluded.

"Yes. Can it be done right away?"

"I'd guess within a month or so."

"Will you arrange for it? All the legal papers—that sort of thing."

"Certainly."

"A Valentine's Day present?"

"Perhaps it can't be done that quickly."

"Well—as soon as possible."

"All right." He held her close in his strong arms. "You know, you really are a wonderful person."

She replied, "I love you."

And by way of good-night, he affirmed, "I love you!"

❧

LETTER TO SHELAGH'S SISTER, ADRIENNE MARKGRAF, IN LONDON

My dear:
I am very touched by your letter about the break-in at our house. I find that it matters a great deal—your reminding me of that passage in Virginia Woolf's Diaries, during the war, of finding her house in London destroyed by a bomb and, instead of feeling bereft, feeling liberated from the burden of things, from the responsibility for things. Yes, you have helped to clear the air—literally, for I have felt the air here poisoned by the vandals; whereas now I feel lighter and more clearheaded about the abuse of things. I can turn my back on the whole experience. To hell with it!
We had an excellent evening with the children in New York recently. Morgan is being recognized and promoted in his work; and he seems inclined to try writing fiction again. He has a gift for it, but he hesitates. Claire needs to travel and experience different ways of acting in a variety of theaters. I wouldn't be surprised if she visited you in London in the near future. She is so fond of you!
How is Hugh?
How are Sissgull and his South American moneybag?
Oh, I must tell you about Walter Webster. I found out something dreadful about him. Not the boy-o-philia; I've known that forever. Something worse. He has no taste. You remember how he asks at lunch, "Is that the way you like it? Is it done properly?" I always thought that was courteousness, a solicitous, thoughtful attention. Not at all. He just can't decide for himself. Chester and I saw a new piece of sculpture in Central Park that we both loved immediately. Walter didn't know whether he liked it or not. Figure-toi. No instincts. No intuition. What would Father have thought? I suddenly realized that Walter wouldn't have spent a lifetime studying Poussin (or is it Clouet?) if someone else hadn't told him to—told him they were "the real thing." Isn't that the living death? To have dwarfed instincts and stunted intuitions. I mean: if you don't have the courage of your own taste—you live someone else's life. You don't have self-approval. Here's a man in his sixties, who is loaded with honors for his distinguished career in the scholarship of art history, who doesn't know what he feels. He doesn't feel on his own. Who needs a "go-ahead" signal from some Authority before he can determine whether he likes something he sees. It appalled me.
You, of course, are a model of self-approval and have always known your own mind. I myself feel that confidence more strongly as I grow older. In fact, I'm making a few absolutely personal decisions these days that can be understood solely on the basis of my trust in my own intuitions, instincts—my taste. And I like myself all the more because of it. If that's cryptic—so be it.

Still: I'll try to explain indirectly. When you saw the cigar burn in the lace mantilla and the olive-wood chest of drawers, you said something like "If you're going to make use of things, you have to run the risk of their being used up." I thought that callous and unworthy of you at the time. I was wrong. You have the right attitude. I was a victim of sentimentality. I'm getting over that. As I am getting over the loss of the Archimboldos and the orchids. It is use that is all-important; not protection against damage or the pain of loss. To use is to use up. To pretend that it can be otherwise is to walk about with blinders on your eyes and to get stabbed in the back by reality.

I see more because of what you said. I will not be done in because of sentimentality.

Sleep warm.

❧

DIARY ENTRY

The horse knows the way—even if he doesn't know whether there's any reason for the trip.

I spent the morning in my studio working on the 23rd Psalm until I realized that the contract is up. I had signed and returned the letter of cancellation, deposited the check for the second half of the advance due. It's all over. There I was at the drawing board out of habit, despite the fact that no one wants what I am doing. Evelyn Knops's revenge.

At first I thought I'd finish the assignment for my own sake, if not for anyone else's. Father once told me that the sculptors of the Parthenon frieze completed all the figures in the round, although once the sculptures were raised and in place, no one on the ground beneath could see the hidden side. They did it because the gods could see what is hidden from men.

Perhaps I would have gone on, but the 23rd Psalm reduced me to the blackest mood of despair. The Lord is my shepherd and I am His little woolly lamb; He restores my soul and sees that I'm safe from harm—with enough water to drink and grass to munch. What self-hypnosis. What a metaphor! What price peace and prosperity? I am to God what a dumb animal is to a shepherd who takes care of all his simple needs, his creature comforts. We all know what shepherds make of sheep, why they raise them, what becomes of them. But to delude yourself for a little while, to pray for the security and integrity of a bloody sheep, for crying out loud!—as if to be just one more head in a herd, "protected" in a flock, until driven to the stockyards and the butcher is the ultimately desirable image of being safe and cared for . . . too much! Most of the Psalms are divided between beseeching God for help to

252

defeat enemies in battle and complaints against God for not delivering the help; or praise for His delivering it. At least, they are the prayers of people who knew what they wanted and tried to make pacts, contracts, bargains with superhuman Power to help them gain their ends. But then in the midst of those imprecations appears 23—with its complete sellout, reduction to infantilism, settling for mindless, dumb-animal childhood security. As if an ancient Greek had prayed: Saturn is my baby-sitter, He changeth my diapers, He spoon-feeds me Pablum; no harm shall ever come to me—forgetting that it can last only until He decides to eat me. Too much.

I cannot hypnotize myself into believing I will not die.

But—oh, God—how I wish I didn't know.

In the evening on the seventh of February, Chester and Shelagh sat facing each other before the fire in the library. The books had been repaired and returned. During the previous few days, Chester had rearranged them on the shelves in groups differently located from where they had stood before, so that even where there were faint traces of the paint on bindings, the word that had been spelled across them would never re-emerge. It was like seeing all the fragments of a mosaic dislodged and then returned to their frame to create an entirely different picture.

Chester rose and stoked the fire, then returned to his armchair and reopened the book of Auden's poems he was reading.

Shelagh knitted.

He looked up from the page and said, "I'm sorry, darling, that the transfer can't be made by Valentine's Day. But the inheritance should be theirs by the end of the month."

"Soon enough," she replied.

"I haven't found a cello yet. Something keeps me from choosing."

"You'll look again soon."

"Another cold spell is predicted for this weekend."

"The Weather Bureau is right only two-thirds of the time. By the way, when I picked up *Flaunting*"—she raised her chin to point toward the rewelded gold statuette standing now on the mantelpiece—"at Warner's, there was a gorgeous Japanese kimono displayed on a wooden frame. Deeply rich purple silk with wisteria flowers embroidered on it in lime-green and ivory. Not that it was for sale. Just a window decoration. Unbelievably beautiful. When I left, I stood outside before the window, admiring it, and along came Priscilla Rosenblatt, who stopped and asked me what I was staring at. I don't know what possessed me, but I answered: 'An example of perfection.' She told me she had just a minute to stay, between a meeting of the League of Women Voters and a Parent-Teacher Association committee, and she looked at the kimono as though she must try to see what I saw, but couldn't. 'Imagine how many centuries of refinement went into bringing this about,' I said; 'evolved from a workaday costume into a gown of distilled elegance.' She actually snorted. 'Think of all the tens of thousands of women kept in slavery or wage-slavery during those centuries so that one aristocrat or noblewoman could have such a dress!' I said, 'All right—I'm thinking of them.' 'Well,' she replied, 'the world would have been a lot better off without that kimono, if those women hadn't endured their slavery.' I had to laugh, unfortunately, and she was offended and took off with apologies about being needed at her committee. I am sorry about laughing at her, but the truth is, because of the kimono I have seen something exquisite and I'm all the better for it—whereas I don't feel anything about ten thousand female slaves, and I don't feel the worse for not being able to imagine them or their lot, or feeling the worse for them. I suppose that's hardhearted; but is it?"

Chester grunted. "I'm sure that if Priscilla were shown the pyramids of Egypt, she would 'see' only the ten thousand slaves who were made to build them."

"She is the quintessential do-gooder."

"Well, there can't be too many of them in the world."

"But to wake up in the middle of the twentieth century and hope to make everyone happy and healthy and . . ." Shelagh stopped and then suddenly said, "There really cannot be justice for all, can there?"

"It is not possible to rewrite the history of the world; and that's what it would take. To say nothing of changing the laws of nature."

"The ancients were right who believed the Primal Goddess was—Fortuna."

The arrangements that had been made through telephone conversations with Morgan enabled Shelagh to pick up a new cello for Chester at Morgan's apartment on the fourteenth of February, the day she drove in to give Morgan the Archimboldos. The cello was rented on a monthly basis, with the rental payments to be deducted from the sale price if it was decided to buy it within six months.

The six-month period would end in the middle of August, Shelagh thought—on my birthday. But I will not be alive to know what Chester decides. It doesn't matter.

It was still chilly on St. Valentine's Day, and Shelagh felt the bite of the cold on her hands at five in the afternoon as she struggled with the weight of the cello in its case, lifting it from the trunk of the car parked in the driveway and hoisting it up the steps to the front door of the house. Chester opened the door for her.

"You're early," she said.

"I wanted to prove I can still surprise you."

"I have a surprise for you."

He took the cello case from her hands and kissed her passionately on the lips. "You are a source of endless joy," he said.

"It's only what you deserve."

"I have a surprise for you." Without letting her take off her coat or gloves, he guided her into the living room, toward the fireplace, and then made her turn around to look across at the space over the sofa, where the Archimboldos were no longer to be seen. Covering the area now where the four panels had hung for so many years was to be seen the purple kimono, held in place by invisible wires.

Shelagh clutched her neck with one hand. "Oh, my God. How marvelous!"

"It's only what you deserve."

"But it wasn't for sale."

"I have powers of persuasion in a good cause."

"I think you love me."

"Do you love me enough to listen to my playing a new cello?"

◦◦◦

For the fourth month in a row Shelagh made herself keep an appointment with Dr. Connolley. She wore a gray tweed suit she thought of as dowdy, and a cotton blouse; with little makeup and without any jewelry. She could not think of being in his presence without requiring of both of them: No Nonsense. The doctor made his simple examinations of blood pressure and blood count, asked his superficial questions, wrote the necessary prescriptions for the month's preventive medicines. Yes, she said, the Nembutal was effective.

Leaving his office, with her coat over one arm, Shelagh was on her way through the long lobby of the building toward the pharmacy at the far end when she caught sight of "Young" McGrath sitting by himself at a small table in the cafeteria. She tapped at the window. He looked up and nodded. She waved a greeting. He gestured for her to join him.

Virginia McGrath, the Jackmans' neighbor for so many years, was so old that her son, whom she and Chester referred to as "Young" McGrath, must be well into his sixties. She shook his hand and said she would like just a cup of tea, which he went to fetch from the counter. Shelagh could not remember what he did for a living; he must be retired by now. She saw, when he was seated opposite her, that his parchment-colored skin was beginning to take on a translucency. The mustache on his oval face and the fringe of hair around

255

his bald head were made up of lank slivers, thin as snippets of white sewing thread. His proud smile showed the handsome false teeth of a magazine model, as incongruous as if he had sat there before her in the blue jeans and T-shirt of a teen-ager. He was a neat old man with a mouthful of young teeth.

"I sent your mother a New Year's greeting, but I haven't heard from her. How is she?"

"Oh. Then you don't know." He paused for a moment. "She died just at the beginning of January."

"I'm so sorry." Shelagh felt the sudden presence of a lump in her throat, heavy as a fist.

"Don't be sorry, Mrs. Jackman," he replied. "It was a mercy."

"Why a mercy?"

"She grew steadily worse after we took her up to that nursing home. Funny name for such a big sanatorium."

"Worse?"

"Her hearing went. Her eyesight. Pretty much paralyzed on her left side. And a lot of arthritis in her right. Hands gnarled like the roots of trees." His own hands were concealed under the table.

"Could she read?"

"No. Almost couldn't talk. Confined to a wheelchair for months. One of those battery-run gadgets. All she had to do was turn the switch on or off— stop and go."

Shelagh wanted to ask if she had died quietly, peacefully. "How did it happen?"

"No one up there is sure. Her room was on the same ground floor as the therapy pool. Not a very big pool, but fairly deep. That's where they found her one morning. Drowned."

"How awful!"

"No. No," he comforted her. "It must have been quick. Nobody knows for sure if she did it on purpose or if it was an accident. They just found the wheelchair tipped over at the edge of the pool, her body in the water." His voice fell to a whisper. "It's a relief."

For her or for you? Shelagh wondered.

"Young" McGrath answered the unspoken question. "I'd been hoping for some time it would come to an end for her. She was that bad off."

So, Shelagh thought, there is a limit to pity, too; and when pity is exhausted, you wish for the death of "the loved one." She felt the chilling horror of that destiny and placed both hands around the cup of tea to warm them. But the cup itself was cold by then.

She said, "You have my sincere sympathy, Mr. McGrath."

"Only thing I regret is—no chance to say goodbye."

256

They stood up and shook hands. He gave no sign of leaving. "Thank you for the tea."

"You're entirely welcome."

He sat down again as she drew on her coat, saying, "Take good care of yourself."

The new teeth in his old smile were proof that he did.

DIARY ENTRY

Dread. For two days I've been filled with the dread that "Young" McGrath inflicted on me. It's not a question of What's Virginia McGrath to me? She was another human being; that's enough. But she suffered the loss of everything to live for even to the ultimate torment—to see her own child's pity for her turn back on himself, wearing itself out, to leave him with only the hope that she would die. What a horror. It is terrible enough to be "so bad off" that you want to die; but to know that your son wishes you were dead is Too Much.

I hope she had just enough power to drown herself deliberately rather than by accident. I know I would rather end my own life than watch my children suffer pity for me long enough to wish "for my sake" that it were all over.

I have the means. Quentin said it would take twelve capsules of Nembutal. If I keep four of them each month—by the end of three months I will have enough to do the job. If at least once a week I can bear insomnia, I'll be able to put aside enough . . . Enough! I imagine it will be painless, like freezing to death. Just the gradual loss of feeling, sensations decreasing to Cessation. Like the knob on a radio—very gradually turned to lower the volume until no sound is audible; and then the clicking "Off" of the switch.

I had thought I could keep my dying a secret until the cup and saucer fall out of my hand, when the phenobarbital and the Dilantin could no longer prevent seizures—and I would become an invalid who would have to be taken care of by others for a month or two, before it ended. No one needs to know until then. But why should I suffer any loss of powers and inflict those months of suffering on anyone else as well as myself? And to run the risk of watching pity turn into the wish that I were dead?! I'd rather kill myself as soon as I know there is no time left for me without being such an invalid. I would rather die by my own choice than live two months of torment for my-self and others.

It is not the impossible desire to live forever that is the essence of human misery: the frustration of the wish to live at the peak of one's powers for how-ever long one lives—that's the curse.

What is the obsession over saying "Goodbye" which seems to matter so much to others but that I don't feel at all? Cliff Rostum died twelve hours after a heart attack and Elsie bemoans the lost chance to say Farewell. Virginia McGrath must have been dying for at least twelve years and still her son regrets not having the chance to say Goodbye. Are some people not aware of what is communicated without the use of words?

Perhaps I should write letters. Farewell letters. It won't give others a chance to say Goodbye to me, but I will be saying Goodbye to them. To be sent after I'm dead? Or before? I'll think about it.

❧

Chester called, "She—la?" as he let himself in at the front door.

"I'm in the dining room," she answered softly.

"How odd," he said, when he approached her. "You look so lovely. Standing there by the window. But there's no light on."

"It's nearly—almost—spring. It's still light out."

She wore a long black skirt and a taupe silk blouse with strings of pearls close to her neck.

He repeated, "How odd."

"I felt like such a slattern all day long, I had to get dressed for you, for when you came home. But I haven't done a thing about dinner." She raised her arms and lowered them in hopelessness. "Part of the day I wallowed in my studio and got no work done. Part of the time I stared out this window watching the repairmen working on the McGrath house. It's fascinating how the whole place is being renovated: tuck-pointing, new copper gutters, new window sashes. It is possible to restore a house."

"The new owners must be eager to have it done as soon as possible."

"Yes. There are so many workmen there at the same time. And then I saw six stalks of crocus in front of that basement window," she said, pointing across the driveway between the two houses, "and I kept staring at them, thinking that I might be present at the moment they burst open. But they haven't opened."

"Let me put on some lights."

"No. Wait. I'm still watching."

"Darling—they won't open at twilight."

Shelagh twisted herself around in the space where she stood, as if snapped out of a trance. "Of course," she said, understandingly, as she reached for him and held him in a long embrace. "I've felt so peculiar all day. Like living in slow motion."

"I think you're risking a bout of exhaustion."

She led him back into the living room, where cocktails and hors d'oeuvre

258

were laid out on the Chinese trunk, and said, "The past two weeks have been so full . . ."

"Hectic," he said.

There had been a dinner at the Warners' in Woodbridge, where the conversation was almost exclusively concerned with the question whether the President of the United States might be impeached. A concert at Woolsey Hall of the Vienna Philharmonic. Two meetings with an architect about the new greenhouse; and one with the lawyers over the transfer of Shelagh's inheritance to her children.

"I'm so glad February's over," she said, looking through the front window at the sky not dark at five-thirty, as if checking her wristwatch to confirm it.

"I brought the last of the papers for you to sign." Chester tilted his head toward the hallway where he had left his briefcase.

They sipped their drinks, seated near each other on the sofa beneath the purple kimono.

"Now that spring will be here," Shelagh began, "I'd love to plan a party. A big party. Not sit-down dinner. Let's have a buffet. People can wander all over the place and sit on the floor if they like. That's the way Adrienne gives 'suppers.' Let's have everyone we'd care to see just one more time."

Chester laughed. "It's the only way to come up with a guest list. Yes, I'd like that. When?"

"Later in the spring. Not just yet. There's a month until April. How's April Fool's Day?"

"Super," he replied.

"What do you imagine Claire and Morgan will think of being given the money now rather than later?"

"That you want them to make decisions they're not ready to make."

DIARY ENTRY

Another letdown. There's no other way to put it—honestly. Claire's birthday on the seventh of March. We met halfway. She and Morgan drove up to the Silvermine Inn near Norwalk, and we met them there. Another habit. The dogwood trees were just begging for a chance to put forth buds. There were ducks on the brook and early daffodils in vases at each table. Hardly anyone in the restaurant. The four of us, close together, with lots of distance from anyone else. I gave Claire my pearls as her birthday present. And then, at the end, over after-dinner drinks, Chester announced the transfer of funds to both of them.

I can only say: it fell flat.

Neither of them could ride with it comfortably.

Morgan said, "I thought you were joking."

Claire said, more than once, "I just don't believe it."

To a not insignificant degree, both of them are, now, rich—and yet the shock of it to them brought no immediate gratification to me.

I want too much. I know it. I feel certain about it.

But I cannot do otherwise.

Perhaps I'm wrong. Maybe something wonderful will come out of it— while I can still know. . . .

Shelagh began to write letters of farewell.

LETTER TO PRISCILLA ROSENBLATT

I'm so sorry about what happened at Warner's store the other day. We were looking at a glorious Japanese kimono and I laughed when you talked about ten thousand female slaves—I regret that. But it did strike me as incongruous. If one applies a standard of social justice against the value of every work of art, then, I suppose, not any work of art in the history of civilization can be found admirable. Somebody—always—was suffering; something was always unfair. It is not that I am indifferent to suffering: I know what troubles you, and I am—in principle—sympathetic with it. But there is nothing for us to do now, in retrospect, to alleviate the misery of wage slaves of three hundred years ago. On the other hand, there is much that a kimono from that epoch can do for us. It enhances our lives by its beauty. Should we refuse to gain from it, or even look at it, because ten thousand women lived unhappily under the conditions of the culture that made it possible?

It goes without saying that I respect your serious concerns for humanity, your concern for the underdog. But you and I are not underdogs, and our compassion might be construed as "patronizing" by one of the thousand wage slaves.

Shelagh could not bring the letter to a conclusion. She despaired of it and threw it in the wastebasket next to the desk, saying out loud, "Pretentious twaddle."

LETTER TO CONRAD TAYLOR

That was a lovely evening we shared at the Warners' last week. I am impelled to write you because I recall your vivid description of your father and mother: he was a lawyer in the Army during the First World War and he brought home a French bride, who lived the life of a St. Louis matron for two decades; after he died, she returned to France in the late 1930s and disappeared when the Nazis occupied all of France. What I want to say, in gratitude for your telling me that story, is that (as you know) Chester was on the Adjutant General's staff during the Second World War, and he brought me back to the United States as a "war bride." Changing one's citizenship is not what's significant. I believe that women do that much more easily than men. But "throwing in your lot" with a man is—precisely—the character, the nature of a woman's fate, no matter how little or how extreme the changes of place or status might be. Men make their way in the world, and the women they love follow them even into strange locations. Women, being more responsive, must be more resilient than men. Of course, I wonder, from time to time, what my life might have been like if I had married someone other than Chester—and if he had married someone other than me. It is the question of a lifetime. Impossible to answer. Nevertheless, a real question—not phony. And should be taken into account especially as one approaches the Last Judgment. I'm not implying that women wonder whether what they've done was right or wrong; that is always a matter of degree, anyhow. What I do mean is: how well have they used their chances. Or is such a Psychological Economics the same thing as Ethics?

The fact that your mother returned to France after your father's death doesn't at all suggest that she made a twenty-year-long mistake. There seems to be something universal about wanting to return to our beginnings when we look forward to the end.

"This will never do," Shelagh muttered to herself, and pushed the incomplete letter aside toward the edge of her desk.

LETTER TO KATE WARNER

I did thank you for the pleasures of your dinner party, but I write you now about something else.

Six months ago, when you came here for an impromptu lunch and we had a conversation in the library, while your children drew pictures in my studio, we talked of how difficult it is to raise children satisfactorily; how easy it is to be worried, upset about them: anxious. I tried to put your mind at ease. There was something wrong in my attitude, and it's bothered me ever since. Mainly, I think I pretended that I did not experience such anxiety when my own children were young. Not only is that not true—or rather, was not true then—but it isn't even true now that they are in their middle twenties. I don't believe I was being deliberately dishonest. I only wanted to encourage you. But

I'm very sorry if I made it appear that I am more fortunate than you, because that is not the case, even now.

On the draft of a letter to Evelyn Knops, Shelagh got no further than one sentence: *"I am so sorry . . ."*

DIARY ENTRY

I have destroyed all the letters I tried to write this morning. They were quite impossible to do. The whole idea was a mistake.

Normally I like writing letters, but these were to serve a different purpose, an ulterior motive, that of saying Goodbye; and all I found myself doing was apologizing or pontificating. These letters were supposed to put my end to certain relationships—whereas ordinary correspondence serves the healthy purpose of fostering a relationship. Every letter ends with the assumption that the correspondence is "to be continued." These were not letters. Some kind of testimonial?

Out of nowhere, I am reminded of a review my father wrote for the T.L.S. years ago, criticizing an art historian's book which he found both trivial and prolix. He wrote something like "We all know what it is to have the germ of an idea. In this case, the author has had but the idea of a germ and he inflated it into a full-blown disease."

I have been misled by the idea of saying Goodbye to people into attempting to do something entirely inappropriate: to express in a letter what matters only in living, in conversation, in a gesture, in acts of friendship or love: to inform and to entertain—without any ulterior motive. Instead, to try to say Goodbye, to set things right, to defend myself or express regrets is something like Settling Accounts. That's such a commercial form of returning to zero. Not being overdrawn—so that the human-relations balance sheet shows that income and expenditures were equal. Better I should reckon on being deprived of Last Goodbyes—and that I so choose to deprive others—not because I lack awareness of something "owed" to them, but because my sense of how to Finish my life is satisfied by an abrupt End rather than a Conclusion and a Coda. It is to my taste.

This has been one of the sacrifice days. I am getting through the night's sleeplessness without Nembutal and the morning's headache with aspirin, so that the "Enough" collection of capsules begins to grow.

We are now in the rejuvenation of early spring. The tulips and irises are in flower in the garden. The builders are just beginning to work on the new and larger greenhouse. We will start collecting orchids again. The cleaning man has mowed the lawn. Mrs. Yates and I are planning the dinner for April first.

I read travel guides to Greece and the islands of the Aegean. I have an appointment for lunch with Brita next week.

It seems to me there is no wisdom in the cliché that you ought to live each day as if it might be your last. You would be in a stupor or a frenzy. I know my tendencies in both directions. With a sense of "the last day" one might want to Sum Up or pretend to Prophesy or—worse—pretend to wisdom that one doesn't have. Think of those letters I tried to write: dreadful.

No. You must live as if your life were infinite, endless, and your powers, unendangered, at their peak. You must live imagining the Ideal, so as not to be done in by Truth.

I will try to do that—despite my knowledge of the end, and in spite of the headaches. But with two additional requirements of myself: that I abjure self-pity, which is the contemptible ingratitude of the unreasonable; and that I steel my resolve—to take all the Nembutal I need to end my life on the day the seizures recur—no matter what day that is. No self-pity; no begging for more time; no regret. Be firm. You will know what to do, when to do it.

Incidentally (1) I must have my teeth cleaned, and (2) I think I should buy a new hostess gown for the party.

❧

Matter-of-factly, Shelagh asked, between the omelette and the salad, "Brita—if anything should happen to me, you will help to see after Chester, won't you?"

"What a very strange thing to say!"

"I don't know what possessed me to say it." She sipped her wine. They had met in the lobby of the handsome private club on Park Avenue in this, the first year that membership had been open to women. When she worked at the United Nations, Brita stayed there. The high windows of the dining room on the sixth floor presented them with the skyline of Manhattan, facing north. "But something will happen to all of us sooner or later."

"It's highly probable." Brita smiled. "However, many of us have a tendency to special pleading. . . ."

Shelagh felt herself relax now; she had actually said it. "Yes," she agreed, "many of us long to be exceptional."

"Are you seeing the children this afternoon?"

"No. I'll go shopping. I must buy a gorgeous new dress."

"Try Bergdorf Goodman, and Henri Bendel."

"Of course!"

"How are the children?"

Shelagh chewed a mouthful of mixed green salad. "In a moment." She

263

drank a sip of water, took a deep breath, and began: "I've given them each a great deal of money."

"Really?"

"Well, they are at the most amorphous stage of their lives. Money is freedom."

"Money is power."

"And it should give them greater range. The power to make choices they would not have otherwise."

"It also makes trouble."

"I was so hoping to see something revolutionary, something radical, happen immediately."

Brita laughed. "Like plastic surgery?"

"Yes. I suppose it's foolish of me, but I couldn't resist. It's spring!—and they're young and unformed, and they ought to throw caution to the winds and do something wonderful."

"Well . . . ?"

"First of all, I think each of them is in a state of shock and can't make plans. Oh, well, yes—they speak of the most tentative and modest of plans. A long summer vacation. Morgan might go to the Middle East. Claire is thinking of the Orient."

"That's the sort of thing you might have expected, isn't it?"

"Yes, but it doesn't excite me."

"And what would?"

"Oh, Morgan's writing a novel. Claire's buying a theater."

They laughed with each other.

"Actually," Shelagh added, "it seems only to be making difficulties in their affairs. Morgan's asked Christina Greene to marry him and she won't do it unless he promises *not* to take the Church seriously."

"Ah, she's one of the new-style women."

"And Claire wants her boyfriend, Simon, to travel with her all summer and he says he won't do it unless they're married."

"Otherwise, he'd be her kept man. Her gigolo. That makes him one of the old-style men."

"I wonder how it will turn out."

LETTER TO ADRIENNE

Sister mine:

Your letter filled me with sorrow.

How could you have broken up with Hugh? I thought him the best man you've ever been involved with. What a shame! And Lord Byrne is so much older and less attractive. I just don't understand. I don't want to understand.

I wanted you to be happy with Hugh. To stay happy with him. It's so unfair to you. You don't give yourself the chance to go beyond romance—beyond being in love—to loving devotion, which can still be volatile, but grants you your only sense of eternity. This way, you are always preparing for the best of life but never knowing the experience of it. I'm so unhappy for you. It doesn't matter that Lord Byrne is showing you a good time; you are not letting yourself have a good life.

Forgive me. We always did judge each other harshly, and forgave each other. What else is a sister for?

No. None of the vandals has been arrested. I doubt that we'll hear either from them or about them again. It was only a hate attack. Chester, I fear, will always carry a scar from it. But he doesn't talk about it. When I see him look at the books in the library, however, I feel it with him: the sense of having been mugged. It was not his body that was attacked; but one's home, books, paintings, flowers are the extensions of one's soul—more than trappings: like clothes, they embody one's values. And for those to be abused is to suffer psychic manhandling. Chester is a very strong man and can take a lot; but he is not without personal sensitivity. Like Hugh!

Last week, in New York, I bought a spectacular dress. Do you know the designer Scaasi? It's knit jersey. In three tiers. Over the shoulders and bosom and the length of bell sleeves it's in ecru; from beneath the breasts to below the hips it's in pale gold; and the long skirt is flecked tan. It makes me feel like a cascade of Champagne.

I'm giving a dinner party for a large number of friends tomorrow night and I can't wait to wear it.

Mother would have looked wonderful in this dress. Odd, my thinking of that. I must be more grateful to her than I'd realized.

Peace!

❧

The next morning Shelagh wrote a letter addressed to Chester, sealed it, and locked it in the center drawer of her desk. It read:

Farewell, my darling.

I write this well in advance of my death, so that you will find it waiting for you when the time comes.

There is a tumor growing in my brain that is incurable, inoperable; fatal. I plan to take my own life before I become a hopeless victim of physical pain and inflict psychic pain upon you and our children. To my taste that will be the best resolution of the situation.

In a sense, I am not sorry to leave you or to think of you without me. That is because I could not love you more or better than I have done, nor do I believe that you could love me better than you have. We have enjoyed to the fullest everything good that we've had to offer each other. More would be only repetition. In that regard, you do not need me anymore, and I do not need you. It would be pleasant to go on like this—but that's not possible.

In working on illustrations for the Old Testament, I think I was more affected by these lines from the Book of Job than by any others:

> . . . as water wears away stones,
> And a rainstorm sweeps away the soil from the land,
> So thou wiped out the hope of man.
> Thou dost overpower him finally, and he is gone.
> His face is changed, and he is banished from thy sight.
> His children rise to honor, but he sees nothing of it;
> They sink into obscurity, but he knows it not.
> He grieves over himself, and he mourns for himself.

All that I regret is not knowing what will become of the children. It pains me, but it does not torture me. I entrust them to God—which means to the rest of the world.

When you and they think of me, I beg of you not to concentrate on my death but rather imagine my life—which in fact includes this secret plan. We all keep secrets from others and even from ourselves, in order to keep our balance. Mankind as a whole keeps the central secret from itself—that People Die. Humanity can take that truth in very small doses, infrequently, and then must put it out of mind so as not to go insane with unhappiness.

If you grieve for me, I pray that it will be for a short time. For I judge that I have used my life well—and been made good use of—and now, it is used up. There is neither pity nor shame in that. There is only: fulfillment. What else could one have wanted?

I honor my father and my mother.

I bless you and I thank you.

I commend my children to the world, which I beseech to treat them kindly.

For the last time, I go to sleep saying: "I love you."

Your

    Shelagh

᠄᠁᠄

On the evening of the first of April, Brita von Bickersdorf was the first to arrive. "What a gorgeous dress!" she exclaimed. "Is that what you bought in New York?"

"The day we had lunch, yes."

"Turn around. Oh, it's breathtakingly beautiful."

"Well, you're no slouch either. I've always admired that brocade suit."

"Comfortable as an old shoe. I love coming to a party early. It's the only chance to see your hostess."

"Let me show you something magnificent." Shelagh led her into the living room. "Look at that Japanese kimono on the wall."

"Fabulous. Oh, to have worn that at some Imperial ceremony! . . . Who else is coming this evening?" She looked to the dining room, where Mrs. Yates was arranging the platters, bowls, and plates.

"The Warners, the Taylors, Walter, Professor and Mrs. Marvin Flower, Elsie Rostum, the new dean of the Law School, a few of Chester's fellow judges, the golf pro from the country club. Dr. and Mrs. Rosenblatt. Freddy Tiejens and his wife."

"Who?"

"He used to be my editor. Now he's teaching at a prep school here in Connecticut."

Brita looked the room over. "What lovely flowers." Fresh violets and lilies of the valley stood in silver vases on end tables, the mantelpiece, the Chinese trunk. "You bring together so much of the goodness of the world. And your own greenhouse? Is it rebuilt?"

"Let me show you." Leading her through the hall to the library, Shelagh said, "It's entirely new. More ambitious. But the shelves haven't been installed yet, and there are no orchids."

Chester and the bartender stood at a round table converted into a bar for the evening. Brita greeted Chester with a kiss on each cheek and the question "Do you have your tickets for Greece?"

"We certainly do."

"You'll enjoy such a good time."

"What would you like to drink?"

As the rest of the guests arrived, the cocktails and the wine served, the introductions made, Shelagh watched her friends and acquaintances form themselves into groups of two or four or six, standing at the bar, in the hallway, seated on the sofa, circling the dining-room table. She realized that there could be no general conversation with so large a number of people. There would be little one-act plays performed simultaneously, and she could stand back and be the audience to this one or step onto the stage and become an actor in that one. Separate pools of drama, and she could swim into or out of them or merely between.

After Isabel and Conrad Taylor took their drinks into the living room, Shelagh asked Brita at the stairs, "You are on the search committee for the next provost, aren't you?"

"Yes."

"Is it likely to be Conrad?"

"Very likely.

In the library, Shelagh joined a small group considering materialism. Freddy Tiejens, who had been fired from Harvest House, was talking with Henry and Kate Warner about the effect of lusting for luxury in American society: ". . . the aims for our material life having been raised from comfort-for-all to luxury-for-all."

Kate asked, "A Jacuzzi in every studio apartment?"

"A masseuse," Shelagh said, "twice a day."

"My recollection of the greatest luxury Kate and I ever saw," Henry said, "is in a kitchen in Portugal. On vacation a number of years ago, we took a tourist drive north from Lisbon and stopped at a monastery built, if I remember correctly, in the sixteenth century."

"The kitchen was *enormous*," Kate added. "Walled with squares of painted tiles—floor to ceiling. Everything was huge: the fireplaces, cold chests, chopping tables . . ."

"They had to feed an army of monks. At one end of the great room there was a large rectangular opening in the floor."

"Tiled!" They would tell this story together.

"Water streamed through it."

"The monks had built the monastery over a trout stream and seen to it that the source of fresh trout would be incorporated into the design of the kitchen."

"Fresh trout for the having."

"All you needed to do was drop in a net as they swam through. Indoors!" Shelagh said, "Ingenious."

"To this day?" Freddy Tiejens asked.

Henry said, "It isn't a monastery anymore. It's a museum."

Before the living-room window, Conrad and Marvin Flower discussed the work of Marcel Proust. Conrad insisted that the richness of the title was untranslatable because of the double meaning of *temps perdu*. "The past that is gone, on the one hand; but on the other, it's the idiom for free time. So it could just as easily be translated as In Search of the Past or as Looking for Some Free Time. In French it's a play on words you cannot make in English."

"You mean it's a pun?"

"Two ideas for the price of one."

Marvin Flower scowled. "Oh, hell . . ."

•

268

Dr. Rosenblatt found himself standing with his back to the living-room fireplace, flanked on one side by his wife and on the other by Isabel Taylor, before a semicircle of the Warners and two of Chester's colleagues on the bench. He considered Isabel in her lush beauty, the latent forcefulness in her striking figure, dressed in a long black gown, strapless, offering her naked shoulders lightly brushed by her coiled blond hair; and on the other hand, his plain wife in a shirtwaist dress of pale green, not so much fitting her as disguising whatever modest figure she formed. "I feel like Ego standing between Id and Superego."

Everyone laughed but Priscilla, who said to her husband, vehemently, "I hate it when you make fun of me like that."

He crumpled. Instantly his face showed that he had no defense.

Henry Warner made light of it. "It was only a joke."

"On me!" Priscilla said, and moved toward the dining room, elbows punching the air behind her.

Her husband followed. "I'm sorry. I'm terribly sorry. I never should have said . . ." She did not stop at the dining-room table. He followed her into the kitchen.

One of the judges shook his head, saying, "Marriage . . ."

Kate Warner said, "People . . ."

The bartender silently refilled glasses. Shelagh urged her guests to serve themselves. The pungent odors of the food overwhelmed the delicate fragrance of the violets and lilies of the valley. People fed themselves from plates balanced on their knees. There was the quality of gaiety as at a picnic.

Brita asked after Dr. and Mrs. Connolley.

Without explanation, Shelagh answered, "I don't see them socially anymore."

Soft ballroom dance music from the 1930s played from the hidden stereo set. Shelagh smiled at the thought that the one experience shared by everyone brought together in her home that night was the same songs sounding in the background of every mind.

Priscilla and Dr. Rosenblatt returned, reconciled. She had cowed him. Attentively he filled a plate for her and brought it to where she sat on the sofa. He squatted on the carpet at her feet.

Mrs. Yates moved among the guests retrieving the used dishes.

Then there was an invisible stretching and yawning, an intake of breath and straightening of the spine, preparation for the home stretch. The actors regrouped for different one-act plays.

Shelagh joined the men on either side of Isabel Taylor.

Professor Flower took the pipe out of his mouth and moaned, "Woe . . .

Let me think of an answer."

Shelagh asked, "What is the question?"

"I've challenged these gentlemen," Isabel said, "to describe their most ecstatic experiences—other than sex. I'm wondering what else there is that
takes you out of yourself, what's called 'mind-blowing' these days."

"The truly ecstatic," Walter Webster said, "should be body-and-mind-
blowing."

Isabel nodded agreement.

"Well, I'll tell you," Marvin Flower began, crossing his arms over his
broad chest. "I remember distinctly. I was fourteen years old and I stayed up
until dawn reading Dickens' *Tale of Two Cities* from beginning to end.
When I finished it I realized I had lost all sense of time and place. I was *in*
the book. Or rather, the book had been me. And then it came to me in a flash
that the book was not an event in real life, something I merely observed. It
was the conception of Charles Dickens, who no longer lived. He had created
it; and it was re-created in me. I was in awe. I discovered, on returning from
the ecstatic experience, that literature gives one the only opportunity in life to
think and feel with someone else's mind."

Shelagh patted his cheek. "Wonderful." She wondered if his statement
was a prepared speech. It had the ring of the lecture hall in it.

"Too intellectual," Isabel said. "I want—something more emotional."

Marvin Flower looked away from her with disdain. "Oh, woe . . ."

"Ah!" Walter Webster looked bright. "In that case, I'll tell you about an
experience I remember as ecstatic. In a spiritual way. In Paris, years ago, I
went to Mass at Notre Dame one Sunday. The great Gothic cathedral was
filled to capacity. There must have been thousands of people there. I had to
stand, in one of the transepts, surrounded by a standing crowd pressing
against each other. A marriage ceremony was performed, and then there was
a great swell of chanted prayer; everyone's voice rose together as one voice.
Between the shared singing, the idea of wedding, contact with all the bodies
against mine—I lost the sense of my physical limits as well as consciousness
of being an individual. I really felt that I was one with both nature and
spirit." He blushed. "It probably lasted for ten seconds. I was relatively young
then. But I've never forgotten it." He looked aside for an ashtray where he
could put out his cigarette.

"Very spiritual," Isabel commented drily.

Chester joined the group to stand next to Shelagh. Marvin told him what
the topic was.

"Well, this is mine," Shelagh said: "It was between the wars, in England. I
was a child. My father took me up in an open plane. Just the pilot in front of
us. I sat on my father's lap. The airplane rose quickly, and I felt instantly that
everything inside me had slipped away. And then as we careered in the

270

sky"—she paused to think how to put it—"I felt without any surface separating me from the most formless of all the elements, air. I was merged with the air of the world's sky, moving at its speed, not mine; in danger of never being transformed back into my own body with its own flesh; yet at the same time, safe."

"I like that." Isabel smiled. "Visceral."

Shelagh continued: "What was unique about it is, it was *I* who was *flying*. Nowadays the plane is flying, but you, inside the monster, do not feel you are flying. It was glorious! You remember"—she turned to Chester—"don't you?"

"No. How could I?"

She looked shocked. "But you're my father."

The group was dumbfounded with embarrassment.

Chester took her hand in his. "No, I'm not. You've called me a lot of things in our time together, but never that. I'm your husband." He tried to chuckle.

The other three could not comprehend what had happened, until Isabel tried: "Have you drunk too much?"

"I? What did I say?" Shelagh replied, recovering herself with the support of Chester's hand firmly clasping hers. "Yes." Shelagh, who had been sipping Perrier water all evening, lied: "I must have had too much to drink. What an odd slip of the tongue." She carried it off as though the lapse was inconsequential, in no way unnerved her, concealing the intensity of her new fear in discovering that—if only for a moment—she had lost her mind. Forcing herself to regain her control, she insisted, "Come, we must take fresh plates from the table. Time for dessert."

Then she turned to other guests. The Tiejenses found themselves content with the golf pro. Elsie Rostum looked over the shelves of books like a librarian checking inventory. The Dean of the Law School asked Brita questions about the World Court. The judges talked with each other about deep-sea fishing.

As she went through the motions called for on the surface, Shelagh felt she must suppress the terror; that she must bear this too.

Chester came to her side, put an arm around her shoulder, and squeezed her affectionately. "You mustn't let it bother you," he said. "A slip of the tongue."

She kissed him full on the mouth.

"All these guests in our home . . ." Chester began. "Your gift to them is like a caress."

Shelagh's eyes filled with tears. "Let me have your handkerchief." She turned her back and dried her eyes. "I'll have to check my face," she said, starting for the stairs.

•

271

When she returned to the library, Shelagh showed the wives of the other judges her collection of brass objects on the side table. Brita and Kate approached and joined them.

As she stopped talking, Shelagh looked distracted, self-absorbed. Absently, she backed away until she stood against the glass door of the greenhouse.

Kate Warner looked up from the table to see the glazed look of Shelagh's eyes. She moved toward her to ask, "Are you all right?"

Shelagh whispered, "If only I knew what God thinks of me."

"What?"

Shelagh mumbled, "Maybe instead of a Last Judgment—our *lives* are a Judgment on God."

"You must be joking."

Shelagh snapped back to her social self and smiled. "Could I be driven mad by jealousy?—I don't have a trout stream in my kitchen."

Kate Warner felt uncertain whether Shelagh was toying with her, putting her down. Not wanting to find out, she excused herself.

When all the guests had left, Mrs. Yates and the bartender had cleaned up, all the lights were out, Chester slumped back on the sofa in the living room. Shelagh sat down next to him and rested her head against his chest.

"Good party!" he said.

My last party, she thought. I wonder if any of the friends or acquaintances here tonight keeps a diary. Well, someday they'll know: it isn't true that we didn't have the chance to say Goodbye.

❧

The catastrophe that befell Claire toward the end of April was announced to her mother in a panicky telephone call, begging her to come and talk with her, to help her. Claire felt paralyzed, unable to move out of her apartment; otherwise she would go up to New Haven. Shelagh left a message for Chester on the front-hall table and arrived at Claire's two hours later.

Simon Monroy was living with another woman.

"How did you find out?" Shelagh asked.

"I went there. I took a taxi and I gave the driver his address on the Lower East Side. I'd never been there before, but I knew the address."

"Why had you never been there before?"

"He said he shared an apartment with two other bachelors. He never invited me there."

"Why did you go?"

"Ah . . . oh! For the most thrilling of reasons. I'd decided to marry him."

"To agree to his wish . . ."

"To acquiesce, to yield, to comply. The Man wanted me to be his Bride, his Helpmeet. Yesterday morning I woke up in this one-room efficiency by myself—a Sunday morning, with spring light making George look like a Christmas tree—and I felt appalled by how foolish it was for me to be here alone, when I could be with Simon every morning when I wake up."

"Yes." Shelagh stroked her daughter's hand. They sat next to each other on the daybed.

"I realized I was only half a person. He is the other half. I was charged with determination. I wanted him. I wanted us to be married. That isn't something you say over the phone. I got dressed in ten seconds. I wanted to be with him always." She broke down in sobs. Her mother comforted her.

"The driver found the address. A crummy building. Simon's name alone was next to one of the bells. It was a three-flight walk-up. My knock on the door was answered by a girl."

"Had you ever seen her before?"

"Never. I asked if it was Simon's apartment and she said 'Yes.' She didn't invite me in. I asked if he was there and she told me he'd gone out to buy the newspaper. I asked if she lived with one of his roommates and she burst out laughing. '*I'm* his roommate,' she said."

"Oh . . ."

" 'And you—who are you?' she asked. I gave her my name. That wiped the smile off her face. 'How long have you been living with him?' She said, 'Since December. We met in Toronto in November.' I recognized then that the soft, rounded sound of her words was a Canadian accent."

"What does she look like?"

"Twiggy. A skinny tall thing, without makeup. In blue jeans and a sweat shirt. 'You're the actress,' she said, with a supercilious sneer. 'You're the Uptown babe Simon wants to marry for her money.' " Claire burst into tears, covered her face with her hands, rocked back and forth in misery. Her mother threw her arms around her and held her close, rocking with her.

Claire went to the bathroom, washed her face, regained her composure, came back red-eyed but calmer. She stood looking out the window in the early-evening light.

"What happened then?" Shelagh asked.

"I don't think I should tell you."

"You slapped her."

"No." Claire tried to laugh. "It's not what I did, it's what I said."

"I think I know all the words you know."

"I asked her to be kind enough to deliver a message to Simon for me. Tell him to go fuck himself. And then I stomped down the three flights of stairs in a blind rage."

273

"Good for you." Shelagh heartily broke into laughter, and feebly Claire laughed with her. "Did you run into him?"

"No. I saw a cab in front of the building as I came out, and I grabbed it. I think I was back here about thirty-five minutes after I left. That's all it took for me to find out that all this while he's been shacking up with that broad—and that he wanted to marry me only because of the money."

"That's the last thing I would have hoped the money could do for you."

"But if it hadn't been for the money, I might not ever have found out."

"What?"

"That he was two-faced; he didn't mean what he said; he wanted only to take whatever advantage of me would be to his benefit; that he didn't love me. I didn't know that! I'm so ashamed. I feel such a fool. I'm afraid to go out of the house."

"But it's not like being jilted."

"What do you mean?"

Shelagh told her daughter the story of how Adrienne was to be married to Trevor Cartwright and how she had been jilted just as she was about to leave for the ceremony. Their father had gone alone to the Registry Office to tell their guests that it was "off."

Claire said, "That's horrible. It was all played out *in public,* in front of family and friends."

"Still, as you say, it's better than not finding out in time."

"Look at what it did to Aunt Adrienne."

That gave Shelagh pause. "In your generation," she began, "there isn't the sense of responsibility for 'doing any of this' *in public.* Family and friends are not consulted; advice is not asked for; permission does not have to be granted. You are free . . ."

". . . to make my own mistakes."

"I had no reservations about Simon. I couldn't have warned you. There was no way for me to know."

"Nor for me either. I believed him. How could I have been so wrong?"

"Were you? Have you spoken with him?"

"He hasn't dared to call."

"What if he does love you, and he does live with another woman, but now, because of the money, he wants to marry you? Would you be his wife; would you have him as your husband?"

"No! I'd want at least my first marriage to be promising enough to last forever."

Shelagh stood up as the waves of laughter from her joined with those of her daughter, and they embraced in the middle of the room.

The telephone rang. Chester was calling to find out how they were, and Shelagh reassured him that while Claire was having "a bad time," she would be all right. She promised to be home in a few more hours. Meanwhile, Claire in the Pullman kitchen poured them each a large glass of Sherry and suppressed her giggles, constantly shaking her head in disbelief.

"You are remarkable," she said, handing the wine to her mother. "When I phoned you earlier today, I thought I'd never laugh again as long as I lived."

"That shows how young you are. Be assured you will survive this, and if you have bad luck, there will be other disappointments that you will survive as well."

"Still—how can it be that you love someone for months and months and then, in one day, learn something that makes you recognize he no longer has any meaning for you? He's forgettable. Disposable as a paper napkin. How is that possible?"

"Everything depends on what you need to be yourself."

"I don't know what I need to be myself."

"You'll find out more every time you say No, and every time you say Yes. Consider Adrienne. She was jilted." Shelagh then began to tell her the story of Trevor Cartwright.

Claire interrupted. "But you said that before."

"Did I? That's awful. I'm so sorry. Just believe it's not your fault—in any way."

At midnight, after telling Chester what she could of Claire's situation, without mentioning anything of having repeated herself, Shelagh, lying beside her husband ready to go to sleep, suddenly asked, "Do you remember the night we took the children to the opera last fall?"

"Of course."

"*Tristan and Isolde.*"

"Yes."

"The potion to bring about eternal love was the mother's gift to her daughter. The tragedy comes about because it is swallowed under the wrong circumstances."

"Yes, my darling."

"I wonder if Isolde's mother ever learned of what happened."

Morgan came to dinner one evening in the middle of May. "Have the new people moved into the McGrath house?" he asked.

"Yes," Shelagh answered. "Mother, father, and four miniatures."

"Have you met them?"

"I don't want to have any new experiences."

Morgan looked at her with surprise. "But you're going to Greece."

275

"I have known Greece all my life." She did not say, "I want to enter the watercolors of my Great-aunt Greta."

With a wry smile, Morgan said, "It must be wonderful not to want any new experiences. . . ."

"That's not for you. You're too young. You should want nothing but new experiences."

"I agree. That's why I've broken it off with Tina."

"You have?" his father asked.

"Yes. I cannot marry anyone who won't recognize that I must be free to take some kind of spiritual life seriously."

Shelagh asked, "How about Transcendental Meditation?"

Morgan dropped his knife and fork onto the dinner plate. "Why do you make fun of me? Because I'm looking for a sense of significance above and beyond ordinary life?"

It was Chester who said, "Ordinary life is wondrous enough for us."

"No, you can't have it," Chester said, alone with Shelagh in their bedroom as they undressed that night. "No. No. You can't force it. People develop according to their own natures and the conditions of the world they live in. You gave them the money because you thought it would hasten the process, ripen them faster. There hasn't been enough time. You cannot hope for them to grow up faster than they can grow up."

"I cannot see them fully formed."

"Not yet."

"Unsuccessfully greedy?"

"That's it."

"I always trust you to set me straight."

"You're lucky that way."

They laughed, getting under the sheet and light quilt, coming to hug each other close. "I can't imagine not wanting to help them along."

"But from their point of view, it's interference."

"And my helping you in your life?" she asked brusquely. "What is that?"

"That," Chester said, "is being blessed."

❧

After the beginning of May, Shelagh ceased to date the entries she made in her diary. They became shorter and tended to run into one another.

On days when I take Nembutal, I find myself clearheaded, alert, but immobile, passionless. Sometimes I discover that I'm sitting up in bed and don't remember having left the kitchen or my studio. In the middle of this afternoon I found myself seated at the open window in the library, facing the street, listening for sounds—a baby crying, a cardinal bird's call, the rhythm of high heels snapping against the cement sidewalk—as if it were important to hear them, but not grasping for an instant why ever I should think that.

It is a state of painlessness but pointlessness. I stare. I have been staring for I don't know how long at the brass collection on the round table. I don't feel anything about the objects; I just see them.

Adrienne writes with an invitation from Lord Byrne to join them during the month of August. He has a house on the Isle of Rhum off the coast of Scotland. Why don't you celebrate your birthday with us? she asks. Will you and Chester bring the children? There are red deer, wild, all over the island. Acres of heather and bright heath. The air is perfume.

I answer with thanks. We'll think about it. What a lovely invitation. Everything I do now about the future possibility is a pretense. I do not desire the future.

I do not desire.

When did Chester and I last make love? I can't remember. In the past, when he went away, as he is away this weekend at a conference of judges in Hartford, I used to masturbate. I can't do that anymore. I do not feel any sexual desire. I cannot "turn it on." Numb.

Good. Another letdown. Every letdown makes it easier to let go of life. To be willing for it to end. I have felt so much tension over keeping my secret that it exhausted my will. After that I found it only tedious. Now it's boring. Perhaps the advantage in this is that I will find myself so bored by the waiting, the end will be a relief. I will welcome release.

Yes. I think that's possible.

This is not being at the peak of one's powers. This is unraveling.

I give no thought to the disposal of my things. When Adrienne and I were little, we'd whisper in the dark about Mother's diamond ring and her opal earrings—which of us would get them, if she died.

I haven't given any thought to a new Will and Testament since the inheritance money has been transferred to the children. And I won't. I have no in-

terest in Who Gets What. Let the survivors . . . "She is survived by————"
. . . dispose of things as they see fit.

My fingerprints will be on them.

I can't do anything more for my son or my daughter. Your children may grow great or they may fall into insignificance, but you will not know; you can only grieve for yourself.

I put nothing in order.

I cannot "wrap things up."

So I am left with their incompleteness. The design of my children remains a sketch. I will not see the finished drawings. What is my complaint? I will not hear the sounds of their individuated voices—in the sense that one respects what is unique in an author: nobody else could have said it this way. Or: only you could have said that.

But even now, they have their own dignities to protect.

I think they'll be all right.

I do not know whether I repeat myself. Ever since Claire showed me I was starting to tell her again the story I'd already told her of Adrienne's being jilted, I have been fearful of repeating myself without knowing it. But now I speak with almost no one but Chester. Well, not exactly. I see people, but not for conversations of any length. It is probably (perhaps?) only with Chester that I run the risk of repeating myself and not knowing it. Could that be happening, and he refuses to make me conscious of it? to spare me? I wouldn't be surprised. Do I want to know? No. Better this way. And slips of the tongue? Does he suffer them, while I remain unaware? Is he living with me now feeling that he must watch me progressively lose my mind?

I am grateful when he is away overnight; then I can endure insomnia and add to the collection of Nembutal more easily. By now I have almost all I need.

I don't know whether I want to go to Greece. To take the plane over and a ship back. Yes, of course, it will be a change, a rest. But so many things might go wrong. I could get dysentery. That's really very funny; it just made me laugh. I could get sunstroke, blood poisoning, bitten by a scorpion. The plane might crash.

What books should I take with me to read on the ship?

•

278

Sometimes I feel a tendency for my left leg to drag. It seems too heavy to clear the ground. I stand still until I feel strong enough to lift it.

From time to time, I have the strange impression that my entire left arm is not mine. As if it belonged to someone else. But who could that be?

No self-pity. Steel your resolve.

It makes me unhappy that I cannot be honest. I cannot blurt out what I think or feel regarding what is most important to me. I must try to understand why I had always believed honesty was so desirable. Yet, where did I learn it—at my mother's knee?—that you shape what you say to fit the ears of your listener. It is one thing to be so in tune with yourself that you can state what you think or feel; it is another to know what your Other can take. That insight into what is good for him or her is the measure of your sympathetic understanding of the other person. You can't be honest in a void; you can only be honest to someone. So sound reciprocal relations depend on sympathetic honesty. Your judgment of what the other can take best determines the limit to what you can say. Isn't there some other word for "sympathetic honesty"? I can't think of it just now. Perhaps it will come to mind.

I've decided not to take this diary with me to Greece.
There is nothing more for me to reflect on.

LETTER FROM ATHENS TO CLAIRE

Darling girl:
The past isn't what it's cracked up to be. Or perhaps I should say—what is left of the past is certainly cracked up. There is the most overwhelming sense of chipping, breaking, falling apart, decaying, moldering into dust of the marble glories that remain here. Centuries and centuries of entropy, the iron fist of time beating everything into a powder. I think the overall impression these nearly two weeks of June have laid on me is that . . . two hundred years from now, nothing of the Glory that was Greece will remain to be seen. This is the last chance. Hurry! Why not come back from the Orient by way of Greece? But then, you probably have the next hundred years in which to get here. There might still be a few stumps left.
We have been to Delphi, Corinth, Mycenae, Macedonia, the museums, the temples, the Acropolis, you name it. We have destroyed two pairs of

shoes and at least one gastrointestinal tract. But we are indomitable travelers.

The present isn't in such good shape either.

We see the effects of years of drought everywhere. This is not a green and lush land. It is dried out. The sparse grass is gray-green and limp. The sheep are limp. The hills are limp. Hot. Tired. Weary. The cypresses are not a vivid green. They appear dusty and starved. The people are dusty and plump; but dangerously—as if they might burst. Or are they all characters in an Eric Ambler novel that is being filmed here without our knowing it?

Yet through it all, there are the remnants and relics of grandeur to be met with. The statue of a charioteer; a silver drinking cup with an overlaid scene of hunting; an amphora in black and brick red of a horny satyr pursuing a nymph. There are universals in human life; and there are moments in which they are captured at their best—forever. Well, for as long as they last.

By the way, I hope you're taking care of yourself. I mean: eating better. You've become too thin. Try lentil salads. I think they are the secret of the beauty of Frenchwomen. Or have I told you that before?

We shall be back in time to give you a gala going-away party. How about dinner and dancing in the Rainbow Room? Wouldn't that be fun?

Your father tends to be morose. I think it's because he's discovered there is no golf course in Greece.

Be strong!

Yours ever

LETTER FROM KYROS TO MORGAN

My dear son,

Ten days of sailing among the Aegean islands! How exhausting pleasure can be. (How do the young put up with all their joys?) Enervating. But we are at the end. Tomorrow we will board the ship to take us home. O home! Routine. O happy, unexciting routine. I long for it. If one has good habits, then your spirit is free to soar, to create, to imagine. But, Jesus, when you're concerned about where you'll be able to go to the toilet again—that drags you down to the level of combat soldiers in a dugout. Well, we haven't been that badly off. We sleep on the ship every evening. And during the days roam about the islands.

This is, to put it simply, what Paradise must look like. But the people here are not living there.

Still, the sky is an incomparable robin's-egg blue, the sea is liquid sapphires; the houses are white cubes, built in tiers that rise from the small ports up onto the hills surrounding the main squares of towns that are thousands of years old.

We have been to Naxos, the part of the island that remains. The rest was blown away by an earthquake (a volcano?) long before Plato was born. It is believed that there the ancient Atlantis actually existed. Why not believe it did exist there? That there was the El Dorado of the ancient world even the ancients dreamed of. For the Hebrews there was the Garden of Eden. For the Greeks the island of Atlantis. I imagine that both are true. And that neither loss is to be regretted. Nostalgia has a great deal going for it. It's a lot easier to take than the pie-in-the-sky of a utopian future. Always trying to get back to perfection . . .

Oh, how these words pervert our lives: past, future, perfection, hope, regret, nostalgia. I want you to be a writer, a user of words. But not to be taken in by words. They are only the nameplates on the things that matter to us: what we think and what we feel. Of course, I'm like the lady who has to hear what she says in order to know what she thinks, but that isn't all bad. Speak. Speak! and you'll find out whether you agree with what you say or not.

This letter should reach you before we dock in New York. What do you say to a gala Bon Voyage party before you take off on your long vacation—at the Rainbow Room? A night on the town to say Goodbye. With or without words.

My best love

❧

Already by eleven in the morning on the second of July, the weather was intensely hot and humid. Shelagh, dressed only in a bathrobe and slippers, responded to the ring of the front doorbell. Through the glass pane she saw that Quentin Connolley stood there alone, looking disheveled.

"May I come in?"

"For a minute."

"Thank you."

"Do you want a cup of coffee?"

"No."

He looked as if he had slept in his clothes.

"Let us sit here." She led him into the library. They faced each other in armchairs.

"Why should you come here like this?" Shelagh had no makeup on, and she felt weak.

"I've been waiting for you to come back from Greece."

"We've been back for a week."

"No one's answered the phone when I called."

"I heard about it," she said.

"My son? You heard that he was killed by a hit-and-run driver."

"Yes. I can't tell you how sorry I am."

He was speechless. Dry-eyed. Hollowed out. "It was my fault," he finally said.

"How?"

"He died for my sins. It's my punishment." He ran his hands back and forth on his legs from his knees to his hips. His lips looked parched.

"I can't believe that."

"I do."

He looked the shell of the man she had known. Shelagh asked, "Why are you telling me this?"

"I'm here to beg your forgiveness. Wherever I've done wrong, where I've given offense—to those against whom I have sinned—I will penitently go and beg to be forgiven."

"What good will that do?" Meaning: will it bring back your son?

"It will lessen my guilt. It will keep worse punishment from befalling me and those I love."

"I don't think the world works that way. Rewards and punishments are for children and slaves. By the time you are an equal in life, it's only your own powers and the world's luck that matter."

"It's not luck. This is a moral universe. I transgressed; and what I valued most in this life was taken from me."

"It was of even greater value to him," she said.

He looked at her as a man who had no more tears left. "Please forgive me. I behaved badly. I am covered with shame. I beg you."

She stood up, pulled the light bathrobe tightly around her, and walked to the bookshelves on the right of the fireplace. She removed two of the books on the shelf at eye level and withdrew the crystal balls she had taken from his examining room. Cupping them in both hands, she offered them to him.

He took them from her, in silence, and pocketed them.

Then she said, kindly, "I thank you for keeping my secret."

The next morning, Shelagh cut a mat to frame one of her drawings of the Garden of Eden for Claire. The knife suddenly flew out of her hand to hit the door of the studio. Her hand twitched uncontrollably. Both hands trembled. Her arms grew light. She felt she was swooning. The only thought that occurred to her was No cup, no saucer breaking on the floor, but the moment has come. She blacked out, with the shock waves of a seizure raking through her body.

When she came to, her first impression was that night must have fallen—she had so little sight. But in all probability, only five minutes had passed.

She lay on the floor, the back of her head sore against the leg of her drawing table. She had bitten her tongue, and the taste of blood was sickly-sweet in her mouth.

Now! It is now or never, she said to herself, rising up on her hands and knees, forcing herself to stand. She moved through the hall to her bedroom, to the chest of drawers, where the pillbox was kept. She clutched the object—an oblong plastic box imitating tortoiseshell—and carried it in her fist to the bathroom, where she ran the water until it was cold and began swallowing the capsules, one at a time, with cool draughts of water, until she had swallowed them all.

She took off her bathrobe and put on her new dress—a cascade of champagne. Then, suddenly frightened that she would not have enough time, she rushed back into her studio, to her desk, unlocked the center drawer, found the letter addressed to Chester, and took it back to the bedroom with her. She laid it on the surface of his dresser.

She stepped out of her slippers and lay down in the bed. The hollowed impression of Chester's head remained on his pillow. That was where she laid her head. She pulled the sheet and the light summer cover over her and drew herself into a fetal position.

She lay there blindly for what seemed a long while, as her pounding heart gradually grew calm.

Shelagh wanted to remember her father's face, but what came to her was the sight of the two Atlases holding up the archway of the apartment building of her early childhood in Vienna.

Then she saw the linden tree in the garden of the Cortauld Institute.

She wanted to see her children.

Morgan appeared as an adolescent, at Rumpelmayer's, kissing his fingers and saying, "I think I'm in heaven."

Claire appeared on the stage, naked from the waist up, secure in her bravery, in the peach light of the stage scene—remote, protected.

She craved for Chester. She could not see him. Only feel his arms as he held her firmly, carrying her up the front stairs to the safety of the bathroom. She longed for the sight of him, but she saw, instead, a detail of Bronzino's *Allegory,* the secret thrust of Venus' tongue undulating into Cupid's mouth.

Her body was radiant with stilling calm. And then she remembered Kyoto. She stood in the garden of the temple; Chester was close against her. She watched the ice carving of a pagoda begin to melt in the warm air, dripping itself into the pool below. Then she saw the drops fall, looking up from below, for she was in the pool; she was one with the pool. She was the pool.

After that, she saw and felt and thought nothing more.

EPILOGUE

The funeral was delayed long enough for Morgan to return from Jerusalem, and for Claire to fly back from Taiwan. Adrienne could not be reached on the Isle of Rhum. Shelagh's body was laid to rest in the Jackman family plot of the cemetery in which her husband's ancestors had been buried for two hundred years.

They returned to the house alone—just Claire and Morgan with their father.

"I'd forgotten how cool the house is in hot weather," Morgan said. "Thick walls."

Claire looked drained; she had not slept for nights. "Brita was very broken up," she said. "But where were the Taylors? and the Warners?"

"Henry and Kate are in Maine," her father said. "Conrad's somewhere in the Southwest, and Isabel"—he sighed, but then said it—"is in a sanatorium of some sort for alcoholics—to dry out."

There had not been a formal service. Each of them had read a poem. Morgan chose the Landor with the lines: ". . . Nature I loved; and next to Nature, Art. I warm'd both hands before the fire of life; It sinks, and I am ready to depart."

Claire recited Elizabeth Barrett Browning's "How do I love thee? Let me count the ways . . ."

It was Shakespeare's sonnet "Let me not to the marriage of true minds admit impediments . . ." that Chester spoke.

"It's unbelievable, still incredible to me," Claire said.

Morgan asked, "How about a drink?" He brought gin and tonics to each of them in the living room. They sat on the sofa and in the armchairs at the Chinese trunk.

Chester had shown Shelagh's letter to both of them. It lay, returned to its envelope, on the surface before them.

Claire continued: "I've read the letter. I try to understand, but the fact is: she was so cheerful, so warmhearted during the past six months, I don't see how we can believe she *knew*, all along, she was dying. Unbelievable. How is it possible she could have kept that secret?"

Morgan said, "Courage."

"Do you remember her dancing at the Rainbow Room only ten days ago? Her verve? Her *joie de vivre*? That woman knew she was about to die?" Claire's eyes flooded with tears. Morgan handed her a handkerchief.

"We should have guessed," Morgan said. "When she gave us the money—while she was still alive. We ought to have understood then."

His sister said, "Well, we certainly didn't."

Chester looked up at the purple kimono on the wall above the sofa. "I'll have to return that to Henry Warner when he gets back. It's his grandmother's. He only lent it to me for a few months. I promised to return it. . . ."

"When?" Claire asked. "By when did you promise to return it?"

"Oh, vaguely, I said something like before the end of the summer."

"I don't understand."

"I asked him to lend it to me for a few months. To make your mother happy."

"A few months? Did *you* know she was going to die?"

"Yes."

Claire sat bolt upright on the sofa. "How did you know? How long have you known? Did she tell you?"

"No. She didn't."

Morgan asked, "Were you so close—you were able to sense it?"

"No. I read her diary."

"How could you?" Claire demanded.

"I don't remember exactly how it began. But it was after Morgan was born, and Shelagh had to stay in bed for a while, when I started the practice of making tea for her every morning. It was then, while the tea was steeping, I'd look around the rooms—she left the book all over the place—and I'd read whatever was there, if she'd written in it the day before."

"How could you?" Claire repeated. "She always said we shouldn't—if we found it lying about."

"I have no defense. It was a secret pleasure. You must know I loved her very much."

Claire asked, "And she was never aware that you read it?"

"Not as far as I know."

Morgan asked, "Then—for how long have you known that this was coming on?"

"Since late October, when she came back from London."

Claire said, "She pretended she was all right, and you didn't call her on it? You didn't tell her you knew she was ill? You weren't able to tell her how you felt?"

"It was what she wanted! She was pretending, but—as I knew—it was acting: remember? I could only admire the way she played her role."

"You gave in to that wish?" Morgan asked.

"Claire, Morgan," Judge Jackman began, "I don't think you understand. What do you imagine a marriage is all about?"

286

Claire said, "Mutual pleasure."

"I'll tell you what it's about," their father said. "At first you think it's the best condition under which to satisfy each other's desires. That's wonderful. But beyond needs and desires are fancies, whims, hopes." He sighed again and looked up at the kimono. "Ultimately you discover not only wishes but unspoken wishes, the merest gesture toward a wish. If you can satisfy those, you can give each other something neither of you was even sure had been desired. I don't think that can happen in any relationship other than marriage. I think that is what makes a good marriage the best thing in life."

"You mean to say," Claire asked, "that you deliberately—knowingly—satisfied Mother's wish to be taken for healthy when in fact she knew she was dying? You knew it too. But you went along—you poor man!—with the charade, because that is what you understood was her wish: that no one should know."

"Yes."

"You knew it since last October?" Morgan asked. "And never caved in? Never betrayed it? . . ."

Chester said, "Almost never. The night we came back from Florida and found the house broken into and damaged. That night—I remember—I wept: out of all proportion to the damage. I wept because of the fear of loss of her; I think I even said something like 'It will never be the same'—yes, something like that. I felt I had broken down at the time. I was nervous afterward about whether I'd given it away. She never referred to it."

"But she might have known, then?" Claire said.

"She might have; but I've no reason to believe she did."

"And she? Did she never give it away?" Morgan asked. "Almost give it away?"

"No. I can't remember any 'mistake' on her part. Except, perhaps, her remarks about 'completeness.' Of course, I understood her wanting to give her money to you as quickly as possible. She wanted to see the effect on your lives during the time left to her."

"Bad show" was all Claire said.

"I'll get us fresh drinks," Morgan said, and did so quickly; but the three of them then sat in silence.

Finally, Chester said: "In the end, I was left with the impression that your mother believed the last judgment on a life is whether it makes a good story."

Claire asked, "Whatever for?"

"Because then," her father answered slowly, "it can be seen as an end in itself, rather than only a means to other ends."

Morgan asked, "Life become art?"

"Yes. I know what I think of as her predominant characteristic. I believe that your mother had, to an exceptional degree, a sense of the balance between a person's being solitary and being bound to others, at the same time. The parity."

Claire asked, "Parody?"

"No. Parity—equal claim. Equally valid claims. She understood that. She lived it."

"Her life made a story?" Morgan asked.

"I'm hoping you'll write it," his father said. "You can read all the diaries. Gather together her letters—if they've been kept."

"Not a biography? But to make a novel out of her life?"

"Yes."

"What's the plot? How does one tell a life's story?"

Claire mocked him: "What's the plot?!"

Their father said, "That's where the artistry comes in."

Morgan said, "I wish I could do it."

"Your mother did tell me, when she came back from London the last time, that she'd met a fellow who said: if you zero in on just the right title for a novel, the rest of the book will flow from that."

"Do you think," Morgan asked, "there's any truth in it?"

"It can't hurt to try."

Claire asked her father, "If you had to choose the title for a book on the life of Mother, what would you call it?"

Chester slumped back in the armchair. He shrugged his shoulders and then grunted. "I'd call it *Sir Hans Markgraf's Daughter*."

"I'd say, *Memories of My Mother*," Claire suggested. "Or *Judge Jackman's Wife*."

"No." Morgan looked around the room and then back to his father's face—already imagining. "*If* I can do it—I'll call it: *Secret Understandings*."